REBEL WITHOUT A BRA

Dedicated to my running buddy, Linda Watt Dolph

By Vicky Wicks-Goggin

Kindle Direct Publishing First Edition, April 2021

Published in the United Stated by Kindle Direct Publishing. Amazon and Kindle are trademarks of Amazon.com and its affiliates.

Rebel without a Bra is a registered trademark of Vicky Goggin.

Quote from "A Case of You" by Joni Mitchell, on her 1971 album Blue.

Cover illustration by Karen Strum. Cover model and photography by Kirstin Farley. Back cover photo by Photography by Westlake.

ISBN: 978-0-578-81464-3

I'm frightened by the devil,

And I'm drawn to those ones that ain't afraid.

-Joni Mitchell

CHAPTER ONE

Bay of Campeche, Mexico - August 1981

The Birds

"Quieres coger? Quieres coger?" The short, sun-darkened crewman repeats over and over again as he tightens one of the ropes on the dinghy next to me. Maybe he's asking about my birds. I know just enough Spanish to ask, "Where is the hotel?' or "How much for a beer?"

"Quieres coger?" Like an annoying bee buzzing around my head, the man leans in closer, *"Quieres coger?"* I involuntarily flinch from his onion-laced breath, shake my head no and hope he'll stop. When he looks over his shoulder to see if anyone is around, I take the opportunity to move toward the cargo hold where my birds are. He watches me out of the corner of his eye, but thankfully doesn't leave his post to follow.

My birds squawk loudly from inside their shrouded cage. I want to check them, but don't want to draw more attention. We've traveled through the cool of the night and a steady thickening of the moist, salty air settles across the water and holds the diesel exhaust like a suffocating sauna. I'm nauseous.

Jeffrey's friend Harry assured me that people take parrots around the Yucatan Peninsula from Belize into Mexico all the time. Well, maybe that's true, but not one hundred birds and especially not a lone young woman. I got a lot of stares from the crew last night as I boarded the boat, especially from this guy.

As the sun breaks on the horizon, the crew shouts back and forth to each other repeatedly. One crewman at the bow peers into the distance and yells instructions that are then reiterated by the next man and the next until it gets to the captain steering the vessel. Every once in a while, the fog clears and land appears in the distance. This part of my journey will be over soon.

The birds were Jeffrey's idea. He was tired of working part-time jobs and wanted to make some fast money. Living less than ten miles from the Mexican border in south Texas brought out the entrepreneurial spirit in most of the people we hung out with. The small airstrip and hangar where he worked attracted an assortment of pilots and mechanics who called themselves, The Crash Gang. When they weren't working on a plane or flying a charter, they were likely involved in trips and transports which were better not to know of.

The place also attracted the occasional transient passing through. The Gang let one dude, who had some exceptionally good weed, sleep on a cot in the back room while he waited for a ride. A few nights of beer drinking and pot smoking led to some exaggerated stories and quick money schemes. This time it was parrots.

"The price for exotics in the United States is only going up." Jeffrey said to me one morning after partying at the hangar the night before. "I can go down to Belize and capture some parrots, bring them back and make some quick cash. If that stoner can do it and make twenty-thousand dollars, I can make forty easy."

No matter how many times I questioned the wisdom of his idea and the dubiously inflated numbers, Jeffrey assured me he had it all planned out. If he borrowed my much smaller plane for the trip, he could keep his costs down. He even expanded on the idea to include building cages in my backyard to house the birds and mate them once he brought them back.

In March, Jeffrey flew my Piper Cub down to Belize. My teaching job didn't allow me to go along, so every two or three days, he'd call and update me on his progress.

His last call was different. "Babe, now that you're on summer break, why don't you come down and stay with me while I finish up getting the rest of the birds? We can fly them back together."

"I just got finished teaching. I want to do some stuff around the house." I lay on the bed with the phone cradled between my ear and the pillow, working the curled phone cord around my index finger. "How many more birds do you need to get?"

"At least a hundred total to make it worth my while, so fifty more."

"You've been down there almost three months." I watched the fan as it gently moved the gauze mosquito netting draped over the four-poster bed. "Is it going to take another three months to get another fifty?"

"With two of us, it will be faster."

"I can't just pick up and leave, I have a dog and a house that I gotta think of." I stared up at the ceiling and tried to imagine Belize.

"Where's your sense of adventure?" He asked. "I thought you were an independent chick. Dan and MG love dogs. They can take care of Lucero."

The harsh afternoon light was fading to a golden glow. The room's four corners softened and the window blinds marked the curtains with dark horizontal lines. "I need to think about it."

"Come on, Genny," his voice softened. "I miss you, babe. A short vacation would be fun. Just come and stay for a couple of weeks. I need to see you and be with you." His voice deepened. My senses responded to his urgings as he told me which parts of my body he'd kiss.

I caught a commercial red eye that night and was in Belize the next day. As the plane taxied to the end of the runway, I spotted a small crowd through the window waiting for passengers at the end of the tarmac.

Jeffrey, a head taller than everyone else, stood out immediately. It always gave me a little flutter to see him. I stepped off the plane and jumped into his arms and he swung me around as easily as a child with a doll.

We hopped into his rented jeep to head back to his hut on the beach. His long blond shaggy-dog hair blew freely as we drove through town. The sun had darkened his skin to a reddish brown with flecks of freckles tumbling down his arms. He gave me a goofy smile that showed off his gold front tooth and made me laugh. He was the epitome of a surfer dude.

The next two days were spent in bed making up for lost time. Every once in a while, we wandered down to the beach bar where a mixture of locals and off-beat tourists hung out. One afternoon we arrived to find Harry, the resident expert on everything in Belize, holding court on the subject of diving. He sported floral swim trunks and an old faded T-shirt that barely covered his beer gut. His sun-weathered skin made it difficult to tell his age.

"Yeah, we get lots of people who come down here to dive that don't know nothin' about the steep cliffs and swift currents. Those guys take you out diving don't give a shit what happens to you. There was a couple of novices diving for the first time." He paused to take a swig of beer and then continued with gusto. "The dive master didn't do a head count at the end of the dive and the poor saps got carried out to sea. They were never heard from again." His audience of rapt tourists gasped at the ending, but wandered off looking for some weed when Harry said he didn't have any to share.

Jeffrey took advantage of the lull in conversation to introduce us.

"Is that story true?" I asked.

Harry smiled slyly. "Don't let the truth get in the way of a good story. Besides, these tourists need somethin' exciting to tell their friends back home."

We laughed at his little secret. His broad smile showed several missing teeth.

"Jeffrey's told me a lot about you." He said straightening his long brown hair back into a pony tail. "It takes a lot of balls to leave Ohio and move down to Texas."

"It really wasn't that brave. I couldn't find a job there and was offered a teaching position during a job fair at college. I basically fell into the situation."

"Even so, most people wouldn't have taken the chance."

Jeffrey nodded and headed over to the bar to grab some beers.

"How long you staying?"

"Only a few weeks, I'm going to help him catch parrots, so he can get home faster."

Jeffrey came back with the beers in time to hear Harry's next question, "What method you using to catch the birds?"

"I got some approved traps from the government," Jeffrey answered. "It's slow going though."

"There's an easier way." Harry took a long swig of beer and cleared his throat. "Buy some mist nets with a tight weave and string them across some trees, then sprinkle berries on the ground to attract the birds. You have to take the nets down immediately when you're done."

"Wouldn't it be easier just to leave them up?" I asked.

"No. The nets can tangle birds overnight and they can die."

Jeffrey questioned the process, and Harry gladly answered as long as the beers were free for the taking.

"I know a place that hasn't been worked much." Harry pulled out a pen and drew a crude map on the back of a napkin.

The next day, Jeffrey and I drove to the spot Harry had mapped for us. The path was overgrown with vegetation, but still distinguishable. Our jeans and long-sleeved shirts were sweat-soaked before we even got out of the jeep. Working this new area of the jungle, we caught twelve birds the first day.

On the second day, we set up our nets right before a heavy rain soaked everything and kept the birds away. Empty handed and disappointed, we walked towards the jeep in silence. I was wet, I was tired and I wanted a cold beer. About halfway back, I tripped over some rope, fell face down in the mud and started to cry. Just as I was going to scream with frustration, I heard screeching a few feet away. A small red-headed parrot was caught in an abandoned net. Jeffrey helped me up and we both went to rescue the helpless bird. I took my knife and carefully worked around the trapped creature while Jeffrey cut the abandoned net completely down, so other birds wouldn't suffer the same fate.

The poor creature was wet and cold with one of its legs injured from the struggle. I put it in my front pocket and felt its heart beating fast next to mine.

"How could someone leave the nets up? Harry was emphatic we take them down each time."

"I don't know, babe." Jeffrey put his arm around my shoulder. "Lots of people just don't give a shit. Good thing we found this little dude before he died."

"Oh my gosh, there're so many jerks in this world." I wiped the tears off my face. "How can we make sure our birds stay safe when we sell them? I don't want them to get hurt."

"We'll be as careful as we can, babe, but this is a business. We're in it for the money."

CHAPTER TWO

Truth or Dare

In the following days, Jeffrey went to the jungle on his own to capture the rest of the birds while I went about doctoring my little fellow. I put a small splint on his leg and tried to get him to eat bird seed. He was too weak to do anything for himself, so I chewed the seeds in my mouth and fed it to him in little bits. It took several days, but he finally ate and drank on his own. He stayed on my shoulder or hopped around the table when I was in the hut. Since he was still weak and smaller than the others, I made him a tiny, separate cage out of bamboo, so he wouldn't have to be in with the rest of the birds and get hurt.

After a week of non-stop trapping, Jeffrey came back to the hut and announced, "We got the magic number."

"Oh? What number is that?"

"Just like the Dalmatians, one hundred and one. I already know you'll never let me sell him." He pointed to the red-headed imp on my shoulder.

"His name's Rocky." I got up from my chair and gave Jeffrey a big hug." Cuz he's a fighter." Rocky squawked, mimicking a rough version of his name.

We laughed at the new member of our family.

"Let's go celebrate and say our goodbyes," Jeffrey said with a smile, his gold tooth catching the afternoon sunlight.

Harry sat on his usual bar stool. "Haven't seen you two for a while," Harry said shaking Jeffrey's hand. "You're all smiles. What's up?"

"We finished catching the last of the birds. The only thing I need to do now is the paperwork on the last thirteen birds and then we're gone," Jeffrey signaled the bartender for three beers.

"Aw, man." Harry started, then shook his head, "Dude, you must not have heard."

"What?" Jeffrey asked.

Harry explained how a new government had been voted into power and would revoke all the prior governments' permits. They would take the birds into quarantine. The new rules would take effect in three days.

"Fuck," is all Jeffrey uttered as he and I slumped in our bar stools.

"You need to chill out." Harry said after dropping the news on us like a bomb. "Just grease some palms with the new government and the problem will go away."

"Dude, we have just enough money for the fuel to fly Genny's plane back to Texas." Jeffrey protested and stared at the beer in his hand.

"And we only have legal papers for eighty eight of the hundred and one birds we've captured."

Harry examined the remaining contents of his bottle before he brought it to his lips, tilted his head back and finished the last mouthful.

As if inspired by its contents, he dramatically pronounced, "It's only rules, man. Rules only apply, if you get caught."

"What?" Jeffrey looked up like someone had awakened him from a long sleep. He narrowed his gaze. "What did you say?"

"Stop fucking around here, man, and get going," Harry pressed.

"It's only *rules*. What's the worst thing they can do to you? Figure out the other thirteen birds later. Maybe it will be *your* lucky thirteen."

The next morning I arrived at the airport to fuel the plane for the long trip home and file the flight plan. Technically, all cargo must be declared, but no one ever checked the plane physically. We'd house the birds inconspicuously in wrapped cages, come back later and load them secretly and then take off.

The man who serviced my plane taxied it to the fuel pumps while I filed my itinerary upstairs in the control tower. The all-glass room gave the two men manning it a three-sixty view of the airfield. The first man directed a small plane on a short air strip by radio while I sat in the corner and filled out my flight proposal. The second man watched a screen in front of him as he radioed back and forth to another aircraft, directing it to the longer runway.

Out of the corner of my eye, I saw a large aircraft coming in for a landing. The roar of the engines was deafening and the room shook as it came in. Both men stood suddenly to get a better look at some ground activity. I watched in silent horror as the air turbulence from the jumbo jet picked up my Piper Cub, the plane I bought with the inheritance from my Nanna, slammed it into the hangar and totally destroyed it.

I stood to get a better look at the scene below, but a hand pushed me down into my chair again and ordered me to stay in place. I watched helplessly as parts of my plane were blown through the air, along with all of my plans. One plane pulled up at the last minute barely missing one of the detached wings and the two men scrambled to divert any more incoming flights as the debris tumbled across the airstrip. Total bedlam ensued for the next hour as ground crews quickly recovered what was left of my plane.

Once the emergency was over, fingers were pointed at me for negligence. My shock quickly turned to anger as I reminded them it was one of the airport workers who had detached the plane's tie downs to fuel it. I argued it was their responsibility and, therefore their liability. After several hours arguing with the air controllers and airport manager, I filed a crash report along with an insurance claim.

I was allowed access to my plane to salvage anything from the heap of metal piled on the side of the field. All of the legal documentation for the birds was gone. I retrieved the plane's title, along with its sales receipt from a plastic pouch locked in the side door panel. It was a total loss. Even the Crash Gang wouldn't be able to fix that metal heap.

Thank God the birds were still with Jeffrey on the beach and not in the plane.

Shaking with rage and dread, I left the Belize Airport and headed back to tell Jeffrey the news.

"Let's just set all the birds free except Rocky and go home," I cried, my anxiety level reaching a fevered pitch.

"I can't give up that quickly. I'll go home broke, and besides, you can't just let the birds go. Their wings are clipped. They wouldn't survive in the wild now."

I sat down next to the birds defeated and exhausted.

"Let's go talk to Harry." Jeffrey took my hands and pulled me up into his arms. "He'll know what to do."

As we walked down the beach, Jeffrey put his arm around my waist and stroked my lower back. By the time we reached Harry's hut, we were joking a little and laughing. Harry was on the front deck of his hut smoking a joint and casually offered it to us. Jeffrey explained the whole situation as Harry stroked his chin where the stubble of a few days beard was forming.

"Man, all you need to do is take the birds by boat around the Yucatan Peninsula. People do it all the time. Most people don't have planes anyway." He laughed at his little joke.

Between his nonchalant attitude and the pot, my anxiety almost completely abated. Maybe going by boat wouldn't be that big of a deal.

Then Harry threw a big wrench into the mix. It would be smarter, he said, if I went by myself.

"Blond Surfer dude Jeffrey with a hundred parrots would stick out like a sore thumb in Mexico. They'll know immediately he's doing something illegal. Just look at him, dude."

A sick feeling came over me, "I can't go by myself. I don't even speak Spanish."

"This is the eighties." Harry went into his hut and came back with a Spanish/English dictionary. "You chicks are always saying you want to be equal," he said, handing me the book. "This is your chance."

CHAPTER THREE

Translation

The boat makes a hard landing as we dock in the Port of Veracruz. The birds and I are unceremoniously deposited on a long wharf crowded with large wooden crates marked *Hecho en México*. The seaman who'd harassed me during the trip scurries to the opposite side of the boat without a backward glance. Men unpack carts stacked with bananas, mangos, and other various fruits from a nearby boat that docked right after us. A strong smell of dead fish pervades the air. Seagulls dive-bomb the wooden fruit carts and fly off with their bounty.

The morning clouds burn off and the bright sunlight illuminates the brilliant colors of my birds' feathers. A rainbow of red, yellow, and white-headed parrots jump from one perch to another panicky from the current move. Crammed together for safe transportation, their movements are purposely limited to prevent them establishing a dominant pecking order and fighting in the cages. They have just enough room to rotate from their wooden poles to the water and feeding dishes.

Now that I'm standing in Mexico with everyone speaking Spanish, I have the grim realization that my worries about this trip were warranted. Buying fruit from one of the vendors on the wharf is a difficult exchange of sign language and broken English. Thankfully, I exchanged some of my money to pesos before I left Belize. Money will certainly help my awkward translations.

I distribute mangos and pomegranate evenly in all of the cages, so the birds feast. The vendor helps me cover the cages with the light sheets I brought to shield the birds from the harsh sun. I need to get the birds to a cool, safe place. I look up and down the street, unsure of what to do next.

Harry assessed one thing correctly. There are no tall blond men in the crowd. I realize just how conspicuous Jeffrey would have been here. I, on the other hand, blend right in. My skin is tanned a golden brown from living on the beach for the last five weeks and my long, dark-brown hair reaches almost to my waist. My hippie-style peasant blouse and long skirt complete the façade. Now if I can just find someone who speaks English.

The plan is to rent a vehicle where I can hide the cages in an inconspicuous way and drive up to one of the border towns, so I can cross into Texas. I ask a few people if they speak English and finally a short woman with two long braids, clutching a chicken under her arm answers my distress call.

"Yes, yes, yes. My cousin. He talk *inglés.*" She points to the auto shop across the street. "He will help you. My cousin name is Arturo. He speak good *inglés.*"

I cross the street, all the while trying to keep an eye on my birdcages stacked on the dock and hopefully out of the fray. I ask for Arturo and a tall thin man comes out from under the hood of a car. He has grease all over his hands, and wipes them before offering to shake mine.

He does indeed speak English.

"I used to pick tomatoes outside of Detroit," he states.

"I have some birds I need to take to Texas." I point to the cages across the street.

"I got a guy who takes stuff over the border all the time. I'll get him to take you and the birds."

"I just need to rent a van and drive them there, myself."

"*Señorita*, you do not understand." Arturo looks at me with sheer pity. "If you want to take those birds across any of our borders, you will need a driver. You will not make it otherwise." There's no drama in his voice, no bullshit, just plain unadulterated fact. Each state in Mexico has its own checkpoints with border guards, he explains, and each of them expects to get a kickback. It's going to cost me five hundred dollars, plus any bribe money. He can have his driver ready in the morning around nine. He acts like this is a common occurrence; someone shows up on his doorstep every day of the week with one hundred birds to smuggle into the United States.

He strides across the street to look at the birds. He circles the large cage twice appraising the whole situation. "This cage can't fit in the back of a van," he says.

"It's really four small cages that interlock with these clamps." I demonstrate how to disassemble the four units and how the water bottles at the top of each cage automatically refill the birds' drinking trough, with a similar contraption to distribute birdseed.

I wonder if Arturo knows that even though the birds are very young, they're worth between $100 and $300 each in Texas. My conscience gives me a small stab as I hear my mother's words in my head, "The price of everything, the value of nothing." Jeffrey made it clear the birds are his money making scheme, but they're living, breathing creatures relying on me to keep them safe. There's got to be more to this than just money.

Arturo says he has a place where they can be kept for the night.

He looks at all of the birds and whistles a short tune, calling them to attention. They flap their wings and respond to his melody as he reaches his finger into the cage and strokes a few of the birds' breasts. Arturo's small connection with my birds calms me.

"I have a few yellow-headed parrots of my own," he says. "They talk and sing all the time."

We walk to an old wood-framed building with rusted corrugated tin siding next to his shop. The floor is dirt and sunlight filters through the metal slats. It looks well ventilated and relatively cool inside.

"The birds'll like it in here." Arturo extends his arm like a game show host, as he proudly shows me the shack that could blow away in the next storm. "It'll give them a place to cool down before the drive tomorrow."

There are no other apparent options, so we move the birds into a far corner of the building next to some wooden crates. I have several bags of bird seed and make sure the birds have plenty of food. Arturo looks closely at the birds' water supply and flicks the rubber tubing with his index finger. "They need clean water." He takes considerable time to clean the water bottles at the top of each cage and fill them with fresh water, all the while singing and cooing to the birds. I relax a little more.

Maybe this really will be as simple as Harry said it would be. I found a safe place for my birds and someone to help me cross the border. At twenty-one years old, I feel I'm a good judge of character.

We agree to meet tomorrow morning at nine o'clock and Arturo points me in the direction of a hotel and restaurant in the center of town. I follow the sound of steel drums playing softly in the distance and smell delicious spices being cooked in open-air shops framing the town's plaza and sit at one of the small mismatched tables close to the bar and try to read the menu. I recognize the word *taco* and feel relieved. The waitress comes over to take my order. I try to keep it simple and say tacos pollo.

She asks, "*Tortillas dearina o de maíz?*" I quickly look up the words in my little book and see "tortillas of flour or corn".

I answer, "*De maíz.*" She asks a couple more questions and I try to look up the words. She finally gives up and walks away.

I glance at a group of people at a large table near me and say to no one in particular, "I don't know what I ordered, but I hope it's good." The group of young Americans and Mexicans invite me to join them. I'm happy I won't have to eat alone, and hope someone can help with my Spanish translations.

It's a light atmosphere and I quickly become part of the party. The Mexicans are students from the university and speak English quite well. Some of the Americans at the table came down for vacation and never left. I wish now I had taken Spanish in high school instead of Latin. Mexicans are more like the Europeans and learn multiple languages. It's only we Americans who don't feel the need to learn our neighbors' languages.

We're having a good time, the beer's flowing and the conversation is light and cheery. I pull my Spanish/English dictionary out of my backpack to look up the words the man on the boat kept saying.

"What words do you need interpreted?" Asks one of the male students.

"What does, '*Quieres coger*' mean?" The entire table goes silent.

"*Señorita,* who would say such a thing to you?" The student looks offended.

"I was on the boat coming here around the Yucatan and a seaman kept saying it to me." I stammer the words quickly as I head off any offense I may have incurred. "I'm sorry if I said something wrong. I really didn't understand him. Maybe I'm pronouncing it incorrectly."

"No, no, *señorita*, you are pronouncing it correctly. It means, 'Do you want to fuck?'" His face turns bright red.

My jaw drops and my face burns. I'm sure the look on my face says everything to the group. "I'm so sorry. I didn't know what he was saying."

Everyone laughs and says he must have been a *pendejo*, and we continue partying.

The conversation turns to the subject of stealing. An American at the end of the table relates his story to the group. "When my girlfriend and I first got here, some guy who spoke English befriended us in the plaza." His girlfriend nods her head in agreement. "Very friendly guy… he asked if we wanted our picture taken. So we handed him our camera and walked to pose in front of the church steps."

"When we turned around for the photo," the girlfriend interrupts, "He jumped into a waiting car and speed out of the plaza. Boy, was he quick. We tried to report it to the local police, but they just laughed at us." Everyone is still laughing when one of the Mexican students says, "The people here don't believe they are really stealing anything. The only 'sin' in stealing is getting caught!" Everyone laughs again, but me. This underscores just how little I know about the people and culture here. My heart beats faster and my stomach lurches.

The guy on the boat was quick to try and take advantage of me. Is Arturo the same? He knew exactly how to stroke the birds and smile to calm my fears and get my confidence. Sister Mary Clement Marie would call this a sin of pride... false pride, really. I was too quick to think I knew Arturo's heart. Trust is earned, she would say.

I've put the birds at risk. What will Jeffrey say if I lose them? A bead of sweat forms on my forehead. I check my watch. Two in the morning and most of the people have left the bar. I pay my tab and excuse myself. I'm tired, but a shot of adrenalin courses through me while I walk quickly across the plaza. I picture Rocky in his bamboo cage and break into a run.

I'll tell you what can go wrong, Harry, when you don't follow the rules.

Summer 1970

"Run back to third base," screams Coach Santoni as he scrambles out of the dugout.

"Why?" I yell back.

"You didn't touch third base," he screams louder. "Go back. Run!"

My feet are frozen. My mind tells my feet to go back, but it's too late. Judy, on third, runs and tags me with the ball. I'm out. The other team is up and my team is heading in.

Instead of joining them, I run into the bleachers and into my mother's arms. I bury my face into her chest.

"Genny, you need to go to the dugout," she says softly, so the people staring at us don't hear. I shake my head.

"You're part of a team, Genny. You can't just leave them."

"Please don't make me go back."

"If you leave now, this is how everyone will remember you."

"I don't care what they think," I look up into her face.

"Is this how you want to remember the day? You're their best hitter, show them how well you can hit."

My feet finally take me to the dugout. Next turn at bat, I focus solely on the ball coming to me. The bat connects perfectly with the ball and I run. I run fast. I touch all bases. I remember the day.

CHAPTER FOUR

Not a Sin

The plaza's bright illumination fades into long shadows as I sprint down the deserted streets to the warehouse. When I turn the corner, a lone streetlight buzzes and crackles from across the way. I quickly stack a few wooden crates and scramble up the makeshift ladder to find the key above the door. I run my shaking fingertips back and forth over the rough doorframe, finally retrieving it.

The streetlight flickers as I unlock the door and enter the quiet room. The dry earthen floor crunches softly under my feet and I hear my birds rustle quietly in the corner. A wave of relief washes over me. It's too late to get a hotel room, so I put the key back in its hiding place, disassemble the stacked crates, and go back in. My knees feel weak as I walk toward my precious cargo. I reach into the bottom of one of the cages and retrieve Rocky's small bamboo cage. He's sleeping and very still, but I put him on my shoulder for reassurance and comfort.

I sit on the ground and curl up next to my birds with the backpack propped up against the wall as a hard pillow. Like big drops of rain hitting me, a cold wet reality pricks my skin. I'm illegally transporting one hundred birds. I look at Rocky...one hundred and one. I'm in Mexico and don't know the language or the culture. I'm in over my head. I can't do anything, but wait for the morning to come to me.

There's a noise outside and I bolt straight up. I must have dozed off at some point during the night's vigil. I check my watch. It's five o'clock. The room is dark, but my eyes have adjusted to the faint light filtering through the cracks in the walls. I grab Rocky and put him in his cage. Silhouettes of two men walk into the room, one tall and thin, the other shorter and rounder. There's just enough light from the open door to see that the thin one is Arturo. They move quickly toward my birds.

I stand straightening my aching legs. *"Hola, Arturo."*

Both men stop mid-stride. Arturo takes a moment to respond, "What are you doing here now, *señorita*?"

"My birds like to be fed early in the morning or they get sick. I didn't think you'd mind me coming here."

Arturo turns to the man and they speak in Spanish for a few moments. The other man lifts his hands up and shrugs his broad shoulders.

Showing up four hours early, doesn't really incriminate them. Technically, they didn't get caught stealing, so there's been no "sin" committed. If I act like nothing was going to happen, maybe this will still turn out okay.

"Is this the man who's going to drive me to Texas?" I ask innocently. "We can get started right away if he wants. We don't have to wait until nine."

Arturo introduces me to Humberto. I shake his hand, rough with calluses.

They both work in an orchestrated effort now. Arturo rolls up the garage door on the opposite side of the warehouse while Humberto pulls his van around and parks it with the rear facing the doors. When Humberto opens the van's double back door, the dome light illuminates his dark features. His straight black hair is slicked back into a stubby ponytail and his dark skin looks like it's been grafted from the hide of an elephant. He could be in his forties, but I really can't tell. He eyes me and I smile.

Arturo unlatches the four cages for easier transport and we load the birds into the back of the van. I cover the cages with the sheet to quiet their squawks. Rocky's small cage is still on the floor and he's flapping his wings to get my attention. He settles as I reach down and pick up his cage.

Hopefully, this part of the trip won't take too long.

"How much do I owe you for storing the birds last night?" I ask Arturo.

"Give me $50.00 and I'll be happy plus half the $500.00 for the transportation to Texas." he smiles as he holds his hand out palm up. I reach into my pocket and hand him two twenties. "I'll give Humberto the $500.00 when I get home…safely. You can get your half from him later."

Arturo looks to Humberto who quickly says, " ¡Oh! Si! I pay you when I return." Arturo looks disappointed, but stuffs the money into his pocket.

Humberto moves toward the driver's side of the van… I get in the passenger side. I place my backpack on the floorboard between my feet and set Rocky's cage on my lap. He hops over to peck my fingers, so I take him and put him on my shoulder. Humberto smiles when he sees Rocky attack my hoop earring.

The inside of the van is a shrine to the Virgin Mary. There's a rosary hanging from the rear-view mirror and a statue along with some shag carpet glued to the dashboard. There are many offerings around the little statue. Humberto makes the sign of the cross, kisses his hand then touches the statue of Mary. He looks at me in an expectant way, so I make the sign of the cross and kiss the statue the same way. He nods in approval. We drive away from the warehouse and Arturo closes the doors. I assume the van isn't equipped with AC. It's better for the birds to have the breeze from the windows partially rolled down. As long as they have water, the heat shouldn't hurt them.

The first rays of the morning light shine through the darkness. We drive in silence at first, but I look down on the console and notice an English-Spanish Dictionary between the two seats. I reach into my backpack and pull out my matching volume to show him.

I page through the book and turn to Humberto, "*El día es muy bonita*".

He smiles, "Yes, today is very pretty. You speak to me English words, *por favor*? I speak English to other Mexicans, they English no good. But you speak *real* English. I know you correct. I know English more better, I make more money."

I smile. "*Sí*, I speak English to you, you speak Spanish to me." With that, we relax a little more in our seats.

I look up the word for money-*dinero*. I try to pronounce it. Humberto corrects my pronunciation and I correct his when he speaks a word in English. We start with getting some nouns memorized. He knows quite a few English nouns already, so I'm really the one learning from him. The first full sentence I learn is, "*Hay un molino en el campo*." The phrase has no practical use in the real world. Who cares if there is a windmill in the field, but it's an accomplishment to learn something other than, "*Dos mas cervesas, por favor*."

Humberto hands me a small bag with five tacos in it and says,

"Two for you and three for me." He smiles.

I take two and hand him the bag. With the first bite, my eyes are watering and my tongue feels like it's on fire. I open the tortilla to see what's inside. There are eggs, chorizo and green chilies that appear to be Serrano peppers.

Humberto smiles even more, "*Mi esposa* is good cook. Everyone say she make best tacos."

How could I refuse? I take another bite and start to sweat. I pick up the bag and examine it further to see if it might have a napkin in it to wipe my brow. On the other side of the bag is written, "*mi papi*"

I try to pronounce the words and Humberto corrects me. "What does it mean?"

"My wife is from Columbia. She calls me *papi* to show her love and respect." He looks at me with a bashful grin. "Now all my friends and family call me *papi*, too."

April 1972   Ninth anniversary of Dad's death

"He called me his gypsy," Mom says with a faraway look in her eyes. She doesn't tell me what she called him. She says she loves how many children he gave her, four before me and one after. He died too soon. I was three, my baby brother was eighteen months. I stare at pictures and try to feel him, remember something. But sometimes I think I just remember the pictures.

CHAPTER FIVE

No Road Map

The drive along the coast is slow on the two-lane road with no wriggle room on either side for error. The road cuts into the cliffs with sheer drop-offs. We view the Bahia de Campeche below us. Large rocks have tumbled from the sides of the mountain and landed on the beach making it look as if they're marching into the sea after a violent fight. The sharp, black boulders cover the white sand with a magnificent jagged edge that continues into the sea. The waves roar up the beach and meet the rocks with a spray of water twenty-feet high. The fight between earth and sea continues as we drive the coastline.

Since the narrow road is used as an agricultural roadway, we aren't making very good time. The bus in front of us picks up people along the road and it's hard to pass. Some of the people carry chickens or small pigs, so take a long time to get into the bus. Each time the bus takes off again, a huge plume of black exhaust fills the air and chokes out any clean breeze coming from the coast. We finally pass the bus and get our speed up to fifty miles per hour. The distance between Tampico and Texas should be a ten-hour trip. At this rate, it's going to take two days.

Our course changes and we head west into the foothills. The road narrows as we continue up a steep incline. On the hilltop, sits a Spanish style, white stucco house surrounded by lush landscaping. Humberto parks the van in the shade and opens the van's doors to ventilate the back for my birds.

"*Tengo familia aqui en Poza Rica.*" Humberto says. He waits for me to look up the words in the dictionary. I'm not sure how to react to the fact that he has family here.

I just want to get over the border, but I have no choice and say, "*Esta bien.*" I pop Rocky into his cage with the rest of the birds and check their water and food.

"*Esa es la casa de mi primo.*" Humberto smiles and escorts me to the doorway. Again, I scramble to look up all the words. "This is the house of my cousin." Is everybody everybody else's cousin in Mexico?

Humberto knocks on the door as I stand to the side. A girl, a few years younger than me, answers. Her eyes open wide and she calls loudly into the house for the other residents' attention. Three more heads pop into the doorway - another young girl, a woman and a much older man - to welcome Humberto.

It's obvious from hugs and smiles that Humberto is held in high regard. The conversation in Spanish is too rapid for me to understand. Finally, Humberto stops everyone and introduces me. They look at me for the first time and greet me in Spanish.

"*Ella es una gringa.*" Humberto quickly says, "*No habla* español."

One of the girls pulls me aside.

"Who are you?" she asks.

"No," corrects the second girl. "Not, "Who are you?" She turns to me and asks, "What is your name?"

"Genny Rekas," I answer.

They both try to pronounce my name and laugh.

"My name is Socorro," the older of the two girls says. She's taller than me by a couple of inches with creamy light skin, high cheek bones and long dark-brown hair. Her eyebrows are perfectly arched above unusual hazel colored eyes. Her full lips stand out on her face below a small perfectly sloped nose. Her features are European and delicate.

"My name is Juanita," the second girl says. Her stature is more diminutive than Socorro's, but she's every bit as regal looking. Her arms and legs make her look like a young foal that still needs to grow into its full proportions. Her brown hair flows in waves down her back. She's a thinner, younger version of her sister.

"Pleased to meet you," I say.

They both repeat what I say like parrots, then laugh afterwards.

Humberto introduces *la Señora* Victoria and *el Señor* Raul. His cousin, Raul has a strong family resemblance to Humberto; they're of equal height and weight and their faces are round and flat. But where Humberto's face is softer with laugh lines, Raul's face has a permanent scowl and hard lines between his eyebrows. He shakes my hand and bows a little, but gives me no smile. His wife also shakes my hand, and then retreats from the group quickly.

We move from the foyer into the main room which is large and airy and the unexpected grandeur of the house is revealed. Roughhewn log beams stretch thirty feet from the entrance to a far wall made almost entirely of windows. The windows are open and bring a cool breeze from the mountains in the distance and a view of the valley below. The giant room serves as living room, dining room and kitchen. Large rugs cover the shiny tiled floors and a staircase climbs the wall at the end of the room.

Humberto sees me studying the house and explains that important homes of the community are given names. The name of this house is *La*

Casa Ventana, the house with windows.

Raul puffs his chest like a preening peacock. *"Mi casa* is better than homes in *Norteamérica, sí?"*

"O, sí. Su casa es muy bonita." Humberto and I smile at each other as his Spanish lessons have definitely been effective.

Juanita and Socorro take my hands and pull me toward the stairs. I look back at Humberto, but he and Raul are sitting at the dining room table opening a bottle of wine. Raul's wife is in the kitchen preparing an assortment of vegetables. I hope we can get back on track quickly. Surely Humberto won't stay too long. I follow the girls as they disappear up the stairs.

Their bedroom overlooks the courtyard where the van sits below. Socorro cranks the window open and I lean out to listen for the birds. They're quiet and have enough water and food to keep them happy for a while. Socorro and Juanita sit on one of the double beds and motion for me to sit on the other. I set my backpack on the floor.
"What is your name?" Socorro asks as she points to my backpack.
"What name is it?" Juanita corrects her.

"What is that?" I correct them both.

They both look at each other and say in unison, "What is that?" Then they laugh and point to the backpack again and repeat, "What is that?"

I start to answer when we hear some commotion from below. Socorro and Juanita jump to look out the window. A young man stands whistling under the bedroom window. My birds join the chorus and the girls look very concerned.

Juanita calls out, *"No, no mas!"*

Raul and Humberto appear in the courtyard and yell at the young man, who quickly turns on his heels and heads out of the yard. The girls cover their mouths and giggle.

"He is the *novio* of Juanita," Socorro teasingly says.

I reach for the dictionary in my backpack, but Juanita translates for me, "boyfriend."

All of this is very nice, but I really need to get my birds to Texas. I yell out to Humberto below, *"Que pasa?"*

"We need to spend the night, *señorita*," says Humberto, with a toothy grin. "The van needs to rest. The birds are hot and need to be cooled down. Miguel will take care of them."

He speaks to a man with a big floppy hat carrying a hoe and a garden hose and they move the birds to a table under the trees.

He must have noticed my disappointment and says, "Please *señorita*, this takes time." He looks up to the window again. "The girls take you to see the area. *Por favor*, have fun. I stay with my cousin to speak." I begin to correct his English, but decide I can't correct everything.

Calculating the distance on the map, it should have only taken ten to twelve hours to drive to Texas from Veracruz, but that doesn't take into account the conditions of the roads and the slow traffic. I was hoping to drive through the night, but I understand Humberto is tired. We might have had to stay in a rundown hotel…or worse. All-in-all this is as good of a place to stay the night as any… maybe better.

I turn to the girls, "Where are we going?"

CHAPTER SIX

80'S Disco

The sisters look at me and then at each other. The wicked smiles on their faces broaden.

"Disco dancing!" they say in unison,

Disco dancing? Who would have ever thought I'd be going disco dancing in the mountains of Mexico?

A flurry of activity ensues. Socorro pulls clothes from a dresser while Juanita searches through the closet. Several outfits are laid out on the bed for approval and then declined for one reason or another. Finally, perfection is achieved. But instead of putting the clothes on, they stuff them into a duffel bag and lower it out the window with a rope to the courtyard below.

Before I can ask what they're doing, they run downstairs to get some food from their mother and bring me back a couple of tacos stuffed with fish. The tacos taste fantastic and not just because I'm starving to death.

Once we finish eating, we take turns using the bathroom to shower. I have two days' worth of dust on me I'm grateful to wash it down the drain.

The girls' curiosity is exhausting. They take every item out of my backpack and inspect it carefully.

"What is this?" Socorro demands, holding up a cotton camisole my mother made for me.

Naked, with only a towel around me, I snatch it away from her.

"Instead of a bra, I wear this. It's called a camisole."

They laugh at the thickly padded garment as I slip it onto my flat chest and snap the fasteners in the front. Years of competitive swimming have given me high, well developed pectoral muscles, but my breasts are unusually small.

Socorro straightens her back and juts out her chest in a pose to demonstrate how breasts should look. I giggle at her exaggerated posture. Juanita shakes her head and rolls her eyes.

I start to braid my wet hair when Juanita stops me. "Leave your hair down. We want to look good at the disco."

I try to protest, but it's easier to do what they want.

I open my backpack to retrieve my makeup case. I usually use minimal makeup, light blush and lip gloss. The girls watch me intently as I pull out my mascara with a curved brush and start to apply it. You would have thought I held the cure for cancer in my hands. They both jump off the bed and grab it out of my hands and completely take over, applying cosmetics to each other and me. I suggest it might be a little too heavy, but both insist this is how it's done in Mexico. After some resistance, they also apply several more layers of paint to my face. I look at myself in the mirror. I resemble Cleopatra going down the Nile with blue jeans and a peasant top. It's a totally incongruent look, but the girls think I'm stunning and ready to be introduced to their world.

We walk down the stairs where Raul and Humberto are drinking beers and eating tacos. Raul stops in mid-sentence and looks up at the three of us.   Humberto almost drops his taco halfway to his mouth. "*¡O!, Dios mío! Qué linda! Señorita!*" I don't need my dictionary to know my new look meets with their approval.

"She looks like a movie star now," Socorro says approvingly.

Victoria eyes me. "She can't go to the plaza in those clothes." I start to correct her to say 'disco', but the girls give me a look. Victoria leaves the room and returns with a long floral skirt, a crème colored blouse and a concho belt inlaid with deep-blue lapis lazuli stones. She pushes me into the downstairs bathroom to change. The bottom of the skirt has many layers of lace and ruffles and is extremely bulky. When I come out, the entire household applauds. I look in the mirror and the transformation is unbelievable. I look like Carmen Miranda without the fruit on my head. I count myself lucky no one I know will see me.

The girls have changed into similar clothes with long skirts and whirl around the living room in a frenzy. They invite me to twirl as well, but the heavy skirt lacks the same effect as theirs and I look like I'm weighted down with sinkers. If someone threw me into a pool, I'd surely drop to the bottom and not come up.

Humberto pours another glass of wine for Raul and himself. Juanita comes up on one side of me and Socorro the other and they lock arms to usher me out the door for a quick exit. I feel like we're on our way to a Halloween costume party.

Juanita practically pushes me into the back seat of the car while Socorro retrieves something from the bushes. I'm trying to pull the rest of my heavy skirt into the car before I close the door and it's taking longer than expected.

"Hurry, Genny. I want not to be late," Juanita calls from the driver's side of a small Volkswagen.

Socorro slides in the passenger side with the duffel bag and corrects her. "I don't want to be late."

With the layers of skirt gathered in my arms, I finally shut the door. "Let's go." I say.

June 1975 – Prom

Patrick opens the car door for me and I slide in, sweeping up the bottom of my prom dress. Mom spent hours in the basement, sewing the yards and yards of shiny satin to match the complicated Vogue pattern I'd picked.

My best friend, Jackie's in the front seat with her boyfriend, Matthew. She looks back and gives me one of her mischievous winks. Two sophomore girls with two senior boys. I always thought only the blonde cheerleaders got attention from the upperclassmen, but ever since Jackie took me under her wing, I've felt more like I fit in. When Patrick sits beside me and reaches for my hand, I remember what Jackie told me over the phone hours ago, "Just act like you know what you're doing and stop being such a good girl for a change."

CHAPTER SEVEN

A Kiss On The Hand

Juanita speeds out of the driveway, then both girls turn to me in the back.

"We need to change our clothes." Juanita says and returns her attention to driving and swerves to avoid hitting a goat.

"We brought clothes for you, too." Socorro shows the contents of the duffel bag. "Would you prefer jeans or what you are wearing?"

I can't believe the duplicity.

"We are so glad you come to our home," Socorro reaches into the bag and pulls out one of the outfits I'd previously seen laid out on the bed.

"We only get out of *la casa* if we dress proper and you dress proper."

"Our papa can't understand disco," Juanita continues. "Our papa can't understand *mi corazón*."

I look up *'corazón...* heart. Got it! These sisters are quite dramatic. I imagine there are few options in this small village, so their main focus is boys.

Juanita pulls into an alcove of trees on the side of the road to cover our quick change.

It's clear they've done this before.

Socorro changes into jeans, a tight blouse with sequins and high spike heels. Juanita's outfit is a bit more conservative, but equally stunning with floral top and snug black slacks. The change is one hundred eighty degrees from the previous parentally approved outfits.

They give me my jeans and a sexy low-cut sequined blue top. The heels they hand me are true horse cripplers, but my sandals don't work with the outfit. I don't want to leave the concho belt in the car, so I loop it through my jeans and loosely tuck in my blouse. Both nod their heads approvingly. They offer several bangles, earrings and clips for my hair.

They don jewels as well and add even more lipstick, blush and eye shadow.

Never too much makeup apparently.

We head away from town up the side of a mountain with the sun setting fast. There are no street lights and few lights from houses, so the darkness is complete. The stars are brilliant compared to the dark mountains around us. As we pull into the parking lot, Juanita accidentally hits the car next to hers with her right bumper.

She and Socorro inspect the fender of their car and laugh. "No big deal!" both say in stereo.

I look around at all of the vehicles in the parking lot with at least two, if not three dents in the fenders and conclude everyone must play bumper-cars.

The building in front of us looks like an abandoned warehouse with some of the windows broken out. I hesitate, "Where's the disco?

Where are you taking me?"

"This is it! Don't worry, you will like it much," assures Juanita.

The sisters each take one of my arms and we walk into the building in lock step. Once inside, the transformation is astonishing. Fog rolls out from a dry ice machine and the darkness is cut by several mirrored disco globes hanging from the ceiling. Strobe lights flash, giving an unworldly staccato feel to our movements.

It's a mix of *Saturday Night Fever* and a Mexican fiesta. The disco scene is fading at home, but must just be beginning here. The music is loud, but not deafening. I'm more of a Grateful Dead or Joni Mitchel fan, but this isn't too bad.

My eyes must be as wide as saucers for the girls smile at me and casually say, "This is good as *Norteamérica, ¿sí?*" I nod my head and start to speak when a very tall man grabs Socorro from behind. I'm ready to help her resist, but she laughs sexily and swings easily into his arms.

Juanita turns to me and says, "That's Roberto. He wants to be the *novio* of Socorro and marry her. She does not wish for that."

"Of course not," I say with an air of authority. "She's too young."

"She has nineteen years and I have eighteen," counters Juanita.

"In Mexico, she is not too young. But that is not why she won't marry him. She wants to marry a gringo and live in United States. She wants more freedom."

I look at them laughing in each other's arms. Both are strikingly beautiful. Creamy colored skin and dark hair, a perfect Hispanic version of Barbie and Ken.

Juanita whispers so Roberto can't hear her. "Papa does not approve of him because he's poor. Papa only thinks about money."

"What about college?" I venture to interject a little elderly wisdom. "Have you two girls thought about what you're going to do in the future?"

"Papa wants to marry me to some old man." Socorro says turning from Roberto, "I want to go to America. I want to travel the world."

"Yes, he wants to arrange a marriage," Juanita excitedly continues.

"He wants her to marry a rich businessman from Tampico, so Papa can get more money too."

"He would have married me to someone on my fifteenth birthday," Socorro agrees. "But Mama stopped him. She is the only one who protects us from him."

"He does not approve of this place either. We should be able to go where we want."

I nod in agreement. At eighteen or nineteen, I would want to be making my own decisions. This place seems harmless, but it's definitely not the quiet night their father imagines.

Juanita and I are left to our own devices when Socorro goes to the dance floor with Roberto. With her arm still entwined with mine, as if to make sure I won't escape, she leads me deeper into the throng of people. Heads turn our way and I feel a blush come to my cheeks. I'm not used to being the center of attention. Why do I always feel guilty when I haven't done anything wrong?

A picture of Sister Mary Clement Marie pops into my head shaking her head and warning. "Just look how you're dressed... sequins and revealing top. Of course people are going to stare at you... and not for the right reasons."

Juanita ignores the attention and scans the room for people she knows. I push down my feelings of anxiety and let her lead the way. She finally spots a group of people standing in the corner and waves to them. We work our way slowly through the crowd.

Juanita's friends start speaking Spanish. I wish I could slow them down or even rewind the conversation. I hear a few words I understand:

Norteamérica, no habla espanol, Socorro. But there are a few new words that are said over and over I don't understand: *bonita, novela, and joven.* I wish I hadn't left my dictionary in the car. I slowly back up to the corner, so I can be less conspicuous.

Juanita starts to say something to me when a handsome man walks up to the group with an armload of beers. While he distributes the beers to the group, he turns and sees me. His eyes move up and down very slowly. For the first time in my life I understand the saying "he undressed me with his eyes." I feel naked and exposed in front of him.

Oh, Sister Mary Clement Marie, maybe you're right.

He quickly asks who I am and Juanita responds. They exchange a few short phrases.

Juanita says, "Genny, I introduce you, Ernesto Soto."

Ernesto extends the last beer to my left hand and takes my right hand in his. He brings it to his lips and gently kisses the tops of my fingers. I feel a shot of electricity shoot through my entire body. I stumble backward in astonishment. Ernesto smiles widely seeing the intended effect he has on me.

Juanita turns him towards her, and speaks in a harsh tone. Ernesto laughs, "Nice to meet you, Genny," he says and turns to the others in the group.

"Stay away from Ernesto," Juanita whispers. "He thinks he is a playboy. He is my friend, but I do not trust him with your heart."

"Why? What has he done that's so bad?"

"He has taken the flower from two of my friends and left them with no promise of marriage."

It takes me a second to understand what this means and I giggle at the statement.

She scowls at my reaction. "And whatever you do, don't look into his eyes."

"¿*Mal de ojo*?" I question.

"No, much worse than the evil eye, he will capture your soul." Juanita laughs gently. "He will make you believe you are the only woman in the world for him. His eyes lie to women and the women want to believe them."

I laugh. "I'll be gone tomorrow and I'll never see him again." I turn my attention back to my beer and take a deep drink. She really believes he has that kind of power over women.

Another man in the group comes over and introduces himself as Juan. He asks me to dance. When I decline, he promptly asks Juanita who accepts. I realize he's being polite and I smile at Juanita who hands me her beer and moves toward the dance floor. As she leaves, Socorro reappears, breathless with excitement. Her coiffed hair is no longer rigidly styled and her skin is glistening with small beads of perspiration. She's quite beautiful in this messy state.

She takes a sip of Juanita's beer and with a conspiratorial look at me, says, "Let's dance."

I look around like a trapped rabbit. I don't think I should be dancing in this place. Like a tourist in a museum exhibit, I want to watch,not participate. I hold up my hands with the beers, as if to show her I can't go - I have a different duty to perform. But she takes the beers from me and gives them to the others in the group. I dutifully follow her.

The smoke from the dry ice lends an eerie feeling to the dance floor and the strobe lights are hypnotic. Socorro moves her arms rhythmically above her head and dances like a flamenco dancer. She takes my hands and motions for me to follow. I awkwardly mimic her dance steps, which are part John Travolta and part salsa. My long hair falls gently down my back and tickles my elbows. Socorro twirls around on her heels and I do the same. I'm trying to relax with the music and enjoy the moment despite the unfamiliar surroundings. The more Socorro moves, the more I follow, intoxicated by the foreign and exotic music.

The music suddenly stops and I realize the dance floor is empty except for Socorro and me. All eyes are on us and everyone starts to clap. I'm both embarrassed and invigorated by the attention. I imagine Sister Mary Clement Marie shaking her head and wagging a finger disapprovingly at me.

Socorro curtsies to the audience and takes my hand to walk off the dance floor. Apparently, Socorro is used to this kind of attention. The crowd thins and the girls begrudgingly decide to leave. On the way home, we pull over to the side of the road and change back into our proper costumes to squelch any suspicion from the family. Before we go into the house, I check on my birds. I feel more than a little guilty that I'm neglecting them, but Humberto and the gardener are taking good care of them.

The area around the house has few lights so the stars are brilliant. I can see why so many people come for romantic vacations in Mexico. The area appears untouched by the rest of the world.

We quietly enter the house and climb the stairs. The girls have two double beds in their room and say they will share one so I can have one to myself. I change into my night shirt and dive into the bed. The girls quickly settle into their bed and I into mine. I look at my watch and see it is 1:45.

I want to get an early start in the morning, so I'm glad the girls don't want to talk any more. I'm asleep as soon as my head hits the pillow. In what seems like a minute or two later, I hear a rustling outside the window and am up with a start. The girls are already at the window when I join them. Below are the silhouettes of three men. At first, I'm alarmed, but one of them starts strumming a guitar and they start singing.

We're being serenaded. *I truly am on a different planet.*

The girls giggle as the young men sing slightly off-key, but it's the most romantic thing I've ever witnessed. Juanita reaches out the window and pinches off a bloom from a nearby bougainvillea branch and throws it to the young men below. Encouraged by this action, the three start a second song. This time the voices are stronger and less tentative. They are more expressive and passionate as they sing. The lights downstairs come on just as they're about to sing a refrain and Raul yells out his window.

Once lit, I recognize the faces of the three singers. The first one is Roberto, who first danced with Socorro, the second is Juan, who danced with Juanita, and the third is Ernesto. Ernesto looks directly at me, bows and blows me a kiss. The three run off and I hear the motor of a car start up in the distance.

Victoria comes up to the room and tells the girls and me to get to sleep. The soft light from the hall shows her long hair flowing around her slight frame. The sisters beckon their mother to come into their bed. All three of them giggle like school girls at a slumber party. I can only imagine the mother must have had similar nights as a young woman and doesn't want to spoil the moment for her daughters.

I lie in bed wide awake and hear them softly whisper among

themselves. I look at my watch in the dark. It glows 2:30. I'll be dead tired tomorrow on the drive to Texas. Gradually I fall back asleep reliving tonight's adventure - the excitement of a kiss on the hand, dancing in the center of the floor, being serenaded by Ernesto. I feel like I'm being pulled into some sort of strange fantasy, not sure if I want to stay or go.

"Mom, these things are so fake looking." The three way mirror in the changing room shows every angle of the heavily padded bra on my flat chest.

"They look like they have cones in them."

"What about the one with all the flowers?"

"You'll be able to see the flowers through my uniform blouse." I hold my blouse and flowered bra together to show the transparency. "All the boys will laugh at me."

"I'm sure they won't laugh, Genny."

"Mom, they already laugh at me for being flat chested, accentuating it with flowers won't help. Please, can't you make me another camisole? They fit so much better than these things and they don't make me look fake."

"JoAnn's fabric is on the other side of town," she resists.

"Pleeeaase! You know you're the best seamstress this side of the Mississippi."

"You used to say in the whole wide world," She picks up the heap of rejected bras and hands them to the disgruntled sale's girl who gave up hope of a sale long ago. "I've been dying to try a new material that the girls in the sewing group mentioned."

"Can you make it with the hooks in the front?" I hold the door open for her as we leave the store. "It's hard for me to put the camisole on after my swim meets."

"It would be easier if you dried off completely before you put your clothes on." She smiles. "You're always in such a hurry."

"Thanks, Mom." I give her a quick hug. "You're the best seamstress in the whole universe."

CHAPTER EIGHT

Back in Time

I'm dead tired, but jump out of bed quickly when I see I'm the only one in the room and it's almost 7:00 in the morning. Hot shower, pull on my jeans from the previous night, dig in my backpack for a fresh blouse and fish out another camisole. Thank God, mom made one for each day of the week. I don't know why they're the butt of Socorro's ridicule. I love them.

I run downstairs.

The girls are in the kitchen lazily eating while Victoria cooks breakfast. They motion for me to sit at the end of the table.

No rush here. This truly is the land of mañana. I feel like I'm going ninety miles an hour while everyone else is standing still.

"Son juevos con camerones," Victoria says as she brings the fry pan from the stove, serving the steaming food onto my plate.

I move the food around with my fork inspecting the scrambled jumble. Eggs are recognizable, but there are small bits of white meat and what looks like corn chips mixed in.

"Eggs, shrimp and tortillas," Juanita translates.

The girls watch me expectantly as I take a few bites. I grab a glass of water to cool my mouth when the hot spices kick in.

"Eat some cheese," they laugh.

"Do all your foods have to be so hot? I ask.

"It is good to sweat. It keeps you cool." Socorro picks up a hot

50

pepper and takes a bite with ease.

I reach for a red clay bowl on the table to examine. In its center is a picture of a man's profile with a large nose. He's holding a challis to his lips. "This is pretty cool."

Socorro takes the bowl from me and says, "Yes, cool. Papa bought it at the market yesterday." She hands it to Juanita who stashes it in a wooden crate under the table.

"Where's Humberto?" I alternate eating some eggs, then biting some cheese.

"He and papa went to town for the day. They will be back late," Socorro answers. "What do you want to do today?"

Before I can react negatively to this news, Juanita says, "Papa and Humberto are very close."

"They don't get to see one another often, so they will be together today," Socorro hastily adds.

"My birds need to get home." My voice rises in desperation.

"Humberto has taken care of your birds. He fed them this morning and keeps them out of the sun. They will be good," Juanita assures me.

"We will take you to the pyramids today," Socorro springs from her chair. She and Juanita almost pick me up off my feet to usher me out the door.

Like a stubborn mule I dig my heels into the ground as we head to the car. "I need to check on my birds." Someone has cut up several pomegranates and the birds are feasting on them. The cages are clean and have plenty of water and seed. None of the birds are molting or showing signs of stress. Perhaps this shady spot under the banyan tree is helping the birds recover from both the boat trip and hot ride in the van.

The birds squawk as I reach in and retrieve Rocky along with some pomegranate. I place him on my shoulder and grab a cloth satchel from the top of one of the cages before joining the girls.

The three of us pile into the car along with Rocky. Socorro drives, Juanita rides shotgun while I'm in the back seat feeding pomegranate to Rocky. He still likes taking food from my mouth, so I put one seed at a time between my lips and he pecks it lose with his beak. My shoulder is quickly stained with purple-red juice and my hair is tangled from his constant pecks.

"You have a pyramid?" I ask.

"*Sí, Señorita* Genny. We have a pyramid. It's Socorro's and mine," Juanita giggles.

Socorro laughs at the little joke, but explains further. "It is called *la piramide de calendario*. It is fifty kilometers from here. There are bird men there too."

I'm captive for another day. M*añana mañana mañana*… Resistance is futile, acceptance comes with prayer. It's time to pray that I get home soon.

The girls are excited. I can only guess they rarely have this kind of freedom away from the watchful eyes of their parents.

Socorro turns the wheel of the car sharply and we head down a dirt road. Juanita starts to protest, but the car stops quickly. Socorro beeps the horn and Roberto runs up to her window. They speak Spanish, but Juanita interprets, "Socorro invited more people for a picnic. I hope it is fine with you."

"Yes, of course." *What else am I going to say?*

Roberto runs back to his house while Socorro turns the car around. Juanita sits back in her seat resigned to her sister's schemes. Now both Juanita and I are along for the ride.

The roads are like deep scars scratched into the sides of the mountains with switchbacks and washouts that barely clear one car at a time. The absence of guard rails adds an extra measure of danger. As we drive through small dips in the road, we are totally enveloped in small patches of fog with zero visibility. Each time we escape one dense cloud, it's like escaping a near death experience. Socorro looks over to Juanita and grins broadly and then grinds the gears while she navigates hairpin turns. She tests her driving skills and Juanita's patience. Neither of them is particularly a good driver as far as I'm concerned.

We make a hard right turn at a fork in the road which narrows quickly and is overgrown with thick vegetation. As we slowly creep our way down the overgrown road, tree branches scratch the doors of the car or spring back from the mirror. A small burro hurries off the road with a short horn blast. Just as I'm about to ask if we're lost, a clearing appears and we park.

I put Rocky into the cloth satchel and sling it around my shoulder before we all climb out of the car. I stretch my limbs, stiff from dancing the night before. I notice neither of the girls is particularly sore. They're thin and lithe and in very good shape so I ask, "Do you girls run in races or workout?"

"What are races?" Juanita queries.

"You know, running or working out? How do you get your bodies so strong?"

"We dance." Socorro stands straight with one arm above her head and the other centered in front of her body.

"You and Juanita are dancers?"

"Yes, we dance the flamenco and the calypso all over Mexico in many shows."

Last night at the disco suddenly makes sense. They're the center of attention naturally when they perform. Last night was a performance. Socorro pops the trunk and pulls out a couple of blankets and an empty ice chest. Within minutes, Roberto, Juan and Ernesto pull up beside us with drinks and ice along with individually wrapped tacos. Socorro hands the blankets and ice chest to Roberto, who dutifully obliges her.

Socorro and Roberto lead the way up the steep incline with Juanita and Juan following right behind. Ernesto and I bring up the end.

The path is narrow and the encroaching jungle fights to recapture the land. Clearly, they've come here often so they walk at a fast clip barely noticing their surroundings. Small lizards and field mice scurry across the path as our small procession disturbs their quiet morning routine.

Ernesto points to a light mist as it floats up from the warm earth and catches a small rainbow within it. "The people here call it *The Breath of the Earth*."

I slow my pace as much as is prudent to watch the stunning scenery. There's a thick veil of clouds hiding the view, but the heat of the morning sun quickly burns it off and gives me the opportunity to see the higher mountains in the distance.

When we reach the edge of the ridge, the sun burns off more low lying clouds and reveals three enormous pyramids. An electric charge shoots up my spine. This must be how the Spaniards felt when they saw this valley for the first time hundreds of years ago. It's as if we've traveled back in time many centuries. I suck in my breath and get light headed.

The others continue down the path, but Ernesto stays by my side.

"What's this place called?" The words catch in my throat.

"*El Tajin.*" In a low hushed tone, he whispers in my ear, "This place is sacred to us."

"Where are the people who built this?"

"We are the people. They are our ancestors. This is my heritage." He moves closer.

"Hurry, Genny, you will miss the show," calls Juanita.

"Show? What show?" I run toward Juanita and the others.

Socorro's lying on one of the blankets with Roberto sitting as close to her as possible. It's obvious he likes her more than she likes him and she knows the power she has over him. Juanita appears to be the good girl in the family and Socorro is the flirt. Juanita passes some sodas from the cooler before she sits down next to Juan. There are a few apples and some cheese passed for a light snack. Ernesto sits next to Socorro and starts to tease her. They laugh softly as Roberto watches, wishing, I'm sure, he could be as suave and charming as Ernesto. I sit next to Juanita and Juan who are holding hands.

More people come from every part of the jungle, carrying blankets and refreshments to set up along the hillside. A small man dressed in brightly colored native garb comes around to each group and collects a twenty-five cent fee for the show from each person. Ernesto pays for our group.

I dig into the satchel and retrieve Rocky to put him on his perch next to my ear. His claws dig a little into my shoulder as he shakes his entire body to straighten his slightly ruffled feathers. Juanita holds a small cup of water to him and he drinks a few gulps. There's soft chatter in the crowd as we wait for the show to begin.

Sweet music from a flute floats through the air and Rocky jumps down onto the blanket. He cranes his neck to listen and bobs his head up and down, dancing to the rhythm of the music. He starts to whistle and mimic the sound coming from the jungle. I pick him up and give him some pomegranate to distract him while the crowd quiets. The sound gets closer. We look toward the jungle to see what's coming.

CHAPTER NINE

Bird Men

In the distance, five men slowly parade out of the jungle playing primitive instruments. The first man leads the group like the pied piper with a small flute to his mouth. Soft drumming accompanies the melodic flutist as the remaining four men twist small hand-held drums back and forth in their hands and dance in a serpentine path through the crowd. I'm mesmerized and transported back centuries by the hypnotic music . with the ancient ruins as a backdrop.

They wear ceremonial costumes with bright colors and small headdresses. Their clothes are tight-fitting to their dark, lean bodies and thin sashes are tied around their waists. As they make their way to the top of a small mound, the music stops. The men start to climb, one by one, up a tall fifty-foot pole.

When they reach a small square platform at the top, they stand to face the crowd below. Four of the five men tie ropes around their waists while the fifth man positions himself at the center and starts to play the flute once again.

A collective gasp emits from the crowd as the four men dive head first in unison from the platform toward the crowd below. The four ropes attached to their waists are released slowly from a wheel at the top of the pole. The men's weight and the centrifugal force unwind the ropes as they fly to earth. They flip upright just prior to touching the ground and the crowd claps enthusiastically.

Tears stream down my face as I look up to see everyone staring at me. "I'm sorry." I stammer. "That was so beautiful. I cry at everything, I'm very emotional." I start to laugh.

The others laugh too and I feel foolish by my outburst of emotion.

"I'm glad that you cry." Juanita hugs me. "It makes us remember how important this really is. We forget. We see it all the time. I see it through your eyes today. *Muchas gracias.*"

The group is quiet and I want to change the subject. "Tell me about the pyramids. And tell me about those men."

"The main pyramid has three-hundred-sixty five *bloques cuadrados.*" Roberto points to the small stone cubicles making up the pyramid. He decides to be the professor. "Each day an offering was made to the gods in the *cuadrados.* These ceremonies are passed from father to son to son. This ritual honors the former gods and ancient people who walked this area long ago. The men's regal beak noses confirm their ancestry. They are called the *Bird Men.*"

"They were amazing," I say. "I've never seen anything like it."

"When the seasons change on the solstice, the light hits the pyramid to line it up exactly with the moon and the stars." Roberto stands taller as he explains this to me.

"What kinds of things were sacrificed?"

"Mostly, crops and small animals." He continues. "There were some human sacrifices, but rarely."

I shiver a little at the thought.

As we walk around the ruins, he points out the perimeters of the ancient village that has all but faded into the jungle. There, along the outer walls, trees grow atop the stones with their roots totally entombing the ancient structure, trying to drag it back into the earth's heart.

"The *Flying Bird Men* are from a lesser tribe of the Mayans." Roberto continues. "The translation may be wrong since it came from the Spaniards, but they are called the Totanaka tribe. Most of them were slaughtered by the Spaniards."

"What do you mean?"

"When the Spaniards came here to make everyone Christians, they killed most of the lesser tribes." Roberto's face looks pained from this piece of history. "Every place there was an altar, the Spaniards tried to make a Catholic Church or mission. More blood was spilled by the Spaniards than by any of the tribes making sacrifices on their altars. They killed hundreds of thousands of native tribes in order to convert them to their true faith."

"I learned about this in school, but it never seemed so tragic until now. How did they keep these traditions alive?"
"Some of the people fled into the jungle." Roberto continues, "The Spaniards just wanted the gold."

"The government is still robbing these people," Ernesto interrupts. "All of the history of this land is sold to the highest bidder. There is even a rumor that another pyramid exists hidden in the jungle, but only the government knows where it is. In that way, they can have a constant supply of artifacts and take the profits for themselves"

Socorro playfully jumps on Ernesto's back and he catches her to carry her lithe body. She rubs his hair and messes it up while she teases,

"Are they yours, Ernesto? Do they take *your* precious artifacts?"

"They belong to *all* of us." Ernesto's voice rises. "The grave robbers take everything and sell it in *Norteamérica*. All of us should be angry. The museums in New York have better examples than we have in Mexico."

"That is an old story," Socorro chides Ernesto, "No one really believes that. And no one could keep that a secret for so long."

"If a poor farmer finds an old bowl in his field, he has two choices," Juan starts. "He can give it to the government and get nothing.

Then the government sells it for lots of money."

"Or he can sell the pot for more money than he can earn in one year farming. He would be *un pendejo* if he gave it to the government," Roberto finishes.

"Our country is not for sale." Ernesto gently puts Socorro down and faces the group with a serious look in his eyes. "We need to stop this robbery."

Socorro's smile fades and she looks to Juanita with a worried look. "Genny does not need to be concerned with our political problems," Juanita interrupts. "Roberto, please tell her about our Bird Men."

Roberto continues with his history lesson as we make our way to the car and our tour comes to an end. I give Rocky some more seed and pomegranate. The picnic wasn't enough food divided among the six of us and I'm suddenly hungry. Socorro says what I'm thinking. "Mama will have food prepared for us."

There are deep secrets hidden here, so much pain and pride. On our way back, my mind wanders over the giant stones and into the jungle to the top of the pole with the Bird Men. They fly through the air to honor their heritage – what was lost and what is saved. I feel it too. It's all part of me: feathers, wind, and most of all --height… the higher, the better.

Summer 1972

The excitement begins when my foot touches the bottom rung of the ladder. With each step higher, my heart runs faster. The sandpaper sensation as I step onto the top board and the view from such heights sends shivers up my spine.

After Mom found me jumping off the garage roof with an umbrella, she enrolled me in classes at the YWCA. Since then, the pool has been my second home and the high dive my refuge. From this height, the world and all my troubles seem small. I am safe on this perch, above it all.

First bounce -- the board meets my feet and bends my knees, second bounce -- my feet barely touch, third bounce --I'm airborne, flying to the sky, arms outstretched to heaven. Free.

CHAPTER TEN

La Fiesta

My heart sinks when I see Humberto's van. It's loaded on top with a lot of unmarked, wooden crates and now a small trailer has been attached to the rear, full of more items. Did he load my birds into the back compartment in this heat? I jump out of the girls' car with my heart racing to check on my poor birds. Rocky clutches my shirt as I make my way around the van and see the gardener, standing by the shaded cages, feeding fruit to the birds.

"*Hola.*" I say on my approach.

"*Buenas tardes, señorita,*" he turns toward me and smiles.

"*Habla inglés?*"

"*No, señorita. No hablo inglés.*"

Just as I'm about to reach for my dictionary, Juanita comes up behind me and saves me from having to struggle with Spanish. "*Hola, Miguel.*"

"Please thank him for taking care of the birds so well." I carefully scrutinize the birds. The water and food troughs are full and they're calm.

"Has he noticed any of the birds fighting?"

"*No, señorita,*" he responds.

"Does he need more food for them?"

"They really liked the pomegranate, so he cut up other fruits and flowers for them to eat." Juanita conveys his responses. "They like that better than the dry seeds in the bags."

"Yes, Rocky loved the pomegranate too." I point to Rocky on my shoulder and the juice stains on my blouse. The gardener smiles at the mess.

I look at the birds and feel guilty I'm not the one taking care of them. I coo to them softly. Rocky responds by bobbing his head up and down. Some of the other birds do likewise. I pick up a handful of sunflower seeds that are in a bag next to the cage and put some in my mouth. Rocky takes a seed out of my mouth. I bring my mouth close to the cage and feed some of the other birds the same way. Miguel looks at me with a measure of surprise and approval. I put Rocky in his little cage and Juanita and I walk back to the house arm in arm.

The sun's setting and I'm surprised the entire day's gone so quickly. I wonder if Humberto plans to drive through the night. Since the van is packed, I assume we'll leave soon.

Inside, Victoria has set the table with a roasted pig placed in the middle of the table. It looks like a party is about to happen. Humberto and Raul sit on the sofa drinking wine. There's definitely a celebratory mood in the house.

The men stand when they see me. Both are quite animated when they say, "*Hola, Genny,* cómo estás?"

"*Muy bien,* señors, *Gracias.*"

Humberto smiles broadly, "You are learning Spanish quickly *señorita.* One more week and you will be speaking like me.

"One more week. We aren't staying for one more week?!"

"No, no *señorita.* We go in *la mañana.*" He smiles broadly and continues, "But tonight we have *una fiesta.*"

Several people enter through the front door carrying food and drinks. Victoria walks in from the kitchen area carrying more wine. The girls know instantly to run up the stairs to prepare. I'm in the middle of a tornado wondering what direction this will take me next. I hear the girls call me from their room. As I walk up the stairs, more people and lots more beer arrive through the front door. It looks like Raul and Humberto can put together a party at a moment's notice too. The food does look good and I'm definitely hungry. What harm can come from a little party?

The girls whirl around like little dust devils before a storm. The air's electric and I can feel the excitement in their voices.

"Should I go somewhere while you and your family have your party?" I ask tentatively.

"Genny, don't you want to come to our party?" Juanita stands completely still and reaches out her arms and holds my shoulders firmly with her delicate hands. It looks like I've slapped her in the face.

"Of course, I want to come to the party", I stammer. "I just don't want to intrude. This seems to be for your *familia*."

"Oh no, Genny. This party is in your honor; your honor and Humberto's. Humberto says you bring him luck. He and Papa have many things to take to *Estados Unidos* for their business and you will help him."

"I will help him? Of course, I'll help all I can but I don't know what I could do."

"He will help you get the birds across the border and you will help him make the crossing with his merchandise. He is very happy you are here. *We* are happy that you are here. This party is to show you our happiness."

"Then I'm happy, too." I'm still a little confused by the reaction to my bringing "luck". I'm not sure how difficult it will be to get the birds across the border and can't imagine how we're going to do it.

"*Sí*, Genny. We are so happy you are here." Socorro says,

"Tonight is your night. We will all celebrate. You must get dressed very special. You are going to be the center of the party. I have some clothes that will make you very sexy."

I'm about to protest, but if they want to have a party in my honor and dress me for their occasion, who am I to stop it? *I will never see these people again.*

The noise from downstairs gets louder, but the girls focus on every detail of their wardrobe and mine. I let go of any resistance and don't even bother to look in the mirror for I'm sure to be unrecognizable, even to myself.

As they apply my makeup with experienced hands, I think back to my first experimentations with makeup and girly clothes. My mother's bureau was stacked with dark red rouge, lipstick and glamorous clothes. The back of her closet held exotic leopard skin mufflers and beaver coats I paraded around in. The high heels were for playing Cinderella with my little brother as Prince Charming. Lipstick never stayed within the lines of my lips and mascara only gave me black eyes, and with three older brothers for an audience I soon stopped trying. Becoming a tomboy was easier and much more fun at the time. With the girls' enthusiasm, I'm almost enjoying this transformation. There's liberation in anonymity. I can be someone totally different without the scrutiny from my family and old friends. At some time in the future, I might explore my feminine mystique. This gives me a window from which to look, at least. They pull my hair into a tight bun and slick it back with hair gel to match their perfectly coiffed hairdos.

At first, I believe I hear a stereo playing music, but I peek through the upstairs window into the courtyard and realize there's a mariachi band playing. Finally, the finishing touches are applied and the girls pronounce us ready to go downstairs. Socorro goes out of the bedroom first and dances her way down the stairs. Juanita waits until her sister reaches the bottom stair, takes a deep breath to stand taller in her frame before she exits through the door. She raises one arm above her head and the other in front of her torso in a calypso stance and floats down the stairs to the awaiting audience. People clap as she hits the final step.

I'm frozen in place. Surely, they don't mean for me to come down the stairs in a grand entrance. I peek around the corner of the doorway and see the girls dancing and whirling around the crowd in the grand room. The tile floors reverberate the clicking of their shoes and their full skirts open wider as they spin.

I'm totally focused on them and their movements when I see someone staring up at me from the bottom of the stairs. It's Ernesto. As soon as our eyes meet, I retreat behind the door frame and try to press my body as close to the wall as possible. Honestly, I wish I could evaporate right at this moment. I can't breathe, I can't move, I can't open my eyes.

Maybe I can stay here the rest of the night.

I silently say a prayer to quiet my mind and force myself to breathe deeply. Just let things happen naturally.

When I open my eyes, Ernesto is standing in front of me, watching me with a quizzical eye. He reaches for my hand, "Do not be afraid, *Señorita* Genny. It does not hurt to walk into a room of people. I will help you."

He leads me through the doorway and down the stairs. The room is full of people, but my entrance is no longer a high expectation. No one claps or even acknowledges me as I hit the last step. Ernesto smiles, "Now see, that didn't hurt."

I'm a little embarrassed I worked myself up for nothing, but everything seems to be taken with a grain of salt here. Maybe I take myself too seriously for my own good. The girls certainly don't take themselves too seriously. They float through the room smiling and laughing instead of being weighed down.

Ernesto guides me through the French doors to the courtyard for a better view of the band. The lead singer strums his guitar and practically cries the words to his song. The audience is enthralled by his performance. He brings a hand to his eyes and dabs away tears flowing freely.

"What are they singing? What do the words mean?"

"The name of the song is *Mi Viejo*. The literal translation is 'my old man', but it is an endearment for 'my father or sometimes my grandfather'. The song talks of an old man's eyes dying and how much they have seen. It also says how much he will be missed when he is gone."

"Oh, that's so beautiful. It reminds me of the music my uncle used to play at parties when I was young. It sounds like it has a Middle Eastern melody in it."

"Yes, some of the origins in our music are from the Middle East. Music is the language of the heart and soul," he says, then takes my hand and places it over his heart. "You can feel it here." I can't help but look into his eyes. *Juanita said not look into his eyes.* I force myself to look down.

As if on cue, Juanita comes over and pulls me away from Ernesto and into the crowd of people. "Watch out, Genny," she says breathlessly.

"He is not good for you."

I turn back to Ernesto to wave goodbye, but he's already walking toward another girl in the crowd. Maybe Juanita is right.

The party dies down to a lone guitarist singing slightly off key. As tired as I am, I can't sleep. The Bird Men, the pyramids and the serenade explode in my mind. It's like I walked right out of my own shoes and into someone else's.

CHAPTER ELEVEN
Vanilla Capital

My ears perk up to noises from the rooms below. The girls sleep soundly in their bed. I'm curled up under the covers and must fight my way out from under the tangled sheets. I look out the window for signs of activity. The moonlight is fading to the dawn's brighter light. My birds sleep under the trees and everything is quite still. I pull on my jeans and shirt and rush downstairs to make sure Humberto is readying to leave.

I want to scream when I hit the bottom of the stairs. The guests are still here and the party's going strong. Raul and Humberto are in the corner singing and playing a guitar. As I come into view, they both simultaneously raise their Corona beers to salute me.

"*Señorita,* you have finally returned to la fiesta. You sleep *bien? Quieres una cerveza?*"

All hope of leaving today vanishes.

"*Señor, por favor*! When do we leave?"

"*Ah, sí, sí, sí.* Now. *Señorita.* We leave now." He pushes himself up from the table to a standing position. Ernesto and another man quickly flank him on each side and catch him as he passes out. Three other men quickly pick up the rest of his heavy body and carry him to a room on the other side of the house.

Everything caves in on me. I'm never going to get out of here. This is a Mexican twilight zone. I cover my face with my hands and run outside to my birds. They flap their wings and bob their heads up and down to greet me. My poor, poor birds. I feel guilty that I've left them for the gardener to take care of, guilty that we are still not home and settled, guilty that Jeffrey trusted me to deliver the birds safely and I'm so helpless. I start to cry and the birds squawk at the distressing noises.

"Genny, this is how we are," Victoria says putting a hand on my back. "It takes time to prepare for a trip to *Norteamérica*."

"I don't understand. The van is packed. What else needs to be done?"

She wraps her arm around my shoulder and softly says, "Sometimes people don't come back from *Estados Unidos* for a long time when they go. Humberto needs to be prepared to stay there for a long time." She crosses herself as she says this.

It takes a minute for it to register with me. Victoria speaks English perfectly.

Now it makes sense. Of course, I should have put the pieces of the puzzle together quicker. If he crosses the border illegally, he may be held indefinitely.

"Oh, I'm so sorry." I'm both contrite and afraid. "I never thought of that." Some partygoers start packing up their things. Another wave of shame blasts me. I've created a scene. "I'm so sorry I made everyone leave the party."

"They needed to go home hours ago." Victoria smiles at me. "I went to bed shortly after you did. I have had enough of them for today. You and I will go for our own little trip."

I start to object, but feel too drained to offer much resistance. Victoria and I walk to the car and get in. The girls rush to the driver's side of the car to question their mother but she's more than prepared to quell their protests. "Genny and I are going to Papantla. The two of you stay and clean the house. I have made menudo for everyone when they wake up."

The girls look disappointed, but go back into the house. Miguel is at the birds' cages cooing with them as we drive off.

"What's menudo?" There are always so many questions to ask and sometimes I feel silly asking them, but I want to learn as much as possible.

"It is a soup for hangovers. I am sure that everyone will need some to feel better. "This is a perfect day for us to go to the mountains," Victoria looks sideways at me as she drives. "Everyone will be sleeping all day and we can play. I will show you parts of Mexico the *touristas* do not see."

Once we're on the road, Victoria drives with an intensity usually reserved for race car drivers. She's grips the top of the steering wheel and her entire body pulls forward so her head is as close to the windshield as she can possibly get. I don't want to distract her. My first inclination is to settle back into my seat and watch the landscape change as we climb into the mountains, but something strikes me as funny when I look at her. I've studied my host closely, but not my hostess. Raul looks to be in his mid-sixties, maybe even early seventies. I'd assumed that Victoria was in her forties or fifties, but upon closer inspection, I see she is much younger. "Victoria, How old are you?" I ask tentatively.

"I have thirty-three years,"

This shocks me. Since Socorro is eighteen years old and Juanita is seventeen, my quick calculations estimate that Victoria must have had

Socorro when she was fifteen years old.

She looks in my direction and our eyes meet. "I married Raul right after my *quinceañera*," she says in a quiet tone.

Afraid to take away the gravity of the moment, but lacking any kind of diplomacy I ask, "What's a *quinceañera*?"

"A *quinceañera* is a party that a family gives their daughters on their fifteenth birthday." She smiles, but instead of feeling a joy from the smile, I feel a deep sadness from it.

"That sounds like a lot of fun!" I say, hoping I'm misinterpreting her mood.

"There are many customs in Mexico an outsider would not understand. I'm sure that it is fun for some girls. A girl becomes a woman after her *quinceañera*."

"She becomes a woman at fifteen. What does that mean?" I ask.

"It means the girl can be married off. It means her childhood has died. She can no longer act as a girl, but has to think like a woman."

Either Victoria drives a little slower or the world slows a bit around us.

"Oh, Victoria, that sounds terrible." It occurs to me that she's speaking about herself. "Couldn't you say or do anything?"

"Raul is a very rich man. Most people think I am very lucky. I have a beautiful home and two beautiful girls. Some would say that is enough for a woman."

"I read an article once that said lots of societies paired older men with younger women because it was actually better for the girls to be introduced to sex by an older, more experienced man."

"Then they only asked the men if the sex had been better, the girls' answers would have been much different."

I try to reply, but she puts her hand up to silence me. "It was Raul's greatest moment. He got a virgin. It was my worst day. I cried for three days after that night and no one would listen to my tears. My mother said I should be proud I had such a powerful husband."

"Marrying for love is the *only* way I will marry someone." I sit higher in the seat and bring myself to full indignation.

"You will be surprised by some of the actions you will take in life and some of the reasons you do them. I used to think the same way as you, but as I grow older my reasons and expectations change. I can't change my destiny now."

"But why can't you? What's stopping you? You're still young and very beautiful. You could get divorced and find real love."

"Apparently, it is not just Mexicans who are romantic. Young American girls can be romantic, as well." she smiles broadly.

"You could leave and start over," I suggest.

"We all have our crosses to bear." Victoria's voice has resignation in it when she continues, "Everything we do has consequences down the line. I will take my consequence for my sins when the time comes, but my girls should not be made to pay for my problems. Raul would kick us all out. He would destroy me and my girls. I will do everything in my power not to let him do that."

"How do you know what Raul would do?"

Victoria gets quiet and gives full attention to her driving again. When she speaks, she weighs her words carefully. "You are a stranger to me, but it is almost easier to talk to you than it is to my priest. Knowing I will never see you again lets me say things that are inside of me, but I could never tell someone else what I am about to confide in you."

"I won't betray a confidence. You can tell me anything you want."

"Raul first saw me when I was thirteen and has told me over and over again it was love at first sight." Victoria's eyes become glassy and she narrows her view. "He believed he *deserved* to have a virgin to marry. It was his right. I believe that Raul killed his first wife in order to marry me. If he did not actually kill her himself, he at least hastened her death. It all seemed convenient that she died right before my *quinceañera*. The man is not harmless."

I gasp and try to offer some kind of apologies, but my mouth is suddenly dry and I can say nothing.

"Raul is not to be trusted in any manner. I live with him, but I do not trust him. I wait for times like these to get away from him and have time to live. When he is in a drunken stupor, I drive away. It is my time for me." I touch her shoulder to comfort her.

"*Cabron!*" she mutters in Spanish. I make a mental note to myself to look *that* one up.

We continue driving in silence up the mountainside and into the small village, Papantla. The vegetation is thick and the air is sweet with the smell of vanilla.

"This is my heaven. This is where I come to live." Victoria parks the car on the cobble street. "Let me show you some of the village." Victoria almost skips down the street. Her long peasant dress sways back and forth as she climbs the steep street to the shops ahead. I follow one step behind to take in the sights.

Victoria directs me to breathe the air deeply. I do as I'm told. "Do you taste it on your tongue?"

At first, I don't understand what she means, but on my third deep breath I notice the taste of vanilla on my tongue.

Victoria smiles as if a beautiful secret is passed from her to me. It's an odd mixture of the time in the car and the wonder of the moment that captures us. She puts her arm around my shoulder and we walk down the street like old friends, not strangers. I'm seeing life through her eyes now. Mexico's going to forever change me.

"I want you to meet someone that is very special to me." Victoria tilts her head to mine.

We walk past the market and around a corner with small houses lining the lane. The yards are small, but neatly gardened. We walk under an arbor, up a small walkway to a faded yellow house with a Spanish façade. Victoria walks in like a family member, not a guest.

"*Hola, Hola.*" She calls out.

"*Un momento, por favor.*" A male voice returns the call from a back room.

CHAPTER TWELVE

Blind Love

A Mexican soap opera is on the television in the corner of the room. A rustling from the back of the house announces the entrance of a tall, medium-built man through a small doorway. He's wearing blue jeans and sandals, but no shirt. His skin is brown and smooth with no hair on his chest. He first looks at Victoria, then at me, then back to Victoria. He looks nervous; his eyes quickly look around to make sure no one else is around. We've definitely surprised him.

Victoria tells him I'm a friend, but his stance stays rigid. She looks somewhat embarrassed by the circumstance and asks, "Can you sit on the sofa and watch television while Hector and I visit?"

"Of course, no problem." As I sit on the sofa, Victoria moves toward him and falls into his arms. It's as if she has been holding herself upright until she could reach him. He gently embraces her to his bare chest.

I've become instantly invisible. They're no longer aware of me being in the room. He kisses her deeply as she moves hers arms around Hector's shoulders. He dips down and catches her under her knees, and carries her into the back room.

This is where Victoria *lives*. I'm now woven into her little secret world as if I were yarn in one of the blankets the people sell in the market. I hear sounds of crying and soft laughter. Now I understand the magnitude of her secret. This is how she lives *around* her circumstances. As embarrassed as I am to be here, I'm also totally engrossed in the occasion. It's like gawking at a car wreck on the side of the road. I really shouldn't watch, but I can't look away. How extreme do people's lives have to become for them to live this kind of double life? And what about the risks involved? I quietly slip out the front door and walk toward the market.

Events have taken me so off-course, I wonder how such small actions can snowball into huge avalanches. When I bought my plane and started taking flying lessons almost two years ago, I needed "flying time" with an experienced pilot, so I asked a friend of Jeffrey's, Lightning Jackson. He agreed to help me as long as I didn't talk too much. He said he liked his heavens to be quiet when he flew.

On one occasion, when the quietness of heaven was just right, I asked Lightning how he got his nickname. He spoke like I wasn't there, like he was talking to God, not me. "I knowed I was in trouble. There was a lot of smoke. But I thought I could make it over the next ridge and bring it on in home. My rig started losing altitude and it got real quiet. Then I heard the voice clear as day. "Frank, get out!" I knew it was over. I ejected. Guys on the ground spotted my chute. Said they saw lightning shoot across the sky. I practice silence whenever I fly now, in case God ever wants to say something to me again."

Lightning taught me simple rules. The most significant lesson was to fly straight. He said even one degree off could take you hundreds of miles off course in the long run.

He recounted the same story several times about when he once rigged his own auto pilot system, since his old plane didn't come equipped with one. He'd wanted to take a quick nap and had strapped the hand controls with his belt and set a timer so he would wake up in twenty minutes. During his nap, the belt loosened a little and when he awoke he was a hundred miles in the wrong direction. He always smiled at the end of the story. "Fortunately there weren't no mountains that trip."

I walk through the narrow streets of Papantla and wonder how many degrees off I've gone? I wonder when my first degree off course happened.

Fall 1974

    Jackie stretches on the couch and files her nails, "I don't want to get married and live in the burbs."

    "That would be like death to me," I say, aware that my words are a bit dramatic. "I want to get my teaching degree and join the Peace Corps."

    "We need to tour Europe before we get jobs, we can get tickets for the Euro-rail. We can start in Italy and visit my family. Then we'll go see your family."

    "I don't think we can go to Lebanon," I say. "They're in the middle of a war right now."

    "They're always in the middle of a war," she says. "That'll make it even more exciting to go."

    "We're going to fail our chemistry class if we don't get back to studying."

    "My mother loves me coming over here. She says my grades have gone up drastically."

    "My grades have to stay up to get a scholarship. I don't have a choice." Jackie picks up her notebook, "If I get a B or higher on my test, I'll have my mom make cannoli."

    "Deal."

CHAPTER THIRTEEN

A Different Side

Victoria and I drive back from Papantla in silence, her faint smile fades when Socorro and Juanita run to the car when we pull up the driveway. They report how they've suffered all day cleaning the house and feeding everyone the menudo to sober them up. Victoria's demeanor instantly changes. She's no longer the self-assured lover, but becomes the concerned mother.

Victoria walks into the house with the girls, covers her clothes with a brown apron, pulls her hair into a bun and places a headband over her ears and forehead. Like a chameleon, she blends into the background. Now I understand why I didn't notice her when I first came to this house.

She doesn't want to be seen. She looks back over her shoulder, gives me a quick smile and goes into the kitchen with the girls. I return her smile and then hunt for Humberto. There are still a few people scattered around the place, sleeping off the effects of the night before. I check the downstairs, the courtyard and finally find him in the backyard passed out in a hammock. There's no point talking to him now.

I turn to go back into the house, but someone catches me by one arm and twirls me around like a dancer with a quick move. It's Ernesto. He gives me an impish smile, puts his finger to his lips and points to Humberto to show we need to be quiet, then guides me away.

"Have you been here all night?" I ask.

"No, I drove a few people home who had too much to drink and went back to my house. I came back to see if anyone needed my help today."

"Socorro and Juanita cleaned while Victoria and I went out. I'm sure they complained the entire time."

He chuckles, "Would you like to see where I work every summer?"

I study him, "What do you do?"

"I work with the National Geographic Society."

"I'd love to see what you do."

He takes me by the hand like a little boy leading a friend to a secret. It's two o'clock and I'm off on another adventure. I look over my shoulder to see Victoria looking out the window and wave as Ernesto guides me to his small car.

"You are very popular here. *Everyone* wants to be with you, even Victoria. Where did you and she go?" he slowly drives out the driveway. "We drove around the mountains and had lunch," I lie. I don't know how much to say about Victoria, but I think it's safer to say as little as possible. "She's a very special person. She works hard for the girls." He glances at me to see my reaction.

"She's a very good mother," I say, and change the subject. "I'm having a fantastic time. I never thought it'd be so fun here. I've only heard bad things about Mex--- . I'm sorry. I don't mean any disrespect. I've always heard it's dangerous, so far it's been good here."

"*Señorita* Genny, do not be fooled," Ernesto looks at me and his brows furrow into a serious expression. "Mexico is still a dangerous and corrupt place, but young people like me are trying to change that."

"I hope you're right."

"Did Juanita tell you I am in my last year at university to become an attorney?" he asks.

"Juanita only told me you're a playboy and not to look into your eyes."

He laughs nervously and clears his throat. "I have worked with National Geographic for every summer for the last six years. I wanted to become an archeologist, but soon realized I could do more good for my people if I became an attorney and stopped this corruption."

"What kind of corruption?"

"That is what I will show you."

He parks the car in front of a rundown building with a sign that says *Museo* on it. It looks more like an old high school than a museum. The guard smiles when he sees Ernesto and ushers us through the door ahead of a group of young children.

We enter a large room with high ceilings. Florescent lights hang from sagging wires. This could have been an auditorium in an earlier time. Along the walls, old display cases with cracked glass fronts are filled with broken pieces of clay pots. Maps cover the walls above each display case indicating excavation sites with photos from each dig.

"The pottery comes from various tribes that lived in the area before Columbus arrived in the Americas. I was at that dig." Ernesto points to a photo on the wall above us. "We found some beautiful jade carvings there."

I look at the photos of the jade, but the display case contains only shards. "Where are the carvings now?"

"They had to be sent to the museum in Mexico City. This place doesn't have the security needed." A momentary look of disappointment crosses his face, but it's replaced quickly with a smile when a little girl tugs on the bottom of his shirt and asks him a question. He motions for her and the other children to follow him. We move to the center of the room where a wooden platform holds several large stones etched with hieroglyphics.

He picks up some rice paper from one of the shelves and places it over a stone, then gently rubs a piece of charcoal over the indented stone. More children gather to watch him and ask questions. He takes several minutes explaining about the picture. The children thank him politely and move on to the next display with their teacher.

Ernesto turns his attention back to me. "The natives practiced human sacrifices, so a lot of the art depicts bloody scenes in their lives." He hands me the charcoal imprint of a man holding the severed head of another man. "This is for you."

It's both gruesome and beautiful at the same time. I put another sheet of rice paper over the picture and roll it up.

The macho swagger is gone. He doesn't even act like the same person. He's just excited to share these things with me. Maybe Juanita is wrong about him.

We stare at the next display case together. "Most of the pieces are broken." I say.

"Yes, that is the main problem. We usually get to the grave sites after the thieves have already picked the place clean."

"What happens?"

"There are many mounds in the jungle. Some of them are natural formations, some are burial sites."

"Why can't they be guarded?"

"There are hundreds of them, maybe thousands, and we don't know where all of them are," he answers. "At first, when the villagers found one, they turned it over to the government expecting to get paid. Corrupt men in the government took the best pieces for themselves and the shards went to the museums. It didn't take long for the villagers to realize they shouldn't tell any government officials. They dug it up themselves and sold it to collectors directly. They earned a little money, but it was better than nothing."

"Well, you can't blame them for wanting to feed their families."

"I blame the government," Ernesto says. "They take the best for themselves and leave the people starving."

"What can you do about it?"

"I am teaching people about how important our heritage is and if they find something, they will get money for it. The National Geographic Society has helped me form a local foundation. They give me money to help keep our heritage alive and not sold away to wealthy dealers."

"What will you do when you're an attorney?"

"I am going to work for a non-profit group associated with the National Geographic Society. They have more influence on our government than the people do. Hopefully, we can change the system. I want our government to protect our heritage instead of taking bribes. I am going to help make those changes."

"That's very noble, Ernesto."

"I didn't want you to think that I was just a playboy. You're different than the girls here in Mexico. You're not silly and only thinking of boys and getting married." He looks me in the eyes and says, "I wanted you to know I love my country very much."

"I think I understand. I want to make things better in my country too. I teach English as a second language to the students on the border."

"Education is the key for all of us."

Ernesto looks around the museum and sighs deeply. He takes my hand and leads me out of the museum. "I have much work to do here, but I know I can make it better."

"Thank you, Ernesto. This was very nice, but I need to get back to the house now. Hopefully, Humberto is awake and we can leave in the morning. I want to get my birds home and get back to my boyfriend." I feel a blush come over my face. *I've almost forgotten about Jeffrey since I've been here. He's probably worried sick.*

"Your boyfriend is a lucky man."

"Thank you."

When we get back to *la casa Ventana,* Victoria is preparing dinner. Humberto and Raul are awake and everyone eats.

After dinner Ernesto and I walk out to check on my birds.

"Thank you for such a wonderful day, I won't look at Mexico the same way when I get home."

"You're an unusual girl, *Señorita* Genny. It was my pleasure." He takes my hand and softly kisses my fingertips. It's not quite the jolt of the first time, but it's pleasant and leaves me with a warm feeling as I watch him drive away.

Tomorrow I will leave this place. I may never see these people again, but something tells me I will never forget them.

CHAPTER FOURTEEN

Adiós

I look out the girl's window into the courtyard below to see the gardener load my birds into the van. I breathe a sigh of relief. The girls are asleep, so I quietly go downstairs. Humberto and Raul drink coffee while Victoria prepares her usual hearty breakfast of *camerones con juevos*. *This place does have its benefits.* I eat a taco and walk outside.

I try to give Miguel five dollars for taking care of my birds so well, but he refuses to take the money, so I shake his hand and thank him. Humberto climbs into the van and crosses himself. Raul, Victoria and I do the same. The girls wave good-bye from their bedroom window and

Victoria comes to my side of the van to hug me as I get in. She whispers in my ear, "*Vaya con Dios.*"

The birds squawk loudly and flap their wings when Humberto starts the van. I'm a little sad to leave, but excited to get home. Once we hit the road, we keep a steady pace of fifty miles per hour and the birds stop hopping around and settle into the rhythm of the road. I take out my dictionary and start looking up several words I haven't had time to check. Humberto wants to help me. I start with *bonita, novela, and joven.* He's quick to translate those.

Then I say the word *cabrón*. His brow furrows and he's quiet. It must be some kind of swear word. I look it up in the dictionary before he has a chance to say anything.

"Old goat," I say.

He looks at me sideways and says, "*Sí, sí, sí.* It means "old goat." How did you hear this word? Did someone call me a *cabrón*?"

The word must have a second meaning. "Why would anyone call you an old goat?"

"It means my wife is cheating on me."

To tell him who said it would be a mistake. "The girls and I were in the market and they didn't want to buy lunch from one taco stand because it was *cabrón*." I smile broadly at Humberto to hide my lie and he accepts it. I need to be more careful. This can get touchy.

After about an hour, we slow down as we approach a roadblock with a guard. "*Señorita*, don't say a word. If they know you are a *gringa*, they will charge us more. I will do all the talking."

I nod my head.

Humberto stops the van and turns off the engine. The day is heating up and the interior of the van gets hot fast with the windows partially rolled up.

Humberto speaks with the guard, who barely looks inside the van. I put the dictionary in my lap and fold my hands over it. The guard looks over to me and says something to Humberto about the *libro,* which I now know means book. Humberto says something about *inglés* and both he and the guard laugh. Humberto hands the guard some money and he starts the van again. That didn't seem too bad. I think back to Arturo standing on the dock in Tampico. His explanation of the border crossing may have been self-serving.

We drive a little further and stop for gas and something to eat at a roadside taco shack. Although I'm acquiring a taste for hot sauce, this is hot enough to blister my tongue. Humberto laughs a little when he sees my eyes start to water. He takes a fresh chili pepper and bites into it to show me how easy it is for him.

I can barely breathe with my mouth on fire. He proudly says, "Is good for your *estómago*."

I don't remember falling asleep, but I awake when the van comes to a halt at another guard stop. "Where are we?" I ask before noticing the guard standing at the driver's side window, smiling like a Cheshire cat. Humberto gives me a pained look. I forgot to stay silent. Now, what's going to happen?
The guard comes to my side of the van and asks me, "*Señorita*, where are you from?" I look to Humberto who's scared silent.

"*Hola, señor*. I live in the United States. I'm visiting *mi tío*."

Humberto quickly chimes in, "*Sí, sí, sí. Es mi sobrina*." He gets out of the vehicle and speaks Spanish rapidly.

Humberto pays the guard and by the look on the guard's face, he got more than he should have. Humberto gets back in the van and we move down the road. He makes the sign of the cross and kisses the statue. I do the same with earnestness. We definitely have a guardian angel looking after us today. I understand now why Arturo said I couldn't do this alone. And I'm grateful for Humberto. *Mi papi*.

We finally see a sign which says, "United States border, 50 kilometers." We're getting close. It's late in the afternoon and Humberto pulls the van over to a small taco stand. He asks me to get him two tacos and something to drink. When I come back to the van, the birds are going wild. They're squawking and flapping their wings like crazy. "What's wrong with my birds?" I ask.

Humberto smiles and says, "*Señorita*, nothing is wrong. They are just drunk."

My jaw drops and my eyes widen as I look at my poor birds trying to fly or just walk. They're staggering around in circles. I look accusingly at Humberto. "They love tequila," he says with an impish smile.

Rocky looks up at me and falls over. "Oh my God. You killed my favorite bird!"

Humberto reaches into the cage and picks Rocky up. "No, *Señorita*, Rocky is just passed out." And he hands him to me. Rocky's still breathing and I can feel his tiny heart beating. I put him in my shirt next to my heart to keep him warm. I'm in shock. I don't know what Humberto is doing or why.

Humberto quickly explains, "*Señorita*, it is illegal to take the birds over the border. *Me entiendes*?"

I nod my head.

"The birds are noisy, *¿sí?*"

I nod my head again.

"We need to hide the birds to get them across the border without getting caught. *¿Sí?*"

I nod my head once again. I feel like a bobblehead.

My heart sinks.

I thought we would have to pay more. I didn't think it was going to be real smuggling.

Humberto works fast transferring the birds out of the cage putting them in cloth sacks. Most of the birds have passed out, so the task is fairly easy. He yanks the cages out of the van and cleans them with a hose at the back of the taco stand. Feathers fly everywhere and float down like snow.

He puts the cages on top of the trailer and ties them down. The birds are on the floor of the van with a tarp over them. He must have done this many times before. I feel like such an idiot. I never expected this. Humberto tells me I have to drive the van across and he has papers I need to get signed. He will walk across the border and meet me on the other side.

I'm about to faint when he reaches over and hands me the bottle of tequila. "Drink this. You must not look suspicious."

I must not look suspicious? *I do look suspicious. I look guilty as sin.* I take the bottle from him and gulp hard.

"*Señorita,* this is something *you* must do. I did everything in my country. Now you must do everything in your country. Tell them you are importing pots. That is what is in the trailer. The receipt is here." He hands me several pages. "Get them to sign the paperwork here." He points to a place for a signature. "I will meet you on the other side."

I take another swig of the tequila and get back into the van, and watch Humberto walk off. I now realize *I* am a smuggler. *I wonder if my mother will visit me in jail.*

The Virgin Mary stares at me from the dash. Is she protecting me or judging me?

1968 - St. Mary's Elementary, second grade

"You need to pray louder, Genny, God needs to hear you."

"O my God, I am heartily sorry for having offended Thee, and I detest all my sins... Sister, please may I stand up. I promise not to chew gum in mass ever again."

"No, Genny, think of Jesus' pain on the cross, dying for our sins," Sister Mary Frances stands in front of the door with opaque glass blocking the view into the hall. "Your pain is nothing compared to that."

"Yes, Sister Mary Frances," I take one more step forward on my knees as I say another act of contrition. Sounds of children laughing float through the open transom above Sister's head. Tommy was the one who tempted me with that bubble gum. He dared me to blow a bubble. When I was caught, he stood next to Sister Mary Frances with his hands folded in prayer and a smirk on his face.

"Sister, my mom is supposed to pick me up after school. She's going to be worried when I don't come out."

"Don't worry about your mother, I'll tell her your sins. I'm sure she'll understand."

"Sister, my knees feel funny."

"Take another step forward, you're only halfway across the room," Sister looks at a shadow framed in the door's window.

"Sister, I don't feel well." The shadow knocks hard on the glass. I hear my mother's voice call for me. A cold sweat comes over me and my body collapses to the floor.

"What did you do to her?" My mother's voice sounds like she's under water.

"She was sacrilegious. I was showing her how Jesus suffered for her sins." Sister Mary Frances' voice echoes in my head.

"She doesn't understand sacrilege. She's seven years old." Mom lays my body flat on the floor, takes off her coat, and props my feet up under it. The voices begin to sound clearer.

"She was chewing gum at mass and blowing bubbles," Sister Mary Frances says with a steady, strong voice.

Mother stands to face Sister Mary Frances and squares off with her. "You will never torture my daughter again with your archaic cruelty."

"She's a strong willed girl. I will do what needs to be done to bend her to the teachings of Christ," Sister insists. "She needs to be taught a lesson,"

"Then I guess the lesson is she can go to public school for the rest of this year." Mother picks me up in her arms. Her cool hands gently touch my face.

"It's all right, Genny," she says. "It's all right."

CHAPTER FIFTEEN

It's a Small World

The truck behind me honks its horn, coercing me to move one more car length forward. The line into the border crossing is long, with about fifteen cars in front of me and apparently one inpatient asshole behind me. Most of the cars lack mufflers and spew heavy smoke. My hands shake and sweat drips down my back. I'm sick to my stomach. I stare at the Virgin Mary and make the sign of the cross. Sister Mary Clément Marie is probably turning over in her grave right now. I deserve the wrath of God for this one.

It's finally my turn to talk to the border patrol. He's older than me by about ten years and probably tired of this same old job. He comes up to the van and says, "Are you a United States citizen?"

"Yes, sir. I am." I hand him my driver's license.

"You're a long way from home, aren't you?"

I look at him a little funny and then realize I never changed my license from Ohio to Texas. "Yes, sir. I am. I came down to Mexico to import pots...clay pots." Just then Rocky wakes and crawls around under my shirt.

"I'm from Niles, Ohio. It's about twenty minutes from you," the guard says.

"Wow!" I say a little too loudly as Rocky pecks around my belly button.

"Your last name is Rekas. Any relation to Joe or Ted Rekas?" he asks.

This can't be happening. "They're my uncles." I smile brightly, hoping to distract him from looking at the contents of the van.

"I'm an old pal of Joe's son," he says signing the importation paperwork with a flourish, handing them back, leaning in close enough to smell the tequila on my breath.

"It's truly a small world." I stutter out, suddenly sounding like a six year old.

"Tell him Curtis sends his regards." I look up at his name tag, C. *Reddendich.*

"Will do," I squeak, then drive one hundred and one smuggled birds into the U.S.

Humberto sees me and waves his hat for me to follow him behind a store into a narrow alley. Rocky peeks out from under my shirt when Humberto comes to the window.

"*Señorita,* you are a very good smuggler. You could be a professional."

I take another swig of the tequila and step out of the van. Suddenly I feel the true weight of the situation and throw up next to a large garbage bin.

Humberto laughs a little. "I did that the first time I cross the border. You get used to it."

"I hope not. I'm never doing this again."

"I say that every time I make a crossing. I have been doing this for twenty years now. Life is boring without it now. I need to do it once or twice a year so I feel life."

I stare at him. "I'm *never* doing this again." I'll never get tired of being bored again.

We open the back of the van to check on the birds. Humberto pulls the cages off the trailer and loads them back into them. The birds are a little ruffled, but all of them are alive. Rocky is now sitting on my head and tangled up in my hair, but I don't do anything to put him in the cage. I need a little diversion anyway.

Humberto drives to the outskirts of Laredo and we pull up to a small block house with a large garage. He honks the horn and several people come out.

"These are my cousins," Humberto says with a smile. His cousins swarm around the van. As he drives slowly toward the garage, they inch along with him. When we stop, they form an assembly line to unload the boxes and carry them into the garage.

Humberto and I watch as they open the crates and remove the top layer of orange clay pots – the kind that are sold at every market place and roadside stand. I wonder how much money he and Raul can make selling them in the U.S. The cousins continue to the next layer of items, which are wrapped more carefully with paper and cloth. I move closer as the cousins work more slowly now, carefully pulling the wrapping off to reveal well preserved pre-Columbian antiques. They place the relics in a separate display case. They're much better than the ones in the museum. I almost vomit again. If I had been caught with these, I would have been in jail for the rest of my life. My knees weaken.

Now I understand why Raul was so happy I came along when I did. They were waiting for an opportunity to smuggle these relics out and I was the way to do it. When that border guard signed those papers, the shipment became legal.

Poor Ernesto, what will he think when he finds out his friends are the ones stealing his national treasures? My stomach lurches and I run outside the garage and empty my guts again. Of course, I can't point any fingers. I just smuggled my birds across. Who am I to be so outraged? I'm no better than they are. I need to get my birds back to Mission, Texas. Jeffrey should be there now and I want this journey to end.

"Humberto, it should only take us a few hours to drive me home. Can we please finish this tonight?"

"*Si, si, si.* We will leave as soon as we unload the pots and eat."

It can take days for Humberto to get ready to leave. I look around desperately and see a man about my age in the group. He's not really helping unload the boxes, but is talking and laughing with the others. I hear someone call him Charlie.

I ask Humberto if Charlie can drive me now. Humberto looks hurt by my request, but calls him over. "Charlie, can you drive me and my birds to Mission? He smiles and says he will.

I sleep most of the way home and wake up as we come into Mission. I direct Charlie the rest of the way and want to kiss the ground when I get out of the van.

Jeffrey runs up to the van and hugs me. He and Charlie unload the birds while I collapse on the sofa and cry. Charlie slips out the side door and I hear the van leave.

Rocky's still tangled p in my hair and Jeffrey gently pulls him away from me. Rocky pecks Jeffrey softly, but offers no real resistance. Jeffrey sits next to me and tries to pull me into his arms, "You look like shit, babe." I cry even harder.

"Why do you have to go so far away to get a job?" She hands me a folded pair of pants to add to my suitcase. "I'll never see you."

"I promise I'll be home for Christmas."

"You're only twenty years old." She picks some lint off my shoulder.

"I'll be twenty-one in three months."

"Maybe you should go back and get your master's degree in remedial reading like I did. With your 3.9 GPA, you could get in the master's program easily."

"All I've ever done is go to school. While everyone else was having fun in the summer, I was going to school. I need a break."

"I could get you a job in my school district." She reaches up to move a long strand of hair fallen into my face and tucks it behind my ear.

"Mom, I've told you I don't want to teach those snotty rich kids in your school district. These are migrant students. I think I can make a difference in their lives."

"Not all the kids I teach are rich." She sighs as she looks around my empty bedroom. "I could talk to the principal and get him to give you a special assignment."

"I've got everything all set. The recruiter said I would be perfect for the job."

"You know," she pauses ever so slightly, "Patrick called the other day to see how you were doing. You two made such a cute couple in high school."

I try to make myself rigid, but my body shudders at his name. If she knew what a jerk he had been when we broke up, she wouldn't be so eager for me to speak to him now.

I look around my lavender room before I hug her one last time. I see her tears, but I have to leave before I lose courage all together. "I'll call you when I get to McAllen." I pick up my suitcase and walk to my car.

On the rear window, my brother has written in white shoe polish TEXAS or BUST!!!

CHAPTER SIXTEEN

Almost Busted in Texas

"I want to go home."

"Babe, you are home." Jeffrey rubs my back and shoulders in a slow motion.

My pillow is wet from tears and snot. I divide my time between crying and sleeping and then crying in my sleep. Smuggling birds was the dumbest thing I've ever done. Jeffrey comes in and out of our bedroom with a worried look on his face. I haven't showered and I look like a mad woman when I take a peek at myself in the mirror. I hear him descend the wooden stairs, run the water in the kitchen, and call for the dog.

I am home. But it doesn't feel like home. This isn't my real bedroom.

I miss my family, my mom, the house I grew up in.

But this is my home, the one I made for myself. The life I was sure I wanted. The day I bought it, I had so much hope for it… and me.

Fall 1979

"Honey, this one's going to take a lot of work. Are you sure you can handle it?" Donna, the real estate agent, seems hesitant to show it to me. "It's a real fixer-upper."

"My parents had rental properties while I was growing up." I explain. "Every time a renter moved out, my brother and I had to go paint and clean and fix things. I'm pretty handy."

Two acres of lush banana plants, a few bushes full of pomegranates and several palm trees hide the 1920s farmhouse from street view. An abandoned orange grove to the east, an irrigation canal to the west, it looks like a Garden of Eden completely surrounded to ensure total privacy.

"Well, this might be the place for you," Donna says. "The former owner started renovating and left several projects unfinished."

As Donna and I walk from room to room, the floors creak under our weight. She points out everything wrong with it, "the shiplap walls are exposed, the kitchen is practically dysfunctional and the laundry room drains out into the yard."

I'm ready to move onto the next house when she says there's one last feature to see. We climb the narrow, wooden stairs to the widow's watch on the roof. The treetop view from the pinnacle of the house closes the deal. I'm in love.

"A lot of girls right out of college rent a place for a few years." Donna clucks like a mother hen protecting her chick. "Are you sure you want to take this big of a project on?"

I nod and begin signing my name. I don't say that I need to do something that's completely for me - completely free of anyone's expectations... that I've been waiting my whole life to make a decision on my own.

CHAPTER SEVENTEEN

Who's Spying on Me?

The total cost of my farmhouse was twenty-seven thousand dollars with monthly payments of two hundred and eighty dollars, a lot of money on my meager teacher's salary of eight thousand dollars a year. Even the secretary at my school made more money than I did. I'd inherited a little money from my paternal grandmother and used part of it for the down payment. I was determined to make this *my* home.

The kitchen should have been the first project to finish, but instead, I chose turning the widow's watch into my bedroom. I enclosed the entire room with floor to ceiling windows and put my bed in the center. Gauze curtains afforded me little protection from the Texas sun, but I awoke each morning to a three hundred and sixty degree view of heaven.

Planting a garden was next on the list. Maybe I could get away with a semi-functional kitchen if I grew my own food, I reasoned. I dug beds for tomatoes, squash and other various leafy vegetables. But I also planted orange trumpets and bougainvillea so my yard would have vibrant colors blooming all year round.

The heat and humidity were brutal, so I wore little or nothing while digging and planting and then showered afterwards with the garden hose in my private backyard. The sub-tropical climate in the Rio Grande Valley made the growing season pretty much all year round, so the area fields were constantly sprayed by crop dusters from the nearby airfield. I didn't give the planes much thought at first. It never occurred to me someone was watching me from above.

Over the course of several weeks, one plane flew lower and lower over my property. I felt like Cary Grant in *North by Northwest* when he was being chased down. It wasn't as dramatic, but I finally realized that someone was definitely screwing with me. I bought a pair of binoculars and got the numbers of the plane. Armed with this damning information, I drove over to the airfield and started to complain to the first person I saw -- a guy in a jumpsuit bent over an engine hanging from a hoist.

"Finally, I wondered how long it would take you to come here. I've been trying to get your attention for months." He took his baseball cap off and his long blond hair fell to his shoulders. All of my righteous indignation went right out the window.

"What do you mean?" I stammered. I couldn't help but be flattered. I blushed as he walked toward me stretching his hand out. "Did you ever think to drive over to my house? You obviously know where I live."

"Well, no I didn't think of that. I didn't know if you'd be home."

"Stop buzzing my house or I *will* call the police next time." I turned and walked out of the hangar.

"Wait, this isn't how I wanted things to go." He quickly caught up to me. "I just wanted to meet you. Would you like to fly with me?"

He smiled broadly showing a gold front tooth which caught me off guard and made me laugh. He took this as an acceptance to his invitation. Several crop duster planes were tied down on the field adjacent to the hangar and he grabbed a set of keys off the wall. He yelled over his shoulder to a guy in the back he was borrowing one of the planes.

We flew around the valley for hours. I could feel my heart soaring to new heights. This was how I wanted to move through the world, above the tree tops through the clouds with no strings to hold me down. He told me he'd been living in the Rio Grande Valley most of his life, his parents had moved from Pennsylvania when he was six and now they lived in McAllen. He slept in the back of an old cargo plane he had bought last year that he was still working on.

I can't say that it was love at first sight, but we both had adventure in our souls and wanted to explore it. I didn't have any expectations of him. I didn't want to end up like most of my classmates, married with kids and no life of their own. There was plenty of time for babies later. Maybe meeting Jeffrey pushed my life off course a degree. Or maybe I'd already started to drift. He moved in with me within a week.

I hear Jeffrey climbing the stairs. Every time I try to tell him what happened, I cry.

He decides to ask pointed questions so he can know the worst.

"Were you raped?"

"No!"

"Were you molested?"

"No."

"Were you robbed?"

I shake my head.

"Were you in an accident?"

I shake my head again.

"Genny, I'm running out of bad things that might have happened. I can't look at your ass and read your mind. Tell me one thing you did."

"I went out disco dancing."

The look on Jeffrey's face is a combination of surprise and merriment. He's totally perplexed now. "You're crying because they made you go disco dancing?"

"Yes. I mean no. You don't understand."

"I'm trying to understand. Tell me something else they made you do."

"We went to see some pyramids and then the family had a party in my honor."

"Then why are you crying? It sounds like they were really nice to you."

I start crying again.

Unexpectedly, the phone rings and Jeffrey, who usually avoids answering the phone at all costs, springs out of bed to pick it up. His face sours immediately. "Yes, ma'am, she's right here." He straightens his arm full length as if he's holding something putrid and gives the phone to me.

"Hello?" I say tentatively.

"Genevieve Anne Rekas, are you okay?" I come to full attention as only my mother can command. *I should just go ahead and kill myself right now.* This isn't going to be good.

"Genny, can you hear me? Are you okay?"

"Of course, Mom, I'm great. I just got back from Belize, so I'm a little tired."

"You got back from Belize via Mexico, didn't you?"

My mouth drops to the floor. *This woman must have a direct line to*

God. "How did you know I came through Mexico?"

"And you brought your birds through Laredo, didn't you?"

"Mom, I had to. At first I was going to fly them home, but my plane got blown off the runway in Belize and broke apart when it hit the hangar. The Belize government took away the permits and they were going to confiscate them, so I had to take a boat around the Yucatan peninsula and drive them up through Mexico and across into Laredo. But I'm home safe now, so everything's okay."

I want to stop myself from talking, but all the words gush from my mouth uncontrollably. I have truly lost my senses when I suddenly stop and say, "How did you know about Mexico?"

"That nice border patrol man called your uncle Joe and said he thought you might be in over your head."

"The border patrol officer called Uncle Joe? Why?"
Jeffrey's mouth drops open and his eyes get big as saucers when I mention border patrol.

"Thankfully your Uncle Joe represented Curtis's younger brother in a case and got him out of trouble. He thought he would return the favor. You have no idea how lucky you are. He said it was obvious you were smuggling birds across the border illegally. He said you even had feathers in your hair for God's sake."

"Mom, I would have brought 'em in legally if the Belize government hadn't screwed up."

"Genny, you should have just stopped then. It was dangerous for you and Jeffrey to bring them through Mexico."

"We thought Jeffrey would stand out too much with his blond hair and blue eyes, so he didn't come with me. He flew home by himself to get the cages ready for the birds."

"You went into Mexico by yourself? Are you out of your mind? Do you realize how dangerous that is?"

"Mom, everything is fine. I met some really nice people."

"Genny, you need to come home right now and forget about this foolish bird thing. I still have your old room set up just the way you left it. You can come home, get a teaching job and maybe start a family."

I stiffen at her words. She's always treated me differently than the boys in our family. Their curfew was midnight or later, mine was ten. I had to fight hard for independence and credibility with my family. "Mom, this is the eighties. Girls make it on their own now. They don't stay home and live with their parents until the 'right man' comes along."

"They shouldn't transport birds into the United States and only by the grace of God not get arrested for smuggling. Genny, you really need to take a better assessment of the situation. You were brought up better than this."

"Oh, Mom, please don't worry. This was a one-time thing, I promise. I'll never do it again."

I can hear my mother's heavy sigh on the other end of the phone signaling complete resignation. She believes I started going off track when I began listening to Joni Mitchell. Joni corrupted me into believing I could be wildly independent. Now all I am is wild and my mother is beyond worried.

Jeffrey gets up and puts the Joni Mitchell *Court and Spark* album on the record player. Instantly, her sweet high voice drifts through the air and lifts my mood. I want to be like her. I want to live life that honestly.

CHAPTER EIGHTEEN

Back to Normal

Jeffrey and I fall out of the hammock and hit the ground hard when a cacophonous chorus of horn honking, dog barking and bird squawking wakes us from a Sunday afternoon siesta. We scramble to our feet and run to the front yard to address the mid-afternoon intruder.

"*Hola, Señorita* Genny. Como estas?"

"*Hola*, Humberto. Bien, e tu?"

He points at Lucero and asks, "Es okay if I get out?"

Lucero circles the van several times before finally sitting next to me. The imposing black German shepherd was a present from my brother.

"*Sí, sí, sí. Pasa le*," I answer.

Humberto's a little hesitant, but gets out of the van carrying a large grocery bag with handles, I introduce Jeffrey.

"*Es su novio?*" he asks, shaking Jeffrey's hand vigorously.

I'm a little embarrassed, but acknowledge that he is indeed, *mi novio*.

Jeffrey and I escort him to the back of the house and climb the stairs to a newly built deck which allows us to watch the planes taking off and landing at the airfield.

"It's been three weeks since I left you at your cousin's." I hand Humberto a beer. "I thought you'd be back in Mexico by now."

"I've been selling all of the things we brought from Mexico. It takes time to find the right people for those pots." He gives me a side glance. "One dealer bought all but a few. He auctions them in New York. The dealer said some of them didn't make the cut."

"That took three weeks?" I quiz him.

"My cousins and I celebrated for a few days. They were happy to see me again."

"I'm glad your cousin, Charlie brought me back here, then," I tease. "You're a popular guy, Humberto. Parties in your honor could take months"

He laughs at my joke and picks up one of two binoculars on the deck railing to search the area, focusing on the airfield.

Jeffrey picks up the other pair and a friendly question and answer session ensues between the two of them about the area and the different kinds of planes flying in and out.

"Whose big plane is that?" Humberto asks, focusing on the largest plane tethered on the airfield next to the hangar.

"Mine." Jeffrey answers.

"You are a pilot?" He looks Jeffrey up and down, appraising the man in front of him.

"Yes, he's a very good pilot," I interject quickly. I don't tell him I'm a pilot as well. Flying under the radar is the new me.

After some more small talk about Jeffrey's plane and the birds, Humberto says, "*Señorita* Genny, I will be meeting with Arturo when I get back." He looks uncomfortable. "He will want his half of the money. You never paid me for the trip."

"Oh, my God! I'm so sorry. I completely forgot." Now I'm the one who's embarrassed. "I was so tired and your cousin was the one who took me here. How much do I owe you?"

Looking around our place, I see him calculating. The price seems to be going up, the longer he takes to answer.

"One thousand dollars," he finally says.

"What?"

"Seven hundred fifty."

"No, no, no. That is not what your primo and I agreed on. He said five hundred dollars plus bribes. I don't think you spent five hundred dollars on the bribes. Besides, I got the pre-Columbian artifacts across the border for you and they were stamped as legally crossed."

Humberto realizes I understood the real value of the border crossing. They made a lot more profit from me bringing the pots across than if they'd done so alone. The border guard had known I was smuggling in pre-Columbian artifacts, I would've been put in jail and the key thrown away.

"*Sí, sí, sí,* es bueno. Two hundred fifty dollars is good," Humberto quickly says.

He and I both laugh and shake hands on the price. He knows he should be paying me, not the other way around. Arturo will probably never see a dime of this money.

"This is to say *gracias* for helping me. The dealer wouldn't take these and I can *not* take them back to Mexico." He reaches into his bag and pulls out two clay pots.

They are obviously pre-Columbian. One of them is all black with almost a shine to the exterior and a fluted top. The other is more open and has a ceremonial pattern imbedded in the base of the bowl.

"Oh, these are beautiful. Thank you so much."

They're better quality than the ones I saw in the museum with Ernesto. I wonder what the other pots I smuggled looked like. They must have been magnificent. I can see why Ernesto is so fanatical about the illegal trade. Ernesto doesn't know it, but he's working to put his friends Raul and Humberto in jail. I hope he never finds out.

As Humberto leaves, I clutch the two bowls guardedly to my chest. I'm holding a piece of his country's history that I shouldn't possess. I silently vow to return them someday.

CHAPTER NINETEEN

The Needle Moves

"Miss! Miss!" Seven year old Maria waves her hand anxiously in the air for permission to answer the question.

School started in mid-August, but harvesting crops up north continues well into the fall months, so the migrant students trickle back slowly. There are only eight students in my class now, but by the end of the year, there'll be thirty-five kids.

My recent trip to Mexico gives me a deeper appreciation for my students' culture and language. I can empathize with their frustration over learning a foreign language.

"My family has five peoples," Maria answers.

"Try saying it, 'my family has five members' instead." She correctly repeats the sentence and smiles proudly. I give her a treat to feed Rocky who perches on my shoulder while I teach.

Sometimes it's easier for the shy kids to talk to Rocky rather than to me, so I let the students teach him new words to say. The rule is they can only teach him English and no bad words. I've been told it's a unique way to teach English as a second language and the kids look forward to my class.

Jeffrey does odd jobs around the valley, but isn't making any steady income. Each time we plan to sell some of the birds, we come up with a reason not to. With no money coming from sales, it's getting expensive to care for all of them and the number keeps growing. Word got out that we were saving birds so, people who no longer want their pets, bring them to us. One African grey came to us from a former opera singer and sings beautiful soprano arias. Another yellow-head must have come from a drug dealer because it constantly says, "Quick! Hide the stash!" We are known around the valley as the Bird People.

With the addition of more birds, Jeffrey builds more cages. The pen gets bigger and more elaborate, and now includes individual mating areas and side nesting pens. It's like a giant Barbie Doll apartment complex. We joke that we've become slaves to the birds.

The parrots aren't the only birds in our lives. All of the banana trees and pomegranates in the yard act as a lure for wild birds to come around, as well. When the fruit hits the ground and opens up, a feeding frenzy occurs. Small birds come to eat the fruit which, in turn, attracts larger birds of prey. There are several ospreys, hawks and a few eagles constantly circling our yard. It's like sharks around chum. Lucero works to keep them at bay with his constant patrol of the perimeter of the property.

Jeffrey and I are into the clickety clack of a relationship that's just rolling down the railroad tracks. A comfortable routine develops for me of teaching, taking care of the animals and getting together with the gang on the weekends. Money is getting tighter, but I keep up with all of the bills. I can tell that Jeffrey wants more, but I keep reminding him we have a lot to be grateful for.

"You're bogarting again. Take a toke and pass it." Lightning reaches to take the joint from me. His heavily stained fingers pinch the roach, he sucks deeply and passes it to Jeffrey.

"Oh, sorry," I say. "This is pretty good shit."

"Yeah, I picked up some Acapulco Gold the last time I was doing a run."

Jeffrey takes the last hit and deposits the roach into a small ashtray reserved specifically for them. The roach stash is saved for the *second level high* when they are unrolled and made into another joint with the potency of hash. I get high enough on regular shit, so I never partake in the "second coming".

Every weekend we go to Lightning's trailer, set deep in the middle of a forty acre orange grove, for some barbeque and target practice. Around the trailer are a few palm trees and some oaks that give shade. Lightning rarely goes into the "tin can" since it gets so damned hot in there and most of his furniture is outside. The trailer is basically used as storage. Lightning takes some rolling papers and a small bag out of the wooden humidor in front of him and carefully sprinkles the small dried leaves into the rolling papers. He quickly rolls the paper and lightly licks the side to seal the fat joint. He pulls his long greying black hair back with one hand and sticks the joint in his mouth with the other. His beard and mustache are stained with a light brown tinge he affectionately calls his last stash and picks up the Beretta next to his beer, "Who's ready for target practice?"

Lightning says Jeffrey and I should have in-depth knowledge of guns and shares his extensive and ever changing arsenal. We practice with a different gun each week. I assume he trades his weapons, but know enough not to ask.

Living in Texas is a huge culture shock. There are basically two cultures here, Wild West cowboy and Mexican. And *all* Texans are proud of their guns and use them as often as they can. Most of their stories have encounters with dangerous animals or snakes and always end the same way, "Then I got my gun and shot it!"

After shooting at some empty beer cans propped on the top of the wooden fence, Lightning tosses an empty coke bottle into the air. I follow the trajectory and shoot. The glass shatters into a brilliant rainbow of colors and falls to earth like confetti.

"Not bad for a chick from Ohio," Lightning chuckles. "We'll have you shooting like a Texan in no time."

"I still have a hard time with the breathing part." I shake my shoulders to relax them. "I want to hold my breath instead of exhaling."

"That takes time and practice." He's a man of few words, so I'm surprised when he offers this tidbit into his personal life. "Well, I'm almost done."

"Done with what?" I ask.

"Done with flying into Mexico." He says it like I should know the answer is obvious.

"When did you fly there?" Since he has never really said he was flying into Mexico in the first place, I take this as an invitation to talk about his adventures there.

Lightning at first looks at me like I'm addled, "I guess you haven't been around here long enough to know that's what I do." He quickly forgives my ignorance.

"No one around here says anything about you when you're gone, so I didn't think it was any of my business to ask."

Lightning nods his head, satisfied with my response, and starts cleaning his gun.

"So, what did you do?" This is my chance to ask questions, but the window of opportunity can close as quickly as it opens, so I speak fast.

"Well, I try to make both trips work for me. I take things into Mexico like electronics and take things out of Mexico like farm products."

"Like this?" I hold up the joint. Both of us smile.

"I never take any hard stuff." He continues, "Weed is all. And not much of it. Just personal use and for friends. A small enough amount so I can pitch it out the window if I need to. No coke and nothing else. But it's getting harder than it used to be."

"You mean the border is getting tighter?"

"Hell, no! No one can catch me in a plane." He says this without the least bit of modesty. "I'm so much better than those yahoos that they got at the border patrol. None of them flew in Vietnam with live gun action all around them. That's what makes me the pilot I am. Running for your life makes you fast and agile. If you don't learn that, you're dead.

And I'm still here."

I can't help but look at him with admiration. He's probably right. There are few pilots with his knowledge and pure guts. He has nerves of steel and he doesn't flinch when he's flying. I can't tell if it's because he doesn't fear death or if he loves life so much that he holds on to every ounce of it.

"Hell, the two of you are better pilots than any of them yahoos that I seen," he says this almost as an afterthought.

"So why are you quitting now?"

"I finally paid off the land and have enough money to build a house. I'm tired of sleeping outside. All I have to do now is work enough for my food and my taxes on the land. The taxes won't be too bad since it is zoned agricultural and I do get some money off the crops." He leans back into the chair and takes a long toke.

"If you aren't afraid of the border patrol, what are you afraid of?" Jeffrey has been listening in silence up until now.

Lightning pauses long enough to measure his words. "I'm afraid that too many people are getting into the business and that greed is taking over. Once people get greedy, they can't be trusted. There's never enough money for some people. The more they make, the more they want and they will try to get yours too."

"What's the biggest caution to take in going down to Mexico?" Jeffrey asks, pumping Lightning for information.

"Don't go!" Lightening doesn't mince words,

Jeffrey tries to laugh it off but says, "Come on Lightning, if I wanted to start going down there, what advice do you have?"

"Three things." Lightning sits up straighter in his chair. "Never give up your passport. No matter what. They got you by the short hairs if you give them that. The second thing is don't tell no one what you're doing. The less people know, the less chance of them fucking you over.

The third thing you do is stay in the legal import-export business." Jeffrey laughs, "Yeah, right."

"I'm serious as a heart attack. Stay legal, at least on this side of the border."

"What's that supposed to mean?"

"Our government is the most important. You need to stay on

good terms with the U.S. of A if you want their help if something goes wrong down south. Only take things down to Mexico that are legal on this side of the border. I take, or used to take, electronics down to Mexico."

"How does that make money?"

"They love T.V's and radios. I can buy them cheap here and sell down there high. Mexico has huge taxes on electronics and the costs are almost four times higher down there. As far as the U.S.A. is concerned, they would much rather help you get out of Mexico if you are being an entrepreneur than a smuggler."

I certainly don't like how this conversation is going and chime in, "Well, I'm glad you're done." I hold up my beer to salute him. "Here's to quitting."

Everyone takes a long drink of beer. But Jeffrey's lost in his own thoughts. He has that wistful look that he gets when he thinks that life is more than what we have. We drive home in uncomfortable silence. I feel the needle of the compass move off course, again.

January 1976

*"Are you sure you and Patrick don't want to double date with Matt and
me tonight?"*

*"I'm so sure, Jackie." I hesitate, "Should you really be going out on a
Sunday night? We both have tests this week. Ever since you started dating Matt,
your grades are going down."*

*"You're sounding like my mom, now," she laughs. "For once stop being
such a good girl, Genny."*

"Can't I worry about you?"

*"No, Genny," her voice is firm. "That's not your job. You're my friend,
not my keeper."*

*"I'll see you in class tomorrow." I hang up the phone and turn to my
books.*

CHAPTER TWENTY
Part Of The Gang

"And then what happened?" MG asks as she inhales from the joint being passed around.

"Then Humberto handed me the tequila, told me to drink and to drive over the border," I answer and take a quick hit before the next question.

Trip gasps and puts her hand up defensively across her chest. "Jesus Christ, weren't you fuckin' scared out of your mind?"

At first, I didn't want to discuss my trip through Mexico for fear of getting a knock on my door by the U. S. Border Patrol. I don't know what would be worse - having my birds taken from me or being hauled off to jail. But as time passes, real consequences seem more and more remote.

"I was never so scared in my life. It was the dumbest -- "

"Then what happened?" MG interrupts. She wants to extract as much information as a police interrogation. Her dark-green eyes penetrate me with her fixed stare.

Everyone is looking at me. Even though the women are the ones asking questions, the men listen intently. They want to glean as much information as they can with the hope that it can save their asses if they ever get in a similar jam.

"The border patrol guy started asking me questions about Ohio," I say.

"What? Ohio? Why?" Maggie interjects. Up until now, she's been sitting quietly next to Lightning with her hand lightly on his knee.

"Well, my driver's license was still from Ohio. I just changed it to Texas."

"But what's that got to do with it?" Maggie's more than curious. To her, it's a crucial point in the story. Using her walking stick as leverage, she leans forward in her chair to hear my answer better. Her body shifts stiffly from one location to another and struggles to find a comfortable position.

"He recognized the town on my license. He grew up in a neighboring area and started asking me questions. It turns out he knows my family, or at least my uncle."

"Wow, what are the chances?" MG mutters. She twists her fingers absentmindedly around her long ringlets of coal-black hair and blinks repeatedly. "Hard to imagine."

"So, what'd he do?" Trip asks.

"Well, my uncle is an attorney and got the border patrol's brother out of trouble a couple years back so he thought he'd return the favor. He gave me a break and let me pass."

"How do you know this?" MG is picking apart all the details carefully.

"He called my uncle after I left and told him I was covered in feathers and it was obvious I was bringing the birds in illegally." The more I tell this story, the luckier I feel.

"No fuckin' way!" Trip exclaims and takes a swig of her beer.

"Unbelievable, I always thought you were a goodie two shoes. This changes everything. You're pretty ballsy."

"Then what happened? MG asks.

"I crossed the border and Humberto waved me over to an alley." I wipe my mouth instinctively, the bile taste bubbling up into the back of my throat. "Then I puked my guts out."

"And you did all this alone?" Maggie asks. The concern in her voice reminds me of my mother's and tears prick the sides of my eyes.

"Yeah, where's Jeffrey when all of this is happening?" Trip asks.

Before I can answer, Jeffrey jumps up and asks, "Who's ready for another beer?"

The story ends satisfactorily enough for the group so the final question fades into the smoky blue haze of pot and is quickly forgotten. But it's been nagging me since I got back. Why didn't Jeffrey come with me? Was he afraid? He avoids talking about it and changes the subject when someone else brings it up.

The conversation moves onto the other people's illegal activities, planes, who got busted, planes, pot and how to get it, and planes. We never discuss politics, religion, sports or world events. The way the gang talks, it sounds like everyone in town is involved in some sort of illegal or illegitimate business. This isolated realm gives us a very narrow view of the world and therefore a myopic view of our options. It's like we're living in our own echo chamber.

There's only one airplane mechanic who has worked steadily at the airport for more than five years. His name is Dead Wrong Dan. He got his name by always being right. He doesn't say much and is always deep in thought. He chews his top lip, really the bottom of his mustache, trimming it with his teeth. Then he spits the small hairs into the air absentmindedly as he ponders a situation. He rarely gives his opinion on anything, but when he does his view is well thought out.

Dan's girlfriend, Triple A, is the exact opposite of him and can talk your ear off. Alison Anne Albright got her nickname, Triple A, in elementary school. Now everyone just calls her Trip. She's stunning with long blond hair, a small waist and very long legs, but her very large breasts are the part that defines her. When I first met her, I couldn't help but think she should have been called Double D.

One of the other regulars at the hangar is Stump. He's tall and lanky with long hair that curls at the ends. He's constantly wearing a bandana that presses his hair flat against his head. I'm not sure how he got his nickname and am too embarrassed to ask. I do know that his girlfriend, MG, is the one who gave it to him, so I can only guess. I try to find out his real name, but no one knows. I end up calling him Stump like everyone else, but worry that I'm offending him somehow.

I haven't figured out why they call Stump's girlfriend Machine Gun, MG for short, but I'm sure I'll find out soon enough. It's hard to ask direct questions without causing some kind of paranoia to take over. They all hide behind false names and identities. I guess that's why their nicknames are so funny.

Lightning and his old lady, Maggie, are the clan's leaders. Maggie is the oldest and has been living with Lightning for almost eight years. Sometimes she looks like she's in her late thirties, and then other times she looks ancient. She's dark-haired with a broad face and a sharp nose. She's from the Lakota tribe and speaks short disconnected sentences. I think it's from too many drugs in her younger years, like a burned out hippie. MG and Trip defer to her in a respectful, hierarchical way. There's a definite pecking order in the group.

Maggie's philosophic about her relationship with Lightning and constantly says, "I love him cuz he sleeps on his side of the bed." Since they sleep outside most of the time, I really don't understand her comment, but they get along with each other. Lightning's gruff personality softens when she's around and he gives her deferential treatment that he gives to no other person.

Up until my escapade through Mexico, I was looked upon as Jeffrey's girlfriend and of no real importance. I was allowed to flutter around on the sidelines like a not very social butterfly but conversations were kept to a minimum and I wasn't really trusted. Now I have bragging rights to the best smuggling story of the year. The fact that I'm female adds double points to the difficulty factor by the group's standards. I've grown a pair in their eyes. With this badge of honor, I have a seat at the table and am now officially part of the Crash Gang.

CHAPTER TWENTY-ONE
Ten Rounds And No Bell

Jeffrey and I fight over money now more than ever. His solution is crazy; mine is much simpler. He wants to get into the import/export business. I want him to get a real job.

Lightning's retirement is not helping either. Now that he's no longer making his trips to Mexico, he has a million stories to tell the group without fear of being turned in. He's obviously the king but I'm considered the new queen.

Jeffrey's jealousy is palpable. When he starts talking about living in Belize and capturing birds, everyone turns to me and says, "Yes, but she's the one that brought them over the border."

He wants his own story to tell and for me to take a lesser role in the group. He wants me to contact Humberto and arrange a round trip exchange like Lightning was doing.

"Why don't you just pick up where Lightning dropped off then?" I ask.

"I tried to talk to him about it but he says he doesn't trust his contacts anymore."

"But you're willing to trust mine?" I ask.

"Nothing happened to you," he says. "Besides, I'll only do two or three trips so it won't be predictable. Some quick cash and then I'll quit."

Now I understand why Humberto continues to smuggle. It's like the thrill of gambling, you think you're going to win, even with all the odds stacked against you.

The more I resist calling Humberto, the more Jeffrey persists. It's as if he's seducing me to get what he wants and he's using all sorts of enticements he hasn't used since we first started dating. I know I'll eventually capitulate, but I postpone the inevitable in order to keep his testosterone at heightened levels. I've never withheld something to get sex before and I like the power that it holds. It's a huge aphrodisiac.

But it's more than a power struggle. I have a bad feeling. And feelings are hard to define to someone else. Jeffrey's arguments are logical, so it's hard to tell him "I have a bad feeling about this." It's a weak retort. The lovemaking is passionate, but the arguments are getting intense.

"Babe, I could pay off the house for you and we could take it easy for the rest of our lives." The promise of easy money and comfort are very appealing.

"That's what you said about the birds and that didn't make any money," I retort.

"I've brought people over but you said they weren't good enough," Jeffrey says. "You never let anyone buy them."

"For God's sake, the last people you brought over didn't know they needed to provide water and food. They thought the bird could live in their backyard without a cage."

"What about the one with the kid?" he asks. "They would've done okay."

"The kid thought he could take Rocky's eyes out like a doll's. My birds go to good homes or they don't get sold at all."

"They're not your birds," he says. "They're mine."

"Then why was I the one who brought them over the border? I could've been arrested and thrown in jail. They're more mine than yours." I keep my voice low, but I'm fuming.

"You're being ridiculous," he says. "You're treating me like one of your students and you're going to teach me a lesson."

"Jeffrey, this could get crazy," I soften my words. "I was incredibly lucky when I came across. Just cuz you're in a plane doesn't make it safe. It's not Humberto I'm worried about, it's Raul. He's dangerous."

"Babe, it will be different with me," he continues his pitch. "Raul will treat me different 'cause I'm a man. Just like they treated you different 'cause you're a woman."

"That's my point. They were easy on me because I'm a woman." I pause to find the right words and something that Victoria had said comes to mind. "They're not going to give you any slack. Raul will be ruthless if you fuck up."

"This is a business deal, pure and simple, Raul will understand that." He slams the door to make his point. "I won't fuck up!" he screams from the other side.

But I never ask the question: Why didn't you come with me?

Lightning and Jeffrey spend long hours in hushed conversation going over details of Lightning's forays into Mexico and some of the pitfalls he encountered. They've charted several flight plans so Jeffrey has contingency plan upon contingency plan. I hear snippets of the discussion and can tell that Lightning is getting a vicarious thrill out of the preparation. It's like a secret boy's club and I'm not included in the plans.

Jeffrey's like a dog with a scent. Every time I put up a road block or offer some kind of reason not to go, he has ten reasons why he should. I believe I'm trying to give this venture a sanity check, not just be controlling. If nothing else, I'm forcing Jeffrey to examine every detail of the operation. I finally capitulate and call Humberto.

"Un buen idea," Humberto shouts through the phone. He's thrilled to hear from me and says he'll contact Raul to work out the details. Now I'm doubly sure this escapade is a bad notion. But I can't undo it. Jeffrey will fly a planeload of electronics into Mexico and fly pre-Columbian artifacts out. Technically, the pre-Columbian is illegal on both sides of the border, but there are ways to doctor paperwork. Humberto has a dealer in the United State who sells to different auction houses, including Christie's. He's secretive about his dealer's name, which protects the dealer and ensures that he, as the middleman, gets paid. He won't even tell Raul who the dealer is.

The gang is optimistic about the trip, but I'm not. Unquiet thoughts keep tumbling around in my mind like a rock churning in a roaring stream, the edges are worn down and smoothed and rounded, but still heavy. I wish I hadn't smuggled the birds through Mexico. I lost something of myself in the process. I would like to go back in time and change every decision. But I can't. It cost me something I can't calculate. Now Jeffrey's going to the exact same place. Will he be as lucky as I was?

1976

"Mom, can you pick me up from school today? I got another detention."
I hold the receiver closer to my ear and turn my back to the school secretary for
some privacy.

"Did you roll your uniform above your knees again?"
"No, I was talking too much again. The other kids were talking too, but the nuns
pick on me."

"Genny, you've been counseled by Sister Mary Clement Marie many
times. What did she say to do?"

"Be quiet."

"That's not all, what else?"

"To pray before I speak."

"Last detention you had to write five-hundred times, 'I will not talk
during mass'. What's the penance this time?"

"Ten Hail Marys and scrub the girl's restroom with a toothbrush."

The heavy sigh on the other end of the line signals the end of the call.

CHAPTER TWENTY-TWO
Flying Solo

It's 1:00 AM and Jeffrey is going through the start-up sequence with the male division of the gang. My emotions bounce up and down like a *superball*.

It's Thanksgiving so Jeffrey and Lightning think the timing's right to fly into Mexico. The U.S. Border Patrol runs a skeleton crew during holidays and is less likely to bother with a small engine plane, if they even see it.

Since school is on break, I could accompany him on the initial delivery, but Jeffrey says someone needs to stay with the birds. Of course, it's his lame reason to keep me here but I'm tired of fighting. So, I'm here and he's on his way to Mexico.

Damn it!

As a child, any time I was in a bad mood, my mother said, "You're stewing in your own juices." And that's what I'm doing now. I wanted to go with Jeffrey to make sure everything went well…at least the first trip, for God's sake. But he's adamant. He says he can handle things and that I'm just a control freak. Those are the words I'm stewing in right now, sitting on the back deck, looking into the night sky. I'm pissed.

I hear the familiar sound of the plane's engine startup in the distance. Fuck him! He can just have his big adventure without me. I go inside and get a beer.

Damn it!

Regret taps me on the shoulder. What if this is the last time I see Jeffrey and I wouldn't even go to the airport to say good-bye? Jeffrey can be stubborn, but so can I. The difference between the two of us is I was raised Catholic and automatically feel guilty about almost everything..

Rocky paces back and forth on the kitchen counter. "Jeffrey," he mutters over and over again. "Jeffrey." He's tired, but won't go in his cage. He's picking up my vibes right now, mirroring my every move. It irritates me to have such a constant reminder of my neurotic behavior.

He's learned to whistle the song, "*Dixie*" from Jeffrey. He flaps his wings and starts whistling it now and won't stop. It's driving me fucking nuts, but I'm too tired to redirect him to something else.

Finally, through the open kitchen window, I hear the plane take off. It circles around the airport and flies over our house. I look out the back window and see Jeffrey tip his wings first to the right and then to the left before he finally flies to the south. I'm glad I wasn't out on the deck. I don't want to give him the satisfaction of knowing I'll miss him. He'll be gone for at least three days.

I walk over to Rocky and extend my arm to the counter. He walks up my arm and perches himself on my shoulder. He finally stops whistling. "Give me a kiss, sweetie," he says before I put him in his cage for the night.

The king-sized bed feels too big so I position myself in the middle with pillows on both sides of me. Lucero jumps up and lies by my feet. Jeffrey won't be missed as much, if the bed is full, I tell myself. But the truth is, I will miss him. A warm sensation rushes through me as I think of our love making from the night before. I may feel guilty about not saying a proper goodbye, but I'll never feel guilty for something that feels so good.

My Catholic high school was full of sexually repressed nuns teaching warped ideas that shaped an entire generation of students. Sister Mary Clement Marie taught, during health class, that it might be prudent if we tied a rosary around our hands, so we don't sin during the night. Of course, some of the "bad" girls in school had already figured out she was full of baloney, but there were plenty of us who took her knowledge as the gospel truth.

Premarital sex was forbidden, of course. But even sex with one's husband was a duty one simply endured. A woman shouldn't have fun during sex. What rubbish. I only wish Sister Mary Clement Marie could see me having sex. That would spin her in her grave.

On second thought, Sister, if you're up there, please don't watch.

The gang invited me to their feast of turkey, mashed potatoes, gravy and a valley tradition, tamales, but I declined. Right now I'm taking guilt out and wearing it like a hairy undergarment for atonement until Jeffrey returns. My Thanksgiving dinner consisted of a cold ham sandwich and half an apple. Never one to suffer in silence, I rehearse the list of grievances I've suffered in Jeffrey's absence and how I've agonized.

My mother used to call me the perfect martyr, the Sarah Bernhardt of my time. Just to confirm my mother's label, I read several books about the actress in order to perfect my dramatic emoting when I wanted to show my suffering. It cracked my mom up.

I'm suffering now. I wish I could talk with my mom about this situation. But with her prying questions, I know I'd spill my guts about everything. She can't know. No one can know.

Two days pass fairly quickly, but the third day is excruciatingly slow. I know he can't call me, so I work hard to distract myself. I listen intently for the peculiar sound of Jeffrey's engine. It doesn't exactly sputter but it isn't perfectly smooth either. By noon, I walk over to the airfield to hang out. The long walk helps me calm down a little.

In the hangar, Dead Wrong Dan is hunched over a pulled airplane engine. It's resting on two wooden platforms and secured by thick chains from the rafters for double support. The propeller is lying on the ground along with several pans of oil scattered among the debris.

Dan looks up, "I wondered when you'd be over here."

Suddenly feeling self-conscious and sheepish, I take in a deep breath and stand a little taller. "I just wondered if anyone had heard anything."

"We haven't heard about any crashes, if that's what you're asking. But we won't know if his plane got caught for a while."

I know there's some kind of underground info center which gets telegraphed between airports about crashes. Even flights that hadn't been filed are somehow quickly reported. Since Jeffrey is literally flying under the radar, we wouldn't be privy to any formal reports.

I must look truly dejected when I turn to walk back home because Dan asks, "You want to help me with this engine?"

I walk over and hand him a wrench he points to. We work for several hours in silence except for a few expletives when a part doesn't fit.

"Jeffrey can't fly back until it's dark outside," he finally says. "Go home and wait. No news is good news. Thanks for the help,"

I walk home tired and worn.

Fall 1967

I find my brother Chuck in the driveway washing the car.

"What's an orphan, Chuck?" I know not to ask Mom.

"It's a kid with no parents. Why?"

"The cafeteria women said I could have a free lunch since I'm an orphan."

"Tell them to go to hell. You don't need a free lunch. I got a job and so does Floyd and Joe just went into the navy. We're taking care of the family. We don't need charity."

"What if Mom dies? Mikey's only five and I'm seven. We're too young to get jobs."

"Don't worry, I'm the man of the house now. I'll take care of things. We don't need their pity and we don't take charity."

CHAPTER TWENTY THREE

The Gang's All Here

Voices and the sweet smell of weed drift into my bedroom. It's 2:19 in the morning. Jeffrey must be home. I throw on my jeans and a top and fly into the living room where a small fiesta is happening.

Jeffrey passes a joint to Stump. "Hey, Babe; I wondered when you'd wake up."

The gang's all here. This isn't the homecoming I'd rehearsed. My inflated indignation collapses like a popped balloon when I see the room full of people.

"Hey, yourself," I walk over and give him a kiss. I have to teach in a few hours so I skip taking a hit and pass the joint to Dan. He smiles and takes a toke.

As this was a collaborative effort to get Jeffrey through his first smuggling job, everyone is eager for details. Stump encourages Jeffrey,

"So, tell us about the trip, dude."

Jeffrey takes a long drink of his beer and forces himself to sit back in his chair. I can tell he's buzzed on adrenaline and trying to calm himself down. Lucero sits next to him getting as much affection as he can.

"I took off toward Zapata and flew just above the treetops all the way there," Jeffrey looks over at Lightning who gives a slight nod. "I stayed close to fields and orchards and avoided houses where someone might hear me and report it."

Everyone around me nods like this is standard procedure.

"I watched out for the landmarks Lightning said led to the high tension power lines, Jeffrey explains. "And kept low to the ground all the way there, since both the U.S and Mexican governments' radars are set to pick up low-flying planes near the border."

Jeffrey has center stage and beams at the attention. "Once I found the correct spot, I flew under the wires and made a quick touch and go under the lines."

"You really flew under the wires?" Stump asks.

"It wasn't that bad," Jeffrey continues. "Lightning told me to approach it from the North-West toward the South-East."

"How'd you find this place, Lightning?" Dan asks.

"It's a service road for the electric company," Lightning answers. "It's not paved, but they keep it fairly level with caliche so you can take off and land pretty easy. I scouted it after I lost a couple of keys in the desert.

When I came back to look for my stash, it was gone. I couldn't tell if someone found it or I lost my landmarks."

"Someone must have found them," Dead Wrong Dan offers. "You never would've lost your coordinates. Never."

"I don't understand," I say.

"A lot of pilots dump their loads from the air as soon as they cross the border and then land their planes," Jeffrey continues. "Even though the pot is pretty well bundled it can explode on impact and make a mess to try to pick up later."

"Anyway, I needed to find a new way to get my stuff across," Lightning continues. "Real handy place to make a quick stop."

"Why's that important?" I ask.

"On the way into Mexico, it avoids the radar," Jeffrey answers. "But if you're coming out of Mexico with a load of weed, you can't land at an airport. It's a perfect place to meet your connection and unload your cargo."

"Isn't that dangerous?" All of them laugh, then I remember the adventure I just had. Another reminder that the naïve Genny is gone. Of course it's dangerous. The Crash Gang feeds off danger and I've become a member of the group.

"Living is dangerous," Maggie interjects. "But in varying degrees."

Everyone smiles. I feel like a novice. I'm being let into this exclusive club and I need to catch on fast. The window I've been afforded could close just as quickly as it opened.

"Keep going with the story, man," Dan says.

"I touched down on the caliche road, taxied under the high wires then took off again," Jeffrey tells us. "It's a good thing there aren't any trees there. The road is short and I clipped some cactus on the way up."

"Yeah, I've pulled some plants out of my wheel base a couple times," Lightning laughs.

"Anyway, once I got in the air again, I passed into Mexico at dawn and started to make out the topo easier than at night. Humberto told me to land at a little strip outside of Posa Rica. It was remote, but an easy field to take off and land on." Jeffrey states.

Jeffrey turns to me and says, "Humberto was there to meet me."

"Oh, how's Humberto?" I ask like this is polite conversation.

"He's cool," Jeffrey answers.

Stump wants to get the conversation back on track. "How was the offloading?"

"No problem," Jeffrey says. "The electronics were offloaded by two guys."

Lightning asks, "Did you keep your hat on and your head down all the time?"

"I stayed on the opposite side of the plane most of the time and spoke only to Humberto. I think the other two guys didn't want me to be able to identify them any more than I wanted them to be able to identify me."

Lightning adds, "Cool, then what?"

"Humberto wanted to have time to inspect the electronics before he handed over the money. I told him that I wanted the money first. At first he hesitated, but he said that since I was the boyfriend of Genny, he would trust me."

"Bullshit." Both Lightning and Stump say in unison. "You did good," Lightening adds.

"Once I got the money, I counted it. I wanted to make sure he knew I was going to check everything." Everyone in the room nods their heads again. They all must have a check list in their heads on how to negotiate a smuggling deal.

"The two men drove off with the electronics and Humberto and I tied off the plane. He said he would load up the plane with the clay pottery in the morning." Jeffrey looks at me as he says, "It took him two days to get around to it."

"Yeah, everything with Humberto is *en la mañana*." I smile. "What did you do while you waited?"

"Humberto took me to stay with Raul and Victoria."

"Really? You stayed with *la familia*? Were the girls there or did they go back to the university?"

"Humberto and I roomed together, but I think I was kept away from the girls on purpose. I got the feeling that the girls don't get out much."

"They get out but, they have to sneak --."

Stump breaks in, "Yeah, yeah, yeah. We need to know the important stuff of the trip. Not the shit about some girls. How long did it take you to load the cargo and refuel?"

"Humberto isn't the fastest person when it comes to getting things done," Jeffrey says. "Drinking beer comes first and work seems to be a distant second. He was excited about getting things across the border without having to talk to border guards, but slow getting everything together."

Trip asks, "What kind of stuff did he want you to bring back?"

Since everyone is pretty high, it's easier to show them than explain the significance of Pre-Columbian artifacts. I bring out the two bowls

Humberto gave me to show everyone. No one gives a rat's ass, so I put them away.

While I'm putting the bowls away, I hear Rocky in his cage and decide to bring him out. He climbs up on my shoulder and we rejoin the group. Another joint is being passed around and everyone starts staring out into space.

Rocky decides he wants some attention from Lucero. He jumps down from my shoulder and hops onto Lucero's head. Lucero startles and runs around the living room with Rocky holding onto his collar for dear life. Rocky starts whistling *Dixie* and intermittently squawks, "Oh dear,

Oh dear."

This puts the entire gang into hysterics. There's nothing like being high and watching a rodeo show with a bird riding a bucking bronco dog in the comfort of your own home.

Once everything finally settles down, Stump asks the all-important question, "Did you get paid for bringing the pots over?"

Jeffrey gets back to business quickly. "Yeah, Humberto left earlier than me and drove across the border. He met me in Zapata and we offloaded the pots under the high wires. He was real quick then. He wanted out of there pronto."

Jeffrey stands and brings his beer up for a salute, "Thanks for all your help."

With all eyes on him, Jeffrey reaches into his pants pocket and pulls out three envelopes and hands them to Dead Wrong Dan, Stump and the last one to Lightning.

Lightning stops him and says, "I didn't do nothing. You don't owe me."

Jeffrey says, "You taught me how to get across. I wouldn't have been able to do it without you."

"If the cops ask, I'll deny everything. You don't owe me. I was just telling tales. You just listened to some wild stories, that's all."

Jeffrey shakes Lightning's hand and thanks him again. I see a change in Jeffrey. An odd feeling passes through the back of my mind like a shadow. The grand gesture feels dishonest and inauthentic. The feeling passes quickly. I'm not sure of what it really is…maybe it's because everyone is high and I'm not.

As everyone leaves, Stump says, "You could make some money

with Bird Dog and Rocky if you want to."

I start to tell him the dog's name is Lucero, but it's too late. Bird Dog is his official name with the group and everyone laughs all over again as they head for their cars.

Jeffrey is now a member of one of the most exclusive societies in the valley – the smuggler's alliance. I am too, by accident, not design.

CHAPTER TWENTY-FOUR

Just Another Story

MG hands me a bottle of tequila as she enters the house carrying a brown grocery bag on her hip.

"What's the occasion?" I ask, following her into my kitchen. Her head's in the freezer and she's shuffling things around to find something buried deep in the back. She pulls out the blue trays heavily coated with frost and empties them into the blender on the countertop.

"It's Maggie's birthday. Trip's picking her up and bringing her here."

"Wow. Maggie's a New Year's baby?" I ask.

"We don't really know when she was born." MG pours a healthy amount of tequila into the blender along with margarita mix and hits the button. "We just celebrate today as her birthday."

"Why don't you know her birth date?" I ask between the whirling noise of the blender and the crunching of the ice.

"She was born on a reservation in Oklahoma and left on someone's doorstep on New Year's Day," MG continues. "She was already a few months old."

"That's horrible."

"Yeah, the tribal elders tried to find the real mom, but never could. The elders figured the mom musta got knocked up and scared and didn't tell no one. She couldn't hide a baby forever."

"Was Maggie sent to an orphanage?"

"No, the elders asked the people who found her if they wanted her, and so they adopted her. But then her folks found out she was special."

"Yeah, I thought she was a little slow." I say, thinking this is why Maggie talks so oddly.

"She's not slow. She's one of the smartest people I've ever met,"

MG continues. "She's a spirit mother. She can talk to the earth."

Just as I'm about to ask more questions, Trip and Maggie come in through the back door and the party begins.

"Happy birthday, Maggie," everyone says in unison. Maggie hugs both Trip and MG and pats me affectionately on the head. The differences between Trip and MG are stark. Trip's a trim carpenter; muscular and very fair skinned. She can be loud at times, especially if she's drinking. MG has light-brown complexion and curvaceous body and does home care for the elderly. Her soft voice hides a sharp tongue that can stab people with her teasing, especially Trip.

MG hands out margaritas to all of us and we clink glasses. Rocky starts screeching from his cage, so I retrieve him before we go outside.

The shade from the large oak that's centered in the middle of the backyard keeps the heat of the day away. Because we usually sit in a circle passing a joint and drinking beer, margaritas make for a nice change.

"So, is Jeffrey here?" Trip asks the obligatory question even though she knows he's gone. It's her way of making sure I'm doing okay so she can report back to the guys if I need anything. I don't mind - it's a relief to talk to someone else about what Jeffrey does. He says I can talk about his trips, but no specifics. Since he doesn't tell me the specifics anyway, there's no real threat to him.

"No, he's gone again. He's really busy." I say.

"Who knew that TVs would be so popular in Mexico?" MG quips.

"Or so profitable," I say. "Jeffrey paid off this house with the money from the last trip."

"That's better than a wedding ring." Maggie claps her hands to underscore her approval.

MG, Trip and I crack up. Maggie doesn't say much, but she's pointed when she does.

"Even better than that, we don't have to sell any of the birds now, which makes me very happy." I smile as Rocky dips his head quickly into my Margarita drink. "We have over a hundred and fifty birds now."

"Holy shit," Trip laughs. "What are you going to do with all of them?"

"I don't really know. We've kinda turned this place into a refuge. I get all sorts of abused or abandoned birds. It takes a lot of time and energy to nurse them back to health. So, I can't bring myself to sell them."

"Yeah, I can understand that." Then she asks, "So, what else is goin' on?"

"Jeffrey's no longer staying at Victoria and Raul's house when he goes down there. Jeffrey says Raul didn't like him around the girls."

"Yeah," agrees MG. "Mexican fathers are beyond over-protective when it comes to the chastity of their daughters."

"Little does Raul know how wild his girls really are," I say as it's my turn to take a toke.

"How are your Spanish classes going?" MG asks.

"I think they're going pretty good." I giggle a little and say,

"Jeffrey and I play a game in the bedroom to learn body parts. Jeffery learns the names faster than I do."

"I can't imagine Jeffrey speaking Spanish," Trip says. "Especially with his accent."

"You're one to laugh at someone's accent," MG teases. "It's funny enough to hear Spanish coming from a blond, but when you throw in a 'ya' at the end of each sentence, it's hilarious."

"Hey, that's just how we speak in Wisconsin," Trip puts her hands on her hips. "I can't help it. Every time I go back to Wisconsin to visit family, it gets worse."

MG can start with good-natured teasing, but sometimes Trip gets hurt feelings for days.

"I just got off the phone with my mom." I change the subject. "She and my stepfather just retired and might move to Florida. I think it upset her when I didn't make it home for Christmas."

"Will she ever come here to visit?" MG asks.

"She doesn't like to fly and it's a long drive. I told her I'd get there at spring or summer break. She said they were putting the house on the market." A shadow passes over my heart as I realize I might not get to say goodbye to my lavender room. Like packing up dolls to say farewell to childhood, it feels like my security blanket is slipping away.

Rocky climbs from my lap to my shoulder as the conversation turns to past boyfriends and ex-husbands. The girls are pretty unabashed about their past and their stories of "bad boy" relationships have an air of one-upmanship about them. Maggie starts off talking about her exes.

She's been married five times and tired of the routine. She and Lightning aren't married and says this is her best relationship.

"He knows I can leave any time." Her voice is deep and rough from years of smoking cigarettes and pot. "He also knows I can shoot a gun and make it look like an accident."

Everyone laughs at this, but I pause. "I don't know if I could ever shoot anyone."

"Honey, you can shoot someone if you hate them enough," Trip snorts. "I put a picture of my ex on my target and hit it nine out of ten shots. The tenth shot I'm usually aiming for his crotch, but since it's such a fucking small target, I miss."

The girls all roar, but I ask, "What did he do to you to make you want to kill him?"

"It's not what he did, but what he didn't do."

"Okay, what didn't he do?" I ask.

"He didn't protect me." Her pretty face hardens.

Now I'm scared to hear the next part, but it begs the question, "What happened?"

She pauses for a moment and brushes her hands through her long blond hair. "Tim and I were in Matamoros shopping for some liquor. We'd just gotten out of the market and started walking toward the bridge. We always parked on the U.S. side and walked across since we had a better chance of having a car when we got back."

Rocky's pecking at my hair and wants my attention. I put him down on the ground in the middle of our little circle. Since his wings are clipped, he walks around pecking at the ground.

Trip continues her story, "Anyway, my ex was carrying two bags loaded with bottles and I had one bottle in each hand when a car pulls up next to us and the guys inside start whistling at me. I ignored them and they drove off. When we get another two blocks down we decide to take a shortcut through an alley to get to the bridge a little quicker. Those fuckers were waiting for us at the end of the alley. One of them gets out and puts a gun to my head and tells Tim to keep walking and me to get into the car with them."

I gasp at this news. "What did Tim do?"

"The fucker kept walking!"

"What did you do?"

"I told the guy he should go ahead and shoot me now cuz I wasn't getting in the car with him. When the other guys in the car started laughing at him, I kneed him in the nuts and swung one of the bottles at his head. It connected and he went down. The guys in the car took off and I ran for the border."

"Oh my God," is all I can say.

I'm startled back to reality when I hear Rocky squawking, "Oh, dear, oh dear!"

Rocky is halfway between our circle and the bird colony and is waddling as fast as he can toward the bird cages. He's whistling *Dixie*, which has become his way of signaling an alarm. I've been so engrossed in the story I've not paid attention to my surroundings. Rocky's out in the open and is aware of a danger I can't see. Suddenly I hear the sharp, piercing caw of a large bird. A red-tailed hawk is circling above.

Rocky screeches for his life. I jump up to run to get Rocky, but trip over the chair. He's helpless in the open and unable to fly. Just as the hawk dives for the kill, Lucero leaps from the shadows of the tree. With the fur on the back of his neck raised and his tail straight, he lunges at the bird, but misses. The hawk is scared enough to change course. I struggle to get up, but my feet are caught in the chair and I'm frozen in place on the ground. Rocky's making his last dash to the cages. The hawk recovers mid-flight and dives again for Rocky.

A blast shatters above the fracas and a volcano of red feathers explodes everywhere. The hawk is totally evaporated.

Trip stands with her right arm extended in front of her. The strong smell of gunpowder wafts through the air. Her face is dead calm. She looks down at me on the ground, "You really can kill when you hate something bad enough or if you love something even more."

I get up and quickly pick up Rocky with trembling hands. I vow to myself that I'll be more aware of just how vulnerable he is. The girls start chatting again like nothing has happened. To them, it's just another story that ends with, "Then I got my gun and shot it."

CHAPTER TWENTY-FIVE

International Mail

Dear Genny

I hope this letter finds you well. In the beginning, these letters were a fun distraction, but now the girls and I look forward to each one. Socorro reads them first for news from the United States. She always likes to know the newest songs so she can buy them and learn the words in English. She dreams of going there soon.

Our friend, Ernesto, just finished the university and is officially an attorney. He wanted to continue working for National Geographic Society but their funding is depleted. He is joining an office in Tampico called Garcia and Garcia Criminal Attorneys.

Juanita wants to go to the university in Mexico City to become a teacher. She will start in the spring. Socorro is concentrating on her dancing and has been performing solo. Raul let her travel to Tampico and stay the night alone. This never would have happened a year ago.

I have not gone to the mountains lately. Raul and Humberto are very busy buying things to export and need my help. We travel to remote villages and have found a lot of exotic pieces. Things continue to change in our lives. It is hard to believe our fortune since you came here. It is like you started a chain reaction. Thank you for your friendship.

Vaya con Dios

Victoria

Jeffery acts as a mailman and delivers letters back and forth between Victoria, the girls and me. The letters from them are in Spanish and mainly about what the girls are doing, but it keeps me connected to the family. In the beginning, it took Jeffrey and me several hours to interpret them, but now only a few words need to be looked up. After the first few letters, Jeffrey got bored and said the girls are too young and silly, but I enjoy it.

The trips to Mexico are almost routine business now. Jeffrey has been there eight or nine times and each time he comes back with more stories to tell. He has brought back several lesser pre-Columbian artifacts for me that wouldn't bring much money at auction. But the most recent trip, Humberto gave me an unusual piece in the shape of a bowl stacked on top of another bowl. The outer walls have fighting dogs biting each other's necks. There are four sets of dogs on the first tier and three on the second. It's quite an intricate piece and probably worth a lot of money.

It's an honor to have such a nice gift.

Jeffrey's getting ready to make another trip and seems unusually excited about this one. Jeffrey constantly has several projects going at once in various stages of flux: an engine disassembled here or a birdcage being built over there, one mess or another. But in the last two weeks, he diligently finished his projects in order to concentrate on this trip. He tells me repeatedly he plans on staying a little longer this time and has told me repeatedly not to worry.

As usual, everyone comes over for a small party. Jeffrey's the star of the moment and he eats it up. I'm the woman behind the man. I don't like being center stage anyway. I enjoy being with our birds and Lucero in our little home.

I start cleaning the house as soon as his plane circles overhead. This is an unusual opportunity for me as I will get an entire week with my house in order and no Jeffrey to disrupt it. We're acting like an old married couple, he has his activities and I clean the house. Despite yearning for something different, I wonder if I've fallen, more or less, into the life my mother imagined for me.

January 1980

"What are you running from?" Jeffrey asks, tracing his finger along my bare arm. He's been living with me for two months and we've made love every night and every morning.

"Nothing," I say, watching the sunlight stream through the bedroom windows.

"Come on, Genny. Everyone down here is running from something." He turns to the bedside table, pulls half a joint out of the ashtray and lights it.

"I'm running from a world where people don't get high before breakfast," I say.

He extends the joint to me. It's Saturday, no school today. I inhale and feel the burn in my throat.

"Good girl," he says, watching me toke like a pro.

"Don't call me that," I snap and pull my knees to my chest.

Jeffrey smiles, gold tooth glinting. "So that's it!" he says, wrapping his arms around me. "Don't worry, babe. Your secret's safe with me."

CHAPTER TWENTY-SIX
Keep Smoking

Like an ambulance hurtling to get to a wreck, Stump's pickup truck speeds down our road kicking up a cloud of dust as he pulls into the driveway. I wonder who needs life support?

MG rushes to my side while Stump hangs back to pet Lucero. She hugs me quickly and ushers me into the house. With her arm around my shoulder, she moves me with such force my feet don't feel like they're touching the ground. The seat of the chair hits the back of my knees before I even feel gravity take over my body.

She fumbles around in her purse, pulls out a joint and lights it. She takes a deep inhalation and hands it to me. "Take a hit," she orders. I obediently take a hit and hand it back to her. She shakes her head, "Take another one."

Her hands shake when she takes the joint from me and brings it to her lips. After taking a few deep inhalations, "Jeffrey got busted down in Mexico."

"What?" Everything's happening so quickly I can't think. "What does that mean?"

Stump walks into the room, takes a long drag of what's left of the joint, "It means Jeffrey's in a Mexican jail."

I have no idea what to say. MG hands me another joint. Lightning and Maggie show up with a case of cold Bud and hand me one. I hear the distinctive rumble of Dead Wrong Dan's truck pull up. Dan and Trip enter the room slowly. Trip looks like she's been crying, but she smiles as her eyes meet mine.

I try to meet her smile with one of my own, but my lips feel lopsided and my smile is more like a grimace.

"What happened?" The words catch in my dry mouth. "What went wrong?"

"The federales were waiting for him when he landed," Lightning answers.

"I thought he was using a new landing strip, so they wouldn't expect him."

"Someone must have tipped them off," Stump responds.

"The only people who knew where he was landing were Raul and Humberto," I say. "Why would they turn him in if he was making them so much money?"

"You never know what's going on south of the border," Dan chimes in. "Humberto was the one who called the hangar. He asked for you. I knowed something was wrong as soon as I heard an accent asking for Genny."

"What did he say?"

"He was very shook up," Dan answers. "He didn't know a lot, but said they had Jeffrey and it didn't look good."

"What about the electronics?"

Stump takes a deep hit off his joint and coughs out, "They got the electronics and the plane. There's no bargaining there. He didn't even make it out of the plane to deny the plane was his. They got him cold."

"Did they get his passport?"

"No, he didn't take it with him," Lightning says. "Jeffrey said he didn't want to have to give it up if he got caught."

"Does that help him at all?"

"He can claim to be someone else, so it doesn't go on his record," Lightning gives a small smile. "He has an alias, but that won't help if he needs the American consulate."

"What do we do?" I stammer. "What do I do?"

"You were right the first time." MG takes my hand, "What do *we* do? We are all in this together."

Lightening leans back in his chair, deep in thought, "The *only* thing we can do is buy his way out of jail. That's the bottom line. It'll take money and more money. That's it."

I fall back in my chair. I don't have a lot of money. All the money Jeffrey was bringing in went into the house and the birds. "I guess I need to sell my birds." Tears start streaming down my face.

"Don't get ahead of yourself here." MG squeezes my hand, "Jeffrey has a stash of cash at the hangar."

"He does?" This surprises me, but I'm so high now I can't think of anything to say.

"Yeah, honey," Trip adds. "All the boys do. It's their dirty money."

"They have it for emergencies," MG continues. "They all started stockpiling the money a long time ago for emergencies. This qualifies." MG looks around the room to make sure all the boys are in agreement on this. No one protests.

I never heard of the money before and can't imagine that Jeffrey would keep something so important from me. "Where do they keep it?"

"We keep it in a safe cemented in the floor of the hangar," Lightning answers.

"Doesn't the owner of the hangar get suspicious of you having a safe in his floor?"

"We all own the hangar," The guys say in unison.

"All of you? Even Jeffrey?"

"It was his idea. The hangar came up for sale a couple of years ago, so we all chipped in and bought it," Dan explains. "That's why Jeffrey slept there. He put all his money into the hangar and couldn't afford nothing else. It was the smartest thing we did."

"How much dirty money is there?"

Dead Wrong Dan takes out a piece of paper and pen and calculates. "We've been contributing for the last ten years, Jeffrey for about six. So I guess there has to be over twenty thousand in the fund."

I'm in total shock now. How could Jeffrey have failed to tell me all of this? "What do we do next, then?"

Lightning takes a long drink from his Bud. "I hate the idea, but we need to get an attorney in Mexico to buy him out. We need to start slow. If they know we have that kind of cash, they'll take it and more."

My mind races. "I know an attorney there who I can probably contact." I think of Ernesto and a strange feeling overcomes me. "He's young and just passed the bar. He probably wouldn't be as expensive as a veteran attorney. He's very idealistic, which might be in our favor."

"Now ain't that unique," Stump scoffs. "An idealistic attorney, especially in Mexico. That won't last long. Wait till he sees how the system really works."

"Should I call him?"

"Sure, sure, sure. I'd rather start with an idealistic attorney than a crooked one. At least he'll start off on our side," Lightning interjects. "He might be bought by the other side sooner or later or even work both sides, but we got to start somewhere."

When the beer is gone and the pot is smoked, everyone drifts to the door. Hugs are given, even by Lightning and Stump.

Dead Wrong Dan pats me on the head. "Call your lawyer friend tomorrow and maybe Jeffrey's parents. They probably need to know."

CHAPTER TWENTY-SEVEN

Nice To Meet You, Too

Manicured lawns divided by tall walls and fences. People leading separate lives. The drive to this part of the Rio Grande Valley is a trip to the inner sanctum of the valley's elite. The house is a white colonial in pristine condition, right out of a box. Did laid-back Jeffrey really grow up here?

The phone conversation with Jeffrey's mother, Susan, was unsettling. She was hesitant about getting together, but finally agreed. It was clear Jeffrey never mentioned me to her at all.

My hands shake when I knock on their door. Familiar blue eyes answer the door. The resemblance is striking. Susan doesn't have his wild mane, but Jeffrey is definitely her child. Her shoulder-length blonde hair is perfectly coiffed and stiff with hair spray. She shows me into the living room where Jeffrey's father sits on the sofa. Starched khaki's with a permanent crease exactly down the middle, he stands up to meet me. He shakes the tips of my fingers, not my entire hand. His cardigan sweater drapes over his shoulders and ties in a loose knot at the front of his chest. His hair looks plastic. Barbie and Ken have grown old and live in the wealthy part of town. His name is Jeffrey, too. Everything is quite formal and civilized.

"I'm sure you want to know why I've come to see you."

They look at each other and exchange an expression I really can't interpret. Jeffrey Senior says, "Look Genny, we're not rich people, so if you want money for *whatever*, we don't have it."

"I don't need any money."

"So," Susan pauses and looks at me sideways. "Are you in some kind of trouble, dear?"

"No, not really."

"Perhaps trouble isn't the right word," Senior ventures. "Shall we say, in a family way?"

"What are you talking about?"

"The baby, dear," Susan insists. "What are you going to do about the baby?"

"Baby? What baby?"

They both reply simultaneously, "You're not pregnant?"

"No, I'm not pregnant."

"Then why are you here?"

"Jeffrey's in a Mexican jail," I blurt. I had planned to be more diplomatic, but it comes out before I can think. Barbie and Ken's little boy is in jail.

They look like I just shot them. I pictured a few hugs and sympathy…not this.

Like cops interrogating a subject, they ask questions in rapid succession, alternating between the two of them.

"What exactly happened?"

"Jeffrey flew into Mexico with a cargo of electronics and was arrested by the police down there."

"Who flew the plane? And wouldn't they be the ones to get arrested?"

"Jeffrey flew the plane." My armpits drip sweat and it trickles down my sides.

"Jeffrey doesn't know how to fly."

"Actually, he's a very good pilot." The sweat is ponding around my waistband.

"When did he learn to fly?"

"He's been flying for five years. I've been learning for almost two years now." *They don't give a shit. I wonder if they can see how wet my top is now?*

"Who else was on the plane with him?"

"He was alone."

"Why are electronics illegal?"

"The Mexican government taxes them heavily. Flying them directly into Mexico avoids paying the taxes." *This isn't how I rehearsed things.*

"I'm really trying to understand all this, so please forgive me. Who *exactly* are you?" Susan asks.

Oh, for God's sake. Why didn't Jeffrey tell them about me? He's living with me. He says he loves me. How much more should I tell them?

"I'm a friend of his." *No one really important in Jeffrey's life.*

With that said, the questions start again, but this time with less pressure on me and more on Jeffrey's situation.

"So, Junior's in a Mexican jail. How do we get him out?"

"I don't know. I came here for suggestions." I could just abandon ship right now and hand this whole mess over to them to deal with. But I love Jeffrey and I want to help if possible.

"We don't know anything about Mexican law," Susan states.

To qualify my status I say, "Well, I'm a school teacher--.

"That's nice, dear," she cuts me off. "But a school teacher won't be of any help in this situation now, will it?"

How rude. I wish I hadn't come.

"Some of our friends and I are trying to help. They have some money they can chip in for an attorney. I can keep you in the loop if you want."

Their silence and stony faces signal they are finished. I stand and walk to the door without an escort. Thank God, I'm not pregnant.

June 1976

"What do you mean she's no longer a good girl? She's a great girl."

"You're too young to understand," Mom's voice is soft to calm me down.

"I understand. She's my best friend and made a mistake. She shouldn't have to go away."

"She has to go away to have the baby, Genny."

"Does her boyfriend have to go away?"

"Well, that's part of the problem. Mathew left town. No one can find him."

"Mom, we should be helping her now more than ever, not sending her away."

"It's not easy for Jackie's mother right now. She's trying to keep the reputation of the family. Jackie has two younger sisters she needs to think about."

"Unbelievable. Is she going to keep the baby?"

My mother looks down at her feet and tears come to her eyes. She doesn't have to answer the question. "Genny, I love you very much, but I need to know. Are you still a good girl?"

CHAPTER TWENTY-EIGHT

Not A Snitch, Not A Crybaby

I drive home from his parents' house shaken and deflated, but determined to help Jeffrey. My head hurts and I feel sick to my stomach. The meeting keeps looping over and over in my head. The first thing that popped into their heads was 'Jeffrey got a girl pregnant'. He never told them about me or that we're living together. And he didn't tell them he can fly a plane. He certainly keeps a lot of secrets from them. But with parents like his, maybe Jeffrey was smart not to tell them what's going on in his life.

It's certainly different than how I was raised. My mother insisted on knowing everything. If I didn't tell her, she found out somehow anyway and it always made things worse when she did. I instantly cringe when I think about how she found out about my adventure in Mexico. They obviously have plenty of money. I can't believe they don't want to help their son. I thought parents had all the answers. I was hoping they would come to the rescue and take over. I don't know what to do. I can't just bail on Jeffrey, we were working towards a future together. He even paid off the mortgage on my house. A stab of guilt hits me in the solar plexus like a quick punch. *How will I ever pay Jeffrey back?*

I need to call Ernesto. Victoria had listed the name of his law firm in her last letter. When I get home, I head to my desk to the stack of letters next to my Spanish-English dictionary. As I search the pile, I notice one I hadn't seen before. The letter has some words underlined. I look up the words in the dictionary and they are underlined in there, as well. Jeffrey must have read and translated it.

Dear Genny,

Everyone in Poza Rica is getting ready for <u>Easter</u> celebration. This year, Juanita is going to be the Spring Princess. She is a little upset Juan will not be her partner, but the boy who will be escorting her is very nice.

Socorro has been very busy too. She dances in many places, even Mexico City. She now has a <u>boyfriend,</u> but has not told anyone who he is. Raul is <u>upset</u> about the <u>secrecy,</u> but that's to be expected from a father. He wants her to marry someone with money, so she can have an easy life. I can't tell him money doesn't always insure happiness.

She will find her own way. New traditions are coming to Mexico slowly.

Vaya con Dios,
Victoria

The letter is very benign, but I have mixed feelings about him not giving it to me. On the one hand, he may be practicing his Spanish, but I don't like the fact he read it without me. Maybe he was preparing for his trip to Mexico and wanted to know what the family was doing. Maybe he forgot. Right now I can't think about this transgression. I'll discuss it with Jeffrey when he gets back. In the U.S., he'd be out on bond in two or three days. Hopefully, it'll be the same there and he'll be home in a couple of days.

Unsure of how to find a phone number in another country, I dial "O" and ask for an international operator. I could have called Victoria directly, but I don't want to get her involved. Fortunately, the operator is bilingual and stays on the line long enough to get the number for Ernesto's law firm. She connects me and even waits for Ernesto to get on the line. I hear Ernesto's voice and I'm suddenly scared to talk to him. The operator tells me to go ahead and she clicks off.

"*Hola*, Ernesto. This is Genny. How are you?"

At first, there's a hesitation like he can't remember who 'Genny' is. Then I hear him say, "*Sí, sí, sí*. Genny. How are you?"

"Oh, Ernesto I'm fine, but my boyfriend's in trouble."

"What's wrong *Señorita* Genny?"

"He was flying electronics into Mexico and was caught on the landing strip. He's in jail right now." I don't dare tell him about the artifacts he was supposed to bring back to the United States.

"*O Dios mio, señorita!* That is a very serious charge. What can I do to help?"

"I thought since you're an attorney now, you could get him out."

"Who was he selling the electronics to?"

"He brought them to Humberto and Raul."

There's a long silence on the other end of the line. I'm implicating Ernesto's friends with this mess. I can tell he's weighing his ethical duties. He finally says, "I will try to help. Has he told the authorities about his partners?"

"I've told you all I know, but I'm fairly certain he wouldn't tell them anything. He understands what it means to snitch on someone."

"What does snitch mean?"

"Betray."

"*Sí, sí.* Okay. I will talk to my partner and let you know what we need to do. When are you coming here?"

It's my turn to hesitate. *I hadn't thought of going back into Mexico.*

"I'll have to talk to some people and then get back with you."

1968

    "Cry a little harder, we can't hear you," my brother Chuck taunts from below. I'm wedged between boxes of Christmas decorations in the attic, but still my wails are heard throughout the house.

    "I'm telling Mom that you had your girlfriend over when you were supposed to be babysitting me and playing Go Fish with me."

    "What a snitch, Genny," he says. "There's nothing worse in the whole wide world than being a snitch except maybe being a cry baby."

    "Oh yeah?" I scream and cry for the next two hours until our mom gets home.

    "What on earth did you do to her? She's lost her voice." I cling to my mother's legs still sniffling while she interrogates Chuck.

    "I didn't lay a hand on her," he scowls. "She's a spoiled brat."

    I stick out my tongue at him from behind my mother's dress.

    "If she can't talk by the morning, she can't go to school tomorrow. And you'll have to watch her again."

    Later that evening, Chuck brings me salt water to gargle. "Crying shows you're weak," he says. "Be a good girl. Don't cry and don't snitch."

    In the morning, my voice has miraculously returned.

CHAPTER TWENTY-NINE

Money

Dead Wrong Dan starts, "I heard Trip took out a problem hawk for you."

"Yeah, she's one hell of a shot. Rocky hasn't left my shoulder ever since."

"Yeah, that's one lucky little pecker." Everyone laughs. Rocky seems to know he's being talked about and sings softly. He starts to rub his beak against my ear.

As everyone relaxes, I break the silence, "I went over to talk to Jeffrey's parents. They didn't know anything about him going into Mexico. It was a complete surprise to them."

"I can't really blame him for that. His parents are very straitlaced. I think they're big in the church and such." Lightning explains. "He don't fit in with his family much."

"I don't think they'll give any money to help get him out."

"That don't surprise me, either," Dan adds.

"Well, we need to just do this on our own," Lightning says. "If we want to do a reconnaissance operation, we need to do it asap."

"I agree, but I'm not sure what to do. I called the attorney I know and he said I probably need to go down there personally to take care of it."

"That's what I think we should do too." Lightning moves to the front of his chair and presses his elbows into his knees. "We need to go down there and see what it takes to get him out. I could fly you down there and do a quick touch down, refuel then take off."

"I know, but I can't go by myself."

"All my contacts down there can identify me now." Lightning moves in his seat and seems to weigh his options here. "I can't afford to lose my plane down there."

"Yeah, but I still need someone with me."

Trip coughs a little and says, "I can go, if it doesn't take too long."

"No offense, but the last time you went into Mexico, they tried to kidnap you. I want to look as inconspicuous as possible. You would be like holding up a neon sign saying, 'Please mug me'. Thanks anyway."

"Well, I speak Spanish and traveled in Mexico a lot in my younger days," MG says.

"Great. Spring break starts on Friday." I quickly accept her half resume/half offer as a yes. "I told my principal I needed to help a sick friend and needed a few days off. Since most of the kids in my class have already gone, she said it wouldn't be a problem. Can we leave tomorrow?"

MG looks at Stump who nods. "I guess so."

"Great. I'll meet you at the hangar at six in the morning." Lightning nods his agreement.

"How long are we going to be?" MG asks.

"I'm sure we can get him home in four or five days," I say. "Maybe a week, at the most."

Everyone stares at me in silence. Maybe I'm being a little too optimistic, but I'm sure this can all be taken care of with a little cash. I saw how easy it was for Humberto to bribe the guards. I'm sure twenty thousand dollars will take care of this. This is just a little set back. Jeffrey will just have to get a real job when he gets back.

After everyone leaves, I call Ernesto to tell him I'll be traveling tomorrow and will see him the following morning. He sounds excited, but I can't tell in what capacity...as a client or a friend.

Summer 1977

"Where are you moving to?"

"Mom's decided California would be a great place to live," Jackie says.

"You can come and visit once we get settled.

"Why can't you stay here and at least finish out your senior year and graduate with our class?"

The smile fades from her face, "I can't handle it here anymore. The girls either talk behind my back or pretend to be my friends just to pump me for information, especially Elizabeth."

"I would never do that." I hug her close.

"Mom says I need a fresh start." She wipes a tear from her cheek.

"Don't worry, we'll always be sisters."

"Promise?"

CHAPTER THIRTY

Machine Gun

I can't bear to leave Rocky behind, so I give him a little tequila to calm him down and put him in a sling around my neck. I can hear him snoring softly within fifteen minutes. MG and Lightning are waiting for me when I drive up. Stump will stay at my house and take care of the birds and Lucero.

"Genny, you don't want to flash hundred-dollar bills in Mexico, so I stuffed this with twenties and ten's." Lightning pats a bulging money belt. "We're only giving you two-thousand dollars to take now."

"Only two-thousand dollars?" I can't believe they're not going to give me all of it.

"This is a lot of cash down there." He doesn't mince words, "Are you sure you can trust this attorney?"

"Are you just going to leave Jeffrey to rot in jail?" I ask.

"No, of course not," MG and Lightning both stammer.

"Honey, maybe I should handle the money," MG takes the money belt from me. "Ernesto will be less likely to mess with me. I'm older and I don't have as much of an emotional investment in this. We need some room to negotiate."

"Isn't this Jeffrey's money?"

"No, it's one fourth Jeffrey's money," Lightning explains. "This is an emergency fund for all of us. We need to be sure it lasts for *all* of our emergencies."

I feel panic come from the pit of my stomach up to my racing heart. I don't know how to respond. I lean back against the plane.

"Aren't you going to give me the twenty thousand?"

"If you show them twenty-thousand dollars, they'll take it and ask for more." MG puts her arm around my shoulder. "Let's start slow. Tell them you're a poor school teacher with only two-thousand dollars and see how far that gets us."

"You'll get yourself killed if you flash that kind of cash," Lightning is more direct. "We ain't giving you the money unless you listen to us."

"We're only talking to an attorney about the case," I say. "How's that dangerous?"

"You never know who they'll tell about the money down there," Lightning says. "If they know there's twenty big ones to be got, they'd kill their own brother for it."

They're trying to scare me, so they can control the money. I thought I'd give the Federales twenty-thousand dollars and they'd give me Jeffrey. That seemed a lot quicker than dishing out two thousand at a time.

"You have to play this game by the Mexican rules." MG gives my shoulder a little shake and says, "It's *all* about the money. They like to negotiate. You have to think like them or you'll be dead in no time. Believe me, you need to understand their culture. If they think you're a damsel in distress, they'll try to protect you. The men down there are especially prone to thinking they know more than women."

I really don't have a choice. It's their money, not mine. I have to try to get this done as quickly as possible to save Jeffrey without hurting

MG or me. I nod my head and agree I'll do it their way.

We fly in silence. The three-hour flight feels like forever.

The small, grassy landing strip outside of Tuxpan is just north of Poza Rica and south of Tampico. It's short and Lightning engages the flaps immediately in order make a quick stop. Any other pilot would have been sweating like a pig on this set up, but Lightning didn't even have to think about it. Lightning must have been a bird in a previous life.

We taxi up to what looks like an old, abandoned barn. Lightning has a beat up old jeep stashed here he used when he flew into this part of the world. Most of the time, he flew into San Luis Potosi where it's more mountainous and easier to find places to hide or evade other planes.

Tuxpan is flatter and closer to the coast, so Lightning felt this would be an easier place for MG and me to start.

The jeep's floorboard is missing in places and the seats have springs coming through the threadbare cushions, but it starts up right away and has a full tank of fuel. Lightning quickly fuels his plane from a free-standing fuel distribution tank that's hidden by the trees.

"You two need to stick together if you're going to get this done." Lightning shakes his index finger at us, "If either of you want to leave right now, we can all get back in the plane. Jeffrey will be on his own, but he knew the risks and took his own chances."

I shake my head. "I can do this, but if MG wants to leave, I understand."

MG shakes her head as well. "Thanks, Lightning. We can take care of this. We'll call you when we need to get out of here."

Lightning gets in his plane and tips his head to us. "Good luck."

MG and I watch as the plane quickly gains speed and lifts off at almost a seventy-five degree angle to clear the trees. You have to admire him as a pilot. There are few with his skills.

As we watch the plane disappear into the clouds, my bravery begins to fade. Rocky pokes his head out of the sling and sings, "We're off to see the wizard." He must have picked up another song from one of the rescued birds. MG and I look at each other and laugh. Rocky always makes me feel better.

The last time I was in Mexico, everyone was a stranger. At least this time, I'm with MG. Maybe this isn't going to be so bad after all. We load our gear into the back of the jeep and MG drives while I ride shotgun. The roads are more than a little rough and Lightning's choice of vehicle is perfect for the rugged terrain. Rocky sits on my shoulder as we bounce along, his wings flapping every so often.

Ernesto's office is in Tampico which is north of us and right on the coast. I check the glove compartment and find a map and a list of places to stay and eat. The map has small numbers on it corresponding to the restaurants and hotels on the list. Lightning really is pretty thorough with intel.

I show the map and list to MG and say, "Being in the military must have sharpened his organizational skills."

"Or his smuggling sharpened them," she responds.

"Yeah, I hope the hotels are at least clean."

"He probably didn't pick the hotels for their cleanliness, but more for their isolation. He was successful in this business a long time because he was careful, never showy." She slows around a curve and barely misses a small monkey crossing the road. "You stay under the radar. You surprise people that way."

The jungle is thick and we each point out different sights and animals along the way. I settle into my seat as best I can, but a spring keeps popping through the seat and stabs me every time we hit a bump, making it hard to enjoy the drive.

"This jeep is held together with bailing wire and tape." I laugh.

"Yeah, but did you notice it started immediately? Knowing Lightning, the jeep's engine is perfectly tuned. That's not an accident."

I need to get my mind off the constant jab of pain from the spring. "MG, I've been meaning to ask you for some time. What's your real name?"

"Linda."

"Linda? I thought MG would at least be something with your initials in it, like Triple A has three A's for her name. So, how did you get the name Machine Gun?"

"Are you sure you really want to know?" she giggles. The manner in which she says this makes me immediately start to blush and I'm not sure I want to know the answer.

MG blushes too. "Well, in my younger days I was a little more adventurous and experimented with sex more."

Now I know for sure I really shouldn't have asked the question, but she continues, "I had the habit of eating a lot of sunflower seeds. I even had a bowl of them next to my bed if I got hungry in the middle of the night."

"What's that got to do with sex?" I regret the question as soon as I say it. This is going to get kinky.

"I was on top of this crazy Cajun, just rolling along nice and easy, nothing spectacular. I reached over to my bowl of sunflower seeds, scooped up a handful and popped them in my mouth. Right when I did that, he reached up, grabbed my breasts and pinched my nipples and did something wild with his pelvis. I came instantly." She laughs loudly.

"I still don't see how that gives you the name Machine Gun."

"I was coming so fast and hard with multiple orgasms that the sunflowers seeds started shooting out of my mouth like a machine gun. That stupid Cajun told everyone. I had an instant reputation and was followed around by different men for several months who wanted a repeat performance. I eventually had to leave town. I rarely tell anyone how I got the name."

"If you moved to get away from the reputation, how come you didn't go back to telling people your name is Linda?"

"A lot of my friends knew the nickname, so it stuck. Besides, Linda just doesn't fit me anymore. I think people grow into their names. I outgrew Linda, but I still have a lot of room to grow in MG."

I'm glad she trusts me enough to know her nickname and her *real* name.

We work our way up the coastline and note some of the restaurants and hotels Lightning has on his list. Some of the restaurants are no more than a shack on the side of the road and most of the hotels look like they'd blow away during a spring rain storm. We decide we could take a chance on some of his restaurants, but we need to pass on his choices of hotels.

The closer to Tampico we get, the better the hotels look, and we breathe a little sigh of relief. We make it into Tampico as the sun is about to set.

Before we check into a hotel, MG lets down her hair from the bun and arranges the long curls gently around her shoulders and down her back. She directs me to get behind her and not to speak. As she approaches the registration desk, she holds her head high, brings her shoulders back and straightens to her full 5'7" statuesque figure. She greets the hotel receptionist in perfect Spanish. The woman behind the desk comes to full attention as if the Queen of Spain has just arrived.

Who is this person? I look at her with a more critical eye. How does a stranger see her? She's in her mid-thirties with high cheekbones, an angular nose and round full lips resembling the Spanish elite.

She's negotiating the room rate in a very professional manner and asks questions about the quality of the room, the service, the view, as if to make sure this hotel is worthy of her. She isn't the person I thought she was. Talk about flying under the radar.

The hotel clerk asks about me. MG tells her I'm her sister.
We follow the bell boy and MG sniffs the room when we enter as if to put them on notice that nothing will get past her attention.

She doesn't start laughing until the door is closed and the bell boy is far enough away as to not hear. What a performance.

"So, *Linda,* what's your last name?"

"Rodriguez."

We both laugh. I mentally register I need to ask people their last names as a matter of course.

We'll find Ernesto's office in the morning.

CHAPTER THIRTY-ONE

Her Majesty

MG studies her reflection in a store window and releases her long hair from the tight bun on top of her head. She arranges her ringlets to frame her face evenly then applies a modest amount of deep-red lipstick. She puts on a black tailored jacket which understates her curvy form and turns sideways to check her image one last time. The transformation from average chick to regal queen is complete. She steps off the curb and crosses the street to Ernesto's office with me four steps behind.

Ernesto's office is a small, unassuming brick building located near Tampico Bay built in the 1950's. The receptionist looks up from her paperwork and immediately comes to full attention. "Please take a seat, *señora*. I will get *Señor* Soto and *Señor* Flores immediately." She addresses MG only. I'm ignored, just part of her majesty's entourage.

Ernesto and another gentleman enter the lobby for brief introductions, and then lead us to a conference room. Julio Flores is the firm's senior partner and has a warm smile to go along with his good looks. His hair is greying around the temples and his skin has no lines or wrinkles. He's probably in his early forties and could easily grace the cover of a GQ magazine. The polite conversation is in English in deference to me.

"Genny, I'm very sorry to hear about your boyfriend's trouble." Julio looks me directly in the eyes and sounds genuinely concerned.

"Ernesto and I will do everything we can to get him home soon." Both men focus on me and ignore her majesty.

MG pulls out a notepad from her large purse. "We have some questions."

Julio puts his hands on the conference table and folds them together as if in prayer, "MG, are you related to Jeffrey?"

MG mirrors Julio's actions and folds her hands on the table as well. They are both sizing each other up. She smiles and softly says, "No, señor. I'm a friend. I'm here to help get Jeffrey released." She looks at me,

"Genny's young and doesn't know our customs or anything about the laws here. I'm here to help her."

I blush to my core and worry Ernesto will think I'm just a silly, young girl. I shouldn't care what he thinks and should be more interested in getting Jeffrey home without worrying about my bruised ego.

"Ernesto and I have discussed la señorita Genny and want to protect her too."

"Genny is a school teacher and doesn't have any money." MG takes charge of the situation. "What are the charges?"

Julio puts on reading glasses, looks down on his clipboard and reads briefly before he answers, "Jeffrey has been charged with several counts of smuggling electronics and one count of smuggling arms into our country." He pauses, "this is very serious."

Shock grips me, "Smuggling arms? What kind of arms?"

"Jeffrey had one handgun with him." Ernesto interjects, "A Smith and Wesson."

"One gun and he's charged with arms smuggling?" I can't believe how unfair this is.

"I'm afraid so, *Señorita* Genny." Julio looks grim.

MG reaches over and touches my hand. Her expression changes slightly, and I can tell she's more concerned than before. She calmly asks, "What's the first step?"

"We need to arrange for food and blankets to be delivered to the jail," Ernesto answers.

"What do you mean?" I feel light headed. "He's in jail and they won't even feed him?"

"The Mexican government wants to discourage people from crime," Julio says. "They provide small meals of rice and beans, water and tortillas. There is an entire business set up outside the prisons to make money off the prisoners."

MG clears her throat, "How much does it cost weekly? Is it cheaper if we pay monthly?"

"Monthly? I thought we could get Jeffrey out in a couple of days, a week at the most."

Julio shakes his head. "No, *Señorita* Genny. He will be here for several months before he even goes to trial."

"But it was only one gun. I'm sure he didn't intend to sell it. It was probably for protection."

Ernesto reaches across the small conference table and pats my hand. "Genny, I know this sounds bad, but I think we can get him out. It will take time and --. He stops and looks at MG before finishing his sentence. --"money."

"We don't have a lot of money," MG says evenly. "We'll try to get some more from Jeffrey's parents. How much do you need right now?"

Instead of answering the question, Julio pulls out some papers from the clipboard and hands them to me. "I need you to sign these papers, if you want us to represent Jeffrey."

I look down at the unintelligible words. "This is in Spanish,"

"We are in Mexico." Julio smiles at me like he has the upper hand.

A small squeak escapes from my mouth. I'm getting dizzy from this conversation. I reach to get some water from the middle of the table and Ernesto pours a glass for me. I take a sip and try to talk, but all I do is squeak again. I'm helpless.

"We need to read these first." MG scoops up the papers and takes me by my elbow to rise. "In the meantime, how much money do you need to just get Jeffrey food and a blanket for a week?"

"Twenty dollars should be enough for the first week," Ernesto says.

Julio frowns at Ernesto, but puts his hand out for the money. Maybe Ernesto should have asked for more money?

MG dips quickly into her purse and hands him a twenty-dollar bill as we leave.

When we get back to the hotel room, MG pulls the contract out and her notebook and lists questions she has.

After two hours of reading and writing, MG finally looks up and says, "Jeffrey's screwed."

I flop down in a small chair next to the window like a ragdoll. "How can you be so pessimistic?" I ask.

"Genny, you have to be realistic. We're in a foreign country.

Jeffrey has broken their laws, and gotten caught. They have a totally different set of rules to play by."

"We have to do everything we can to get him out."

"Just with the electronics charges, it's going to take a lot of money to get him out, but with this arms charge, he could be looking at years here."

"What does the contract say?"

"It says we pay them lots of money up front and they may or may not get him off."

"We at least need to try and talk with Jeffrey. Maybe he has some ideas. Maybe he wasn't even carrying a gun."

MG frowns and says, "All the guys carry a gun with them when they go into Mexico. It's stupid not to."

"We can't just let him rot here. Let's at least go back and talk to Ernesto."

MG pulls her chair right in front of mine and looks me straight in the eyes. "Desperate people do desperate things. You might not like it, but I'm here to provide a sanity check on this entire operation. We can talk to Jeffrey, but we need a plan. No shooting from the hip. Do you understand?"

"You're treating me like a child. I'm twenty-one years old." I bite my lower lip to stop myself from crying, but the tears spill from my eyes.

"*You* can do whatever *you* want, but not with the group's money and not while I'm with you. I don't mind helping as long as you're cool, but as soon as you want to do something crazy, I'm bailing on you."

"Fine. I understand. Can we go see Ernesto again and ask if we can see Jeffrey?"

"Sure," she stuffs the contract into her purse.

I put Rocky on a lamp shade in the corner while MG picks up the keys to the jeep. We ride in silence over to the law office. I know I'm pouting, but I want some voice in this. Even if I have to communicate with my silence.

We drive up to the office as Ernesto is leaving. With all my pent up energy, I practically jump out of the jeep to catch him. "Where are you going?" I ask.

Ernesto smiles. "I'm going to lunch. Do you want to join me?"

"*Sí*," MG and I both reply.

We climb back into our jeep and follow him to a small open-air restaurant looking out onto the Tampico Bay. If the circumstances weren't so dire, this could feel like a vacation and we're three friends having lunch. Ernesto is quite charming and the conversation is light and easygoing. I can see how women fall for him. I wish I could forget why we're here.

After we finish eating, MG takes the contract out of her purse and says, "Ernesto, we need to fix this contract. There're too many problems with it."

Ernesto smiles and says, "I told Julio you wouldn't like some of the stipulations. What do you want us to change?"

I sit in silence as Ernesto and MG hammer out changes to the contract. MG wants several tiers to the contract where the money is paid out specifically for certain duties performed by the law firm. They get their money once they've performed, not before. I can see where this makes sense, but it also means it will drag the process out forever. Whoever said 'the wheels of justice turn slowly' must have hired an attorney.

They shut me out of the negotiations. I may as well not even be here. I pout again.

We drive back to the law firm and after some changes, I sign the contract and MG hands over the first installment. MG gives Ernesto a thousand dollars for the law firm and eighty dollars for Jeffrey's food and care for the next four weeks. MG is quite proud of her negotiations. We're leaving with money in our pocketbooks.

Finally, I ask the most important question, "When can I see Jeffrey?"

"*Señorita,* are you sure you want to see him?" Ernesto looks at me with concern in his eyes. "It is a dangerous place and he might not want you to see him."

"Of course I want to see him. I don't want him to think I've abandoned him."

"I can meet with him and tell him everything," Ernesto says.
I hold up my hand to stop him from saying any more. "I need to see him. I don't care how dangerous or dirty it is. He needs my support."

"*Sí, Señorita* Genny. I will arrange for you to see him tomorrow. You need to get some rest. Meet me here in the morning at 9:00 and we'll go to the prison together."

Ernesto takes my hand, raises it to his lips and gently kisses it. An electric shock bolts through my entire body. My knees feel weak and I take a small step backward. I smile slightly and take my hand away. MG laughs a little, takes me by the elbow and leads me away.

"You are in over your head with this guy," she whispers in my ear.

For once, I don't argue the matter.

Spring 1978

"I've got an appointment next week at the student clinic to get on the pill."

"I thought you were a good Catholic girl." Patrick pulls me closer to him, "You don't need the pill, I'll be careful."

"Like Mathew was with Jackie?" I ask. "No thanks."

"If you got pregnant, I'd do the right thing. I'd marry you."

"I don't want you to have to do the right thing. I want to make sure I'm never in that predicament." He starts to kiss my neck, trying to distract me. I pull back. "You'll have to wait a little longer."

He pulls away from me and starts to gather his backpack. I know he's upset, but I resist the urge to give in. "Exams are coming up, so I can't get back for four weeks," he says.

"Why don't we wait for spring break then and meet at home?"

CHAPTER THIRTY-TWO

In God We Trust

The hotel room seemed big when we first arrived, but it feels smaller and smaller as Rocky and I sit in a chair in the corner waiting for MG to awake. Rocky has eaten half the lampshade, so I know I'll have to pay to replace it. He's on my shoulder rubbing his head against my cheek.

A faint, predawn light glows through the hotel window and I thumb through the *Biblia* from the nightstand. The pages are well worn with many passages underlined. Between four years of Latin in high school and my current efforts with conversational Spanish, I labor at translating verses from the New Testament. I want to believe it holds the answers to my problems. Sister Mary Clement Marie used to say "read the bible and pray for answers. God hears your prayers." But, there's nothing similar to my situation noted in these pages.

There are two double beds in the room and MG sleeps in the one closest to the windows. She finally rolls over and opens her eyes. "I've been awake for about a half hour. I wondered how long you could keep quiet."

"We need to get going."

MG stands and stretches then looks at her watch. "It's only 6:00 o'clock. We can't wait outside Ernesto's office for three hours. Let's take a walk along the waterfront and eat some breakfast. Try to enjoy our time here."

MG dresses in baggy jeans and a loose-fitting top, no makeup and looks me up and down. "You need to change your blouse and take off your jewelry.

"I want to look nice for Jeffrey."

"For Jeffrey or Ernesto?" she teases. "Absolutely nothing flashy. I need to call the guys at the hangar to arrange for Lightning to pick us up."

"Maybe I should stay in Mexico and you can go back without me."

"Bad idea. You need to concentrate your time on teaching school. Jeffrey's a big boy. He can handle himself."

"But I was the one who introduced him to Humberto and Raul. It's my fault he's here." I don't mention the fact he paid off my twenty five-thousand dollar mortgage. I make eight thousand dollars a year teaching. How will I ever pay him back?

"Is that what you're feeling guilty about? Jeffrey wanted to do something like this for years. None of the gang would give up their contacts to him."

"Not even Lightning?"

"Especially Lightning. Plausible deniability is his philosophy. If the government comes knocking on your door and points to one guy, the rest of the gang can deny everything. But if an informant can point to more than one, it can implicate them all. All the guys have their own units and distribution lines and none of them overlap. They trust one another, but none of them trust their Mexican counterparts."

"How did Lightning pick his contacts in Mexico?"

"He started years ago when he got back from 'Nam. One of the other pilots in his division moved down to Mexico. Some of the Mexicans down there approached him to fly some contraband into the United States.

His buddy got so busy doing runs, he asked Lightning if he wanted some of the work."

"So Lightning trusts his contacts?"

"No. Not really. When Lightning is doing a business deal, he approaches all Mexicans like they would kill him just as soon as look at him."

"You're Mexican. How does his attitude make you feel?"

"Doesn't bother me. It's a cultural thing. Gringos don't trust Mexicans and Mexicans don't trust gringos. It's a good working relationship. It keeps everybody on their toes. Besides, he doesn't carry it into his personal life, it's only business."

"Who do you think turned Jeffrey in?"

"It could have been anyone. Humberto is the one who called, so it probably wasn't him. That's not to say you can totally trust Humberto, but he might have been blindsided by this too. He maybe even thinks he could be next."

As we leave the room I put Rocky back on the lampshade, or what's left of it. It's dark outside, but the first light of day is breaking over the water. There's a lot of activity in the streets at this early hour.

"So, who should I trust?"

"Well, so far I would say you have to trust Ernesto a little. Don't ever trust anyone here fully, but you have to trust them a little at a time."

"What do you mean?"

"It's just like that contract you signed. You pay them when they complete a duty for you. You trust them when they do the right thing. You stop trusting them when they screw you."

"I don't want to be that jaded. I have to have faith in people."

"Faith is different than trust. Trust is earned. Faith is a belief from your heart and soul. Have faith in God, not in people. People are fallible, God is not."

I can't argue with that.

We walk along the waterfront in silence and my mind begins to clear. Small fishing boats dart in between the larger commercial haulers and cruise ships which crowd the docks. They resemble the interaction of pilot fish picking off the spoils from slow, lumbering sharks when they're feeding. Bulldozers scrape shacks and old docks into a pile of rubble next to the construction cranes swinging steel beams for new hotels and resorts. Tampico's quaint charm is being pushed out of the way by industrial giants with big wallets.

We cross over one of the many rivers that flow through the city and leads into the gulf. A taco stand next to the wharf has a line of people in front of it. We stop and get some egg and shrimp tacos. The sun's heat makes both of us sweat a little. It feels better than the cold ache I was feeling in the room.

We circle around the entire waterfront and end up in front of Ernesto's office.

MG slides a ten-dollar bill across the top of the desk as she asks the receptionist if she can use the phone to make an international call. The receptionist lets MG into the conference room where she can have a private conversation.

Ernesto walks through the door from his office as MG closes the door to the conference room. I can feel my face blush and my heart beat a little faster. He greets me in the reception area. "*Buenos días, Señorita*

Genny. *Ven a mi oficina .*" He shows me to a chair in front of his desk and sits next to me. He's more formal than yesterday at lunch.

"*Buenos días, Señor. ¿Cómo estás hoy?*"

"Your Spanish is getting better," he smiles. "You could be fluent if you stayed longer."

"I'm afraid I need to leave soon, probably tomorrow."

"Are you sure you want to see Jeffrey now?" Ernesto looks concerned.

I nod my head, but feel my shoulders sag. "I need to see him and find out what he knows. He must have some clues as to what happened."

I look at Ernesto, but he doesn't look me in the eyes when he says. "We may never know how he got caught."

"Did you speak with Humberto and Raul?" I ask.

"They both say they know nothing," he answers.

"Who was supposed to meet Jeffrey at the airfield?"

"Humberto, but he was running late. He says he got there after Jeffrey was arrested."

Since Humberto is chronically late for everything, I can imagine that happening. "Would Humberto have been arrested if he had been there?"

"Absolutely."

"Well, I'm glad he was late then."

Ernesto looks somewhat relieved to hear me say that. He reaches for my hand and says, "We will do everything we can to get Jeffrey out of jail."

There's a soft knock at the door and MG enters. I take my hand away from Ernesto's. MG looks at our hands and smiles.

Ernesto stands and offers her the chair he was sitting in. Always the gentleman.

MG looks at me. "We leave early tomorrow."

"I was hoping to show you my beautiful city." Ernesto frowns a little and says, "Where we are going today obviously is not the best we have to offer."

"Genny and I will need to come often, so I'm sure we'll see better parts in the future."

"How are you going to arrange payments?" he asks.

"We'll bring cash each time." MG answers.

Ernesto nods and pushes himself up from his chair. "I will need to stay at the prison to make arrangements after your meeting, so we need to take two vehicles." He looks at MG and continues, "Do you mind if *Señorita* Genny rides with me and you follow? I want to explain some of the rules for her to follow."

CHAPTER THIRTY-THREE

Rules

Ernesto drives an old Volkswagen beetle with multiple dings and rust spots. As I look around, few cars look new and most of them have dents. He doesn't act self-conscious about the car's condition at all. Fancy, new cars must not be the status symbol here as they are back home.

"Try to say as little as possible," he starts. "Walk tall and do not look anyone in the eyes, especially the prisoners."

"Will there be a glass partition between Jeffrey and us?"

"No, he will be in the same room."

"Don't ask him questions about the arrest or who he was working with."

The scenery changes drastically once we leave the city. I feel his eyes watching me as we pass the rundown parts of town and wind our way through a more rural landscape. Shacks and tents dot the hillside. We round a corner and dead-end into an imposing fence made of concrete blocks with barbed wire all around it. There are more shacks and lean-tos just outside the fence.

"Villages grow on the outskirts of the prisons," Ernesto explains. "Like a giant market place, there are taquerias, fruit and vegetable stands, even pharmacies for toiletries and blankets. This is where we buy food for our clients. These businesses feed off the prisons. We give them money and they deliver the food daily."

Normally, I would find this interesting in a curious way, but today I'm so out of my element I just nod my head. We park outside the gate in a caliche parking lot littered with trash and wait for MG to get out of the jeep.

Ernesto ushers us into a ten-by-ten foot building outside the gate. He speaks to the guard and shows his I.D., then motions for us to show ours. MG holds her driver's license in front of the guard's face while he reads it.

When I walk up and show mine, the guard takes it out of my hand to look at it more closely. He holds it next to my face to compare the picture on the license to me and asks me a question in Spanish. When I answer I speak a little Spanish, he smiles like the Cheshire cat. "Why does a *gringa* come here?"

I answer before Ernesto has time to stop me. "I'm here to see my boyfriend, Jeffrey."

Ernesto jumps in front of me and starts talking too rapidly for me to understand it all. I can tell there's some kind of damage control taking place. I hear the words young and no money from Ernesto, but the guard is unconvinced.

Ernesto turns back to MG and me and whispers, "He wants twenty dollars from each of you to see Jeffrey."

"He can do that?" I ask.

"He can do anything he wants," Ernesto answers.

MG digs into her purse and pulls out forty dollars. Fortunately, they're not charging for Ernesto. Ernesto hands the guard the money.

My hands are clammy and shaking, but I try to keep my head up and avert my eyes as the guard walks us through the gate and into the courtyard. We are silent as we walk up to the iron prison door. My throat is dry and I couldn't talk if my life depended on it. We enter a long hall leading into a room with a rectangular table in the center and six chairs.

I reach to pull out a chair but Ernesto stops me. "Don't touch anything with your hands. Pull the chair out with your foot and don't touch the table."

There's one fluorescent light in the middle of the ceiling with the bulbs exposed. One of the bulbs is broken and the other flickers. There're no windows and the room has a musty smell mixed with urine. We sit silently for about twenty minutes, although it seems longer.

Finally, the door opens and Jeffrey is pushed through it. At first, he acts drugged, but he may just be disoriented. He has cuffs on his hands with long chains attaching to his feet and smells like gasoline. He looks at Ernesto first. Then he sees MG and his face brightens. He turns to me and says, "Oh my God! How did you get here?"

Ernesto jumps in, "Don't say how you traveled here, please."

"I came with MG."

Jeffrey looks back over to MG and says, "Thanks, I owe you and Stump."

MG seems relieved to hear him speak and says, "I'm here to help you and Genny."

I get up to hug Jeffrey, but Ernesto stops me. "Sit down and don't get up again. They won't let you come back if you touch him. If you want to have conjugal visits, you will have to pay for them."

I flinch and Ernesto apologies immediately. "I'm sorry. I just want you to understand all the rules here. I should have told you that one in the car. We only have a short time left, so please hurry and talk. Do not ask questions about the case. Do not talk about money."

I look at Ernesto and then back at Jeffrey, "Are you okay?"

"Yeah, I'm okay," Jeffrey composes himself. "I just want out of here."

I point to Ernesto. "He's going to be your attorney. Another man named Julio Flores will be representing you, too. They'll also be getting you food and blankets. So if you need anything, ask them."

Jeffrey turns to Ernesto and says, "Get me the fuck out of here."

"You cannot speak that way here and especially in front of the *señoritas*," Ernesto says.

Jeffrey immediately bows up and says, "Okay, *please* get me out of here."

Ernesto ignores Jeffrey's sarcastic tone and says, "We will do everything possible to get you out as soon as possible, but this is not the United States. You don't have the same rights here as you do in your country."

"You don't have to tell me that. The highlight of my week so far has been getting sprayed down with kerosene to prevent lice and bed bugs. The guy in the cell next to me says it happens weekly."
Ernesto looks less than sympathetic and says, "We don't have money to feed and take care of our good citizens; we surely can't be expected to do better for smugglers and thieves."

I don't like how this is going, so I say, "I miss you Jeffrey and I know this is hard, but we can get through this together."
Jeffrey turns his attention back to me and says, "I miss you too, babe. How are the birds doing? How's Lucero?"

"Everything is fine. Stump is at the house taking care of

everything."

"Great. Stump's a good guy." Jeffrey looks over at MG, "Tell everyone that I appreciate the support. What else is happening?"

I look at MG and then at Jeffrey, "Well, I went over and told your parents what happened."

Jeffrey's face turns bright red and he looks like he's about to explode. Mindful of Ernesto in the room and the guards right outside the door, he forces himself to *calmly* ask, "Why would you do that? They didn't need to know about this at all."

"I didn't know what else to do," I stammer.

"I didn't call your mom when you were in Mexico bringing the birds across the border," Jeffrey blasts.

"I didn't get arrested," I respond.

Ernesto hisses a warning. "You cannot talk about anything like that past or present. Do you two understand?"

Ernesto's correct. Jeffrey has just implicated me in smuggling birds. This isn't going well. Maybe I shouldn't have come to see Jeffrey after all. "I'm sorry, Jeffrey. I didn't know what else to do."

Jeffrey finally says, "That's okay babe. I understand. Please don't contact them again. They don't need to know any more. Okay?"

I'm about to touch his arm when the door opens and the guards take Jeffrey away. I look at Ernesto and MG and my bottom lip starts to quiver. MG gets up from her chair and puts her arms around me. The guard who took our forty dollars comes in the room and says, "Either get out or pay another forty dollars to stay." We start to leave when he holds up an envelope and says, "Senorita, do you want your driver's license back?"

I feel the blood drain out of my face, "Yes, thank you."

"I usually charge another twenty dollars to give these back," he says. But today it will be free."

As MG drives us back to the hotel, I absentmindedly open the envelope to get my driver's license and a folded paper falls out. On the outside is a series of numbers. I unfold the paper and read.

Senorita Genevieve,

If you want your boyfriend out of jail faster, call me.

Raymundo Garcia.

CHAPTER THIRTY-FOUR
A Faster Plan

MG takes a nap when we get back to the hotel, so I take the squawking Rocky with me to the plaza. It gives me time to think about the note from the guard and if I should call him? I pace between two pay phones in the plaza deliberating the pros and cons of meeting with him.

He probably wants more money. I can always say no.
I dial the number and ask for Raymundo. It takes a while, but I hear his deep voice on the other end of the phone.

"This is Genny Rekas. Can you meet me at the plaza, so we can talk about my boyfriend?"

There's a pause at the other end of the line. "*Sí, sí, Señorita* Genny. Where?"

I tell him the name of the restaurant across from the pay phone. He'll come soon.

The waitress and I talk about Rocky for a while. She's amused Rocky stays on my shoulder and is so affectionate. I tell her he's my little baby, but the concept is foreign to her. She says people shouldn't be so attached to their pets. They are *just* animals.

No. Rocky's my baby. So is Lucero.

The waitress brings a bowl of tortilla chips and Rocky crunches them in my ear. There's happy chatter all around me, lightening my mood. Lunch comes and I dive into my tacos.

The sound of keys clanking and heavy footsteps approaching quiets the room. I look up from my plate as the waitress hurries to the back of the restaurant. Raymundo walks toward my table wearing his guard uniform with the cuff of his pant legs stuffed into his heavy, shin-high, black boots.

Rocky pulls on my hoop earring and whistles into my ear, so I put him in the sling around my neck. He stops singing, but his heart beats fast next to mine.

Raymundo pulls up a chair and straddles the seat with the back of the chair toward the table. He has a toothpick in his mouth and his smile is slightly twisted. In the light of the restaurant, I see his features better than the dark prison room. His black hair is slicked down with hair product, and his dark skin is pitted with acne scars. His thick black mustache covers his top lip completely.

I smile at him. "*Buenos tardes, Señor* Garcia."

He doesn't smile back, "It's *buenas tardes*, señorita. Not *buenos*. You pronounce our language like a gringa. You need to do better, if you are going to be here."

"I will try harder. I have only been here a couple of days. I will learn."

My answer must satisfy him somewhat because he leans back a little to relax. He still doesn't smile. He motions for the waitress. Her hands tremble as she writes his order. I'm not sure, but she looks like she curtsies before she leaves the table.

"Your boyfriend is in a lot of trouble in my country."

"I know. I'm afraid for him."

The restaurant grows noisy again, and I strain to hear him. "You *should* be afraid for him. Without my protection, many bad things could happen to him." He says the words very slowly with a soft menacing voice.

Rocky moves around inside the sling. He may be picking up my vibes as my heart beats faster. He pops his head out from under the sling and looks around.

"I'm grateful you're willing to extend your protection to him. How much will it cost?"

He studies me. "Money isn't always the most important thing in life. I have much money." He looks around the room. "I also have things money can't buy."

"Yes, you obviously have the respect of your community." I look up and everyone focuses their eyes on what is in front of them. No one looks in our direction.

He smiles and puffs his chest out like a peacock. "You need my help and I need yours. We could help each other."

"What can I possibly do for you?"

He lowers his voice. "I need you to take my cousin to the United States."

"I don't understand. Why can't he go by himself?"

He clicks his tongue and stares at me like I'm stupid. "If he could cross the border by himself, I wouldn't need you. He needs to get over the border and into Texas."

"My boyfriend is in jail for doing something illegal in your country and you want me to do something illegal in mine? I can't do that."

Raymundo leans into the table. "I already know you smuggled birds into your country." He reaches across the table and taps Rocky on the head. "Do you have a permit for this bird?"

My face flushes and I instinctively pull back from his reach. He knows I don't have a permit. He must have been listening outside the room when I was talking to Jeffrey.

I'm screwed.

"I need you to take my cousin to San Antonio, passed the checkpoint in Hebbronville tomorrow."

I feel my knees shake and my mouth go dry. I pick up a glass of water to take a sip as the waitress brings Raymundo his food. She says nothing, but gives me a concerned look. It's enough time to regain my composure. "I can't. I leave tomorrow with my friend in *her* car."

Raymundo shovels his food into his mouth and large particles hang from his mustache. He's unconcerned about his eating habits and continues to speak with food falling from his mouth. "Then your boyfriend may not have a comfortable stay in our little hotel."

"I've got to go home, but I can come back in a few days with my own car."

"You don't need your own car. You will drive my cousin's car, actually a pickup truck with a special compartment."

Things are happening too fast and I need to think. Right now Raymundo can take Rocky and hurt Jeffrey if I don't cooperate. "I must go home tomorrow or my friends will get suspicious. I'll come back in two days on a bus and take your cousin across then."

"I will have to trust you to come back and you will have to trust me. You have more to lose than me."

I was just thinking the same thing. "You can trust me."

Raymundo says nothing more. He wipes his mouth with his

napkin, drops it in his plate and gets up from the table. He peels off several pesos from a large wad of bills and tosses them on his plate and leaves. All eyes in the restaurant turn in my direction. The patrons had been frozen while he was here, but now they look at me with concern.

The waitress hurries to the table. "*Señorita*, what are you doing with such a man?"

I keep my eyes on the table. "He's a friend of my boyfriend."

"Then you need to change boyfriends."

"My boyfriend is in trouble and he said he can help."

"That is worse. You are making a deal with the devil. You must not do what he asks."

"I don't have a choice."

January 1981

"It's for sale," Jeffrey says, leading me around the small plane parked behind the hangar. There are a lot of dents in the fuselage and the supports for the wings are missing.

"It needs a lot of work."

"Me and the crash gang can fix it up for the cost of parts."

"I'd love it," I say. "But I don't have much money left from my grandmother's inheritance. I spent most of it on the house."

"I know the guy who's selling it. He got busted and needs the money," Jeffrey says. "I bet I can get you a sweet deal."

"I love you," I blurt out. It's the first time I've said it to anyone outside my family.

Jeffrey laughs and pulls me to him. But instead of saying it back, he nods to the plane. "This will change your life," he says. "Trust me."

CHAPTER THIRTY-FIVE

CAVU

We leave the hotel in darkness and drive the two hours to the airstrip in Tuxpan. Rocky sits on my shoulder and weaves his talons through my hair during the drive. By the time we reach the landing strip, he's hanging upside down in the long strands of my hair like a Christmas tree ornament. MG sighs heavily and reaches up to help, but Rocky pecks her hand away.

"Put him in your sling. Lightning isn't thrilled you brought him. If we get stopped, the bird will be considered illegal contraband."

I stuff Rocky into my sling. I'm deep in thought about Raymundo and his heavy black boots, and what he might do to Jeffrey if I don't take his cousin to San Antonio. This is getting complicated. If I get caught, who will help me?

The soft glow from the sun slowly brightens the early morning sky. We park the jeep and throw camouflage over it to hide it in the jungle once again. The silence is broken by the hum of an airplane's engine. I'm about to flag Lightning down when MG stops me. She pulls out binoculars from her purse and checks the numbers on the plane, then uses a mirror to signal. Lightning tilts the plane from side to side and flies over us. He circles back and lands with a short stop. She nods her head to me and we run to the open door while Lightning turns the plane around.

Never coming to a complete stop, he immediately gooses the engine and we're three feet off the ground. He doesn't say anything for several miles.

We fly west, just above the treetops for several miles to avoid populated areas then circle back following geographical markers. A wide stream cuts through part of the jungle and lets us fly between tall trees, so no one can see us from the ground. We're low enough not to be picked up on radar. Gradually we turn our course northeast until we catch sight of the coast.

Lightning turns to me and says, "Well kid, you need to fly for a while. This is damn near perfect CAVU and I need a quick nap." With that, we change seats and he goes into the back, puts his hat over his eyes and falls asleep.

I love flying, and this is the kind of day I live for; Clear And Visibility Unlimited, CAVU. I follow the coastline almost due north toward home. Even from the air, I can see fifty or sixty feet to the bottom of the deep blue green waters of the Gulf of Mexico. There're a few boats bobbing in the water, but for miles and miles we're alone on this side of the world. MG points out a large sea turtle in the surf and settles into the ride while I maneuver in the heavens.

Flying without instruments is easy to do on a day like today. It's harder when the fog rolls in and visibility is only a few hundred feet. The ground can creep up on you or even worse, you can't tell where the ground begins and the sky ends. Instrument panels tell altitude and pressure levels, but Lightning says he's seen them fail. He claims he can *feel* the ground and has tried to teach me the technique. He's made me land the plane a couple of times blindfolded. It really tests your memory of the airport landing strip. You have to go beyond the fear, he says.

Of course, he has many stories of landing in difficult places in 'Nam which sound absolutely unbelievable, but there are medals at his trailer indicating he has done some pretty heroic deeds.

Just as I'm feeling the rhythm of the plane and getting comfortable, Lightning wakes up and indicates he wants to fly. The three of us trade seats; Lightning takes the controls, I sit in the co-pilot's seat and MG goes to the back. Lightning sets course and flies around the outskirts of Reynosa and then north. Once we get to the border, he tips his wings almost imperceptibly starboard in order to thread the eye of the needle between the high-wire tower and the ground below. It's another twenty minutes until our wheels touch the ground. Home.

CHAPTER THIRTY-SIX

On Hold

When I was five years old, my mother bought bunk beds for my sister and me. A whole new world opened up. I had my own space in a universe where everything, up until then, had been shared with four brothers and one sister. I created a castle under tented blankets and retreated to a dark, warm place to hide and foster a fertile imagination. With my dolls and dog by my side, I fought all sorts of invented battles.

I recall my college psych professor saying people usually recreate certain aspects from their childhoods in order to feel safe in the midst of trauma or chaos. So, I climb into my four poster canopy bed with Rocky and Lucero and close the mosquito netting around us like a cocoon. The light from the windows filters through the gauze and into my inner sanctum.

I watch Lucero roll on his back to beg for a belly rub. Rocky marches over and pecks at Lucero's ears. One lick from Lucero's large tongue sends Rocky halfway across the bed. They repeat this activity over and over. I could enjoy this game all afternoon, but Lucero finally goes too far and Rocky half falls, half flies from the bed and lands on the floor.

I wish I could hide in my bed with the two of them forever, but Jeffrey's situation pushes its way from the fringes of my mind into the center. The universe needs a little push to get things back to normal and Jeffrey home again. I tried to get Jeffrey's parents to help, but they were useless. They wouldn't even discuss giving any of their precious money to an attorney. And the gang's strategy, though thoughtful and generous, feels too slow. I feel responsible for getting Jeffrey into this mess, and if there's something I can do to get him out of it, I owe it to him to try.

I move to the kitchen and my entourage follows me like a circus parade. With the two of them here, I don't feel so alone. They're always on *my side*, unquestioning and unconditional.

Smuggling people across the border is nothing new. There are a lot of people in the valley who are coyotes. They use tractor trailers to smuggle twenty to thirty people at a time. Raymundo is only asking me to bring one person across… his cousin. If I can smuggle a hundred parrots over the border, I can smuggle one person. I'm sure Raymundo knows what to do. I have to trust that he's orchestrated these missions before. And that they've been successful.

I'll drive to San Antonio, leave my car at the bus station and take a bus to Tampico. That way I won't have a vehicle in Mexico that can be confiscated, and I'll have my car in San Antonio to get home fast after I drop Raymundo's cousin off.

I wish there was someone I could talk my plan over with, but I can think of no one who would bless it. They would all think I'm crazy or impatient or too emotional. Before I transport Raymundo's cousin, I'll demand to see Jeffrey. Depending on how he is, I'll reassess whether or not to make the trip.

When night falls, I hear a strange noise coming from outside. Lucero growls softly and his ears perk up. I pick up a flashlight and a bat and head for the back door. The noise is coming from the right side of the yard. Lucero crouches down low and slowly stalks toward a thrashing sound. He gets there just before the light from my flashlight illuminates the dark clump ahead. It's a female deer on the ground struggling to get up and can't. She's obviously injured. Lucero readies to attack when I pull him away and take him into the house.

Animal Control's first question when I call them is, "what kind of animal is it and is it attacking me or someone in the household?' *Bambi is here and she's hurt...*

"...A female deer and no, no one is being attacked," I answer. They tell me someone will be out shortly to help.

"Shouldn't we take it to the vet?" I ask the game warden when he arrives.

"You ain't from Texas, are you, ma'am? You need to go ahead inside."

I hear a gunshot within moments. When I look out the window, the game warden throws the carcass in the back of his truck, tips his hat and leaves.

I let Lucero sleep in my bed. I need to dream of the warmth of an animal rather than the coldness that follows death.

Fall 1977

"Mrs. Romano, is Jackie there?"

"No, Genny. She's gone up to San Francisco for the day with some new friends… to a place called Haight-Ashbury."

"Will you tell her that I called? I miss her so much."

There's a hesitation in her voice. "She misses you, too."

"Do you think I could come there for a visit during Christmas?"

"Genny, she needs to move on with her life and leave the past behind. Maybe you should stop calling for a while."

CHAPTER THIRTY-SEVEN
White Lie

I work the entire day cleaning the bird cages and making sure all of the water supplies are fresh. The humid weather in South Texas makes for a mean breeding ground of bacteria and algae. Jeffrey devised an elaborate system of tubes funneling water from a single source to each individual bird sanctuary. But if the tubes get clogged with algae, the birds could easily dehydrate.

The food system is a little different since some of the birds prefer different seeds. Jeffrey put large feeders on each of the cages that have to be filled once a week. I need to make sure everything is set for my quick trip to Mexico.

The gang arrives and everyone congregates in the backyard under the tree. Dead Wrong Dan pulls out a bag of sinsemilla pot. We are all pretty mellow by the time the conversation turns to Jeffrey.
I tell about the poor deer that met its end in the yard last night. All the guys say I missed a great opportunity for barbecue and if it ever happens again to call them. They would be glad to bring their guns.

"Genny, you need to be very careful for the next couple of weeks." Maggie has a totally different take on it. "Death has come to your house. It's an omen. That animal's a warning."

"I'm not superstitious," I say, but feel the goose flesh go up my spine and settle at the bottom of my neck. "My house must have looked like a safe place."

"The universe sends messages all the time. You can try to ignore it for a while, but eventually the message hits you like a ton of bricks."

"Is that the pot or the beer talking?"

Everyone laughs a little, but she continues, "I used to ignore this kind of stuff too, but now I've learned to read the signs pretty well. Something dangerous is going to happen to you, something that could take your life. Don't be foolish. These guys can play that macho shit, but you don't have to. You won't have nothing to prove if you're dead."

MG changes the conversation by explaining how she negotiated with the attorneys to pay as we go. Everyone nods and agrees that was the smart way to do it.

The conversation continues about Jeffrey and the attorneys when Maggie veers off the conversation. "Genny, what are you going to do if he doesn't come back?"

"I can't think about that."

"You might have to. He might not come back and you'll be forced to let go. Can you do that?"

"I'll keep trying until he gets out."

"No, honey. Wrong answer. You need to know when to put down the shovel."

"What shovel?"

Lightning scowls, but Maggie continues, "When you start digging your own grave, you need to know when to put down the shovel. You can't blame yourself for Jeffrey's problems. This is his karma, not yours. You have your own path."

"I don't believe that. Jeffrey needs me more now than ever. I can't give up on him."

Lightning comes to my rescue. "Maggie might be getting ahead of herself. We have plenty of time to think about the next step if this plan fails."

"Jeffrey looks good." MG jumps into the conversation. "He looks like he's handling the situation fine and the attorneys seem competent. I think one of them is sweet on Genny."

I instantly feel myself flush and retort, "He's that way with *all* women. I'm nothing special to him." Even as I say the words, I wish he'd like me a little more than just another woman to be conquered. Now that I'm farther from him, I feel a connection to him more than I did before. Maybe I just want him to save me from all this mess.

The conversation dwindles like a dying fire. Dan watches an exaggerated yawn from Trip and takes his cue to leave. As everyone is about to leave, I tell them I need to go to San Antonio for a couple of days and ask if Stump and MG could stay at my house and watch Lucero and the birds. They agree.

"I also need you to watch Rocky."

MG stops in her tracks. "You're not taking Rocky? He goes everywhere with you."

I take a step backwards and stammer trying to think of a good excuse. "I'm staying at a friend's house and her mother doesn't like birds."

Maggie quickly asks, "What's your friend's name?"

"You don't know her."

"You don't lie very well."

"I'm not lying. Why would I lie?"

Maggie hugs me tight and whispers, "No one can stop you from doing something stupid. You're about to do something dangerous. I can feel it. You better be prepared. No one here is going to pull you out of the fire. The universe is unforgiving."

1971

"Genny, where did you go after school today?"

"I came home, Mom."

"Don't lie to me, Genny."

"I'm not lying, Mom, I came home."

"Did you go anywhere else before you came home?"

"What?" I feel my face get hotter by the minute.

"Genny, Mrs. Randall called and said she saw you at the skating rink." Her dark eyes pierce through me.

"I came home," I stutter. "That's not a lie."

"You can't make that kind of distinction. When I asked you where you went after school, you should have told me everywhere you went. It's called the sin of omission. You have to tell the truth, the whole truth and nothing but the truth. Anything less than that, is a lie. People will start to doubt everything *you say, if they catch you."*

CHAPTER THIRTY-EIGHT

Coyote

My entire body tingles with anticipation. I want this ordeal over as soon as possible. As soon as I leave the Rio Grande Valley and head north, the lush landscaping of palm trees and orange groves stops and the desert takes over. The sun creates heat mirages in the distance, distorting oncoming traffic. I feel the sweat dripping from every pore of my body. I can barely concentrate on my driving.

I'm wearing a long skirt and a peasant blouse and my hair is braided. I've brought the bare necessities in my backpack. I park my car at the far end of the bus station parking lot and buy my ticket to Tampico with a short layover in Laredo. I've been practicing short phrases in Spanish, so I can understand if someone asks me a question. The man behind the ticket counter doesn't even look up.

I sit toward the back of the bus, put my backpack down to prevent someone from sitting next to me and avoid eye contact. An old man wants to take the seat next to me, but continues to the back of the bus when I don't acknowledge him. The bus takes twenty minutes to load and stops in every town from San Antonio to Laredo in order to either pick up or drop off passengers. The smell in the bus reeks from body odor and food. I'm grateful I don't use this form of transportation on a regular basis.

I change buses in Laredo and continue to Tampico. This bus is full, so I must share my seat with an old woman. She has no teeth and smiles broadly, showing me her half eaten lunch. She has two chickens tied by their feet hanging on the seat in front of her. I sit in the aisle seat and put my backpack in my lap. She asks, "donde va?"

"Tampico," I answer.

She tries to continue conversing, but I barely understand Spanish when it's enunciated perfectly; with no teeth she's unintelligible. With no responses from me, she turns to the person behind her. I lay my head down on my backpack and sleep despite the squawking chickens.

The old lady shakes me awake. "*Señorita*, Tampico is here. Tampico is here."

It takes me a few moments to understand where I am. I stand up fast and knock into several people waiting to get off the bus. I apologize in my best Spanish, but they're annoyed.

I make my way to the front of the bus and exit brusquely to a small platform in the plaza. It's the middle of the night and the place is deserted. I walk stiffly to the hotel where MG and I stayed before and ring the bell. It takes several minutes to get someone to let me in. It's the same person that helped us before, but she doesn't recognize me. I was hoping to see a friendly face but a non-combative person will do. I drag myself to my room for the night.

Maggie says the universe is unforgiving. I only hope it doesn't find me right away.

After my morning shower, I gather my things and check out of the hotel. My backpack feels heavier than before. I shoulder the weight and hail a taxi. The driver eyes me suspiciously. "What does a gringa want at the prison?" *I ask myself the same question.*

I'm alone to face Raymundo.

I get out a block before the prison and walk the rest of the way. The guard raises his eyebrows when I ask for Raymundo, but says nothing. I sit in a hardback chair and look straight ahead. When Raymundo enters the room, he looks at me with a mixed expression, part sneer and part surprise. I feel like prey. I'm ready to fight if I'm cornered.

"*Señorita*, I didn't expect you until tomorrow."

"Did you really expect me at all?"

"I didn't know how much your boyfriend meant to you. I still don't."

"I want to see Jeffrey."

"I'm sorry *señorita*, he cannot see guests today. He has been having some problems."

"Then I will go back home." I stand to leave.

Raymundo hesitates. "I may be able to make an exception for you."

I sit down and he leaves the room. This is turning into a real cat and mouse game. When he returns, I follow him to a different room than before. It has no sunlight and smells fetid. There's a round table and three small chairs. I sit and wait for Jeffrey to be brought in.

I'm not prepared for the heap of clothes and dirt brought to the table. Jeffrey is unrecognizable. He looks up at me with little recognition in his eyes and then focuses more closely on me.

"Genny? What are you doing here?"

"I came to see you. What's going on?"

"These fuckers have been messing with me. You need to get me out of here."

"I'm trying as best as I can. You smell like gasoline."

"It's kerosene. They hosed me down this morning."

I flinch. "Didn't they let you bathe?"

"You have to pay for your shower and apparently your wonderful attorney didn't pay."

"Oh my God. I'll try to fix it,"

"I need to get out of here. Get me the fuck out of here!"

"Jeffrey, there is only so much I can do. Do you know who turned you in? Was it Humberto?"

"No, Humberto was almost caught too so I don't think it was him. I think it was Raul."

"Why would Raul want to turn you in?"

Jeffrey doesn't answer. He seems to be thinking of something, but only says, "I don't know why. Just get me out."

I want to tell him about the plans with Raymundo, but I don't want him to worry. "The attorneys are doing their best. The system here is totally different than the United States."

"No, shit. This is hell."

"You need to be patient. All of us are trying to figure the system out. This is uncharted territory for us. Everyone wants to do this carefully." Maggie may be right about Jeffrey. He did this to himself and now is being unreasonable about his expectations. How can I tell him that? "Jeffrey, it may take months to get you out of here. You need to temper your expectations."

Jeffrey looks like I've slapped him. Tears enter the corner of his eyes and he struggles to keep his composure. "I can't take much more of this. They treat me like shit."

"I'll do the best I can, but you need to have faith."

"Please don't start on that God crap with me. I don't want to hear it. There's no God in here, I promise you that."

I'm about to contradict him when I look more closely at his face.

"What's wrong with your mouth?"

"The guards pulled my front tooth."

"Your gold tooth? Oh my God!" My stomach lurches and I puke in the corner.

"Pay someone off. That's all it'll really take. Get your candy ass attorney to find out who needs to get paid off."

A guard opens the door and drags Jeffrey out. I don't know if I want to cry or throw up again. I start to stand, but my legs are unsteady.

Raymundo comes into the room. He looks down on me and smirks. "Your boyfriend is weak. He does not know how to be a man. We will teach him to be macho."

"You're treating him like an animal. That won't make him a man; it'll make him mean."

"That is what a man should be. It keeps him alive." I don't know if that's a veiled threat or just a testament to his own vicious nature.

"*Señorita*, you and I must meet outside of these four walls."

"No. I'm not meeting you anywhere until Jeffrey gets what he needs." I stand and face him. "He needs a shower and clothes. I know the attorney paid you. If you don't help my boyfriend, I'm not helping you."

"Well, I guess not all Americans are gutless cowards." He snickers, "You are braver than your boyfriend. I will arrange for his shower and clothes. Meet me in one half hour at the café down the road called *Los Caballeros*."

CHAPTER THIRTY-NINE

The Secret Compartment

Even though it's scorching hot, I'm chilled to the bone. My body trembles as I walk to the café. But the walk does nothing to clear my mind. I'm missing something important in the big picture. Why did Raul turn Jeffrey in? I need some answers soon.

The café is deserted, so I sit in a far corner of the outside patio, and ask for *cafe con leche* and a couple of tacos. I'm hungrier than ever before. I gulp it down to calm my stomach. There're no napkins, so I lick my fingers as Raymundo walks up to the table. He sits across from me and stares at me like he's assessing an opponent.

"*Señorita*, you have much hunger to eat so fast."

I pick up my backpack and fish through it to find a napkin and wipe my mouth. I keep the backpack on my lap and rest my hands there.

"Your boyfriend eats a lot as well."

"He says you don't feed him."

"Our country isn't as rich as yours. When someone breaks our laws they must pay for everything or go without. We cannot afford to let a criminal eat our food and let our own people go hungry."

"I will take your cousin, but I won't do this again."

"We all do things we don't expect to do. Only the future will tell. My cousin is waiting in the truck."

"I thought I'd get to meet him first."

"He is in the secret compartment. We have to move fast." He hands me a paper with the same emblem that's on his uniform with his signature at the bottom. "When you get to the checkpoints in Mexico, show them this pass." I stick it in my backpack. He hands me a separate piece of paper with a San Antonio address written on it in. "Take him there."

We get up from the table and walk to a large truck with an extended cab. I look in the back and there's a young boy asleep in a car seat. I turn to Raymundo, "this is your cousin? How is he going to take care of himself when I drop him off?"

"That is my cousin's son. My cousin is under the back seat with his wife."

"I'm taking three people now? That wasn't our agreement!"

"I will work three times as hard to get your boyfriend out."

"Can they breathe?"

"They are fine. You just need to drive fast."

Raymundo hands me the key. "Your boyfriend is under my protection now. I will take good care of him. You have my word."

"I know you will. I'll take good care of your cousin and his family." But my heart sinks. I feel my breakfast trying to come back up, and I swallow hard to push it down. Raymundo's using Jeffrey as a pawn in his game. I'm too emotionally involved to think logically. All objectivity goes out the window. I drive out of town as quickly as possible.

After I smuggled the birds, I wanted nothing to do with any illegal business ever again. I resisted every temptation. And just like that, it's done. The needle moves again and I drift further off course, deep in a world I know nothing about.

The truck doesn't have air conditioning and I'm sweating profusely. I worry that the sweat will make me look guilty. I look back at the little boy and he's sound asleep. He's sweating too, so I know the heat is the cause and not the guilt.

At the first checkpoint the guard's eyes widen when he reads the signature from Raymundo and passes me through quickly. I don't even have to *tell* him who the boy is.

There're three more checkpoints and all of them go the same way. I make my way to the border crossing in Matamoras. I wish I could give the U.S. border guard this paper and pass through as easily as in Mexico, but I know this is going to take some large lies on my part and the grace of God to get through. It's around noon and we've made good time getting to this crossing. The line to get into the United States is long and exhaust fumes discharge from the tailpipes of most of the vehicles. There's a blue haze from the car in front of me as I pull up to the guard. My heart's racing and my throat's dry, but I smile as I get to the guard. He doesn't smile back.

"What is the purpose of your trip into the United States?"

"I live here."

He gives me a puzzled frown. "Are you a United States citizen?"

"Yes, I live in Mission. I'm a school teacher there." I hand him my Texas driver's license. It's new and has my current address on it.

"What're you doing with a vehicle from Mexico then?"

"My uncle lives in Mexico as a missionary." I'm going to hell for sure now. I'm invoking a lie tied to church work.

"Who's the kid?"

"He's my nephew."

"Do you have his birth certificate?"

"I didn't know I needed that." I bat my eyes at him and try to act as innocent as a school child caught in a big fat fib.

He goes to the booth and types my driver's license info into his machine and waits a few seconds which seem like hours. I know he's going to arrest me right now.

He comes back to my window, looks in the back seat one more time, hands my driver's license back, and says. "You can go." He waves me through.

I put the truck in gear and pull out to drive north a few miles before I pull over. I can no longer keep breakfast in my stomach and hurry to the other side of the truck to vomit. I wipe my mouth, get back in the truck and drive fast. There's one more check point in Hebbronville before I can get to San Antonio. I could take some back roads to avoid it, but I need to make it to San Antonio before they suffocate in the compartment and this is the fastest choice.

I take deep breaths to calm myself and slow down to normal speed before the checkpoint. There're several big trucks full of vegetables and fruit ahead of me. Finally, it's my turn.

The border patrol officer motions for me to pull my truck up to his stop. He starts speaking to me in Spanish. "I'm sorry, I don't speak Spanish very well." I say to him as nicely as possible.

His eyes narrow quickly. *"Por que no hablas espanol?"*

"I'm a school teacher in Mission and I teach English. I'm originally from Ohio. They don't speak Spanish there." The man's stance is even more hostile now.

I can see I need to calm the situation. "I'm learning Spanish as quickly as possible. My students are teaching me Spanish and I'm teaching them English." I smile as broadly as I can when I say this.

He looks into the back and asks, "Who's the kid?"

"He's my nephew."

"If I wake him up, will he say the same thing?"

"Oh, please don't wake him up." It's taking all my nerves not to scream and run away. "We were up late last night at his cousin's birthday party and he's very tired." Then it dawns on me, he's been asleep an awfully long time. Of course! They drugged him for the trip. This guy probably couldn't wake him if he wanted to.

The truck behind me blows his horn and the officer mutters something under his breath and waves me through.

I'm going to hell faster than any of the nuns at my high school ever predicted. They said they saw it in my eyes. I wonder if they ever saw me as a coyote transporting migrants into the United States! They probably saw the "sex before marriage" thing, but not even with their direct connection to God could they have foreseen this whopper.

I drive about fifteen minutes, pull over to the side of the road and empty what is left of breakfast. These stops are necessary, but they're slowing progress. I wipe my mouth again, get in the truck, ready to finish the last leg of the trip. I have a San Antonio map in my backpack to locate the address on the paper Raymundo gave me. Most of the stores in the area have signs in Spanish and we pass several small houses badly in need of paint before finding the address. The house looks like it could be blown over with a stiff breeze.

I park the truck and turn off the motor. I lean up against the truck to steady myself before I open the back door and call out. "Hola. *Estamos en San Antonio.*" The little boy awakens and starts to cry. I bang on the seat and repeat, "Hola. *Estamos en San Antonio.*"

Nothing happens. Oh, my God. What if they're dead? What if they smothered in the hole? I quickly pick the little boy up and place him in the front seat of the truck. I lift up the back seat and am relieved to see a man and woman staring at me. The box looks like a coffin. They're frightened, but alive.

The woman sits up in the coffin with her hands above her head and begs, "Please don't kill us." Her clothes are drenched in sweat and she starts to cry.

"I'm not going to kill *you*! Please don't cry."

She crosses herself and says a prayer thanking God. The little boy starts crying again and reaches over the seat to touch his mother. The man scrambles out of the box, helps his wife out and closes the top of the seat.

He's shorter than I am and drenched in sweat too. I hand them my thermos of water and they both drink cautiously.

"Your cousin Raymundo said to bring you here," I say.

"Raymundo is not my cousin." He spits on the side of the road to emphasize his disgust.

"He said you were his cousin. Why would he tell me that?"

"I do not know *señorita*. We paid Raymundo three thousand dollars each to bring us to the United States. How did he get you to bring us here?"

"He's a guard at the prison where my boyfriend is being held. He told me he would protect him and help get him out if I took you to San Antonio."

"Don't believe anything he says. He is an evil man." The man spits on the ground again. "We have been waiting for months to come to the United States and each time we were ready, he would raise the price. Finally, he said he could arrange the trip, but the person taking us was crazy and might kill us along the way. We said we would take our chances. Thanks be to God, you are not a killer."

"I'm not a killer, but you could have died in that box."

"We have no money and the United States has much. We are school teachers in Mexico, so we will make good here. We have been preparing to come to the United States for a very long time and this was our opportunity."

"I need a ride to my car. Can you take me?"

"We cannot drive the truck. Raymundo said he would kill us if we did. There will be a man to meet us. Maybe he can take you."

"I'll get a taxi. I don't want anything more to do with Raymundo or anybody associated with him. Maybe you should leave too."

"We cannot. The man will have papers for us."

The wife and son cry softly.

"I hope you're right." I hand him the key to the truck.

"We will wait. We have the truck and will trade it for our papers."

Down the street there's a pay phone outside a convenience store and I call for a taxi. While I wait, I use the bathroom and get a coke. By the time I get out of the store, the taxi is waiting for me.

I sit in the back seat and try to bring myself down from the adrenaline high. I have sweated through my clothes several times today. "Desperate people do desperate things." MG's words ring in my mind. I catch the driver looking at me in the rear view mirror. Is that what he sees in me now…a desperate person? Those people were scared I was going to kill them and were still willing to take a chance. I must look as frantic to Raymundo as they did. Do we have the same look in our eyes?

The driver drops me off at my car and I drive home.

I hear Lucero barking wildly from inside as I walk up the three stairs to my front porch. MG opens the door with Stump standing behind her. She puts her hands on her hips. Before she can say anything, Lucero jumps and almost knocks me down.

"You must've had one hell of a time at your friend's in San Antonio. You look like shit."

"Thanks, you look great yourself."

Stump is smoking a joint and hands the rest of it to me. I take one drag and put the roach in the ashtray.

When MG gives me a hug, Rocky jumps over to my shoulder.

"Get some rest. We'll catch up with you tomorrow."

I walk them out the door and turn back to go to the bedroom. I catch a look of myself in the hall mirror and see how fried I look. I sink to my knees and cry hysterically. My whole body shakes as I curl in a heap on the floor. I can't believe I got through this one. I'm so grateful to be home and not in jail or worse. Lucero puts his paw on my head to comfort me and Rocky crawls under my hair to nest next to my cheek.

It's the only peace I've had in days.

Spring Break 1978

"Genny, we're so glad you could come to our spring break party," Elizabeth *gushes. "How are your classes going at college?"*

"Pretty good, how about you?" These girls are not my friends.

"What college are you going to?" I wish I hadn't come.

"I got accepted at Ohio State, but Donny proposed, so I'm not going." *She holds out her hand to show her engagement ring.*

"Well, congrats."

"I heard you and Patrick broke up," Susan *breaks in. "I'm so sorry."*

My face instantly turns red, "Who did you hear that from?"

"Patrick told my boyfriend you were dating other guys, so he was moving on."

"But I'm not dating anyone else," I stammer. *"Why would he think that?"*

"Well, he said you were getting on the pill, so that meant you could do it with more than one guy at a time."

"Oh, my God, that's ridiculous."

Just then Patrick walks into the party with a girl on his arm. This is a huge setup. They obviously want a show, I may as well give it to them.

I walk up to Patrick and throw my drink in his face, then walk out the door.

CHAPTER FORTY

The Universe Finds Me

The pounding at the door seems far away at first. Lucero barks wildly. Rocky hangs upside down from my hair as I get up from the floor to answer the door. The man on the other side pushes his way through the entrance. It's a border patrolman and he has his gun drawn. Lucero is ready to attack the man.

"Ma'am, either control that dog or I will shoot him."

I grab Lucero's collar and pull him to my side. I'm confused and stunned at the intrusion. "Officer, what's the matter?"

"Sit down, lady, and shut up if you know what's good for you." I back up to the sofa and sit down hard. I pull Rocky from the tangled mess of my hair and put him on my lap. Lucero growls at my side. I can't believe this is happening.

Another officer walks through my house checking the bedrooms and comes back to the living room.

A third officer walks in the front door and stands in front of me. He looks vaguely familiar, but I can't place him.

He picks up the ashtray and points to the roach. "Are you dealing pot?"

"No. Absolutely not." I'm shocked by the question.

"It's not enough to bust you, but I will if I have to."

"Why are you here?"

"I can't keep calling your uncle Joe to keep you out of trouble."

Now I recognize him. He's the border patrolman at the first crossing I did with Humberto. "Curtis?"

"Well, at least you remember my name. I could take your ass into custody right now."

"For what?"

"Don't give me that shit. I'm not an idiot. I flagged your driver's license and it showed up yesterday. You were driving a truck from Mexico. What the fuck are you up to?"

I'm too tired to think and burst out crying and can't stop. Lucero licks my hand and Rocky whistles *Dixie*. Snot runs down from my nose and Curtis hands me a tissue from a box next to the sofa. He lets me cry without saying anything else. The other two officers go outside.

I stop crying momentarily when he says, "If we had found something here today, I wouldn't have been able to stop an arrest. Tell the truth. What are you involved in?"

"My boyfriend's in a Mexican jail and if I want him out, I have to do what the Mexican guard tells me to do. And they're spraying Jeffrey with kerosene to kill the bugs." I know I'm talking too fast now, but I can't stop myself. "They won't give him enough to eat and I have to pay for his blanket and I don't have the money to get him out, so I had to take this family across the border. They thought I was going to kill them and they were being made to pay more money than they thought."

My confession doesn't need to be coerced. The priests and nuns at my high school forced confessions out of me for twelve years with much stronger tactics. I may as well unburden myself now and get it over with. I feel better instantly.

Curtis sits down in front of me. He must be assessing if I'm telling the truth or not. He studies my face and his scowl softens. "I can't help you again. You have to stop. Your boyfriend will have to handle himself.

Get a good attorney for him."

"But..."

"No. Stop. You'll end up in jail or dead. Stop or I'll arrest you. Your choice."

"Please don't tell my uncle. My mother would just die over this."

"I won't tell him this time. But you have to promise me you'll stop."

"I promise." He and I stand. I'm so relieved I reach up and put my arms around him to give him hug and get tears and snot all over his shoulder. He doesn't hug me back, but holds me by my shoulders and pushes me back to arm's length.

"I'm done watching over you," he looks me in the eyes. "Do you understand?"

"I still need to go see my boyfriend. I can't just let him rot there."

"You can go see him, but you have to call me first. I want to know what's going on. I'll be watching you."

CHAPTER FORTY-ONE

Confession #2

Someone's pounding on the door again. I hope the hinges hold. I stumble to the door and open it. MG, Trip and Maggie file in quickly without looking at me and head straight for the sofa. They sit down in unison.

From the stern looks on their faces, I suspect I'm in for a long lecture. MG motions for me to sit in the chair opposite them and I follow her instructions without saying a word. She speaks first, "We know you're concerned about Jeffrey, but it's time to let go."

I gasp slightly.

"You need to restore your soul." Maggie is the next to speak.

"When a soul is young and has a painful experience, it can wander for a long time."

"What?" I emit a nervous giggle. I think Maggie has one too many acid trips under her belt.

Maggie ignores my inappropriate laughter and continues. "When someone has a deep wound on their soul, they don't want to open it again and again. They do everything they can to avoid pain. That's what you're doing. You're going to extremes to save yourself from pain. That's why you won't let Jeffrey go."

"I'm trying to save Jeffrey," I counter.

"No, you're in self-destruct mode and we're witnesses to it. We're watching you go ninety miles an hour towards a brick wall and we're here to get you to tap the brakes."

Now, she sounds like my mother. At least this is clearer and not so trippy.

"Where've you been?" MG asks. "And don't say, San Antonio. None of us believes that."

There's no use lying. I can't cross into Mexico again anyway. "I went to Mexico and smuggled a family of aliens into the country."

The girls give each other knowing looks and nod for me to continue.

"The main guard at the Mexican jail told me if I brought his cousins over the border he would protect Jeffrey and might help get him out."

Trip chokes as she sucks in air. "And you believed him?"

"I didn't know what else to do."

"That's not true," Maggie retorts. "You do know what to do. You can wait like the rest of us. You have an attorney and we have to follow his instructions."

"The guards beat Jeffrey up and pulled out his gold front tooth. He says he's going to die in prison if he stays there."

Maggie lowers her voice and speaks slowly. "They *all* say that. Jeffrey knew he was taking huge risks. It's like a little kid stealing candy. It's an adrenaline rush. The more he risks, the bigger the rush. Jeffrey's caught. He'll live through this, but *you* might not!"

When she says this, my body flinches like someone slapping me across the face. I cross my arms in front of me and take a deep breath before I continue. "Well, I can't do anything like that again anyway. The border patrol has flagged my driver's license and will search my vehicle the next time I cross. They were here last night."

The girls' faces turn white. MG stammers, "What the hell did you do to bring that kind of heat down on you?"

"Remember, I told you the officer knows my uncle. He's the one who came. He's trying to scare me. I don't think he'll really do anything."

"Oh my God!" MG screams. "Do you hear yourself? Do you think this is a game?"

I roll my eyes. "Don't you think you're being overly dramatic?"

MG almost comes out of her seat, but Maggie stops her with her arm. "It's only by the grace of God you aren't in jail yourself." MG's body shakes with rage. "We're all here trying to help you, but you don't seem to appreciate the weight of your situation. You're putting all of us at risk. What you do to yourself is your business, but it becomes our business when the border patrol comes around. You could get us *all* busted."

I push back in my chair, letting her words sink in.

Maggie takes the opportunity to go off topic, as usual. "You know I've been married five times." I nod my head. "I know a lot about men. You're still young and you should listen to us when we talk about men. Do you love Jeffrey?"

"Yes."

"Lightning's a good man, but he's only as good as I let him be."

"Don't you mean 'as bad' as you let him be?"

"It works both ways. It's about accountability." Maggie struggles to sit higher and uses her cane to gain some height and authority. "About five years ago I felt the presence of another woman. I could feel she was close and within my touch. I knew our circle wasn't big, so I stayed close to Lightning for three or four days. We went everywhere together. Finally we went to a small diner and I knew it was the waitress. She was small and brown and would look up at him shyly."

"Was he having an affair?"

"If an affair hadn't happened already, it was only a matter of time. What man could resist a pretty woman looking at him that way? She wanted him."

"What did you do?"

"I finished my breakfast and we left the restaurant. I went back to the restaurant two days later. I asked the little *señorita* what was going on. At first she denied everything. But then she said Lightning needed a younger woman like herself to make him happy. I told her I was going to put a *mal de ojo* on her if she didn't stop."

"What did she do?"

"She laughed at first, but then I told her the name of a *curandera* I knew. She must have known the woman because she packed up and left town."

"That's an interesting story, but what does it have to do with me?"

"I feel the presence of another woman coming between you and Jeffrey."

"That's ridiculous. I trust Jeffrey."

"I don't trust any man." Maggie laughs softly. "I trust the Great Spirit. You need to start going beyond yourself and look at the bigger universe. I know you don't believe me now, but there *is* another woman. I can feel her and she's the reason Jeffrey is in jail."

My mouth's wide open now.

"You need to understand this," MG takes the opportunity to get her own jabs in. "You need to stop all illegal activities. Do *not* argue this point. You need to understand the consequences of your actions. You could bring us all down with you and we *won't* let that happen."

Up until now Trip's been silent. "You might not understand this now, but we came here because we love you. If we didn't love you, we would just drop you. No contact, *no nada*. A good friend has your back. We have your back, we're not so sure you have ours."

Her words sting me, "Of course I have your backs."

"Your selfish actions say something else. Do you really think Raymundo is going to release Jeffrey?" MG doesn't wait for me to respond. "He'll just want more and more and still not free him."

"You need to let the stillness come around you and listen to the God within you," Maggie softly comes into the conversation. "You're letting way too many things confuse you. There's a right way. Anyone can be a messenger of the universe."

"God could be screaming at you right now and you wouldn't be able to hear Him." MG adds. "Genny, you're scrambling in all directions. You need to promise me you won't do anything illegal again."

This is the second time today I've had to promise no illegal activities. I need to listen. If I want to stay in the gang, I have no choice. Am I part of a cult now? I wonder if there are any dues.

"I promise." I suddenly feel lighter, like the weight of all of this has been taken off my shoulders. "I really appreciate all you're doing for me. I don't want to hurt any of you."

We stand and each of them give me a hug. Maggie hugs me the hardest and says, "Be still and quiet your mind. You won't believe the amazing things you'll hear."

"Mom, please pin it shorter. I don't want to look stupid." I stand on the wooden box in the basement as she pins the dress evenly just below the knees.

"You won't look stupid, you'll look like a good girl."

I sigh heavily. There's no way to roll up the hem of a dress like I can with my uniform skirt. Most of the girls in my class get to buy a dress at the store, but my mother insists on making the dress for my first high school dance. She's just sewn puffy sleeves onto the blue velvet bodice and it really looks great.

"I've asked a couple of the other mothers about the boy who asked you to the dance."

"Oh mom, tell me you didn't. I know what I'm doing."

"Well, in this case you do. They all told me he's a very nice boy from a good family. You need to stay with a group and don't be alone with him."

"Sister Mary Clément Marie has already gone over the rules for the dance with us. We need to keep enough room between us and our dates so our guardian angels can fit in between."

She and I both laugh then she quickly pulls the line of pins out and folds the hem up two inches. Just above my knees.

"You have a good head on your shoulders," she says, helping me step down off the box. "But sometimes you do things without thinking."

I twirl around in front of the mirror. "Don't worry about me," I say. "If I'm ever in trouble, I'll just call for an angel."

CHAPTER FORTY-TWO

Big Bend

The girls come over frequently to give me pep talks. *Peace, Acceptance, Love.* I don't resist them. I know they're right. But sometimes, like a fighter in a ring who has been knocked down, I want to get up one more time, even if it means another beating.

MG told Ernesto I'm too emotional about the current situation and since she can be more objective, all communication should go through her. To me, it sounds like she's telling him I'm mentally incompetent and she's taking over. Considering my recent history, the assessment might not be too far off. She understands the culture and the language better than I do, so it's an obvious choice. I'm working on learning acceptance. *Shut up and listen.*

Ernesto needs more money to continue Jeffrey's defense and MG only wants to transfer the monies in person. Tentatively, she says I can go with her if I go camping with all the girls first. I'm not sure what the correlation between going to see Jeffrey and camping is, but the girls believe the trip is necessary for me to be mentally prepared to go to Mexico again. We're going to Big Bend National Park for out retreat.

The girls say I cannot take Rocky or Lucero with me and I reluctantly agree. I'm willing to follow their instructions even if it pains me, so Stump's going to watch the birds and Lucero. My babies must know they're being left behind and are pacing the floor. *Acceptance.*

We set off in MG's old station wagon on a Thursday evening after everyone has gotten off work. MG drives the first leg of the trip and I crawl in the back of the wagon to sleep. I'm really not sleepy at the moment, but the others insist we all take turns driving and sleeping. Since I'm low man on the totem pole, I'll be taking the last shift of the twelve-hour drive. I fall asleep faster than I expect and am awakened at 3:00AM to do my shift. I drive into the mountains just in time to watch the first rays of the sun hit the tallest peaks. It's incredibly quiet as we roll into the parking area at the base of the Chisos Mountains. I park and the girls start unpacking the car. The scene resembles a nest of ants coming to life.

They're all moving fast and picking up backpacks that look twice as big as they are.

"When are we going to eat breakfast?"

All three simultaneously say, "We eat when we get to the top."

I'm crestfallen. I thought we would just camp at the bottom of the mountain and leisurely walk around the park.

MG comes up to me and asks, "You're Lebanese, aren't you?"

I nod my head.

She continues, "Do they have a royal family in Lebanon?"

"No, they don't."

"Then stop acting like a little princess and get your backpack ready." She hands me a huge bag and says to fill it. I can barely lift the pack, but don't want any more harassment, so I hoist it on my back and fasten the belts. Trip hands me a canteen of water and we hike our ascent up the Chisos Mountains in single file. Maggie is the head of our expedition, then MG. I'm third in line of the four of us and Trip is the tail end.

I describe the scenery as we walk. "Wow that rock formation looks like a man lying down."

MG turns around to address me. "We don't want to know what you're seeing. That's for you only. Part of quieting the mind comes from shutting your mouth."

How rude! Maybe it's time to pout, a natural way of shutting my mouth. I turn my attention to the path, so I don't trip on all the loose rocks. I soldier on. Quiet my mind.

There's a small landing with a rock seat and I make a beeline to take a break. Just as I'm about to sit down Trip says, "Don't sit down."

With all the weight on my back, I can't recover from the squatting position, and I sit down ungracefully. The heavy backpack tosses me backwards and I flail helplessly like a turtle flipped over on its shell.

The girls finally stop.

Maggie pulls out her camera and takes pictures of me in my vulnerable state. It isn't something I want for posterity, but am helpless to resist. After much laughing and many pleas from me, Trip takes my left side and MG takes the right and they pick me up like I'm as light as a feather. All the while Maggie photographs the event blow by blow.

"We have a name for you." Maggie claps her hands together and smiles. "Let's call her 'Turtle'."

It's not the name I would have picked for myself, but it isn't as bad as some of the monikers that could have been attached. All three of them say my new name in unison now as if to baptize me. "Turtle. We like it."

"How far to the top?"

Maggie looks at me with some sympathy, but with the firmness of a mother says, "If we keep stopping like this, it's going to take all day.

Pace yourself and find your inner strength."

MG hands me her canteen. "This is special tea. Drink it. And quit your bitchin'."

"I'm not complaining. I just wanted to know how far it is." I take a drink of her tea and almost spit it out. It has a bitter taste, but I swallow hard.

Maggie smiles at me and says, "Don't worry, the view is worth the trip."

Thank God they have a goal. Up until now, I thought it was just to torture me.

We continue our climb with several stops for my sake. The canteen is passed among us and the climb gets easier. The heavy weight gets easier to carry and my muscles move like a well-conditioned athlete's. I'm really getting into the climb. We reach the summit and I'm proud of my accomplishment.

We huddle together to confer which campsite is best. "I could keep going if we need to."

"Pace yourself." MG and Trip laugh.

Maggie hands me the canteen and says, "Don't drink too much of this stuff. It's pretty strong."

"What do you mean? You said it's tea."

"It's tea from Peru. I smuggled the leaves out."

"What kind of leaves are they?"

"Coca leaves," MG chimes in. "You didn't think you could do it on your own, did you?"

"Well, yes. I thought I was doing pretty well without it."

"You could have done it on your own, but we like to make the trip less stressful for our bodies to recover," Maggie jumps in. "People in Peru chew on the leaves all day so they can climb up and down the mountains without having to rest. There's no shame in having a little help from nature."

"Nature provides for those who take," Trip quips.

Maggie points to an open area under a tree and starts barking orders like a drill sergeant, "We need to camp there. MG, take the tent out of your backpack. Trip, you have all of the cooking gear." She looks at me and says, "Turtle, find some firewood."

I'm not sure we really need firewood, but I think she wants to redirect my energy. I walk around looking for wood and begin to see some of my surroundings from the high plateau. This part of the world is definitely different than the Allegany Mountains where I camped growing up. Those were older mountains worn down from rain and time. The forests were lush and green with heavy undergrowth. Finding firewood there would have been a breeze.

These mountains have a rugged beauty baked by the harsh sun and wind and little rain. I walk to the rim to look out over the edge. At this height, the Rio Grande is a small winding line in the vast valley below. I feel lightheaded and wonder if altitude sickness could be getting to me. There isn't much wood, but I gather what I can. Once I drop the wood, I help MG set up camp.

"I want everything done now, so I don't have to do work during the ceremony," MG says.

"What ceremony?" I ask surprised by the statement.

"Maggie is going to heal you, so you can go to Mexico with me." MG says, laying the tent out on the ground. I hold the stakes while she hammers them to secure each corner.

"What's wrong with me?"

"You're a spoiled brat." She passes the tent poles to me to put together.

"Well, you're bossy." *I didn't think name calling was going to be part of this weekend.*

MG stands in front of me and places her hands on my shoulders to look into my eyes. "Don't get your feelings hurt. We all need to have a mirror held in front of us to really see ourselves through other people's eyes. You have an honest soul and a good soul, but you're seriously fucked up."

"I like the way my soul is."

"You need help. Your spirit has a deep wound that needs healing. You need to make it stronger. It's weak and it keeps leading you in stupid ways."

"No it doesn't." But I can feel my defenses letting go. *Peace? Acceptance?*

"Yes, it does. It leads you places and you never stop long enough to nourish it. It needs nutrition just as much as your body needs food." Always the smartass, I ask, "What does a soul eat? Angel food cake?"

"This is serious, Genny. You're going to get hurt or killed if you don't change how you live. It's not just a matter of changing one or two things. You need to change how you think, how you work and how you create. You need to be stronger, wiser and more self-aware. Right now you're weak."

"What's the ceremony going to do?" I stretch the ropes from the top of each tent pole and MG hammers a stake at each end. The tent is taking form. I unzip the front entrance and duck through to open the small windows for ventilation.

"Maggie performs a guided meditation, but it's just the first step. You'll have to repeat the ceremony every day of your life to strengthen your soul. It's kinda like yoga. You do it over and over again to go deeper and deeper into the practice each time you do it."

"I'm not sure I have that kind of commitment."

"This is your life, Genny. We're only the teachers right now. There's no real test at the end of the course. You either fulfill your life's promise or you fail."

"What life promise?"

"We're all born with potential. You either fulfill that or you live with regrets and resentments. You can either be a beautiful rose or the thorn." She throws four sleeping bags at me to stack in the corners.

"It sounds so black or white."

"It *is* just that: black or white. You have choices and consequences. Each choice has a consequence you have to live with, so you better think hard before you make your choices."

"When do we start the ceremony?"

"We need to eat first."

"You know, I'm really not that hungry."

"That's the effect of the tea. Once that wears off, you'll be hungry."

Trip comes over and starts putting her things in the tent. Maggie walks around the crest of the mountain moving her arms up and down.

"What's Maggie doing?"

"She's praying," Trip answers. "She needs a lot of energy to fix you up."

"Okay, I guess I better have a peanut butter and jelly sandwich then."

MG points to her backpack. "Help yourself, princess."

CHAPTER FORTY-THREE

The Trip

On my thirteenth birthday, my brother, Chuck and his date took me to see the movie *The Exorcist.*

"Why would you take her to that movie?" My mother asked when we got back.

"Mom, she's thirteen. She should be able to watch it without any problems. It wasn't that bad."

"Oh for crying out loud, Chuck. She still gets emotional watching Disney movies. She cried for days after *Old Yeller.*"

"My date thought it was funny."

"Hopefully, your date is older than thirteen. Isn't this movie banned by the church? The nuns have been scaring her and her friends about devil worship. The nuns are going to have a fit if they find out she went."

I still have nightmares about heads twisting around and trying to outrun the devil with a bunch of nuns and priests in hot pursuit.

Now Maggie's going to perform a ceremony on me. Is she a high priestess? Are they going to send the demons away? I wonder if it will hurt. Is it grounds for excommunication? This is bordering on ridiculous. *Sister Mary Clément Marie, please don't watch.*

Trip and MG announce that it's naptime and unroll their sleeping bags under a nearby tree. I'm too wound up to sleep.

"The wood is for the ceremony, Trip says. "That's not enough. Go get more. We aren't going to do the ceremony until after dark."

That's my cue to take off.

The vegetation is sparse, so I wander far from the campsite. This area must have been a real hardship in the pioneer days. Camping gives one an appreciation of just how easy our lives are now. I'm beginning to wonder if I'll even find an armload of sticks, when something catches my eye.

An eagle soars above the cliffs over the valley below. It flaps its wings and flies above the rim, catches an air current and rides down the side of the mountain on the updraft. It repeats the flight over and over as if performing a show for me. It has incredible strength and beauty and I get lost in the moment so much so that the sun starts to set. I hear the girls calling my name.

Maggie looks at me in a strange way and says, "What have you been doing?"

"I've been watching an eagle fly up and down on the air currents. It almost looked like it was watching me."

Maggie raises an eyebrow and looks at MG and Trip in a strange way.

"Okay, it's time to start," MG says. "You need to start chewing on these." She hands me what looks like dried and moldy fruit. I don't dare question what it is, so I pop them in my mouth. They're dry and bitter herbs which I chew as best I can then wash them down with water. As the sun sets, the temperature quickly drops and a deep silence envelops us. The full moon rises over the mountains and reveals the silhouette of a man in repose. We build a small fire in the pit near the front of the tent and MG directs me to sit in front of it on a rolled up blanket. "Get as comfortable as possible. Your ass is going to hurt if you don't sit right."

Trip sits on the ground next to me with her legs crossed. "Don't squirm around a lot. I know you're hyper, but the whole point is to concentrate within yourself. Breathe deeply and just watch the fire." MG brings over a heavy blanket and wraps it around my shoulders. Maggie puts a small glass of water in front of me and takes a seat across the fire from me. MG sits opposite of Trip on my other side.

Maggie picks up a small cylinder with a skin stretched over the top and starts beating gently on the handmade drum. A small giggle escapes my mouth, and all three of them shush me. I straighten my back and stare at the fire. Maggie starts singing in a low rhythmic melody. At first I don't understand the words, but it starts sounding like, "Genny is your child, Genny is a child of the universe." She repeats this over and over to the point where it becomes hypnotic.

Trip and MG hum for a while, but then start singing the same verses. My body moves to the music as the fire starts dancing in front of me. The blues, yellows and oranges of the fire flame in my mind and I see the song float in the air then get carried away by each spark. The weight of my body presses into the ground, but at the same time, I feel like I'm floating above myself.

There's a shift in energy. MG and Trip hold my hands and I feel their energies pulsing through me. I feel each of them separately and together. The energy starts through my fingertips and works its way up through my chest, into my ears and out through my eyes. It's an odd sensation, but not frightening.

I still hear them singing, but their mouths aren't moving. It must be an echo. They're all concentrating on me and I feel a sense of wellbeing and peace.

"What are your intentions?" Maggie asks.

At first, I don't realize the question is directed at me and I passively move with the flow, mentally tallying the energy levels as they ebb and flow through me. But she asks again and I realize I must answer. My mouth is dry and my lips are stuck together. I shout, "I don't know." It startles everyone including me.

Maggie whispers in my right ear and then my left ear. "You need to quiet your spirit. We can hear the softness of a kiss within our spirits. What do you want from life? "

"I want it all. I want all the good and all the bad. I want the highs and the lows. I want everything." I take a deep breath and breathe in my new life and breathe out the past. There are no words, just pictures swirling in the wind. My high school boyfriend floats past me and my first Volkswagen bug, Lucero and Rocky, then my mom and family. Like a million particles caught up in a tornado. They're random and flowing like a river and everything starts melting.

My heart races and it's hard to breathe. I start to hyperventilate and hear MG quietly say, "You're in our arms, you're safe. Just look at one thing you want to happen in your life. We know there are infinite possibilities for each of us, but look only for the next year. Look at one path for now."

My breathing slows. I feel myself in the future. I can see a path and feel my feet press into the ground.

"Don't press too hard on one path. You never know when you'll be called to walk another one." Trip squeezes my hand. "The most important thing is *how* you walk on the path, not the path itself. Walk tall, raise your head up."

I do as they instruct and my feet lightly touch the ground and skip along the path.

Maggie suggests, "Ask for strength and wisdom."

The energy changes again, but this time it comes from outside the circle. Instead of seeing pictures of my future, animals come to me. They don't touch me, but rather go through me. I *feel* them. Each one calls me to be part of them. A bear is far from me and starts galloping towards me, then leaps just before he reaches me, diving through the middle of me. I feel a different kind of energy surge through the top of my head and through my fingertips. The last animal to go through me is the eagle I'd watched flying above me earlier today. He glides through me like he already knows the way. I feel a shudder down my spine. The animals aren't docile per se, but I don't feel threatened.

Maggie moves the energy in a different direction. "Find your past and heal it."

I feel myself resist this directive. I don't want to look backwards. It's exhilarating to see the future. The past feels dead to me. I don't want to go there. MG and Trip urge me to try. I can feel a vacuum sucking me to a place with no bridge and that's longer than I'm capable of jumping. "You'll have to fly over this part to see it. That's what the eagle is for," Maggie says.

I feel the air lift me up and carry me. I'm becoming smaller and smaller or rather younger and younger. I know where this leads and I don't want to go. I'm three years old, standing on my front porch and I'm tearing up a photo of my father. I'm angry at him for dying. I start to cry. Then my father appears in front of me. He takes me in his arms and whispers, "I'll always be with you." And then he passes through me like the animals did earlier. I'm not angry anymore and the tears on my face start to wash my spirit. I feel a truth surround me. I shouldn't fear people or things leaving. They are with me forever.

I'm exhausted and I feel the energy move again. The fire is dying in front of us and I'm getting cold. Maggie whispers, "You need to come home now."

CHAPTER FORTY-FOUR

My Mantra

I must still be tripping from whatever concoction I ate last night. The sky is an iridescent blue and everything glows.

"You're quite a student." MG nudges me gently with her elbow. "It took me seven or eight campouts with the girls to not just sit there and drool. You have a very open spirit."

I smile like I know what the fuck she's talking about.

"She has a young spirit," Maggie chimes in.

"She's got a wild spirit that needs to be protected." Trip adds several logs to the fire. "That's what the bear was for."

They nod in agreement like three wise doctors. This is more than a little freaky. Either we all had a collective dream or I was hypnotized into thinking all of this. I decide I really don't want to know the hows and whys. I'm in a very safe place and these girls are a trip in and of themselves.

Maggie squats in front of me, cups my head with both of her hands and looks into my eyes. Her hands are cold and rough, but I feel a warmth and gentleness from them as I stare into her lined face. Small tears form in her coal-black eyes and roll down her cheeks. I get a mental image of a river and try to blink my way back to some kind of reality.

"She can see better now." Maggie stands abruptly. "Her light is stronger." The other girls nod in agreement. "Now the real work begins.

We need to ensure your intentions will become solid within you. MG, what do you think would be a good mantra for Genny?"

"You're afraid to be by yourself," MG says to me. You don't like the conversations in your own head. I think your mantra should be 'I am not alone.'"

"No, I don't think that's quite it," Trip breaks in. "I think she becomes so close to someone or something that she can't stand to have it taken away from her. Once she melds herself with a person or thing, it's like tearing two pieces apart. It's painful and leaves a jagged edge."

"She can't let them go," MG says. "When her father died, she didn't want him going to *his* next place."

"...even when they've become part of her." Maggie nods her head in agreement.

"Maybe she lets them become too big a part of her." MG stands up and stretches. "She lives inside them too much. She's not living her own life; she's living theirs."

"She'll need a powerful mantra." Maggie looks gravely at MG and nods her agreement. "She'll need to totally change the way she lives her life in order to be her own spirit."

They're talking like I'm not even here. Don't I have a say-so in what I need to say? "Do I have to change everything? Can't I keep some of me?"

"We love who *you* are. You'll just look at life differently." Trip takes a deep breath and exhales her explanation. "There are four parts of your spirit. *You* can change some of the parts, but your spirit mostly belongs to the universe, and in that sense is almost impossible to change. It can be done, but usually collectively. It takes great courage and is usually violent."

"I don't understand what you're saying," I mumble.

"The universe is like a river, it flows from the collective consciousness," Maggie starts like a patient mother instructing a toddler. "Most people go along with universal thought until there's a violent disruption in thought. The best example I can give is slavery in the United States. Most accepted it until enough people said it was wrong."

"People went along with it because it was too big for just one person to fight." MG continues. "But as more people began to see the injustice, it took a violent action to change it. War is the ultimate violent change."

"It doesn't have to be violent," Trip interjects. "Martin Luther King started a non-violent protest, but the other side reacted violently. It's like a jolt to the universe."

I must have a blank look, so she continues to explain, "Like a rock thrown into a pond. It sends out surface waves that eventually make it to shore."

I'm getting more than a little worried now. It's beginning to make sense. I thought we were camping for fun and to bring us closer together. I didn't know I was going to have philosophy class 101 while doing psychotropic drugs. My mind bounces around like a ball in a pinball game.

"This is the hardest part —" Maggie takes my hand-- "to change ourselves."

My first reaction is I don't need to change, but all three of them are here telling me I'm going down the wrong road in life. "What do I need to do?"

Maggie looks deeply into my eyes and searches for some kind of sign I'm truly willing to change. Finally she says, "There are four energies within ourselves that have to be moved at the same time for us to really change." She gets up and goes to her chair.

Trip starts reciting, "The first one is our spirit. It holds the light. It captures the light of the universe and reflects it back. If our spirit doesn't want to change, then the rest of our being won't go along."

"The next one is the heart," MG says. "It's where your compassion is. It must be open to the change. The third one is your body. Sometimes your body is frozen with fear or is too weak, but most of the time, a person can push the body along."

"The last one is the mind. The only way we can change our mind is to quiet it. It needs stillness, so it can hear the universe speak. If it doesn't have silence and has a million things bombarding it constantly, then we can't change anything." Maggie says.

"I can make changes in my life without doing all that fuss," I challenge.

They look at me and shake their heads.

"Okay, okay. How do I begin?"

"Start by praying," MG says. "It'll quiet your mind. Sit down each day and pray for one hour."

"I've prayed the rosary for years. I still don't get it."

"Those prayers might work for some people, but obviously they don't work for you," MG continues. "You need a mantra that states an intention. It needs to be something that centers you. Don't do anything else. You're too scattered, this will focus you."

That doesn't sound too hard. I can do that. "What's my mantra?"

MG pulls out a joint and starts passing it on. Smoking weed is more like what I had in mind when I agreed to go camping. I can do prayer and a mantra if it entails getting high.

"Your mantra should be 'My spirit connects with all things.'" Maggie claps her hands and I repeat it.

We break camp and walk down the mountain. My muscles are screaming at me, but I plod along in a daze. I was hoping for some of that tea we drank when we climbed up the mountain, but apparently that's all gone. The girls think I drank more than my share anyway. I'm not allowed to think of Jeffrey. Just pray. "My spirit connects with all things." I'm at the front of the parade going down this ghost mountain. The eagle from yesterday follows us to the last switchback. He catches an updraft and disappears in the clouds. I feel like I'm picking up vibrations of people and animals that walked this path before... long ago ghosts. I wonder how much of this feeling is from the drugs and how much is really spirits of the dead who spin around me.

My spirit connects with all things.

CHAPTER FORTY-FIVE

One Degree At A Time

Like a crazy person, I walk around and talk to everything in my life and see how they touch me...actually how I touch them. I press my back against the tree in my backyard to see its perspective of the world. The bark is rough, but solid. I watch the leaves move with the wind and how the light filters through. I ask it if it's okay to sit under it and drink beer and smoke pot.

Maggie says I have to do this. The Tibetan monks bless their feet every morning. They know with each step they take, they may inadvertently kill an ant or a spider or any other living creature. So, before they begin their journeys, they pray for the souls of each creature. She says this will help me be less of a brat. Those weren't her exact words, but I get the message.

It's been one week since our trip to the mountains and I'm still high. It's intensifying rather than dissipating. Lucero and Rocky are extensions of me. When I look at Rocky's feathers, I see all of the vibrant colors down to his quills. Lucero's black fur glows with the sunshine and blackens further at night. I talked to the two of them before, but now it's nonstop and Rocky talks back. He constantly chants "My spirit connects with all things" over and over. I can't tell if I'm saying it or Rocky is. It echoes in my mind at night.

I no longer think of myself *by myself*. I see how connected I am to my world like branches to a tree. I'm a mini-helicopter and hover above the world to look down upon it, rather than from my eyes outward. These new feelings keep me a little off balance. The girls come over more and more to touch base with me. My connection to them is off the charts. I feel how much love and effort they are putting into me. I'm ashamed at the risks I took with no consideration for them or the rest of the group. What a jerk I've been. I hope I can make it up to them somehow. They say it's all part of karma. It will all even out.

My anxiety concerning Jeffrey is gone. I know his problems are bigger than me. I'll help as much as I can, but I can't risk my life or anyone else's to save his. I'm staying as positive as possible.

Maggie says she sees me letting go. I feel a connection and at the same time a detachment to the world around me. Maggie wants me to move past misplaced loyalties and focus on listening to what the universe wants me to do. I'm trying to listen. Sometimes I think I hear a whisper in return, it's faint, but I'm tuning in at least.

The girls show up at noon for a quick lunch and we retreat to our circle of chairs under my tree in the backyard. I think the tree likes when we connect to it.

The birds are loud when we first go outside, but calm down and coo within a few minutes of our settling into our chairs. Maggie starts by lighting a joint, inhaling deeply and passing it to MG. MG takes a strong hit and passes it to Trip. I'm the last to receive the smoke. I'm catching on to this pecking order. No one speaks right away. We take time to meditate before we begin our discussions and planning. I see the benefits of this ritual. It quiets the mind, so distractions can move out of the way. A picture comes to mind of someone sweeping the sidewalk, so no one trips over anything on the path.

Maggie starts the meeting with our new intention to keep Jeffrey safe, in or out of jail. This makes the anxiety level for the group lower and more manageable. If the emphasis is getting him out of jail, then our focus feels out of our control. If our intention is for him to be safe, we have more concrete things we can do to provide well-being for him.

MG begins, "I've been speaking to Ernesto. He said he has been to see Jeffrey twice this week and he looks stable. He's still obviously upset, but is less defiant and more compliant with the guards." MG takes a sideways look at me to make sure I'm not reacting to this news in a negative way. I take three deep breaths and look straight at her and smile. Everyone takes a collective deep breath and smiles too.

I hope they see their patience and hard work paying off. I'm moving one degree at a time, ever so slowly to eventually make that one-hundred-eighty-degree return. MG proceeds, "Ernesto has gotten blankets, a pillow, toothbrush, toothpaste and soap to Jeffrey. He has also brought him some books to read. We might bring more books when we go back down there next week." She continues, "We can't keep using Lightning to fly us down there. It uses up a lot of our cash and adds unnecessary risk. We aren't transporting anything illegal, so we should just go by bus."

The thought of my last bus ride prickles my skin and a light sweat breaks out on my face and under my armpits. This new electric feeling touches me in all sorts of weird places. I'm extremely sensitive to feelings now. I relive situations more intensely now than when I was doing the actual deed. Maybe now I have a deeper appreciation of the dangers I was in. During the run to Mexico, I was hyped up on adrenaline. Now that I don't have adrenaline pumping through me, I have a more sane view of my stupidity in motion.

Trip coughs and I shake my head to center my thoughts. Her clear-blue eyes stare straight into my heart. She smiles, tilts her head to one side and says, "Reliving a moment or having a flashback?" I giggle now at their teasing, but it's a little more than unnerving that they are so in my head. Trip points to the bus schedule in MG's hand to bring me back to center.

"We leave in two days," MG continues. "I'm taking enough money for two months' worth of supplies for Jeffrey, so we don't have to go down more often than needed."

I stiffen when I hear her say two months. This could be a lifetime. The weight of the situation presses on me. I wish I hadn't gotten Jeffrey into this mess. All of the girls straighten at the same moment. Maggie turns to me with a very stern look on her face. "This is Jeffrey's path. He chose it. You did not choose it for him. You can't think that way or your own feet will trip. You will fall into a hole no one will be able to rescue you from."

Trip completes the thought, "Stay on your path. No one else can travel your path, only you. He has his."

MG hands me the bus schedule. "Be ready in two days to be picked up. You fuck up, I'll leave you in Mexico on your own."

With that, they stand and leave.

Stump and MG arrive right on schedule and we ride to the bus station in silence. Stump's pickup truck is old, but clean. MG sits in the middle with her long legs hiked up a little because of the hump in the floorboard. She has her left arm leisurely on the back of Stump's seat and absentmindedly plays with his ponytail. Stump's hand is on MG's knee and he plays with a small hole in her faded blue jeans. They've been together for five years and are comfortable in their own silence. Maybe Jeffrey and I can work to have that kind of relationship.

They kiss goodbye and stay in a warm embrace before he sends her off with a quick pat on the ass. He pats me on the head and says he will take care of my place and not to worry.

We both sit in the station and wait for the bus to arrive. I've been waiting for an opportunity to ask MG about Maggie for a week now and this is finally my opportunity. "What's with Maggie?"

MG stares at me puzzled.

I ask again in a slightly different way. "Maggie seems to know a lot about rituals. I'm afraid to ask her. I might hurt her feelings."

"Maggie is a holy woman in the Lakota tribe. Her mother was one and her mother's mother was also."

"I thought you said her mother abandoned her."

"Her mother eventually came back. She thought if she gave her up, Maggie wouldn't have the stigma. Her family had to keep it secret when she was growing up because *they* said it wasn't right."

"Who's *they*?"

"Our government. Her tribe was moved from one reservation to another to keep them off balance. They almost lost their language. They weren't allowed to speak it in school and they were discouraged to speak it in public. She was once beaten by some neighbors when they found her doing a ceremony. Now she only does ceremonies with people she trusts wholeheartedly. You must be very special to her. It took her two years

263

before she would perform one with me."

"Really?"

MG puts her hand over mine and says, "She sees something very special in you. She thinks you could see beyond yourself, if you let yourself be free."

My hand is picking up an electrical current from MG's hand. Fear passes through me at the same time. MG picks up on this reaction and quickly says, "These things take time. She doesn't want to go too fast with you, but she thinks you could see into people's hearts better than most. You're transparent and she can see *you*."

"But I lied to all of you."

"Yes. And we all knew it. You were even transparent in your lies. The important thing to us was the lies weren't malicious. You were trying to help someone besides yourself. That's noble, but misguided. We had to let you come to the end of yourself."

"What do you mean by that?"

"The only way someone will change is when they run out of options and come to the end. You tried everything you could to get Jeffrey freed and failed. Raymundo had his own agenda and that didn't include letting Jeffrey out of jail. The universe is warning and protecting you. It even sent you a border patrolman to protect you. Those are all signs you are ignoring. The universe is screaming at you and you won't listen. Maggie can teach you the signs, but you need time to understand them better. A big part of this is to know and understand oneself. To know oneself is to know the universe."

MG pulls her hand from mine and gently pats my shoulder. The bus arrives and we get on. I need time to think. MG quietly reminds me,

"Take this time to pray." The long road ahead is full of prayers and meditations.

I feel electric.

CHAPTER FORTY-SIX

Signs Everywhere

I'm not prepared for the bolt of lightning that hits me when I see Ernesto. I stumble getting out of the taxi and he's there to catch me as I tumble into his arms. I look from MG to Ernesto and try to hide my reaction, but I'm dizzy and my knees are weak. The universe is so unfair. I have prayed as hard as I can for Jeffrey and the universe throws Ernesto in front of me.

MG and Maggie always say to look for signs. What the fuck is this supposed to mean? I'm at the jail to see my boyfriend and his attorney, Ernesto, catches me in his arms. Are there really two paths in front of me? Am I supposed to decide which one to go down by myself or listen to this push from the universe? I regain my balance and straighten my body and my composure.

Ernesto asks if I'm okay. "I'm so sorry, Ernesto. This place upsets me," I respond. "I'll be fine. Thanks for the help."
MG gives me the eye. I can tell she's assessing me. I stand taller and look directly at her and smile. She can shut me down at any point and tell me to go back to the hotel and I will have to comply. I've given my word I'll do exactly what she says. She gives me a nod before we follow Ernesto into the prison with our eyes forward.

My handkerchief is doused with a heavy perfume which I hold close to my nose as does MG. The rancid smelling outer rooms of the prison catch my nose and lungs making it difficult to breathe deeply enough to calm myself. The space is more cramped than I remember and I notice a dark growth on the walls. I mimic MG as she sits rigid on the wooden chairs, her hands in her lap. No one needs to remind me to not touch anything.

The door opens and Jeffrey shuffles in with shackles on his legs and hands. He's thinner, but clean, and smiles when he sees us. We wait for him to sit down before we talk.

"Jeffrey, how are you doing now?" MG starts. "Are there improvements?"

Jeffrey stiffens and bows up like wet rooster ready to fight. He takes a moment and then exhales. I can tell he's wrestling to control himself. "It's better, but it ain't the Ritz." He tilts his head in one direction and then the other to pop his neck and stretches both arms on the table to flex his whole upper body. In a low and steady voice he continues, "I need out of here."

Ernesto takes this as his cue. "We are working on your defense and things are starting to go our way."

Jeffrey holds up his hand. "I've heard this before. This is a show for the girls, so you can get more money. I need out or I'll tell everything I know."

Ernesto slams his hand on the table and looks Jeffrey straight in the eyes. "This is dangerous talk, especially in front of the women. Control yourself. We are doing the best we can, as quickly as we can. If you do this again, I will stop coming and make sure you rot in jail." He's breathing fast and his face is red.

Neither of them raises their voice enough to get the attention of the guards. They both take time to go back into their respective corners for a time out. I haven't moved a muscle. I'm sitting and watching and for once in my life not reacting. I'm detached, and it feels foreign and yet empowering. I'm catching on to this third-eye voodoo shit Maggie talks about.

MG gives me a *Mona Lisa* smile. I return the smile and turn to Jeffrey. "We brought some books for you and other things. We had to leave them with the guards, so they can search for contraband. They said they'd give them to you later." Jeffrey's demeanor softens a little with the sound of my voice. The pissing match between these two bulls is over. Jeffrey doesn't admit defeat easily. It's what will keep him alive in jail, but I can tell he's changed. There's little lightness in him now which might turn him bitter to life. I can only pray it doesn't.

As I'm about to continue, Raymundo comes through the door and everyone stands. He walks directly to me and shakes my hand. I'm speechless. Raymundo looks around the room as if this is expected behavior. His voice booms. "This *señorita* is honest. A very rare quality in people. God watches over such people." And as quickly as he came into the room, he leaves.

"What the fuck was that all about?" Jeffrey stares at me as he asks.

Ernesto starts to ask something as well, but MG quickly seizes the opportunity to whisper, "Genny took care of Raymundo's cousins in the United States. He's obviously grateful." She expertly pivots back to our previous conversation. "We can bring other things from home if we pay the guards a little extra. Lightning says he has some things of yours in the hangar, if you let him know which ones you want." She proves to be adept at diffusing an explosive situation.

"Did you bring any paper?" Jeffrey asks. "I'd like to write while I'm here."

"I am sure we can buy some things for you in town," Ernesto adds. A truce between the two men is tentatively declared.

With all of the civility and calm, I sort through my feelings better. It's obvious I added a lot of chaos to this situation. As my mother constantly reminds me, *you stirred the pot.* A guard comes in and tells us we need to leave.

Jeffrey walks toward his door and I toward mine. He turns right before he leaves, "Thanks for sticking by me, he says. "You can quit if you need to."

"I won't turn my back on you, Jeffrey. We'll get you out and then see what happens."

I catch up to Ernesto and MG and we step out into the sunlight. It's a beautiful day which makes me feel at odds with the circumstances. MG and Ernesto are smiling, so I smile back. It lightens my mood. We climb into Ernesto's Jeep and head for a restaurant close to the beach. MG wisely sits in the front with Ernesto and I squeeze into the cramped back seat.

I quickly braid my hair, but MG loosens her bun and lets her long hair fly. The long curls spiral upward creating small tornadoes that twist and wrap around the roll bar. She looks blissful with the wind in her face and is oblivious to the tangled mess her hair is becoming. Ernesto plays the radio and we're simply enjoying the day. Under any other circumstances, someone seeing us would think we're tourists on a joy ride.

The weight of Jeffrey's incarceration pushes itself to the

background. I'm determined to be in the moment. No daring escape plan, no backroom deals with the devil, just a realization of the cold facts and acceptance.

Am I changing… finally?

CHAPTER FORTY-SEVEN

Paid In Full

We can't get an express bus from Veracruz to McAllen, so our bus stops frequently and the trip seems to take forever. I nod off often and awaken each time with an uneasy feeling. As we pull into the bus station, I know immediately something must be terribly wrong. Stump paces back and forth along the platform and Dead Wrong Dan sits on a bench watching the bus make the last turn into the station.

MG looks at me and gives my hand a squeeze, "Take a deep breath, honey. Something bad must have happened, if both of them are here. Neither of them likes to talk much so wait until we get home to ask questions." The hiss of the door opening and the blast of hot exhaust fumes slow my exit.

Stump gives MG a hug and helps her with her bags and Dan grabs mine and we're ushered into the truck. Stump gets behind the wheel, MG next to him and I ride shotgun. Dan swings his tall frame into the back of the truck where he crouches just below the rear window with his back against the frame of the truck. He looks straight ahead and doesn't move for the entire trip back to my place. Once we pull into my driveway, the rest of the gang is waiting. Lucero runs to the truck and jumps up on my side of the door to welcome me.

The smell of burning sage welcomes us home. Everyone settles into the living room as the initial joint is lit and passed around. I pass it without taking a drag, I need my wits for whatever is coming. MG looks at me sideways and then at Maggie, and gives a slight nod of her head. It's okay to start.

"We got a call from Ernesto," Trip begins. "He knew the two of you were on the bus, so he spoke to me. A small riot broke out in the prison. A lot of the prisoners were hurt."

"Is Jeffrey alive?" My heart races and my tongue's thick.

"Yes. He was stabbed several times, two pretty deep," Trip answers. "It doesn't look good for him." Trip's deep-blue eyes look straight through me. "Ernesto believes Jeffrey was the target of the attack.

No one else was hurt badly."

"Is he in a hospital?"

Trip shakes her head, "No, honey. They don't let you out of prison to go to a hospital. He's still in prison and he's in pretty bad shape."

"What else did Ernesto say?"

"The attack came from three prisoners. I guess he didn't want to say too much to someone he doesn't know." Trip looks at MG and says, "Ernesto wants you to call him."

"What do we do?" I look to Lightning.

Lightning takes a long drag on the joint and coughs out a long trail of smoke. "Before we make any plans, we need to hear what Ernesto has to say."

MG takes her cue and calls Ernesto's law office. She speaks softly and takes notes. There's a long distance between his world and ours. The gang is quiet except for the occasional exhalation of pot. A pin dropping could shatter the silence. The phone conversation lasts fifteen minutes, but seems like forever. MG finally thanks Ernesto and says goodbye. After she cradles the phone, she looks up and her face is ashen.

"Can we trust this fucker, or is this a way to get more money?" Lightning spits.

MG holds up her hand to stop him. She shakes her head and her long hair tumbles from the hair pins holding her loose bun. "When Genny and I were talking to Jeffrey this last visit, Jeffrey insinuated he would talk if he wasn't released right away." Her bottom lip quivers and she looks exhausted. She speaks slowly and her voice is very soft. "Ernesto got very angry and stopped the conversation quickly. I didn't pay too much attention to it then, but apparently other people were listening."

"I remember that, too." I gulp for air as emotion floods me and begins to overtake my third eye detachment. I'm hovering over the room, but my vision is two dimensional and flat.

"Ernesto says information is as good as money in prison. Since Jeffrey's an American, the guards and inmates spy on him. If he says anything suspicious, they sell the information for money or favors. Jeffrey has no connections to protect him, so he's vulnerable."

"Oh my God, what else can happen?"

MG puts her hand up again to stop the chatter. "Ernesto said everything happened quickly after our visit. He believes some of the prisoners were paid by someone to start a fight in one corner of the cafeteria while Jeffrey was in the opposite corner. When everyone was running to see the fight, three prisoners attacked Jeffrey with knives. Raymundo saw them go after Jeffrey and pulled them off before they could finish him off. He saved his life." She looks at me. "Raymundo told Ernesto he and you are even now."

I'm too shocked to say anything. To think that Raymundo is a man of his word is something I never imagined.

MG looks down at her notes and picks up the pace, "Jeffrey was stitched up by a local doctor who came to the prison. Ernesto says Jeffrey probably can survive, but he'll need help keeping the injuries clean. More prisoners die of the infections than the initial wounds."

"Is he in an infirmary or something?" Trip questions.

"They've put him in a cell by himself which keeps him a little safer than being in with thirty or forty prisoners." MG takes a swig of beer. "Ernesto asked around to see if he can get someone to go to the prison and treat him, but no one will. He thinks someone has paid everyone to stay away or worse, they are afraid to help him and suffer the same consequence."

"Should I go down there to help Jeffrey?"

"I can't keep going down there with you." MG looks at Maggie and then at me. "If you go down, you're on your own."

"You just said no one there will do it and he'll die if someone doesn't help." My third eye is gone. My eyesight is myopic now; I can't hover above the room. My third eye shuts.

"Yeah, but whoever tried to kill Jeffrey wants him silenced." MG paces back and forth. "They won't be happy about anyone helping him." "There don't seem to be much choice." Lightning strokes his beard and looks into the distance. "Those fuckers have closed all the doors and locked us down. It's either Jeffrey dies or Genny helps. Jeffrey would help any of us if we was in this kind of mess. We need to pull together."

Maggie sizes me up and down. "We can do a quick ceremony before you go back down there so you're ready. You'll need to be prepared for battle." I flinch at the words, but I see her point. They're not telling me to go, but there are few options if they ever want to see their friend alive again.

"Can you and Stump stay here and watch the birds while I go down there?" MG nods. "I'll drive down there with my own car, so I can get around more easily." I turn to Maggie, "Can we do the ceremony tonight? And can you include Lucero and Rocky? I'm going to take them with me."

Maggie claps her hands. "I'll need sage, red persimmon, sweet grass and tobacco. We're lucky the moon is new tonight. It'll bring more power to the ceremony. We'll be back at midnight."

"We need to make some modifications to your car and boots before you leave," Lightning reaches down for my boots and I hand him my keys. I'm flooded with gratitude and understand *they got my back*.

CHAPTER FORTY-EIGHT
Boot Camp

The gang returns just before midnight with my car. Stump carries my cowboy boots in one hand and a brown burlap bag in the other. Everyone sits in the living room and Maggie lights the smudge stick. It glows red and MG lights a joint from the flame. Maggie blows out the flame and allows it to smolder. The guys get straight to work with their presentation.

Stump takes position in the middle of the room and boxes an imaginary opponent, breathes deeply, and shrugs his shoulders before he digs through the bag and pulls out a long silver handle. It looks innocuous and I giggle a little at the dramatic staging. He holds it upright and presses a button on the tip of the handle. A long stiletto blade comes to life. I gasp at the lethal contraption. I've never seen anything so sharp and dangerous in my life. Stump demonstrates closing and opening the knife a few more times and gives it to me to try. The blade ejects easily, but it's difficult to retract. Practice will be needed if I don't want to cut myself.

Dead Wrong Dan stands and Stump quickly grabs him around the neck and thrusts the closed knife upward under his rib cage. Stump looks me directly in the eyes and waits for me to be fully focused. "Don't waste your time trying to go for the heart. You don't have the upper body strength. You can do more damage to internal organs this way and not have to worry about ribs. Twist it for good measure." I wince at the information.

He releases Dan and then picks up my right boot and shows me the inside. He's installed a small long pocket in the upper quarter of the boot just below the boot straps to hide the knife. He hands the boots to me and tells me to put them on. The right boot is snug, but feels fine.

Stump sits down and then Dan stands next to me. I've never been this close to him before and I'm a little nervous. He's perspiring and wipes his palms against his pant legs before he speaks. "I'm going to grab you. What's your move?" Before I can say what I would do, he has his arms around my neck and drags me down. I can't even scream. He lets go before I have any time to react further. I want to sit on the floor and cry. If this was a lesson in being defeated, it's a quick one. Dan takes my hand and pulls me to a standing position before I can work up any tears. He takes me by the shoulders and shakes me quickly to attention.

"You need to think fast. You're small, so you have to go for the weakest part of someone's body." Dan points to my boots, "Those can do major damage. Think."

I try to kick Dan in the groin and he grabs my foot while it's in the air. I'm falling to the ground, but Stump comes up behind me and catches me before I hit the floor. I no longer want to cry. I'm angry. "Focus your anger. It's a good emotion, if you use it right. Have you ever been to a circus?"

"What?" The question surprises me.

"Have you seen the acrobats in the circus?" Dan repeats. "The acrobats fly around and catch the swing so easy, don't they?"

"Yeah, I guess."

"The great ones make it look easy. You need to practice. It's not hard, but it takes repetition." Dan grabs me again and says, "Use your boot heel and come down hard on my toes." I'm mad enough I stomp on his steel toed boots. I connect on some toes and smile.

He lets go of me and turns me around. "Keep your eyes up on my face and aim for this part of my shin or knee and try and keep your balance." I do as instructed and it's easier than I thought to inflict some pain without losing my stance. He grabs his leg to rub it when I try another kick. He shields the kick with a forward block and catches my foot with his other hand flipping me on my ass. This time Stump isn't there to catch me.

Dan straightens up and reaches down to pull me up. "Always keep your eyes on your opponent's face. He can anticipate your next move by watching your eyes. You'll be able to do the same with him. Practice snapping pieces of wood thicker and thicker each time until you can snap someone's leg."

Next, the spotlight goes to Lightning. He stands up, but doesn't go through the warm up exercises Stump and Dan did. He reaches in the bag and pulls out a semi-automatic pistol and hands it to me.

"This is different." I feel its weight and consider its size in my small hand. "It's really light and sleek. What is it?" I hand it back to him.

"It's a Glock. A friend of mine brought it in from Europe. They have a clip you can preload fire." He demonstrates releasing the clip. "It only has a little kick. You can double tap your target fast."

"What's double tap?"

"You can shoot twice without recoil. It lets you shoot your target quickly without having to re-aim." He aims at a blank wall and pantomimes shooting the gun. "Once, in the heart and another to the head, fast and deadly. Don't even stop to think about it or you're dead, not them."

"How am I supposed to get this into Mexico? I don't want to get caught at the border."

I follow the three of them out to my car. Lightning pulls the driver's seat out of the car and flips it upside down on the ground. "We're not done yet, but we've hollowed out the seat and are installing a box for the gun and ammunition. There're a couple of other things we still need to do." They put the seat back in place and Stump climbs in to leave. Lightning and Dan follow in the truck. I watch as they drive down the dusty road toward the hangar.

That was quite a show. I hope I never have to use any of those techniques.

In the house, the girls sit around a small bowl with burning sage in the middle of the room. A liberal amount of candles light the space and my long shadow casts a tall thin figure on the wall. I plop into the empty space next to Maggie, harder than I mean to and feel at once the spot on my butt where I hit the floor with Dan. I rub my butt and start to complain, but MG gives me a stern look and I swallow my complaint and quiet my mind.

Maggie lights a joint and passes it to me. I take a hit and pass it to MG. Maggie begins to chant and sing. Everyone settles deeper into their positions on the floor. Maggie picks up the smoldering smudge stick and points it to the six cardinal directions: east, west, north, south, above and below. She fans the smoke over my entire body. Then she picks up a long prayer feather and chants prayers to bring positive, healing energy to me. At first, the prayers are in her native Lakota tongue, but then they change to English. She first acknowledges the Creator whom she calls Grandfather. Then she asks for the blessings of Father Sky and Mother Earth. She picks up a pinch of dried herbs and adds it to the fire. I recognize the smell as tobacco. She changes from a seated to a kneeling position and bows toward the West.

"Buffalo People, you are the most powerful. We ask that you bring your power to this woman warrior." Both MG and Trip bow, so I do, too.

Maggie slowly straightens up and turns to face the north. She taps me with the long feather. "Elk People, bring your spirit to this woman warrior." Once again, she bows and we follow. The next bow is to the South for the Owl People and then to the East for the Black Tail Deer People.

Maggie motions for me to sit in front of her. I face her with my bended knees touching hers. She reaches down with her first two fingers and thumb to a bowl and dips into a red paste. She gently coats the cool cream onto my face in circular motions and outlines it evenly, avoiding my mouth and eyes. "You're the woman warrior. You walk with all of your relatives now. You're a part of all things and they're part of you. The Shadow Man will come to protect you and all your relatives. This is the Shadow Man's mask for you to wear." She smears a second layer of red goop on my face.

"The Owl is your relative. The Buffalo is your relative. The Black Tail Deer is your relative and The Elk is your relative." She taps me each time with the feather and then calls Lucero to come to her side. He eagerly sits at attention while she taps the feather on his head. "The Wolf is your relative." He licks her face and puts his paw in her lap.

Then she whistles and calls Rocky to her. He hops down from his perch on the couch and waddles to her. She taps him on the head lightly with the feather, "The Birds are your relatives. Now they're part of you and you must protect them as you would protect yourself. They will do the same for you."

CHAPTER FORTY-NINE

The Mask

I step over MG and Trip's sleeping bodies on my way to the bathroom. One bleary look in the mirror confirms a rough night. My long hair is plastered to my face and the red paste has hardened into a rubbery mask. I doubt my own mother could identify me.

MG comes into the bathroom and mumbles, "Try to take the mask off as a whole piece." She reaches up to my face and pries under the outer edges of the mask to release it from my skin. My hair is stuck to it, so I yelp every time she pulls. Half my face comes off with it. The mask is one rubbery, somewhat round facial plaster with two eye holes and one for the mouth.

"It looks fierce with all those hairs stuck to it." I place it on the counter.

"When Maggie did this ceremony with me a few years ago, I took mine off right away so mine isn't so out of shape or hairy."

"You did this too?"

"We all did it. Even the guys, but they won't talk about it." MG looks at my face and pulls my hair back. "It connects us with our surroundings and protects us. The Shadow Man is the dark part of all of us. There's a time and place for him to come out. He's the part of you that you use when you need to fight."

"I know I can use what the guys showed me on self-defense." I look at my face, red and sore in the mirror. "I'm not sure how this is going to help."

"Honestly, you better rely on The Shadow Man more. He's the energy deep inside you to fight to the death if necessary. He's like a volcanic eruption directed against your enemies. When you're ready to give up, he fights beyond you."

"Have you ever needed him?"

"I haven't yet, but Trip says she used The Shadow Man when those morons in Mexico were trying to kidnap her. She said it was incredible how large she became. It's hard to understand, but she grew so large that those guys couldn't take her. They saw her bigness too. She saw it in their eyes."

"I hope you're right, but I hope things go well and I won't need him."

"You're going into a very dangerous situation. You'll need everything we've given you. Maggie can see the truth. This may be beyond you. No one would blame you if you didn't go."

"Something inside of me is pulling me. I don't quite know how to describe it. Somehow my future is on this path. I can feel it and sense it, but I can't tell you what it is."

"I've felt that at times in my life too. It's like there's an easy way laid out for most people and I take the one just for me. It's harder, but I'm more alive and stronger when I follow it. I really hope this is your path. Just know that if you need any of us, we'll help as much as possible."

We hear some stirrings from the living room, so I jump into the shower. When I get out, I look in the mirror again and my face is red and smooth. I feel tired and invigorated at the same time. My skin is electric and my mind is sharp. I dress and follow the smell of bacon from the kitchen where Trip is cooking.

Maggie and MG are sitting in the living room talking as I look out the window and see the guys pull up with my car and Dan's truck. Trip shovels the food onto paper plates and we all sit in the living room eating bacon, eggs and biscuits in silence.

Lightning wipes his mouth with a paper towel and clears his throat, "You'll need some money." I start to protest, but he holds up his hand. "We need to keep giving the money to this attorney guy. But it's unsafe for you to carry money on *you*. We've hidden the money in different places in your car. There's a money belt you can wear when you have to carry the money on your person. You'll be able to get the money as you need it. We've also packed medical supplies for Jeff. The stuff down there probably isn't even sterile and they'll charge you a fortune."

Maggie looks at me and then Lightning. "I think she's ready. She needs to practice everything we've taught her, *every day*."

I hope her confidence in me translates into actions. Jeffrey's recovery is in my hands. The gang shuffles out of the house, each giving me either a hug or a pat.

When I start to pack my stuff in the bathroom, the mask is still lying on the counter. I stare at the black, hollowed out eye sockets and mouth. And in that moment between moments, my third eye glimpses the chasm of the dark side of my soul. It electrifies the air and sends a bolt up my spine. I steady my breathing and stance. It's terrifying to see the depth of this shadowy side I want to control. I hope I'm ready for this overwhelming power.

To ensure the mask stays in one piece, I gingerly pick it up and put it in a plastic container and start to pack my toiletries. I instinctively reach for my birth control pills and a shiver runs up my back. Ernesto said Jeffrey and I could pay for conjugal visits in the prison. That certainly won't be happening. I leave them on the counter and sweep my toothbrush, toothpaste and a variety of other items into my make-up case. Rocky and Lucero nervously follow me around while I load everything into the car, and show relief when I finally put them in, too. Lucero's tail wags wildly until he sits in the front seat. Rocky's on a perch that Lightning has fashioned between the two seats, so he can easily walk between Lucero and me and watch the scenery as we drive.

I look at my ragtag team. Maggie has summoned the *Shadow Man* within us to fight the evil forces of the universe. The three of us are prepared for battle, but hoping for a diplomatic solution. I watch as everything in my rearview mirror gets smaller and the world in front of me gets bigger than anything I've ever seen before.

CHAPTER FIFTY

The Fort

I crack the window slightly on the passenger side of the car, so Lucero has just enough room to stick his snout out to breathe fresh air. He leaves a stream of drool flowing down the window and pooling at its base. I don't dare roll the windows down too far because Rocky gets blown around the car from too much wind.

Lucero barks wildly and growls at the guards at each successive border post. The guards don't bother talking to me and wave me through. I wish I'd had Lucero with us when we were bringing the birds through the border guards. Maybe I wouldn't have had to pay so much for safe passage. Apparently, it's not illegal to bring birds and dogs into Mexico, but bringing them back might be an issue.

Before I left for this trip, I called Curtis, the border patrolman, and said I was going back to Mexico.

"Unwise," was his one word response.

"I'm not going to do anything illegal," I promised. "I'm just helping a friend."

"Genny, you've used up the last of my good nature. If you fuck up again, I'm gonna come down hard."

I also called my mother. "It's kinda like the Peace Corps, Mom." I lied. " It's a small organization with a church." I hoped if I mentioned the word "church," she'd relax.

"Is it a Catholic church?" she asked, hopefully. "If it is, I'll call Father Monroe to see if he knows people there."

"No, it's like a missionary group."

"You're not getting mixed up in any cults, are you?"

"No Mom, I promise. I'll call you when I get back"

Ernesto arranged for a cheap place for me to live, but I need to get the keys first. Once I hit Tampico, I head straight to his office. Ernesto quickly comes to greet me and escorts me back out the door.

"*Señorita* Genny, you can no longer come to my office. Get in your car and follow me to the place I got for you."

He jumps into an old truck and accelerates out of the parking lot and into the street. I follow as closely as I can, but nearly lose sight of him a few times. We wind our way out of the city and along the coastline south of town. The road has no guard rails and is built close to the cliffs overlooking the Gulf of Mexico, with breathtaking views of the azure water and virgin beaches. The farther out of town we drive, the fewer houses we pass. We turn into a hidden driveway almost totally engulfed in jungle vegetation. The driveway goes for another one hundred feet and dead ends into a small villa built into the side of the hill.

Ernesto jumps out of the truck and comes up to my car window. Lucero barks wildly, but Ernesto doesn't flinch. "Get him quiet now. I don't want anybody to hear us."

Ernesto holds up a key. "I don't have much time. I have to get back to my work."

I follow him up the stairs of the front porch. Brilliant red bougainvillea covers the front entrance of the villa and sunlight barely filters through the thick palms and overgrown ficus trees. The place looks long abandoned. He pushes the warped front door open. "This is the best I could get for you with the budget MG said to pay."

My stomach sinks. My vision of me as Florence Nightingale nursing Jeffrey back to health is replaced by the unromantic, stark reality. The place is a mess.

"You must be careful when you come and go." Ernesto faces me and grasps my shoulders with both of his hands. "Make sure no one follows you here. No one knows about this place, but me. You are safe for now. But if they find you, they may try to ..." He stops talking and stares at me. "You don't have to do this."

"Who else is going to help Jeffrey?"

"He knew what he was doing. Just because he was stupid doesn't mean you have to be."

My body stiffens at his words. "This wasn't his fault. Raul must have betrayed him. He turned him in so he could get the money and the electronics."

"Genny, you don't know everything. He challenged Raul's honor."

"Do you hear yourself, Ernesto? I can't believe you would defend Raul. Jeffrey lost everything... his plane, all of the electronics he paid for and almost his life. It's a bunch of macho crap. Jeffrey couldn't have done anything worth killing him for."

"You don't know everything Genny."

"I don't want to hear any more. I need to get Jeffrey well and out of that hell hole. I owe him that. I can't think of anything other than that right now."

"You need to think about your own safety. Raul and his thugs tried to kill Jeffrey. They'll try to kill you too if you get in their way. This is as safe a place as we can get. If you go to the second story, you can see the main road in both directions. Keep a constant watch."

"I can take care of myself." I say this with more resolve than I feel. I hope the *Shadow Man* followed me into Mexico. "I need to see Jeffrey and assess his situation."

Ernesto releases my shoulders. I suddenly feel a weight that wasn't there before. "I will leave first. Stay here for at least thirty minutes, then go to the jail. I will meet you there, later."

"Is all of this necessary?" I'm skeptical at his insistence of this cloak and dagger drama.

"Come with me." He takes my hand and pulls me up the staircase to the second floor. The view is incredible. The Gulf goes on forever and the beach is totally secluded below. I can see for miles in both directions. "This place was built by a drug family. They set it up for protection, but even they were discovered and killed. You must take precautions, regardless if you think I'm wrong. You are a woman by herself in a different world. I will help you as much as I can. Please watch for danger."

"Thank you, Ernesto. I know you're doing your best. I just want Jeffrey better." Ernesto gives me a friendly hug and goes down an outside staircase from the observation deck.

I open the car door and Lucero bounds out and Rocky screeches for attention. After I feed them, we explore our new home together. The furniture is covered by sheets and a thick layer of dust. Under other circumstances I'd find this place charming. Because it's built partially into the side of the hill, the windows in the back of the house are at ground level. The kitchen, living room and a small bedroom are downstairs. There's only one bedroom upstairs and an observation platform. I find a pair of binoculars in the bedroom. Ernesto wasn't kidding; the house is built for protection and positioned like a fort. There are so many things I don't understand about Mexico and its culture. There are no rules, just raw power, almost like the Wild West. And no one is who they seem to be. Raul looks like a harmless old man, but if I'm to believe Ernesto, he ordered a hit on Jeffrey.

I suddenly feel vulnerable. I'm alone in a foreign country, so it's prudent to be careful and check the surroundings from the second-floor lookout. The beach sparkles with blinding white sand and the clear-blue sea beyond. How can this place be so beautiful and treacherous at the same time?

CHAPTER FIFTY-ONE

Hope

Getting into the prison is easier than the grand affair it was when I first came. The guard walks me past several closed doors and down a hall past several individual cells. I gird myself for the smells and the filth, but almost faint when I'm taken to Jeffrey. He's laid out on a wooden bed about a foot off the floor with no mattress and no blankets. His clothes are caked with dried blood and his long blond hair is flat against his head and filthy. There're a few plates of rancid and moldy food around him with flies and roaches crawling over them. The guard tells me I only have thirty minutes before I have to leave. Jeffrey's not a flight risk, so he doesn't shut the door.

I kneel on the floor and gently wash Jeffrey's face. He opens his eyes wide with fear and tries to put his arms up to defend himself. "Jeffrey, it's me, Genny." I choke back tears as he falls back onto the wooden slats with a thud and passes out. While he can't fight me, I judge which wounds need the most attention. His eyes are black and swollen and his right ear is cut, but these lacerations don't appear life threatening. He must have used his arms to reduce the heavy blows waged by the attackers because they have deep cuts on them and his knuckles are raw.

My hands shake as I pull his shirt up to reveal two knife wounds into his abdomen with crude stitches holding his flesh together. The wounds are angry red and seeping blood and pus. His body convulses slightly from the sting as I pour alcohol directly onto the knife gashes. I work fast to clean these more serious injuries and apply iodine to the lesser abrasions.

His lips are cracked and bleeding. "Jeffrey, sit up a little." I softly whisper while I lift his head to give him water. He gags at first and then drinks like a man dying of thirst.

He opens his eyes again and smiles crookedly as he recognizes me. He tries to say something, but starts crying. "Oh, Jeffrey, I'm so sorry this has happened to you." Just as I'm about to hug him, Ernesto comes through the door. He sees me and smiles, but his face contorts with disgust when he sees Jeffrey. He looks away momentarily to cough and then turns back toward me with an expressionless face.

"Why doesn't he have a mattress and blanket? We paid for them."

"They had so much blood on them, they had to be burned."

"Why didn't you buy another then?"

"We don't have any more money. I've paid for some things out of my own wallet, but I'm not rich." He looks down and avoids my gaze.

"I'm so sorry. That should have been the first thing I did with you this morning. I wasn't thinking."

Ernesto looks up and smiles at me. "We can do that after we leave. How's he doing?"

Jeffrey tries to sit up, but can't. He stops crying, but tears run down the sides of his cheeks. He's too weak to brush them away.

The guard comes to the door and tells us it's time to leave. Ernesto seems relieved he doesn't have to stay any longer.

"Goodbye, Jeffrey. I'll be back tomorrow." I bite my lower lip, so I won't cry. He turns away from me and his body shakes in waves.

As I follow Ernesto out of the prison, he whispers to meet him at the café on the plaza. We split immediately to go in different directions. I retrieve some of the money Lightning has stashed in the car and am surprised at the cleverness of the hiding place. It's smart all of it isn't in one place. He told me where the first of the monies was stashed, but not the rest. It will be a game looking for it.

I park several blocks from the plaza and walk the rest of the way to the café. So many emotions course through me right now. Keeping my wits about me won't be easy. A short woman greets me and says Ernesto is in the far booth. I keep my head down and walk to the dark corner and sit with my back to the café.

Ernesto's face is drawn and tired. He barely looks up and doesn't smile as he concentrates on adding more sugar to his tea. "Genny, you shouldn't be here. It's very dangerous right now. Animals that are cornered are the most wild with their actions."

"Jeffrey will die without attention. I'll stay at least until he gets better. You need to find a way to get him out of there, please."
He sighs deeply, "It will take a miracle to get him out. Too many men are connected to this. Raul is only the match that struck the fire."

"Please, Ernesto, don't give up." I reach over and take his hand in mine. They are freezing and a slight tremble runs through his fingers. I look into his eyes and his features soften a little. "Before all this happened, Jeffrey said to pay someone off. Is there someone you can call with that kind of power?"

"There is one more way I can try to get him out, but it's a… How do you Americans say, a Hail Mary pass." He looks around the room. "But if this plan fails, you need to be prepared to leave without him. He may be in prison a long time and you cannot waste your life for him."

"I will get him healthy and then see what comes next." I reach into my pocket and hand Ernesto an envelope with cash in it. A look of relief passes his features. He's been working on faith we would pay him.

We order lunch and eat in silence and the strain between us eases with each bite. I leave first and sit in the plaza on a bench and watch some children play. There are so many faces and all of them look at me with suspicion; is it because I'm a foreigner or because they mean to do me harm? Walking back to my car, while trying to see if someone is following me is nerve wracking. When I was with Socorro and Juanita, I didn't feel so out of place. Now my jeans and T-shirt bring too much attention to me. I need to blend in more with my surroundings.

On my way back to the villa, the sign on the bodega advertises TELEPHONE INSIDE and I chuckle to myself. Who thinks a phone is a significant selling point? But then I think about my own situation and it's no longer funny. Things I take for granted at home may prove difficult to find in Mexico. I pull into the parking lot. I need to purchase food, cleaning supplies and some clothes for me to alter my appearance. I browse through the clothing rack to find peasant blouses and skirts. There's a phone booth in the back corner of the store. I examine it to see the coin denominations needed to use it.

"*Señorita*, do you need to use the telephone?" The store clerk comes over to help me. "We have the correct money to use it."

"Yes. I want to call the United States. Can I do that here?"

"Call the operator first and she will connect you." I hand her ten dollars and she hands me the change.

The operator answers and asks the number. She directs me to

deposit the coins for three minutes of talk time. After several rings, MG answers. I quickly begin to speak. MG interrupts, "Genny, is that you? I can barely hear you."

My hands cup over the phone while I keep my back to the clerk. "Yes. It's me. I'm at a payphone. I'm outside of Tampico. I saw Jeffrey and he's alive, barely, but still alive."

"Slow down. You're talking to fast."

"I don't know if I'm cleaning his wounds the correct way." I speak louder than I want. The girl at the counter strains to listen. "What if he gets worse? How will I tell?"

MG starts to explain how to look for signs of serious infection when the line goes dead and the operator asks me to deposit more money to continue the call. I deposit the money and MG is still talking.

"MG, the phone went dead while you were talking. I had to deposit more money. I haven't heard a word you said. We only have three minutes. I'll write to tell you what happens with Jeffrey."

"That's probably a good idea. But you need to phone in every day so we know you're okay. I'm glad you got to see Jeffrey. What did he say hap..." The operator cuts in and says to deposit more money. Three minutes just isn't enough time. Frustration pricks at the pit of my stomach. Between watching for Raul's men, going to the prison, and talking with Ernesto, I'm totally fried.

I pay for all of my supplies and new clothes and leave. All this pent up energy needs direction. I head back to the villa to do some major cleaning. I'm grateful I got to speak to MG. I feel a little more connected with my clan.

CHAPTER FIFTY-TWO

Room For An Angel

I grab the gun from under my pillow at the sound of faint knocking at the front door.   Lucero barks wildly, so I leave him and Rocky in the bedroom while I rush out to the observatory and down the back staircase. I quietly come around to the front of villa with my gun raised to eye level.

There, standing on the front porch, is Ernesto. I lower my gun and hide it behind my back as he turns toward me.

"I brought tacos and coffee." He raises a bag in his hand.

Dressed only in my T-shirt and shorts, I wave for him to come up to the observatory, so we can eat together. I rush ahead, so I can put my gun back under my pillow and let Lucero and Rocky out. I get back to the observation deck just as Ernesto hits the top stair. I moved furniture around when I cleaned the night before and put a small table and two chairs on the deck.

We sit down to watch as the predawn light blooms over the Gulf of Mexico with puffs of pink cotton candy clouds floating over the deep azure waters. Outlines of the small boats on the horizon anchored in the shallow waters bob up and down in the gentle surf. We sip our coffees and listen to the sound of the waves hitting the shore echoing off the walls of the mountains behind the villa. There's a feeling of total peace and tranquility. Ernesto seems to enjoy the peacefulness of the moment.

I study the expansive vista and watch as an old truck slowly drives down the road towards Tampico. I turn back towards Ernesto and see him staring at me. Suddenly self-conscious of my appearance I try to pull my hair back and comb it with my fingers. "I know I must look terrible. I just woke up and didn't have time to—."

He holds up his hand and stops me from saying more. "You look beautiful." He reaches up and touches my cheek gently. "*Mi corazón*," he says and starts to move closer. Lucero growls at him and Rocky half flies, half jumps toward him. Ernesto instinctively pushes his chair to avoid the two of them and flips over backward onto the deck. The spell is broken, and so is the chair.

Ernesto jumps up from his fall and quickly recovers his dignity. *Sister Mary Clément Marie, did you send my guardian angel to sit between Ernesto and me?*

"I need to get to work," he says. "What time are you going to the prison?"

"I want to get there early and stay as long as they let me. I get the feeling that it's the guard's discretion as to how long I can stay. We can meet for lunch if you want."

"The same café then. In the corner booth."

I feed my babies and eat the tacos Ernesto brought. I wonder if I came back to save Jeffrey or to see Ernesto. I'll try to keep my wits, but whatever brought me here is too strong to fight.

I dress in the loose-fitting and unflattering clothes I bought yesterday. For good measure I wear a floppy hat and a pair of cheap sunglasses to cover most of my face. I almost don't recognize myself.

I clock the distance to the prison and pay attention to what kind of traffic is on the two-lane road into the city. I don't know what I'm looking for, so I feel I need to note everything. There are mostly big trucks carrying vegetables and fruit. Once I enter the city, the traffic changes to a few busses and people on bicycles.

Lightning always says routine will get you killed, so I park even farther away from the prison than yesterday and walk a different path. Every day I need to change what I do to stay away from anything predictable someone can use against me. The camp outside the gates of the prison is crowded this morning. Women and children squat next to small cook fires, making tortillas and cooking meat. The smell of fresh coffee and a faint aroma of burning mesquite firewood is a drastic difference from the smells inside the prison. I buy two tacos from one of the stands and a bucket of water and soap.

The cost of entering the prison has gone down to a few pesos with no explanation. No one even looks at me today. I pass through several guard stations to get to Jeffrey's cell. Not much has changed since yesterday. He's lying motionless on the bed, but now there's a mattress under his body and a blanket folded under his head. The dirty dishes have been removed. I call his name and he moves a little.

I kneel down next to his bed and start washing his face. He opens his eyes and smiles a little and tries to talk, but his lips are sealed from dehydration. I lift some water to his lips and he drinks so fast, he coughs half of it back out. He looks at me. "Thank you for coming." Tears form in his eyes, so I redirect his attention to the bag next to me.

"I brought some of your clothes. I'll help you change into them after I clean your wounds." Jeffrey stands and steadies himself with one hand touching the wall. We carefully pull his shirt over his head and I wash his chest and arms. Gone are the strong pectoral muscles and well-defined biceps. Long gashes scar his chest and arms and his skin stretches tightly over his ribs. I wash the dried blood and dirt from his face, neck and arms. He unzips his pants and they drop to the floor. I'm suddenly bashful and embarrassed to see him naked. He washes himself and puts on his pants and sandals. I feel the distance between us widen.

"We can try to wash your hair tomorrow first thing. Once you're stronger, it will be easier if you take a shower."

"A shower will be nice. It's going to be a while though." He tries to sit and barely makes it to the bed before collapsing. Still weak, he lies back down. We talk of small things which won't be remembered, but a peace comes to the room that wasn't there before. And maybe even hope for a future.

Ernesto is waiting when I get to the café and smiles as I slide into the booth. I'm torn between these two men. Ernesto knows I'm here for Jeffrey, but Jeffrey doesn't know I'm meeting Ernesto. My life's already complicated enough without adding fuel to the fire. I need to figure things out with Jeffrey.

We order our lunch and wait for the food to arrive in awkward silence. Finally, Ernesto begins a rehearsed speech, "Genny, I don't think I should come to the villa anymore. It's too dangerous for you. Every time I go, there is a chance someone will follow me. We need to keep apart from each other until Jeffrey is released."

Although that's exactly what I was thinking, I feel hurt and rejected. I wanted to be the one who built the wall to separate us, not him. I burst into tears and run out of the café into the plaza. This is absolutely stupid. He's doing the right thing, but I feel abandoned by him. I sit down in the middle of the plaza and bawl my eyes out. The release of energy is sobering.

People stare at me and I stop to examine myself. I look like a peasant woman who's lost her mind. I walk back to my car slowly, wary of everyone around me. What a mess. I need to focus my energy and finish what's been started.

On the way back to the villa, I stop at St. Mary's church outside the plaza. The white stucco exterior is clean, but in desperate need of repair. When I walk up the front steps a wave of emotions hit me. The soft glow from the offertory candles makes a dancing shadow behind the statue of the Virgin Mary and I slide into the back pew. I press my knees into the well-worn kneeler as tears stream down my face.

"Jeffrey needs your help, God. He won't ask You. He's too proud. I know I have fallen too, and shouldn't even be here, but he is your child and needs your protection. My trust is in Ernesto and You and not with a man like Raymundo. Please help Jeffrey to survive and get him back home."

I get up to leave, but stop myself, "Please guide me safely home, too." I cross myself and leave.

CHAPTER FIFTY-THREE

The Wake

For the last ten days Jeffrey's condition has not changed. He's mostly unresponsive and weak. I clean his physical wounds, but his mental trauma is deep. I sit and read to him some of the books Lightning sent. At times he listens, mostly he sleeps. I ask questions about the characters or the plot, but he rarely engages in conversation. He doesn't cry as much when I'm there, but his face strains for composure at times.

My affection for Jeffrey changes as my role in his life shifts. There are days where I bring a mother's love and sometimes a friend's, but my role as lover slips away and fades. I struggle to remember our love making. I'm sad to lose those touching memories. They're being replaced by a hollow existence and a broken man. I fight to keep pity from the edges of my feelings. It's like having a funeral for a friend who is still alive.

CHAPTER FIFTY-FOUR

From Hell to Purgatory

Jeffrey counts the number of days he's been in prison and says he'll never get those four months back. I count my days here alone and I'll never get my five weeks back. We both realize we're in purgatory and may wait an eternity to be free. I tell myself my job is to get Jeffrey strong enough to survive on his own. I've let go of any notion I can single handedly get him out of prison. Every day, I leave the prison looking for ways to escape.

Tampico's only airport is located south of the city. Although Lightning tries to avoid landing at official airstrips, he may be able to use it to come and rescue me in a pinch.

Sitting in my car, I watch the air traffic come and go. The runways are undersized so commercial craft like cargo planes and passenger jets are limited, but there's a healthy amount of light aircraft holding six to eight passengers.

I move my car beyond a fenced area and walk to a small hangar. A short man hurries out of an office to assist me.

"*Hola, señorita.*"

"*Hola.*" After establishing that he speaks English, I ask if I can buy a map of the area with coordinates on it.

He pauses for a brief moment and says, "Not many people ask for maps. The pilots usually have their own. There might be some in the back of the hangar. Do you have time for me to look for them?" I nod my head and he heads to the back office. After several minutes, he comes back with an armload of rolled up maps. He spreads them on his desk for better inspection.

"Can you tell me what you need these for, *señorita*?"

"I'm working for National Geographic and we're marking old burial grounds. I need to be able to document the area with coordinates."

"*Sí, sí, sí,* National Geographic. That is very important work."

I pay for one map and start to leave, just as two men drive up in a military camouflaged jeep to the hangar. I instantly know I've done something stupid and walk in the opposite direction of my car toward a different hangar. A plane lands and taxies down the runway toward me. The pilot stops just past me and I hurry to open the door for him. "Do you need help with the tie down?" I ask as he disembarks.

He looks surprised, but hands me one of the tie lines and hooks. I casually look over his shoulder to see if the two men are watching me. I no longer see them, but feel like I'm still being watched.

Once the plane is secure, the pilot looks me up and down and asks, "You need a ride?" He's an American, which right now is a relief.

I quickly nod. We walk together toward a jeep parked next to the hangar. Once we jump in, the pilot peels out of the parking area and heads toward the mountains. We drive in silence with me constantly looking behind us for any signs of being followed.

At the top of the mountain ridge, the pilot pulls the jeep over and speaks to me in a kind tone. "You're obviously in trouble," he says. "Do you want to talk about it?"

"Not really. I'm just being cautious."

"Fine. I don't really need to know. But you were as white as a sheet when you came up to the plane. You got in my vehicle without even knowing who I am and you spent the last forty-five minutes watching behind us."

"*I'm* not in trouble. I'm here trying to help a friend who is and I need to be extra careful.

"Why were you at the airport? I'm guessing you know a little about planes."

"I can fly, but I probably need to stay away from *that* airport. Where else can someone land? Is there a smaller airport without a lot of people around?"

"Not really." The answer is what I expect. "This is the only airport for several hundred miles, but people have been known to land on the beach. It's flat and mostly abandoned. I've done it a couple of times south of here when I needed to take a break."

I'm deep in thought when he asks, "Do you want me to take you somewhere?"

"Oh, crap. Yes, please. Take me to the airport. I'll get back to my place from there."

He starts the jeep and we drive back down the mountain to the airport chatting like two old friends. He's from San Francisco and works for a big fruit grower. At least that's what he says. I don't press his story, and I certainly don't want him questioning mine.

He lets me out of the jeep about a half mile from my car. I don't want anyone to see what my car looks like, not even some nice American pilot from San Francisco named George. I hide behind a tree and watch to see if anyone is near my car before I approach. Three weeks in Mexico and I'm getting more and more squirrely. My world consists of Jeffrey and prison during the day and Rocky and Lucero at night. It's like a self-imposed solitary confinement.

On my way back to the villa, I stop at the bodega and buy a large envelope and paper along with a few other supplies. The girl behind the counter is friendly and asks about my day. I remember Lightning's voice: *"Routine is your enemy. Don't do anything the same way twice."* I need to stop coming to this store. I don't want to get too familiar with any person.

When I get back to the villa, I walk around the house and the grounds with Rocky on my shoulder and Lucero close by my side to make sure everything is safe. I feed them and then climb the stairs to the observation deck. The sun has already gone behind the mountains, but the heat has not abated. I'm alert as I sit down and write MG a letter.

> *Hey MG,*
>
> *Hope all is going well there. Jeffrey is doing a little better every day, but seems pretty bummed about his circumstances. He no longer has a fever, but is still very weak. I know he's lucky to be alive. I just wish he would have a better attitude.*
>
> *I haven't been able to speak to Ernesto. He says it's too dangerous for me to meet him at his office. He mostly communicates to Jeffrey and then Jeffrey tells me.*
>
> *I picked up a map at the airport in Tampico and marked on the map where I'm staying. It's a villa across from the beach. Really cool place.*
>
> *Maybe you could come down and visit for a few days. Would love the company. Hope the birds are doing well. Say hi to everyone else.*

I'll call and we can talk, if you or Lightning have any questions.
I'll make sure I have lots of change for the pay phone.
Genny

I hope MG can come for a visit. I need some outside perspective. I stuff the map into the envelope and seal it. I wipe my sweaty hands down the sides of my skirt before I address it. My nerves are shot. Those men at the airport could be in Raul's gang... or not.

CHAPTER FIFTY-FIVE

Deep Cuts

The stiletto knife cuts me once again as I stab the already dead fish carcass on the beach. The button on the handle makes it easy to open and thrust the sharp point into flesh, but it requires the right amount of finesse and firmness to strike, twist and then retract the knife. Most of the times I push too hard and lose my grip on the handle and my hand slides onto the blade. My fingers and hands are constantly bandaged after my combat exercises. I'm getting better though. My cuts aren't as deep or numerous as when I first started.

At first Lucero just sat and watched me attack the dead fish, but now he joins in the aggressive attack. The hair on the back of his neck rises as he crouches on his approach. Once the fish is in his mouth, he sinks his teeth deeply into the flesh and drags it. We're both constantly on the ready for a crisis that may or may not occur.

Lucero drags a large piece of driftwood from the surf and I stack it on top of several others. There are four stacks of lumber now, each taller than me. The game evolved over the past weeks from boredom to necessity.

If an emergency arises and Lightning needs to come and get me, the beach is the best alternative. So Lucero and I keep it clear of debris...just in case. I begin each morning with prayer and meditation and then Lucero and I go to the beach to run a solid three miles. In the beginning, I would find small sticks to throw, and Lucero would retrieve them, but we both tired of that sport. Now I practice the self-defense kicks the guys taught me on the varying sizes of logs. I can break a four-inch thick board in two with either foot now. I'm starting to break boards with my hands albeit much smaller ones.

I haven't seen anyone suspicious since the men at the airport and even they may have been an imagined threat, but I can't take chances. Raul tried to kill Jeffrey. The threat waits beneath the surface. One wrong move and he could be dead… or me.

CHAPTER FIFTY-SIX

The Envelope

"Did you get the envelope I sent?" The payphones have made MG and me keep our conversations under three minutes. We get down to business quickly and keep our answers short.   I get no sense as to what is happening in her world nor her in mine.

"Yes, Lightning says he knows the area pretty well," MG answers.

"I know I'm asking a lot, but can you come down and visit me for a couple of days. I'll pay for your bus ticket."

"You don't have to pay for my ticket." MG doesn't hesitate. "The gang already thought I should come down and check on you and Jeffrey. I'll be on the express bus in two days."

"You don't know how much I appreciate it."

"I spoke with Ernesto two days ago. He says he's working some contacts who are really promising. He's hopeful that they can help, so he needs more money. He says Julio will meet you at the prison to get the payment tomorrow."

"Where's the next hiding place on the car for the money?" I giggle a little. "Lightning sure has some creative ways to hide things. Even with instructions, it took me an hour to find the last one."

As I leave the *mercado,* I make sure no one suspicious is near and head back to the villa. This cloak and dagger is wearing on my nerves. I no longer feel safe anywhere. I'm relieved MG's coming. I need someone to talk to besides Jeffrey.

Lucero and Rocky follow me around while I clean the place for MG's arrival. Afterwards, Lucero and I walk to the beach for a run and a splash in the water. I drag more driftwood to the several piles that I've made along the edge of the beach. The sun sets behind the mountains and it's time to enjoy the last bit of tranquility this deserted beach offers. I light one of the stacks and watch as the flames dance fast then quietly die to low embers. Lucero sleeps by my side until the stars brighten in the sky. A light mist settles on us before we get up and walk back to the villa, stiff and tired. This would have been a great place to vacation, but it only accentuates my loneliness now and the strange direction my life has taken.

CHAPTER FIFTY-SEVEN

A Slip of the Tongue

Jeffrey sits hunched on the bed when I walk in. He looks weaker than he did yesterday. His skin has a yellowish tint to it and his eyes are sunk deeper into their sockets. His injuries are almost completely healed, but he's lost so much weight his muscles hang from his arms and he loses his balance easily and shuffles around his cell like an old man.

I bring him enough food and water to last him all day, but he lacks enthusiasm to eat it all. There are always leftovers when I arrive the next morning.

Ever mindful everyone is listening to us, we speak in low voices. I don't dare tell him MG is coming for fear I might put her in danger. She'll just show up and surprise him.

He no longer asks how long he will be here and I have no reason to give him hope for any changes. This morning is no different.

"I've brought you some tacos from a new stand this time."

He looks at his food, takes a small bite, and smiles faintly. "I can't tell much difference from one to the other, but thanks for trying." He wipes his mouth with his sleeve and continues to eat slowly. "How's Lucero and Rocky?"

"Lucero caught a lizard this morning and was so startled by it in his mouth he jumped two feet in the air."

Jeffrey chuckles softly at the image, but slumps deeper into his position on the bed. "I'm tired today. I might go back to sleep before my attorney comes to see me."

My heart beats a little faster with the mention of Ernesto, but I purposefully deepen my breath before I speak. "What's happening with your case?"

"Same bullshit, different day. He says he's working a different angle and says it's promising."

I perk up at that comment. "I know you don't like me saying this, but I've been praying for you. Maybe Ernesto will get you out of here soon."

"You're right, I don't like hearing about prayers and shit." He softens his voice and changes the subject. "What are you going to do the rest of today?"

Most of the time, our conversation revolves around getting him food and cleaning his wounds, he rarely asks about the world outside of prison. This might be a good sign. Maybe he's getting interested in life again.

"I've been exploring the area. I'll probably drive up to San Luis Potosi."

"That's where they sent Socorro," he says in a matter of fact manner.

"What do you mean, '*That's where they sent Socorro*?'"

Jeffrey's face goes white. "Please Genny, we can't talk about any of this now." He looks toward the hall to see if the guards have heard anything. "Believe me, you just need to drop it. You need to leave *now*."

CHAPTER FIFTY-EIGHT

Hell Hath No Fury

I run to my car. I can't breathe from the jolt to my entire being. My heart is ready to explode in my chest. There are so many lies and so many people hiding things from me...especially Jeffrey. Up until now, I've tried to give Jeffrey the benefit of the doubt. But it all makes sense now. Raul must have found out Jeffrey was fooling around with his daughter and turned him into the federales, but he made sure he secured the shipment first. Victoria stopped writing to me just before the last run, so she knew too. She could have warned me.

I know I'm driving like a maniac. I can see it in the pedestrians' eyes when I pass them. I should slow down, but I can't. The road has huge pot holes and hairpin turns. My mood is black and the air is nauseatingly sweet. I'd forgotten that Papantla is the vanilla capital of Mexico. The cobblestone street forces me to slow down and my mind starts to focus again. The last time I came here was with Victoria. She is the key to this entire mess. Hopefully, she's here for a tryst with her lover and I can ask essential questions.

I drive past the small café where Victoria and I ate lunch and park the car a distance from the plaza. Something snaps in my brain, time slows to milliseconds. Tiny pictures with stuttered speeds click in my head. Scenes of Socorro saying she wants to marry an American, Jeffrey reading my mail from Victoria, talk of honor, respect and betrayal. My focus narrows to a pinhole and it's hard to keep my balance. I grab my large floppy hat and broad sunglasses to cover my face and walk unsteadily to the café.

The view from a table in the back lets me see the entire café and gives me time to clear my mind. I'm cold to the bone, I drink hot cocoa and watch as a sudden rain pours from the skies. The sun is still out, but a cloud releases all of its energy. I feel the same urge to let go and cry the rest of the day. I've been made into such a fool.

I pay my bill and am about to leave when Victoria and Hector run under the awning to avoid the rain. They're laughing and holding hands. How could they be so cheerful when I'm so miserable? They sit at a table near the window and order something from the waitress.

When their food arrives, I walk up to their table and take off my sunglasses. Hector looks up and shows no recognition, but Victoria immediately drops her fork when she looks deeply into my eyes. She flinches back and raises her hands instinctively to stop a blow. I wonder how many times she's been hit, if that's her first response to seeing someone who may be angry with her. Instantly my heart softens toward her; she's in an untenable situation too.

I pull up a chair and sit so I can see the two of them and the entrance to the café. I can feel more than the electrical charge of the thunderstorm outside.

"Genny, I'm surprised to see you."

Hector looks at Victoria and back to me, "Genny?"

"How have you been?" Victoria must be judging how much I know. I don't reply.

After several moments of silence, Victoria continues, "We heard about Jeffrey going to prison."

"He was stabbed and almost died," I say with a more accusatory tone than I intend.

"I heard some things from the local gossip, but Poza Rica is a two-hour drive from the prison. We don't hear about things unless Ernesto tells us."

"You know Raul was responsible. Jeffrey would be dead if one of the guards hadn't helped him. Why did Raul turn against Jeffrey and turn him in to the federales?" I keep my voice low.

"I didn't know what Raul was going to do. He doesn't tell me anything."

"You could have warned me."

"Socorro is my daughter too. I wanted to protect her from Jeffrey. Raul found her bags packed. She was going to run away with Jeffrey. Raul stopped it. I didn't know Raul would order him killed."

It's one thing for a suspicion to bang around in the back of my head, but it's another to have it confirmed. My body flinches and I push back my chair. I've risked my life for a man who betrayed me. Socorro just wanted out of this shit hole. Jeffrey played me. What a dick!

Victoria reaches over and gently touches my hand. "You need to leave soon. Jeffrey is not worth losing your life over."

"Why is my life in danger?"

"Raul thinks you know too much."

"I don't know anything." But immediately I know that to be false. I smuggled Raul's artifacts the first trip. I'm just as big a threat to him as Jeffrey. My stomach turns upside down.

"He's still trying to kill Jeffrey and I know he's looking for you.

He's trying to find out where you live. You need to get out while you can."

"You must be in danger too."

"Socorro and Juanita are staying with my family in San Luis so they are safe from Raul's anger."

Hector takes Victoria's hand, "I will protect Victoria, he says. We will go to my family's place in Guadalajara."

"Raul is supposed to go to Mexico City tomorrow." Victoria smiles fondly at Hector and continues explaining their plan, "We will leave then."

"Good luck," I say. "*Vaya con Dios.*"

CHAPTER FIFTY-NINE

Last Payment

Lucero's muzzle lifts my chin. He's ready to greet the day and needs me to open the back door. The sun barely peeks over the horizon as Rocky waddles around the floor while I fix a quick breakfast for all of us. I packed all my stuff into my car last night and I'm anxious to get things settled in town. Once MG arrives tomorrow, she and I can drive back to Texas together. I'll be out of here for good. I'm still reeling from the confirmation of Jeffrey's affair with Socorro. The duplicity is so calculated and cold. I want to scream at Jeffrey, but I know I can't. Pity and loathing have pushed out all other feelings I have for him.

Before I leave the villa, I add an extra measure of caution by stringing a tripwire across the driveway, so I can check if someone comes here while I'm gone.

The drive into town seems to take longer than usual, but I try not to rush myself. The last ration of money hidden in the car was sewn into the passenger visor. It's now in a money belt around my waist. I can feel the perspiration drip down my back and gather at the cinch around my middle. I park on a small side street I've never parked on before. The walk to the prison is quieter than usual. Most of the campsites and cooking areas are abandoned. As I round the corner to the front of the prison, there are three black sedans parked in a row with American flags on them. A feeling of impending doom descends over me like a shroud.

My feet feel like cement and it takes Herculean effort to move them. I walk through the front door and am ushered into a side room where Ernesto's partner, Julio, is waiting for me. He looks up from some papers.

"*Señorita* Genny, please sit down."

I'm actually grateful to be able to sit, but an overwhelming fear and dread keep me from moving the chair.

Julio stands up and helps me around the table and I half fall, half sit in a hard metal chair. My money belt clangs as it hits the back of the chair. He moves to the opposite side of the table and sits back down, but doesn't make eye contact. He looks at his papers and says, "We need to reconcile your account now." He looks up briefly and then back down at numbers on the last page he shuffles through. "You owe two-thousand-five-hundred dollars and forty-five cents for Jeffrey's attorney costs."

I reach up under my blouse to unhook the belt buckle and swing the canvas and metal pouch onto the table with a small bang. I push the belt over to him and it scratches the table as I do. "There's twenty-eight-hundred dollars in the bag. I need to go back to the United States, so there's a few hundred dollars to pay for his food while I'm gone."

"*Señorita*, he's being released today. Those cars in front are here to take him away."

"What? How did you do that? Why didn't anyone tell me?"

"We had to keep it quiet. Jeffrey is being released to the United States Embassy. Ernesto has been working with the embassy on other matters and was put in contact with Jeffrey's parents. They worked in concert to get him released back to the United States."

I stand up and move to the door, but Julio blocks my exit. "You can't meet with them."

"Why not? I've been here taking care of Jeffrey. I should be able to say goodbye."

"*Señorita* Genny, I'm sorry. Jeffrey was beaten again last night. He will live, but for your safety you need to stay away. Ernesto will be here soon to talk with you. He is finishing the paperwork from the embassy. He has worked hard on this for you. Please thank him much."

I cover my mouth with shaking hands. "Of course. I'm extremely grateful for the help from both of you. I can't thank you enough." Julio bows his head a little, but still won't look me in the eye. "I didn't think we should take this case. It has been dangerous for Ernesto and even a little for me. He is brave to fight against the thieves taking all of our archaeological treasures and selling them in the U.S. That is how he knew the people in the embassy getting Jeffrey out. It is a favor to Ernesto."

My head spins from all of the news. I'm happy, yet suddenly tired. Ernesto opens the door and comes in with several papers in his hands. I stand thank him, but the room becomes hot and tilts to the right. I feel myself sliding down to the floor. Ernesto and Julio catch me before I hit and lower me into the chair. Julio leaves to get some water and Ernesto pulls a chair out to sit next to me.

"*Señorita* Genny, you should be very happy."

"I can't thank you enough, Ernesto. Julio told me all you've done."

"We still are not done. Raul must have known Jeffrey was to be released. He tried to kill him again last night. Jeffrey's parents paid for protection, so the attack was stopped. You need to get out of here. He'll be looking for you next."

Julio comes back into the room and hands me the water. "They are getting into the cars now. You two can leave."

We get up, but my feet still feel unstable. Ernesto puts his arm around my waist to escort me out of this horrible place for the last time. As we round the corner, I see Jeffrey being helped into the back seat of the middle car. His hair is matted and his clothes are bloody. He looks in my direction, but his eyes are glassy and he doesn't seem to recognize me. My knees weaken and my eyes cloud with tears.

I walk like a zombie for several blocks as Ernesto guides me around the corner. He leads me to an old *mercado* with a staircase in the back of the main building and takes my hand as we walk up the stairs to a small apartment. It's sparsely furnished with a sofa, a coffee table and a kitchen table. In one corner, an old desk faces the wall with a cork board above it. The board has so many photos push pinned into it that they overflow on to the wall. Some of the photos are of different pyramids. Ernesto points to a few. "These are some of the raided gravesites. We think they got a lesser chieftain's tomb with this one. We found some jade shards they left behind. That means what they took is irreplaceable. The thieves probably sold them for a few thousand dollars."

I point to a set of pictures that I recognize from La Pyramid de Calendario. There's a picture of all of us in front of the pyramid. Socorro and Juanita are posing in a dance stance. I'm standing between them with Juan and Roberto as bookends. Everyone looks so happy. I look at Ernesto. "That seems like a long time ago."

"Sit down. I'll get us something to drink. Would you like some coffee or tea?"

"Tea would be nice right now."

Ernesto busies himself in the small kitchen while I sit on the overstuffed sofa in the middle of the room. He puts two cups of tea on the coffee table and sits down next to me. "Jeffrey was attacked again last night. There were several people who got paid to save him. He's a lucky man, but Raul is very angry now."

I take a sip of tea and feel my body relax. "I wish you and I could have gotten to know each other better. Maybe sometime you can visit me in the United States." Even though Juanita warned not to do so, I look into Ernesto's eyes deeply. His long dark lashes accentuate his eyes' dark frame. Rich honey with flecks of copper within create the hazel iris. His gaze is unflinching.

"I come to the United States once or twice a year to promote the stopping of illegal trade, so maybe I can see you and Jeffrey there," he says tentatively.

"Jeffrey and I are done." I take another sip of tea. "He and I both stopped loving each other a while back. I just couldn't leave him in prison without help. Now that he's out, we'll go our separate ways." My eyes start tearing again.

"Please don't be sad, *mi corazón*." He gently touches my cheek with his hand and wipes away a stray tear. His touch shoots a bolt through me. I take his hand in mine and kiss it. It's been months since I've been touched at all. My body fills with goose flesh and a rush works its way up my spine. He leans closer and lightly brushes my lips with his. "I've wanted to kiss you for a long time." His voice is deep and smooth. He lightly licks my lips and seeks to open my mouth wider. His tongue finds mine and darts in and out of my mouth to explore.

His chin and cheeks are smooth against my face and he covers me with light kisses. He gently rubs my back and slowly moves my body closer to his. Shivers rush through me and my nipples harden when he brushes over them. *I want his hands all over me.*

He places his hand under my buttocks and lifts me to straddle his lap. My body moves back and forth as he unbuttons my blouse and frees one of my breasts from my padded camisole. The tip of his tongue encircles my areola and he sucks gently on the nipple. *I want his lips kissing me everywhere.*

I unbutton his shirt, so I can feel his skin on mine. It's warm and smooth. He has little hair on his chest. My breath quickens, but I try to match mine with his slow and deliberate exhales. He reaches under my skirt to pull my panties down. I'm drunk from his kisses and my head spins from desire. I want him to take away these last few months and get lost in his arms.

He touches my breasts with both of his hands and slips them out from under the lingerie. I wriggle out of my blouse. I want him now and can think of nothing else. He hikes my skirt up so he can position me over him then pulls me down. My body explodes with both pain and pleasure.

He pushes upward and holds my hips while I move up and down on his cock. My body starts to crash over and over again as he pushes me down harder. My breathing slowly comes back to normal. Ernesto lays me on the sofa and continues to push hard into me until he releases his energy with a deep shudder.

I want him inside me again and again. He pulls me to his bedroom where we make love two more times. The rest of the morning floats away in quiet calm. For the first time in months I feel hope and a lightness of heart.

CHAPTER SIXTY

Dominos

I pull my sunglasses and floppy hat from my large straw purse to disguise myself as I leave Ernesto's apartment. As we said goodbye, I told him MG was coming here by bus and we are to drive back together. He told me Raul has put a bounty on my head. The guards at each checkpoint north of here will be looking for me, so traveling by car will be next to impossible. Jeffrey gets to go home and I'm stuck behind with no easy way out. A heavy weight comes with each step.

I hate admitting that "plan B" needs to be put in place, but it's time to call for reinforcements. I walk down a side street off the plaza to find a phone before I go back to the villa. Stump answers the phone on the first ring. Since he hates to talk on the phone, I'm surprised. "*Que pasa?*" I ask.

"When we got word Jeffrey was released, MG left on the express bus to help you get home. It's scheduled to arrive at 4:00 in Tampico. So she should be getting there soon."

"That's why I called. Raul put a bounty on my head and sent out word to all the border guards. We can't drive back. I was hoping Lightning could fly down and pick us up instead."

"Ok. I'll get in contact with him to come down tonight and pick up both of you. It should take about four hours of fly time and another hour of prep, so give him five hours to land. He knows he'll have to land on the beach."

"It'll be dark by then. Tell him I'll have a fire on the beach to show where to land."

"He's gotten guys out of the jungle in 'Nam under worse conditions. This should be a piece of cake for him."

"I'm sorry all of this shit is happening. I'll make it up to all of you."

"Genny, this isn't your fault. Jeffrey fucked this up. He got greedy."

"He got stupid. He was fucking around with Raul's daughter. That's why Raul turned him into the federales and has been trying to kill him."

"Fuck! We'll get you out. You and MG. We'll get you both out." He chokes on his last words and we're cut off.

I walk four blocks down the road to the bus station. The consequences of Jeffrey's actions are falling like dominoes. I hope I can stop them from falling on MG and me.

The schedule says MG's bus will arrive at 5:00, but it doesn't pull into the station until two hours later. MG gets off the bus holding a baby belonging to the woman disembarking after her, with two other kids in tow. They say goodbye and MG waits for the driver to retrieve her bag from the cargo hold. I make sure no one is watching before I approach.

"MG, I'm so glad you're here."

She turns around to the sound of my voice, but does a double take on my appearance. A smile breaks over her face and I get a big hug. "You look like a commercial for Foster Grant sunglasses. I almost didn't recognize you. You've lost weight or something, too."

"I've been running on the beach a lot. Kinda been practicing those fight moves the guys showed me, too. I can break a two by four with my foot now." I laugh a little self-consciously.

She swings her bag over her shoulder. "How'd you know I was on this bus?"

"Stump told me. We have to go to plan B."

On the drive to the villa, I explain all that has happened with Raul, Jeffrey and Socorro. "So Maggie was right about there being another woman," MG says. "Damn, Maggie sees *everything*."

"It took me forever to see it. I just don't get it. Jeffrey played me all the way to the end. I'm such a fool."

"You're not the fool, Jeffrey is. Guys think with different body parts. They rarely think with their hearts." She switches gear, "So what's the plan?"

"I packed all my shit in the car. I'll have to leave it here and have Ernesto arrange to get it to me later." A look passes over MG's face when I mention Ernesto, but we both know we don't have time for that conversation.

"Lightning is coming tonight to pick us up."

"What do we need to do?" she asks.

"I've been cleaning the beach every morning and stacking the driftwood. We can use the pyres as beacons so he can land. We'll grab Lucero and Rocky from the villa and wait on the beach."

The sun sets behind the mountains as we drive, but a soft glow continues to outline the beauty of the coast. We approach the villa and pull into the driveway. I immediately turn off the headlights and back out of the drive. "The trip wire is gone."

MG stiffens and pulls a gun from her waistband. "Drive back

down the beach and park. Get out of that skirt and put some pants on. You need to be able to move fast."

I grab a pair of jeans packed in the back of the car and change as MG checks the area up and down the beach. I reach under my seat to get my Glock, put the extra clips in my camisole, and fasten the stiletto knife to the inside of my forearm with a strap.

We walk along the foot of the hill on the beach and approach the villa from my usual trail. Along the way, I point out the stacks of wood to light for Lightning. MG nods.

I direct MG to go one way and I go the other way to the villa. My heart's drumming loudly in my ears until I reach the top of the drive where I see Ernesto's jeep. A wave of relief and joy floods through me and I slip my gun into my waistband as I walk through the door. Ernesto and Victoria are sitting on the sofa waiting for me. "Victoria, what are you doing here? I thought you were..." I don't notice until I enter the foyer that their hands are behind their backs.

Raul comes around the corner with a club. I duck and miss the blow that's meant for my head, but it connects with my left shoulder instead. I scramble to the kitchen, missing the next blow. The sound of a gunshot comes from outside and a bullet splinters the doorframe. MG must be coming from the other direction. Raul moves back to where Ernesto and Victoria are as a second shot rings out.

Raul knows I'm not alone. I peer over the cabinets and see him by the front door looking outside. A rifle shot rings out. There's someone outside shooting at MG. Several shots of different caliber guns blast through the air. There's a brief silence before one last indistinguishable shot echoes off the mountain.

Ernesto has gotten free and pushes Victoria out the side door. Raul turns around and shoots just as they clear the doorframe. Victoria runs into the night, but I hear a thud on the porch. Ernesto must have been hit. I hear him moaning. He's still alive.

Raul screams at Victoria to come back. "*Puta. Ven aca. Voy a matarte.*"

He turns his attention back to me. I hear him coming toward the kitchen. I pull the slide on the Glock and fire a shot into the ceiling of the kitchen to warn him. I've practiced shooting over and over, but never at a living thing, especially not a person. Raul retreats and I hear him fumbling with the latch on Rocky's cage. "Genny, I have your bird."
I peek over the counter as Raul grabs Rocky out of his cage and chokes him. Feathers fly everywhere as Rocky screams and screeches. Raul yells,

"Throw out your gun and I'll let the bird go." He shakes Rocky again. I stand to come forward when Lucero bounds through the back window to rescue Rocky and lunges at Raul just as Raul pulls the trigger. Blood splatters everywhere as Lucero's body hits Raul in the chest and knocks him to the floor. As Raul reaches for his gun, I unload my entire clip into his shaking body. I release the spent clip and reload. I'm ready to shoot again when MG comes through the front door and yells for me to stop. I barely hear her and point the gun at Raul's head before it registers. I've killed him.

My hand feels like it's on fire. The smell of gun smoke burns my nostrils. I already know the answer, but I check on Lucero and Rocky. They're both dead.

Outside, Ernesto leans up against the side of the villa bleeding. MG takes command of the situation and checks him out. There's an entry and exit wound through his left arm. She wraps a kitchen towel around it like a tourniquet. "Do you know how to shoot a gun?" Ernesto nods his heads. She hands Ernesto the gun taken from Raul's body and hands me a rifle she must have taken from the shootout. "How many more men are in the woods?" she asks.

"Raul came in my jeep with Victoria and one other man," Ernesto says. "There was another car that followed us here. I think there were two men in that car, maybe three. One of the men is Humberto. I'm not sure who the others are. They parked down the beach."

"We need to get down to the beach, but we can't go down in a group. Genny, you go first. Ernesto goes next. I'll cover the rear. Keep about fifty feet apart, so we have time to react if necessary."

Adrenaline courses through me as I start off toward the beach. I have the rifle slung around my neck and the Glock in my waistband. The gunshots have left a ringing in my ears, so I can't hear anything. I walk carefully down the sloped driveway past a grove of trees toward the gulf when hands reach out from behind the last tree and grab me. The man pulls me close to him. At this close proximity, the gun is useless, so I pull the stiletto knife from my sleeve and thrust it into the soft flesh of his stomach. Instantly, warm liquid pours over my hand. I push the blade upwards and he drops without a sound. I'm numb to violence now. I have to survive.

I quicken my pace and half run, half slide down the trail. I run to the farthest of the three piles of wood and light it. A shot rings out and sand splatters in my face. I abandon my guns and run into the surf. The darkness of the water hides me from further volleys, but I hear shooting in the distance.

The dry driftwood catches fire and casts a glow on the beach. Smoke curls from the base of the pile and quickly climbs to the top. The sound of the surf muffles the sound of something in the distance. It's Lightning. He does an initial pass of the landing site. I see him tip his wings. He waits for a signal. Nothing. He flies off.

The gunfire dies down, then completely stops. When I see MG and Ernesto take cover behind one of the other stacks of driftwood, I come out of the water to join them. Ernesto takes me in his arms and kisses me. MG doesn't look surprised, but cuts it short, "The men have stopped shooting at us for now. Get ready to jump on the plane the next go round. We don't know if the rest of the guys are dead or just waiting for the plane to land before they attack."

Ernesto looks at MG then me, "I can't go with you. I'll stay on the beach and cover you while you take off." He goes up the hill with the rifle. I pick up the Glock.

Lightning circles again and MG signals with a flashlight to land. Lightning tips his wings and comes in fast. MG and I run to the plane as it touches down. Just as we open the door, gunfire starts again. MG jumps in and turns to help me as the plane moves down the beach. I gab her hand just as a large man grabs my leg and pulls me toward him. Before looking down at him, I kick him as hard as I can. "Humberto?" "*Señorita* Genny!"

"Humberto, please let me go." He clings to my foot. "*Papi, por favor.*" With that, he releases his grip and MG yanks me into the cabin.

Lightning can't get enough speed to take off because the beach is littered with debris from the tide going out. He throttles the plane to gain speed and hits something hard in the sand bouncing the plane higher in the air. He takes the opportunity to goose the controls and gains eight to ten feet of altitude when a bullet pierces the cockpit from the underbelly of the plane. Lightning slumps in his seat.

MG grabs Lightning and yells to me, "Take the stick." I reach from behind Lightning and pull hard on the controls to gain altitude. Once we ascend, the g-force pushes Lightning back into his seat and I lose my grip on the controls. MG pinches Lightning under one of his arms and he regains consciousness.

He pulls the controls toward his chest and levels us off. He reaches down and unhooks his seatbelt, "Take the controls, Genny." I climb over the back of the seat as he slides out the side. MG helps him to the back of plane where he lies on the floor next to the auxiliary fuel tank. MG puts pressure on his wound. I climb higher and bank the plane around to head north. A large explosion lights up the night sky and the villa is completely engulfed in flames. Victoria and Ernesto must have torched the place.

I follow the coastline past Tampico toward Matamoros. "How's he doing?" I yell over my shoulder to MG.

Lightning answers, "I'll live. This ain't nothing. Just fly."

"Okay, I like hugging the coast. When do I start turning west?"

"Stay the course until just south of Matamoros. We need to come under some high wires west of Reynosa. You got time."

MG kneels next to him. "The bleeding is slowed."

I concentrate on the coastline and slow my breath. The only sound is the engine. I wonder how Lightning has done this for so long. I feel like I've aged ten years in one night. It's been a long night and it's not over yet.

CHAPTER SIXTY-ONE

180 Degrees Off Course

The plane struggles to maintain a constant level because of the surface winds at the lower altitudes and we bounce up and down on air currents as I try to stay under radar detection. The night sky is black along the coast, but ground light gets denser and brighter the closer we get to Matamoros. I slowly change to a northwest direction, so we can cross under the high tension wires west of Reynosa. This has to be all visual flying. The border area is a hotbed of activities for small aircraft and since I have radio silence, I don't know where other planes might be. I keep just south of the urban areas to avoid any aircraft flying into the cities.

My hands cramp from the tight grip on the controls. I've never flown this long and rarely at night. "Lightning, what landmark am I looking for to turn north? I'm passing Reynosa now."

His voice is weaker than I expect, "There's a border crossing just west of town that's lit up like a Christmas tree. You need to get past that before you head north."

In the distance, I see the checkpoint and circle around using that point as center and keeping an equal distance flight range from it. "Roger, that."

"You shouldn't be picked up by radar anyway, but just in case, keep low."

"You two need to get in your seats and buckle up." MG helps

Lightning into his seat and straps him in before getting into the other rear seat.

I spot the two landmarks and descend slowly, flying toward the high tension tower. Its lights are flashing intermittently. I'll have to time going under it perfectly. I see the eye of the needle and fly towards it. Lights out, lights back on, lights out, I tip my wings slightly starboard. The water tower to the north acts as my focal point. I tighten the grip on the controls and say a prayer, "Sister Mary Clement Marie, work your miracle now."

"We made it." The relief washes over me. "We're twenty minutes from home." We're flying over the valley now. I start my landing sequence, everything seems routine.

We pass the mission in Sharyland and head toward the seven-mile line with the landing gear down. I circle the hangar and tip my wings.

Someone on the ground flashes a light three times on and off sending an "all clear" signal and I come down to land. The flaps are down and I've slowed to 80 knots as I touchdown, but the landing gear is soft and not holding the weight of the plane. Something in the landing gear must have broken when we were taking off from the beach in Tampico.

Lightning shouts, "Hold the nose up. Don't let it drop. Hold it up goddamn it!"

I pull on the controls with all my strength, but can't hold it up. The nose drops and the plane flips over quickly onto its back. I kill the engine. We're suddenly hanging upside down in our seats skidding down the landing strip. I scream as the sparks fly and the metal scrapes along the runway. We slide about fifty feet passed the hangar and come to rest just before the vacant field. My nose burns from electrical wires smoldering.

Lightning cusses, "What the fuck were you thinking on that landing?"

"The landing gear was soft. I couldn't hold the nose up." I scream back at him.

Dead Wrong Dan runs with a fire extinguisher in his hands and coats the plane with white foam. There's lots of smoke, but no fire. Stump runs to the plane and opens the door. MG is passed out and her arms are hanging in the air.

"Lightning's been shot," I call out to Stump, but he heads to MG first. Dan unbuckles her and she drops into Stump's arms and he carries her to the open field. Trip runs to MG's side. Dan turns his attention to Lightning. His belt is stuck, so Dan takes a knife from his pocket and cuts Lightning loose. Maggie runs up to the plane and helps carry Lightning to safety. Finally, Dan and Stump come back for me. My hands still grip the controls and the strap across my hips presses me tightly into the seat. My legs push against the floor. I'm too scared to let go. Dan unbuckles me and I fall into Stump's arms. I right myself quickly and we get out of the plane.

We gather on the grass at a makeshift triage and watch as light smoke from the plane dissipates. MG regains consciousness when Stump splashes water on her face.

Lightning moans when Maggie tries to attend to his wound and he gently pushes her hands away. I bend over to look at his wound. "We need to get you to a hospital."

"No!" Lightning answers. "How ya' goin' to explain a gunshot wound? This never happened."

I can't argue. My body shakes and tears roll down my face. I kneel down on the ground and sob uncontrollably. Trip comes over and puts her arm around my shoulder and cradles me while I rock back and forth. Maggie slaps her hands together loudly bringing everyone to attention. "We need to get Lightning home, so I can take care of him."

I stop crying long enough to respond. "No, take him to my house. It has air conditioning and is bigger. You can take care of him better there."

Stump brings his truck around and they load Lightning into the truck's bed. MG gets in the passenger seat and Maggie jumps in the bed with Lightning. Lightning sits up on his elbow, "Dan, get this cleaned up.

If anyone got the numbers off the plane while we were flying into the U.S., they can trace it back to me. Break everything down and make all this disappear. And kid, you did good. Any landing you can walk away from---"

"---is a perfect landing." I finish.

Dan runs behind the hangar and comes back driving a bobcat. Trip helps me up from the ground and we walk toward the plane. "It's best Lightning isn't here to see this anyway."

Trip and I roll the heavy hangar doors open, hook some chains to the plane and to the bobcat and Dan drags the plane into the hangar's first stall. The metal scraping on asphalt rings in my ears and makes me cringe.

Dan quickly dismounts the bobcat and we attach the chains hanging from the ceiling to hoist the plane up on pulleys. With a quick, almost magical move, he flips the plane upright on the chains. "I'm going to take this mother apart. Police the area. Pull in all of the debris from the landing and hose down the area."

"Before you touch anything, wash your hands." My hands look like they have red gloves on them. Trip holds the hose over my hands while I wash away most of the blood.

The soft light of dawn breaks the night sky as Trip and I finish and walk into the hangar. Dan has cut away the plane's ID number and a lot of the plane is dismantled. It's taken less than an hour for the crash gang to clear everything. They've planned for every contingency and earned their moniker.

"I've done as much as I can with this pile of junk." Dan loads the props in the bed of the truck. "Genny, hop in the back and we'll take you home, then dump the prop and ID somewhere and come over later after we get some sleep."

I nod my head to his commands and jump in the back of the truck. I'm too tired to feel my legs and almost fall when I arrive at my place. The house is dark. MG, Stump, Lightning and Maggie must be asleep. I collapse on the sofa, too numb to move.

CHAPTER SIXTY-TWO

The Door's Gone

The front door explodes with several border agents storming through simultaneously. As I jump to my feet, they surround me and hold my hands behind my back. One of them screams in my face, "Who else is here?"

Before I have time to answer, MG and Stump come around the corner with their hands up. Two men grab Stump and push him against the wall. MG yells for them to stop, but they push her into the opposite wall.

Curtis enters the front door while two men finish their search of the rest of the house and come back to the living room. "The house is clear." Maggie and Lightning must have split while I was sleeping. I show no emotion.

Standing in front of me, Curtis screams so forcefully that spittle hits my face. "I thought you were going to Mexico on a humanitarian mission. What the fuck have you done this time?" "I don't know what you're talking about." A cold calm comes over me. The girl in me is gone. I killed one man last night and maybe a second. I'll do whatever I need to do now to survive.

"Really? You don't know that someone flew from Mexico into the United States illegally and crashed at the landing strip less than two miles from here? You don't know that all sorts of international laws were broken and the Mexican government believes one of their most esteemed citizens was murdered last night? And they tracked a small plane on and off radar coming from Tampico to Reynosa last night?"

I know all of those things. I know more than that. He knows I know more, too.

"Do you have a search warrant?" I don't know what gives me the presence of mind to ask.

Curtis steps back from me like I've hit him. "I have just cause."

"No you don't. You have nothing to lead you here."

"No one is going to save your ass now. There's going to be a ton of bricks coming down on you. Look at yourself." He grabs me by the shoulders and moves me to the mirror hanging on the wall. My shirt is brown with dried blood and my face and hair have flecks of blood splatter throughout. "Tell me what happened."

Looking in the mirror hardens me more, "Where's your search warrant?"

"You fucking bitch." He drops his hands from my shoulders and signals his men to leave. "I'll be back."

MG hurries to my side. "We need to burn those clothes and you need to shower." I head to the bathroom, but she stops me. "You need to shower outside. All the blood will get sterilized by the sun."

Stump gathers all the pillows from the sofa and follows us out the door. "Where's a gas can?" I point to the garage. After I strip, he heads to the burn pile in the back yard.

MG stands over me with the hose while I shampoo my hair and soap my body. The cold water prickles my skin while I scrub harder and harder to wash away what I've done.

"Why can't I just say it was self-defense?" I ask her.

"You just spent the last six months watching the Mexican justice system work. What do you think they'll do to the person who just killed a huge source of income for them?"

After the third shampoo and cleansing, MG stops squirting me down with the hose and hands me a towel. "Stay out here and dry yourself in the sun. I'll go inside and get some clothes."

My body is shivering even in the heat of the sun. My long wet hair dries in ringlets shrinking up my back.

MG comes back with my clothes and shoes. "Thankfully, we ran out of weed a couple of days ago, so there's nothing here."

I pull on my pants and shirt. "Where'd Lightning and Maggie go?" I ask.

"For now, it's best you don't know. Maggie says Lightning's wound isn't too deep. The bullet didn't hit any organs, just deep in the muscle. She got the bullet out last night and took Lightning someplace to heal." She looks around the yard, then back at me, her eyes sad. "It's weird without Lucero and Rocky here."

"Empty." I shake my head to get the last image out of my head. "They saved my life. Raul was going to kill me and Rocky when Lucero lunged at him. I still can't believe all of this shit happened."

MG hugs me, "You gotta remember what Lightning said, this never happened. Forget it."

"Stay off the phone in case they bug it," Stump warns, grabbing Jeffrey's toolbox from behind the house. "Get your story straight. Both of you," he adds. "If you didn't fly here, how'd you get back from Mexico and when?"

"My car's still down there. What do I say?"

"Whatever you say, I need to be your alibi." MG starts. "So we need to have the same story." She picks up the towel and hangs it on the clothesline. "Maggie and Lightning took our truck, so let's walk to the hangar and see if Dan and Trip are there. It'll give us time to practice our story and clear our heads."

"I'll stay and fix the front door," Stump says.

"I think the Shadow Man took over when I was in the villa." I confess to MG as we walk. "It wasn't me. I was hiding behind the cabinets in the kitchen, ready to give up. I could feel something cold touch my face, telling me to let go. I was ready to let Raul kill me. Then I felt something surround me, pushing the cold away, pushing me to kill Raul."

"I've tried to control the Shadow Man," MG says and then falls silent for a long time. "I don't think anyone can. You can't put the genie back in the bottle. He's your protector and pulls everyone and everything to do his bidding. Lucero and Rocky were under his control too... especially Lucero."

"It was scary and wonderful at the same time. I was out of my body, kinda floating from above. I could see everything happening. I knew Raul was evil and had to be destroyed. It was so clear. I knew what needed to be done."

"You need to keep that same clarity now. We need to come up with a story to keep the border patrol and police away from us and let things cool down."

We trade ideas with each other until a plausible story emerges. If we both tell the authorities the same thing, I might be able to skirt murder charges and extradition to Mexico. If we had been caught in Mexico, we would be in the same hellhole Jeffrey was in.

Thank God we're on this side of the border.

CHAPTER SIXTY-THREE

Moved

Huge padlocks dangle from chains on the hangar doors and a sign from the Border Patrol DO NOT ENTER. "These fuckers move fast, that's for sure."

MG and I turn around to walk back to my house when Dan and Trip pull up beside us in their truck. "Hop in the back," Trip calls from the open window. "Is Stump still at your place?"

We drive back to my house and Dan honks the horn. Stump runs out and jumps in the truck bed. We bump along some back roads through neglected orange groves with tall grass to a remote area near Citrus City, northwest of Mission. A white block house sits in a clearing, hidden in the middle of an orange grove. We park behind Stump's blue F-100 pickup next to the front door.

I turn to MG. "Whose place is this?"

"This is our new house."

"Jesus, how did you find it? We're in the middle of nowhere."

"Stump and I sold our old place and bought this one while you were in Mexico. Dan and Trip have a new place in Mission."

"What about Lightning and Maggie?"

"Them too."

"Wow. Talk about cleaning house. I was only in Mexico a little over two months."

"Yeah. The Border Patrol is really going to be pissed off when they find out the hangar got sold too."

It takes a while for all of this to sink in. MG takes me by the hand and pulls me through a guided visit of her new place. Saltillo tile is throughout the downstairs and the upstairs is bare wood with partially finished rooms. "The bathroom needs to be finished and we're putting flooring down, but it's livable." Their bedroom has a balcony and a periscope. I laugh, but then think it's probably a good idea to be able to see over the trees.

After the grand tour of the house, the five of us settle in the living room to discuss the events of the last two months. No one pulls out a joint. No one offers a beer. This feels like a staff meeting, not a friendly get-together. MG begins, "It's time to lay low for a while."

Stump continues, "No drugs. No imports. Not even a parking ticket. Keep our noses clean. It was time to stop this import shit anyway." Everyone nods their heads, even me.

Trip moves closer to me on the sofa and puts her arm around my shoulder. "We know you went through hell. We'll protect you as much as possible."

Tears roll down my face. "This has been a fucking nightmare and I can't wake up. What do I do next?"

"Get an attorney. We already spoke to this guy." Dan hands me a business card. "He's cool. He ain't cheap, but he knows his shit."

"We have some cash from the sale of the hangar to help you," Stump offers. "Sell your house. You don't want the law to seize it."

"Can they do that?"

"Honey, they'll take everything." MG says, looking straight into my eyes and my heart.

"Oh, God. I'm fucked."

"Since they came straight to your house, they suspect you *know* things," MG continues. "But they don't know who killed Raul and they don't have proof you're even involved. The fire wiped out most, if not all, the evidence in the house."

"They don't know who flew the plane," Trip cuts in. "Stump wiped it down for fingerprints and cleaned up the blood. That's the cleanest piece of scrap metal they'll ever check. They can't prove anything."

"What do I say to the attorney?"

"As little as possible." MG hands me a tissue. "He'll ask the questions he thinks the Border Patrol will ask. Keep your answers short. No one needs to know *everything*. Just stay cool. You did real good when they busted into the house. Better than I thought you would." "I don't think they'll extradite you to Mexico. I doubt if your border patrol officer, Curtis, thinks you killed someone, but he thinks you *know* who did."

"How did all of you move so quickly?"

"We've had contingency plans for years." Stump stands and looks out the window. "Once Jeffrey got busted, we put the plans into action. We weren't optimistic for Jeffrey. We just thought we would reshuffle the deck. We never thought it would end so…" He searches for a word. "…spectacularly."

"What about my birds? When I sell my house, I won't have a place to keep my birds." My eyes start tearing and I bite my lower lip to stop. I have no contingency plan. I have nothing. "Can you help me find good homes for them? I don't want to sell them. It wouldn't be right. Rocky gave his life for me. I've got to pay that back somehow."

Trip hugs me again. "Dan and I'll take some of them and you can visit them anytime." "Us too," MG and Stump say in unison.

"Where's Lightning and Maggie?" I finally ask.

"They split for their new place in Taos. Maggie needs to be in the mountains. She says she found a sacred place. We'll go up there and visit them once the heat dies down here." MG sighs. "Maggie can perform a healing ceremony for us."

"I have some errands to run so let me run you back to your place." MG stands to stretch.

"Can we stop at a pay phone and call Ernesto's office?" I ask. I know I shouldn't use my home phone, but I want to call him to see if he's okay.

"I need to stop for gas," MG says. "We can call from the convenience store."

We drive through the orange groves to the nearest store and MG places the call to Ernesto's law office. The conversation is stilted and she turns to me after she hangs up the phone. "Julio sounded guarded. Ernesto is on vacation right now. Julio doesn't know when he'll be back."

"Is he okay? Did he go to a doctor? What exactly did Julio say?"

"He said he went on vacation with his friend Victor. They drove in his jeep to San Luis."

"Okay, that means he's with Victoria and they're with her family. It also means he got his jeep out of there so he can't be implicated in Raul's death by the federales."

"At least that's what you hope it means." MG walks over to gas up her truck. "Ernesto was shot, but couldn't go to the hospital, so he probably went to a private doctor. That's not difficult in Mexico. This tells us two things: one, he got away safely and two, he's okay physically."

"It also says he's probably in danger from the federales."

MG holds up her hand to stop me. "Julio said he'll speak with him this evening and have him call you tomorrow at your place. You need to understand you can't ask him direct questions or use his name when speaking to him. You're in trouble with the law on both sides of the border. Stay cool and lay low. Call the attorney then get in contact with a realtor to sell your house."

"What should I do about my car?"

"Your car is long gone. Don't count on ever seeing it again. I think there's an old clunker we can lend you until you sell your house and get some cash."

MG hugs me when we get to my house. "You're a true warrior now, Genny. Stronger than you know. Take this time to meditate and heal. This mess isn't over.

As I walk into the house, a silence envelops me like a bell jar. Rocky doesn't whistle. Lucero doesn't greet me with a wagging tail. I've lost everything. I hear an unearthly wail. I realize it's coming from me. I can't stop.

CHAPTER SIXTY-FOUR
Crackers

MG kneels next to me and shakes me. "Honey get up. You can't keep doing this."

I try to open my eyes, but they're puffy from crying and glued shut. I've been balled up in the corner for days. MG offers her hand to help me stand. My knees are weak and unsteady as I straighten to my full height. "What day is it?"

"It's Thursday. I've been trying to call you for three days and no answer." She moves around the room and closes the windows and flips on the AC. The cool air blasts out of the window unit and instantly feels refreshing. It's the beginning of May and already hot in the valley.

"I unplugged the phone. If I need to call Ernesto, I go to the pay phone at the gas station. Now that my job ended, the days blend together."

"You look like shit. Come on, I'll make you some breakfast."

"I'm not hungry. Just give me some crackers."

"You can't exist like this. It's been three weeks and you need to turn you attention to your future." MG steers me to the sofa and hands me toast and tea.

"I keep waiting for the Border Patrol to show up again." I dunk the toast into the tea and try to eat it. It gags me. "Why haven't they?"

"I'm sure they're waiting for information from Mexico." MG leans forward, casually looks out the window, and scopes the area. "What's Ernesto say is happening down there?"

"He says the local federales are covering their own asses after the minister found truckloads of artifacts at Raul's warehouse. The President of Mexico says they are national treasures and wants a full investigation. But Ernesto thinks that's just for the public's eye. Everyone wants this swept under the rug."

"What's your attorney here say?"

"He says to just sit tight. He hasn't heard anything from anybody yet." I put my tea down on the table next to the sofa and stretch my arms.

"I got an offer on my house yesterday."

"That was quick. Did you get a good price?"

"The real estate agent said if I wanted a quick sale, I would have to put it on the market under value by five-thousand dollars. The buyer still offered me less. I had to take it. Thankfully, it's a cash offer. I close in two weeks." I look around the room. "They got most of the furniture too."

"It's time to take a road trip." MG stands and pulls me to my feet. "We can go see Maggie and Lightning. Stump can stay here with the birds. I'll see if Trip wants to go too. Pack your stuff and we'll leave this evening. It's easier to drive at night in this heat."

Since Dan and Stump can't work on planes at the hangar, they've engaged their skills on cars and trucks. Trip and MG pick me up in an old station wagon that the boys just finished refurbishing. I can see my reflection in the highly buffed and varnished wood side panels as I get in. "Nice ride, ladies. Let's get out of this place." The sun begins to set as we drive north.

The farther we drive, the lighter my shoulders feel. We take turns driving and sleeping. The rear seat folds down to a long bed and I get the best sleep I've had in weeks. No nightmares, no running away from Raul, no guns shooting, no feathers flying, just peace.

With three women, the fifteen hour trip stretches to almost two days and we pull into Taos as the sun is rising over the mountains. The road to Lightning and Maggie's place is full of ruts and switchbacks leading up the side of the mountain. The road ends when we reach a level area with a view of the entire valley below. A small adobe sits off to the right with a thin line of blue-grey smoke drifting from a stovepipe on the snow-covered roof. The air is crisp and clear.

Trip beeps the horn three quick times. A large furry coat with a black knitted cap runs out of the front door to greet us. Maggie's long salt and pepper hair waves in the wind as we hurriedly follow her into the house to get out of the cold mountain air. She hangs her heavy fur coat on a wall decorated with the bones of dead animals.

Lightning sits in a chair warming himself in front of a crackling fire. He smiles when he sees all of us, but doesn't get up. "My stomach still isn't healed. Maggie says I have to stay in one place or her potions won't work right."

"I'm so glad you're doing better." I reach over and touch his shoulder gently. "I've been really worried."

Maggie heads to the kitchen, speaking over her shoulder, "I've got hot coffee, bacon, eggs, grits and toast. Is everyone ready?"

MG and Trip follow her into the kitchen and I sit next to Lightning. We stare into the fire while the others prepare the food.

Lightning scratches his beard and looks at me, "Have you heard from Jeffrey?"

"No. My attorney contacted his parents and they said he's in Washington or Oregon or someplace northwest. I guess in the agreement they made to get him out of Mexico, they had to promise he'd never come back so his parents moved him as far away as possible."

"He got in over his head, couldn't see his way out," he talks more to the fire than to me.

"I'm so sorry you got hurt. I never meant for it to get so crazy."

Lightning smiles, "Kid, that wasn't nothin'. You should'a seen some of the shit we did in 'Nam. It's over now. We're done. Maggie's happier here in the mountains."

"You and MG saved my life. I'll never forget all you've done for me."

"You saved your own life. I just brought the plane to get you out."

"I still can't believe what I did." My hands shake and turn ice cold.

"We all do what we have to do to stay alive," he says. "Then we move on."

"I don't know if I can forget what happened." I force the next words out of my mouth, but they come out in a whisper. "I *killed* a man. I can still see his face. What's worse… my face is the last thing he saw before he died. I sent him to hell."

"You never forget it. That's the purpose of the Shadow Man. He gets you through the danger and absorbs the rest of the energy. Then it doesn't hold any power over you. It'll eat you up, if you don't give it to him. Maggie wants to do a cleansing ceremony or some sort of shit with you and the girls. She has a special place in the mountains picked out."

"I'm more than ready. I can't stop dreaming of Raul. I'm always running in my dream and I wake up exhausted."

MG calls out, "Food's ready. Come and get it."

Maggie brings a plate to Lightning and the rest of us sit at a large gathering table with wooden benches on either side. The idle prattle is calming. My old life fades away and a new one needs to be imagined. I'm with my clan.

CHAPTER SIXTY-FIVE

No Choices Left

The sound of pots and pans clanging in the kitchen breaks the silence of the night. Lightning stokes the fire as the faint light of dawn illuminates the mountainous terrain through the wall of windows.

The table is set with stacks of pancakes and bacon. Before I can decline the food, Maggie hands me a drink. "I've prepared this especially for you. You'll need this to give you strength."

Knowing I can't refuse Maggie's elixirs, I tentatively take a sip of the green sludge and am surprised how refreshing and delicious it is. "It tastes better than it looks." A self-congratulatory look crosses her face. "After that smelly salve you rubbed all over my body last night, I was afraid of anything you might give me to drink."

Trip hands me a pancake, "You'll need to eat something solid before we hike."

Before I can protest, MG says, "Don't put syrup on it, it will be like a dry piece of toast."

Satisfied that I'm eating, Maggie leaves the table and returns with a pile of clothes and drops them on the floor. "I went to Goodwill and bought lots of ski outfits. Find something that fits."

None of us has anything warmer than jeans, so we approach the multi-colored heap like vultures picking at a carcass. I emerge wearing a pink jumpsuit, green gloves, purple hat and a red scarf. Trip and MG fair marginally better. Dressed in black, Maggie is the only one who has a monochromatic color scheme to her ensemble. "You won't sneak up on anyone today for sure." Lightning stifles a laugh while he sits by the fire. "They'll see you coming a mile away."

Maggie addresses the troop before we head out the door, "We're at an elevation of ten-thousand feet. I've chosen a spot around eight-thousand feet so we shouldn't have problems with altitude sickness. We need to hydrate a lot. I've got thermoses for all you, and a special one for you," She says, handing it to me. I only hope I can handle the next concoction she has for me today. So far, the salves and drinks have been pretty soothing.

The cold air is invigorating as we traverse the serpentine road to a lower level. I can see why Lightning and Maggie chose this place; its strategic location allows views of the entire valley below. There are only a few other houses on the mountain. "Maggie, what are your neighbors like?"

"Most of the people who own the houses up here only come during the summers. The winters can get pretty rough. Lightning wishes we could own the whole mountain, but he's content to have it to himself now. They'll start coming in late May, early June."

We work our way down to a clearing on the south side of the road and follow a path to an old mining site. We slow long enough to admire the small rail line leading from a tunnel in the side of the mountain. Maggie stops at the entrance and picks up a metal pot and spoon and clangs them together. We can hear a few varmints scurry deeper into the shaft before we enter.

It takes a few minutes to adjust to the darkness. Maggie has set up a small fire pit with seats around it. MG takes a lighter from her pocket and lights the kindling. Trip picks up a few old boards and adds them to the fire. A lazy wand of smoke travels up into the recesses of the tunnel and ventilates through crevices in the ceiling.

Maggie claps her hands hard one time to bring us all to attention. "We need to state our intentions before we begin the ceremony."

"Sit down, Genny." MG looks at me with a concerned eye. "There's something you need to know before we do the ceremony."

My knees are suddenly weak and I hit the small wooden crate with a thud. "Am I getting kicked out of the group? I know I've fucked up, but I'm really trying hard."

"Do you think we would drive you all the way up here to throw you out of the group?" Trip asks. "We love you. You will always be welcome with us."

"Then what's up?" I breathe a little easier. "What do I need to know?"

Maggie looks at MG and Trip before she speaks. "You're pregnant."

The vacuum that has been sucking everything from my life suddenly stops. I can't move. Instantly, I know they're right. I thought I wasn't feeling well because of all the stress. "Oh, no. I can't believe this is happening *now*." *The universe sure knows how to hit you upside the head. My mother is going to have a fit.*

My mind bounces quickly to Ernesto and our lovemaking and a shiver of pleasure runs through me. I went back to Mexico for Ernesto, not Jeffrey. *Now what do I do Sister Mary Clément Marie?*

Trip squats beside me, "You'll be okay. We're here for you no matter what you decide."

"I won't give the baby up."

MG squats down on my other side. "We know that, honey. We just mean that we'll help raise the baby if you need us. We know it will be hard, but you have time to figure all of this out. You need to use the time during the ceremony to bring energy to your thoughts."

The fire burns brighter as Maggie puts more wood to it. "Girls, let's get started. Focus our energies on Genny and the baby. Here are some drinks for all of you. This is yours." She hands me a small vial.

"Should I be doing drugs while I'm pregnant?" I ask.

"This contains vitamins and herbs to help with your morning sickness. That's what the salve was last night. MG, Trip and I will be doing a mild cannabis tea. Anywhere your mind can go with drugs, it can go without them. No drugs for you for nine months."

Maggie claps her hands again and everyone takes their seats. I try to focus my bouncing thoughts. I listen to Maggie chant and close my eyes. I can hear my own heartbeat. I wonder about the baby forming in me. I've messed up so many things.

I *have* to fly straight now. All the way home, I dream of my new baby and try to imagine a new life.

CHAPTER SIXTY-SIX

Knock, Knock

I've been rehearsing what I'll say to Ernesto when he gets here. The thought of telling him about the baby thrills me. Although the girls assure me I'll have a boy, I painted the bedroom of my new apartment a neutral yellow. The gang helped me move everything from my house. The girls bought a bassinet and a mobile which hangs from the ceiling of the room the baby and I will share.

The knock on the door starts my heart pumping. My hands are moist as I turn the knob to welcome the father of my baby. My smile fades quickly when I see Curtis on the other side of the door. He doesn't have his border patrol uniform on, just jeans and a T-shirt. No one else is with him, so this isn't an official call. I hold the door slightly closed.

"You must think you're so clever." He looks me up and down carefully. "You and all your friends moved things around like pieces on a chess board, but I'll find out what happened."

I'd been waiting weeks for him to find me. My attorney, James Davis, notified everyone I moved to McAllen, but I was hoping they would forget about me. I stand tall and face him squarely. I put one hand in front of my belly to shield my baby from negative energy like Maggie says to do.

"I really don't know what you're talking about. I had to move because I no longer had a front door."

"Don't be such a wise ass. It's not going to play well in court when I get you there. Most people around here don't like smugglers."

I know he's trying to bait me. I try to shut the door, but he sticks his foot in the doorway to stop it. With one hand, he pushes the door open wider and grabs my arm with the other. "You owe me. I didn't bust you when I had the opportunity. Tell me what you've done."

"You need to go now."

"There's all kinds of heat on both sides of the border trying to find out what happened and you're the key." He grabs both my arms now and his fingers dig deep into my flesh when I try to pull away.

"I don't know what you're talking about. Talk to my attorney." He shakes me and raises his right hand to hit me when a hand reaches from around the corner, grabs his arm and swings him away from me. I pull away from his grasp and the force knocks me to the ground.

When I look up, Curtis is on the ground with Ernesto on top of him throwing punches that connect solidly with Curtis's face. As I scramble to my feet, other people in the apartment complex rush to break the two men apart. Someone asks if they should call the police. Both Ernesto and Curtis stand quickly to defuse the tension.

"It was just a misunderstanding," Curtis breaks the silence. "I'm leaving now." He looks over his shoulder to watch me as he walks toward the parking lot. I stand stiff with my back against the wall until he drives away.

"Are you okay? Who is he?" Ernesto dusts the dirt from his clothes and comes closer to me.

I let Ernesto into my apartment before I explain. "He's a border patrol agent looking into the plane crash. He's trying to put me in jail."

Ernesto pulls me into his arms and hugs me tight. Tears roll down my face. I wanted this to be a happy moment and it's turning into another fiasco.

"He was going to hit you." Ernesto pulls away from me a little and looks into my eyes. "That shows more than him doing his job. He's angry with you."

"My attorney thinks Curtis may get demoted or lose his job with this case." We sit on the sofa. "He didn't follow procedure and now they can't find any evidence. My friends moved and now Curtis can't get the proof he needs to arrest them. He thinks I'm the link between all of them, so he's trying to force me to tell what happened."

"A similar kind of thing is happening in Mexico." Ernesto reaches over and touches my hand. "Now that Raul is dead, the cockroaches have scattered and his men are all hiding."

"Have they contacted you?"

"No. It's a little more complicated. For the public eye, the President of Mexico has to say he's trying to stop the grave robbing, but the farmers who find the treasures get nothing from the government when they turn them in."

"Is your organization trying to help?"

"Raul paid the farmers a lot of money, more than we can afford to pay. They need to feed their families, but it's ruining Mexico's history. We're trying to get organizations *and* the government to work together, but a lot of officials were being paid off by Raul, so it's not easy."

"I'm sorry I brought all of this trouble to you."

"Obviously, Raul was doing this before you came to Mexico." Ernesto shakes his head. "If anything, we owe you thanks for stopping him."

"Are you in trouble with the police in Mexico? Do they suspect your involvement with Raul's death?"

"No. Most people think one of his gang must have killed him over territorial disputes. Others gossip a different story. Since the killing was so close to Jeffrey's release, they say the American's gang came for revenge. A nice romantic story has been repeated over and over. Soon they will sing a song about it."

Both of us smile at the joke, but we both know how close we came to dying that night. A chill goes up my spine and I try to turn the conversation.

"What happened to Victoria?"

"Once you flew off, the remaining men went back to their car down the beach and drove away. I found Victoria and we set the house on fire and then went directly to San Luis. Since I took a bullet in my shoulder, she drove my jeep to her cousin's, who's a doctor. He just stitched me up since the bullet went through me. No permanent damage."

"I'm glad you're okay." I gently touch his shoulder. "How did Socorro and Juanita take the news about their father dying?"

Ernesto bows his head a little and won't look me directly in the eyes. "They both hated him, Socorro more than Juanita. They have been changed by the experience." Ernesto looks up into my eyes and says,

"Socorro wants to help me in my fight to preserve our Mexican heritage. She's working with the museum to recover artifacts."

There's something odd in the way he says this, like he's trying to justify her to me. He knows she and Jeffrey were going to run off together. I don't understand why she's suddenly up for sainthood. "So, is she still looking for another American to marry, so she can live in the United States?"

Ernesto stands immediately at my words. "He tricked her. She was an innocent young girl and he seduced her. It was not her fault."

I stand to face him, "Jeffrey's not the type of man to be so forward. She had to have made the first move. I think she seduced *him*."

"Of course you would say that. You could not believe your man would betray you. How long did it take for you to figure it out?"

"I've gotten smarter in the last few months. Socorro is playing you now. Has she seduced you yet, or is she playing sweet and innocent for a while?" I'm angry and scared at the same time. Hormones course through my body; I'm shaking with emotional overload. I run to the bathroom and fall on the floor crying.

My body stops heaving after a few moments and Ernesto comes in and sits on the edge of the tub. He pulls my hair away from my face and looks down at me as I sit on the floor. "I'm sorry, Genny. I didn't mean for you to find out this way. Socorro and I have feelings for each other and we want to see each other. I wanted to come here first, so you and I could talk."

"Go in the other room." I stop crying. "I want to wash my face and compose myself."

He gets up and walks out of the bathroom. I close the door behind him. *Now what? Do I even tell him I'm pregnant?* I take my time washing my face and brushing my teeth. I at least want to look good when I say good-bye.

I walk back into the living room, but he's not there. He must have left. I sit on the sofa numb to the entire events of the day. I hear soft footsteps coming from the bedroom. Ernesto stands in front of me with a thin smile on his face. "Why didn't you tell me on the phone?"

"I wanted to see your face."

He reaches down and takes my hands, pulls me into his arms and softly kisses me.

"What about Socorro?"

"Ah, *mi corazón,* this is bigger than Socorro. I will have to let her go." Passion washes over me as he takes my hand and leads me into the bedroom and onto the bed. He slowly unbuttons my blouse and takes it off. He kisses my shoulders and gently touches my breasts. They are swollen and tender and respond immediately to his touch.

He kisses my stomach and looks up to meet my eyes. I'm aching for him in me, but he's slow with his touches. He lifts my skirt to remove my panties and leaves his hand between my thighs and lightly strokes them. I pull him to me, so we can kiss. The kisses are more urgent and deeper. I unbutton his shirt and feel his smooth skin on my fingertips. I touch the bulge in his pants and we both moan in anticipation. The excitement is almost too much to control. Our breathing is fast and hot and our bodies move with pure passion.

We lie quietly in each other's arms and Ernesto's breath slows to a sweet rhythm of peace. I feel his chest rise gently and bring that moment into me. *Time narrows to small drops. It clicks by second by second, slowing the world around me. My third eye opens between the jagged moments and I see Socorro calypso dancing, her long dress raises with her spirals as she moves around the room. She laughs and moves gracefully as she leaps into the air, again and again. At first, she's alone, but then a man joins her. I can't see his face, but I know who it is.*

CHAPTER SIXTY-SEVEN

Big News, Mom

"Mom?"

"Where have you been?" She asks, her voice higher pitched than usual. "I've been worried sick. I've been trying to get ahold of you for weeks. Your phone's disconnected and the mail came back saying 'moved'. What's going on?"

"I moved to McAllen and got married." I try to sound upbeat.

There's silence on the other end of the phone for a few moments and then, "Why couldn't you and Jeffrey have come here to get married?"

"My husband's name is Ernesto Soto."

There's a gasp on the other end. "What on earth have you done now? We can get it annulled. You don't have to live with this kind of mistake."

"I'm pregnant."

"Dear God." She covers the receiver, so I don't hear what she's saying to my stepfather. When she comes back on the line, she's crying. "You need to come home, Genny. We'll help you with the baby. Just come home."

Something deep inside of me wants to go home and let someone else take care of me and my mistakes, but I resist. "He's an attorney in Mexico. He's very smart and I think we can be happy together."

"What are you doing for money?"

"I started substitute teaching. Right now I'm teaching English to the migrant workers. There might be a permanent position for me next year." I don't tell her I can't go back to my old teaching position because Curtis visited my principal. I don't know exactly what he said, but since I worked as a contractor with the migrant organization, the school district wouldn't renew my contract.

This seems to mollify her and she tempers her response. "We have big news too. We're selling our house and moving to Florida to retire. I hear there are a lot of migrants there, as well. Maybe you could get a job in Florida?"

"That's a possibility. You never know where life takes you." I've shocked her enough for one day. I don't want to tell her that the Border Patrol is after me and I might have the Mexican mafia after me once they reorganize. We end the call with love and kisses and I'm relieved one giant thing is checked off my to do list.

The next thing on the list is not as daunting, but just as critical; I need to find a doctor who goes beyond Maggie's prenatal care giving. By my calculations, I'm six weeks pregnant.

MG and Trip are coming with me to interview some doctors. The knock on the door coincides with their scheduled arrival, but I check the peephole just in case Curtis wants to harass me again. The girls are standing outside dressed professionally, ready to do battle. I open the door and get hugs immediately. I'm so glad these women are on my side.

MG squeezes my arm, "So, did you tell your mom you're married?"

"I did. I didn't tell her all of the details. I kept it short."

Trip hands me an envelope. "I took some pictures of the wedding these are your copies. You can send your mom a set if you want."

I take the envelope and look through them quickly. MG and Trip both were maids of honor since I couldn't pick one over the other. Stump and Dan mostly stayed out of camera range. Ernesto looked handsome standing tall next to me.

"I'm glad Maggie and Lightning could come. We'll go see them again soon."

"Yes, she expects you to go there to have the baby." MG says, herding us toward the door. "She wants you to have a mountain man!"

CHAPTER SIXTY-EIGHT

Changes

Everything is swollen. My fingers and toes look like small sausages with the skin stretched to the max. I'm at the beginning of my second trimester and I'm already huge. Everyone wants to touch my growing belly, especially the migrant kids I'm teaching. My personal space has expanded to a two-foot radius, but people keep invading it. This is going to be a long nine months.

MG and Trip are coming over to help refinish some old baby furniture. I hear a light knock at the door and open it to see Trip without MG. "What's up? Where's MG?"

"She'll be here later. You're probably better off with just me to help with this stuff anyway. She's not the best painter."

It's too hot to work outside, so I have a tarp on the floor in the living room to contain the mess. We sit on the floor and put on masks. I hand Trip the sandpaper and she works a small area on the wooden chest of drawers.

"I got the pictures developed of your reception last month. I got you a set. I'm glad your mom convinced you to have one." She reaches into her purse and pulls out a large stack of photos and shuffles through them.

"Yeah, my mom was disappointed she wasn't there for the wedding, so this pacified her." I reach for the photos from Trip. "It helped that she and my stepfather paid for the party. I'm scared to spend any money right now. I still have most of the money from selling my house, but the attorney costs a lot."

"We told you we'd help." Trip looks up from her sanding. "The money from selling the airport was pretty good."

"I know, but I need to get through this myself."

She hands me one of the pictures. "You look a lot like your mom." I smile at the two of us posing for the camera.

"Has Ernesto been back since the reception?"

"No, they found several of Raul's warehouses full of antiquities and he's cataloging all of them before they go to the museums. Now that Raul is dead, all of the small-time smugglers are trying to take over the trade."

"He's so handsome. What did your mom think of him?"

I try not to roll my eyes, "She's happy he made an honest woman out of me. She didn't want to have to explain to her bridge club she had an illegitimate grandchild. He's an attorney and Catholic, so she has some bragging rights." We both laugh.

"You two make a cute couple. Your children will be smart and good looking. She can't complain about that."

"Mom likes Ernesto, but she's worried there's too big a culture difference between us. I need to be prepared to make some changes in my expectations from a marriage."

"There are always compromises. You and Ernesto can work around your differences."

"I'm trying, but Ernesto has some strange ideas about sex some times. It's hard to believe some of the things that bother him."

"Like what?"

"He thinks he should be the one to initiate sex. I should wait patiently until he's ready. With all of these hormones rushing through my body, I'm ready to jump him when he comes through the door."

She laughs loudly. "Maybe you should give him a little chance to get his shoes off next time."

"If there is a next time. I thought once I was married, these things would get easier, not harder. Now he's worried he's going to hurt the baby when we have sex. "

"Tell him that unless he's hung like a horse, there shouldn't be a problem."

"It didn't help when Lightning told him he could put a dent in the baby's forehead if he wasn't careful."

She laughs so hard she rolls on the floor. "Oh, no. I didn't hear him say that. What did Ernesto say?"

"Well, Lightning kept calling him Ernie all night, which just made Ernesto mad. I could tell Lightning was pushing his buttons, but when he said the baby was going to have a dent, Ernesto went white and walked away."

"I'm sure Lightning didn't mean anything by it. He rags on Dan and Stump all the time."

"Ernesto is sensitive about all of my friends. He was Jeffrey's attorney, so he knows a lot about Jeffrey's import business. He thinks all of my friends are cut from the same cloth."

"He's not too far off the mark, but he's going to have to get over it for the baby's sake. Just concentrate on the baby and you for a while.

Everything else will come together in time."

MG walks through the door without knocking, carrying a six pack of beer and some iced tea. "I brought drinks to help with the chores. Guess which is yours?"

This is going to be the longest nine months of my life.

CHAPTER SIXTY-NINE

The Sin Of Omission

"I didn't hear you come in. You weren't supposed to get here until the weekend." I walk to the kitchen to pour myself a cup of coffee. The sofa has a folded blanket and pillow on it. Ernesto must have slept there instead of coming to my bed.

"You have a big problem." He pours a cup coffee and sits next to me at the small kitchen table. "Humberto has been arrested."

"What can the federales do to me?"

"He wasn't arrested by the federales. He was arrested by the U. S. Border Patrol. He was trying to smuggle the contents of an entire tomb from Guanajuato into the country."

"Oh no. I feel bad for Humberto but, how is this my problem?"

"Your friend Curtis was one of the arresting agents."

"First, he's not my friend. This still doesn't lead to me."

"Curtis apparently studied Jeffrey's file extensively and figured out Humberto was from the same area where Jeffrey was arrested. He put two and two together and asked Humberto if he knew you."

"Oh, shit." I gasp. "What did Humberto say?"

"He reacted to your name, but said he didn't know you. Curtis is issuing a warrant for your arrest. He thinks he can squeeze Humberto to implicate you."

"How do you know all of this?" My hands shake as I bring the coffee mug up to my lips.

"Julio has been hired to defend Humberto. He's trying to get him extradited back to Mexico." He straightens his body and sits higher in his chair. "We need to meet with your attorney here to mitigate any damage from this situation. I don't want my baby born in jail."

"Humberto was at the beach that night. He was dragging me off the plane. I begged him to let me go and he did. Maybe he'll protect me again." I pick up a napkin from the table and wipe the tears from my eyes. Ernesto makes no effort to comfort me, he just stares into space.

"What can Humberto say about you?" He says, his voice strangely flat. "What did you do?"

This is the question I'd hoped would never be asked. Do I tell him everything?

"Humberto helped me bring my birds into the United States. He got them drunk, so they would be quiet and I smuggled them across the border."

He looks relieved at my answer, but I continue, "He also had a trailer full of other things we crossed too. At the time, I didn't know what they were. But once he unloaded them, I realized they were relics. They were better than the ones you showed me at the museum."

"You lied to me." Ernesto closes his eyes and exhales. When he opens his eyes, he looks at me with contempt. "All this time you lied to me."

"I didn't knowingly smuggle the artifacts. You knew about the birds. That's all I'm guilty of doing."

"Your guilt is of omission. I would never have made love to you if I had known."

"You were defending Jeffrey for smuggling. You knew Raul was trying to kill Jeffrey and me. What did you think? You had to suspect there was more to the story. You were complicit in all of this mess, too."

"Yes. And now we're married. I could have married a virgin and because of you and Jeffrey that is impossible now."

"A virgin?" The image of Socorro dancing flashes through my head. "Socorro stole Jeffrey away from me."

"*He* seduced *her*."

"She was writing letters to me every other week, pretending to be my friend while she was fucking my boyfriend. Just who do you think seduced whom? She traded her virginity for a ticket to the United States. She also had to know what her father was doing with the relics. You want to blame me for all of this mess. How about blaming her? Have you slept with her yet?"

"No, she says she's not ready to give herself to me, yet"

"Oh, so she's still playing sweet and innocent."

"At least she takes her time to bed someone. Not like you. You jumped into bed like some whore in heat."

I gasp at his ruthlessness and cruelty. "I was all alone in Mexico and frightened. I took comfort in your arms. I thought you could see that. You pursued me for months, even when you were taking money from me to defend my boyfriend. You certainly had no conscience about doing that." *The gloves are off. This is going to be a street brawl.*

His face is red and contorted with anger. It takes several moments before he composes himself. "All of us will share the blame, even Socorro. I want to stop arguing."

"No. You don't get to be the one who ends this. You say I have the sin of omission. Yes, I do. But, I think you haven't told the entire story either. I've been thinking long and hard about the money. My money wasn't enough to get Jeffrey out, was it?"

"No."

"You were taking money from Jeffrey's parents too, weren't you?"

"Julio was. I didn't know about it until after Jeffrey was released to them."

"How much did you and Julio make off them?

"We each made fifty thousand dollars."

"Wow. And you have the audacity to point out my sin of omission. Were you ever going to tell me that news?" I'm spitting my words at him.

He looks at me as if I were a stranger. "I don't know how I even got to this place."

"Don't worry, Ernesto. Once I have the baby, we'll get divorced." He doesn't contradict me. He leaves the apartment as I sit and finish my coffee alone. I feel the scales balance. For weeks Ernesto has acted like he did me a favor by marrying me. I won't stay in a relationship where I'm not an equal partner. The baby and I will be fine on our own. We don't need him.

CHAPTER SEVENTY

Courtroom #4

Courtroom number four is where my fate will be decided. I pull the dark double-mahogany doors open and walk into the quiet, dimly lit room. I sit in the back row on a hard wooden bench similar to ones in church. There should be kneelers installed in every courtroom. People probably pray more here than they do in church. I'm here to seek mercy, not justice.

I'm wearing a light oversized London Fog coat with a matching hat my mother bought for me several years ago while she was in London. The hat even has a chin cord which attaches through a loop on the back of the coat to ensure it won't blow away in a stiff wind. My mother thought the feature added to the coat's London authenticity. I thought it was corny, but my attorney, Mr. Davis, says I need to dress conservatively.

There's a large black oscillating pedestal fan in the corner whirling the humid breeze occasionally my way. Every few minutes the sound of the air conditioner comes to life, but chokes off almost immediately and marginally contributes cool air to the stuffy room.

The bailiff startles me out of my meditation when he enters and turns on the lights. He walks to the front of the courtroom and shuffles papers on his desk. Gradually, other people come in and seat themselves according to guilt; innocent in the front, guilty as hell in the back row. No one sits as far back as me.

When Ernesto and I met with Mr. Davis we decided I'll enter a plea of *not guilty* today. Mr. Davis tried repeatedly to have the charges dismissed to no avail. The prosecutor offered a plea bargain if I tell him what happened that night and who was involved. I'm the one who committed all the crimes, albeit in self-defense. I can't point the finger at anyone else and I don't want to incriminate myself. I have refused all offers.

We are twelfth out of approximately thirty cases scheduled on the docket. The room fills up with more people competing for the same air. Small beads of sweat track down my back.

Finally, the bailiff commands us all to rise for the Honorable Judge Jenkins. A door behind the raised bar opens and a tall, thin, dark haired man enters. He steps up to his ornately detailed bench and sits. The bailiff directs us all to sit as well. It's the judge's world now. He will rule like a king from a throne.

Most people are silent, but I hear soft whispers now and then. All eyes are focused on the man sitting at the front of the court. The first person is arraigned and the man is whisked away by deputies within a matter of minutes. I watch as a few more defendants do the same procedural dance with the judge.

I turn to see Mr. Davis enter through the heavy doors and scan the room for me. He moves toward me, but goes back into the hall momentarily and returns with Ernesto by his side. They come and sit down next to me.

Ernesto whispers in my ear, "Why didn't you meet us in the hall?"

"I sat down and couldn't get back up. I'm terrified." I bite my lower lip so I don't begin to cry. "I didn't know if you would come or not."

For the first time in months, Ernesto's face softens and doesn't show the contempt and resentment which has been present since our "blow out". "I will fight for you despite what you did. You will always be the mother of my child."

The bailiff calls Genevieve Soto, and we walk to the defense table. I see Curtis out of the corner of my eye. He's watching me with a curious look.

The bailiff comes to our table and asks me to remove my hat. As I remove my hat, the chin cord tangles in the coat and chokes me. Mr. Davis tries to remove my hat while I cling to the coat, but the two are hopelessly tangled. I remove my outer shell with shaking hands. I'd wanted to shield my baby from my shame.

The bailiff and the judge are visibly surprised by my figure. My belly is huge and my back is swayed from the strain of the weight. Before the charges are read, the judge calls for the prosecutor to approach the bench. The two men confer for several minutes before the judge calls Mr. Davis to also approach the bench. The prosecutor's face turns redder and redder as the conversation continues. The judge looks down at the file, shakes his head and stabs his finger at the papers on his desk.

Finally, the prosecutor turns and scowls at me, and returns to his chair.

As Mr. Davis sits down next to me, I try to ask a question. He shushes me and waits for the judge to speak.

The judge motions to the bailiff, who says to me, "Defendant Soto, please rise."

Mr. Davis and I both come to our feet.

Judge Jenkins clears his throat and quietly announces, "It is the opinion of this court that no charges shall be filed at this time against the defendant, Genevieve Soto because of lack of evidence. This case, at best, shows guilt by association. Therefore, the defendant shall not be required to make a plea at this time. However, it is also the opinion of this court the defendant needs to associate with a different class of people. A change in location may prove beneficial to her future and to the future of her child. Mrs. Soto, you are encouraged to leave my jurisdiction as soon as possible. If I see you in my court again, I will not be inclined to give you the benefit of the doubt next time."

Tears run down my face as I look at Ernesto. He cries too. Mr. Davis ushers us out the door and into the hall quickly, so we can leave before the judge changes his mind.

As the three of us walk toward the stairs, Curtis suddenly appears in front of us. His voice is low and steady. "You think this is the end of all of this? I might not have gotten *you,* but I'm going to hunt down every single one of your friends."

Ernesto steps in front of Curtis, toe to toe. "Leave my wife and her friends alone. You're not the only person with power here. I will press harassment charges against you and get you put in some hellhole town in west Texas."

"No one's going to listen to some so-called attorney from Mexico." Curtis's voice seethes with contempt.

Ernesto calmly returns the verbal blow, "Oh, really? I'm on the Texas' Unity Across the Border committee. I met with your governor yesterday. I could call him this afternoon and we can see which of us has better standing with him."

Curtis raises his arm to punch Ernesto when Mr. Davis steps in, "Do you want assault charges brought against you too?" Ernesto asks. "If you think your job is in jeopardy now, you'll have no job to worry about afterwards."

Curtis's face turns bright red as he turns and leaps down the stairs two to three steps at a time.

"Hopefully, that's the last time we have any trouble from him." Ernesto says as he puts his hand lightly on my back and escorts me down the stairs.

Once we're outside, Mr. Davis leaves me alone with Ernesto. Awkwardness descends upon us again. I don't know how to say goodbye, but feel the need to keep our relationship positive. "I didn't know you were in the Unity Across the Border committee."

"There's no such committee." Ernesto laughs for the first time in a long time. "I made the whole thing up. I never met your governor either." We laugh until we cry. It feels good to release it all.

CHAPTER SEVENTY-ONE

The Bear

Every inch of the station wagon is taken up with my possessions. The baby's crib is tied to the rack on top and covered with a plastic tarp; clothes and baby paraphernalia are crammed into every nook and cranny. Three spaces are niched out to accommodate room for Trip, MG and me. My due date is two weeks from now. With the baby pressing on my bladder, I will need to stop and use a bathroom every hour. It's going to be a long trip to Taos.

The closer we get to Taos, the heavier I get. The baby's pressure makes it hard to breathe. Thankfully, the air is cooler the higher we get and by the time we arrive at Lightning and Maggie's place, I'm almost cold.

Maggie offered to be my midwife and since I have to leave town anyway this is a great opportunity. I told my mother I'm going to a special birthing center and will come to Florida once the baby is born. She offered to come and help, but both of us know it's not a good idea. She had six children and all of them born while she was knocked out. Having a home birth with a midwife and no drugs is totally foreign to her.

Maggie runs out to meet us with hugs and kisses. Lightning's not far behind. He looks stronger and more vibrant than he has in years. The mountain air must agree with him.

"We built a small guest house in the back for you and the baby."

Lightning guides us to the back of the main house.

"Wow. I didn't expect that."

Maggie comes over and hugs me again. "You can stay as long as you need. I've been trying to get him to build a guest house for a long time. This just gave him a little more motivation."

"Yeah, I just want to keep the main house quiet," he laughs. "All you women make too much noise."

The guest house looks like a miniature adobe lodge complete with a ladder leading to the flat roof. MG inspects the outside texture of the walls and whistles, "Lightning, this is remarkable work. If I'd known you could do this kind of work, we would have gotten you to help us with our house."

"Yeah, Lightning," Trip chimes in. "You've been holding out on us."

Lightning is noticeably pleased, but quickly changes the subject. "I built a skylight into the roof so you can watch the stars at night." He leads us into the interior of the house so we can see his handiwork.

The floors are a wide plank wood sanded and smooth to a high shine. There are two built-in bunk beds on opposite sides of the room and a small sitting area in the middle. A large fireplace centers the far wall and is the only source of heat. To the left of the main door is a small hall that leads to a bathroom and a closet.

Maggie is beaming at her man. "He actually put in four skylights so I could track the movement of the bear."

Trip is the first to verbalize what all of us are wondering, "Is there a bear that comes around here? Has he tried to get in the house?"

"No." Maggie assures us. "The great bear in the sky. Our

ancestors saw pictures in the stars just like the Greeks. Our bear is hunting."

I smile at MG. "My baby will be born under the moon and the stars."

"I doubt you'll notice them when the time comes," she jibes.

I rub my belly and laugh. "I'm ready for the baby to be born now." As if on cue, the baby moves and we see the ripple cross from one side of my belly to the other.

Maggie gently pushes Lightning out the door. "We're going to have a cleansing ceremony this evening. Please bring some of the stacked wood in here and start the fire."

Lightning looks relieved he's been dismissed to do a menial job and quickly goes outside.

Maggie directs me to lie down to rest and for Trip and MG to help her in the main house. I lie on the bottom bunk and try to contemplate the enormity of my future.

I wake up to a warm room and the girls wrapped in blankets, sitting cross legged on the floor under the skylights. They invite me to join them. I stretch as I stand and walk over to sit next to them.

Maggie stops me, "Take off your clothes first."

I look to MG and Trip and realize that all three of them are naked under the blankets. I protest, "I'm too fat." I hang my head and look at my feet, "I'm too embarrassed to undress."

Maggie stands up and drops her blanket; her skin is wrinkled and folds of flesh hang over layer after layer. MG stands up and drops her blanket; a long scar runs from her back down under her arm and around to the front of her navel. It looks like she's been cut in two and sewn back together. Trip stands up and drops her blanket; her large breasts are perfectly shaped and hang above a narrow waist and small hips. Just above her pubic hair is a horizontal line that marks an operation. They are honest and unflinching. I strip as fast as any locker-room jock and quickly cover myself with the blanket. Maggie throws more wood on the fire along with some sage and we all sit in the circle in unison.

Maggie glows with the anticipation of the new life coming into this world and begins to pray. "With the warmth of our hearts, with the fluidity of our bodies, with the stillness of our minds and the light of our beings, we are thankful for this union of souls. We come together as the four parts of the spirit," Maggie begins. "MG represents the mind, Trip the body, I the light of the spirit, and Genny is our heart. Without her open heart, we wouldn't have this new life coming into the world. We are complete now."

Maggie begins chanting and slowly, I relax. I don't understand most of the ceremonies, but always come away trusting everyone a little more. The connection is powerful. MG starts rubbing oils on my arms and legs while Trip braids my hair. Maggie directs me to lie down in the middle of the circle and they rub oil on my belly. They tell my baby that it will be loved and nurtured by them, always.

Maggie lies on her back in the opposite direction as I'm lying and looks up through the skylight at the stars. MG and Trip do the same. The four of us watch as the bear moves across the night sky, forever in search of his prey. We are the spokes of an invisible wheel. My child will be born into this wheel and will be just as much a part of it, as I am.

CHAPTER SEVEN-TWO

Honey, It's Time

MG and Trip take turns walking me around the mountain. Maggie stays in the guest house and sings Lakota songs while she meditates. The baby is a few days late, but Maggie's optimistic that the new moon tonight will coax it from its hiding place.

Trip sets a quick pace as we take our mid-day walk. "You really need to walk with a bounce if you want the baby to drop further," she says. "Maggie says you're starting to dilate and the baby's head is in the birth canal exactly how it's supposed to be."

"I feel like I'm carrying a bowling ball between my thighs as it is. If I bounce, I feel like my entire pelvis will fall out along with the baby."

"Are you squeezing your muscles down there like Maggie showed you? You have to pretend there's a pencil up there and you're trying to keep it in. It's easier to do when you're sitting down. Squeeze and release. No one knows you're doing it. It's almost like foreplay." She laughs.

"Is that how you rev yourself up?" I ask, too winded now to laugh at my own joke.

"Hmmm, maybe. I'll have to be more mindful when I'm doing it and see if Dan picks up on it." She giggles as she marches up the next rise in the trail.

There are two large rocks next to each other around the bend and I beg her for a rest. Once we sit down, I ask, "The other night I noticed you have a scar on your stomach. What happened there?"

"I'm not sure I should tell you now." She lowers her head and takes a deep breath. She looks up at me with moist eyes. "I had a baby girl when I was very young. She died at birth."

I want to say something, but I can't. Fear grips me as she continues her story.

"The doctor didn't know the baby was breech until I went into labor. They waited eighteen hours before they finally did an emergency C-section. But it was too late. She was without oxygen too long." She struggles with the next words, "I only got to hold her for a few minutes before they took her away. She looked like a china doll, just so beautiful."

"Oh, my God. I'm so sorry. I didn't know." I start to cry. "I don't want my baby to die. Maybe I should go to a hospital to make sure everything goes okay." I stand up to leave when I feel something hot and wet move down my legs. I gasp as Trip and I both look down.

Trip grabs me by the shoulders and hurries me down the trail. "Don't worry, Genny. There's no time to get to a hospital now. We won't let anything happen to you or your baby."

We rush into the guest house just as Maggie is adding more wood to the fire.

"Her water broke." Trip says more calmly than I feel.

Maggie claps her hands smartly one time. MG and Trip immediately go into action. MG pulls out a small mat, pillows and towels from the closet and sets them on the floor in front of the fire.

Trip ushers me into the bathroom, so I can disrobe and shower. I put on a clean shirt and she wraps me in a large bathrobe and gently moves me to the floor. As soon as I sit on the pillows, a deep contraction tightens my belly and pelvis and I cry out in pain.

MG sits on the floor with her back to my back so I have support while I push. Maggie examines me, "I can see the crown of the head. The baby's coming fast."

Another contraction hits me in the gut and I scream. Trip holds my hand and says to breathe. The contraction subsides.

Maggie asks MG to keep track of the timing between contractions.

"They're coming every ten minutes."

"Okay, we need to ask the universe for our intentions of health and safety." I pray for those things and speed, too.

This process goes on for the next two hours with the time between pain getting shorter and shorter. Finally, I can feel the next contraction start from small spasms and mount to a more intense urge to push. With a rush of intense pain, the baby's head makes its way from my body and into the world. Maggie directs me to push harder and the rest of the baby's body is released. Trip quickly wraps the baby in a towel and places the bundle on my stomach. I try to get up to see the baby, but am wracked with another contraction; the afterbirth is expelled.

"Is it a boy or a girl?" I ask.

Maggie smiles and responds, "Ten fingers, ten toes and a kickstand."

"That doesn't compute. What?"

MG and Maggie cut the umbilical cord and after tying the end, Trip picks up the baby and heads to the bathroom. She answers over her shoulder, "it's a boy."

MG and Maggie clean me up while Trip gives the baby his first bath. After several hugs and kisses, we are tucked into bed. Exhausted and sore, I watch my baby boy sleep on my chest.

A boy... with all my hopes and dreams.

CHAPTER SEVENTY-THREE

Home

The last three weeks in Taos have been amazing. Bonding with my baby and being babied by the girls. But MG and Trip need to get back to their own lives and I need to move to Florida to be closer to my parents. Mom says to stay married for at least six more months, so the shotgun marriage isn't so obvious and the gossip can die down. Ernesto and I agree, and I'll wait and file for divorce in Florida. I'll be back to being Geneviève Rekas, not Soto. It's better that way. I know who Geneviève Rekas is, I was never sure who Geneviève Soto was.   Ernesto came to Taos to meet his son. He's satisfied that the baby is healthy and beautiful, but resists bonding with him. He held him only once. I'm sad for them both. I, on the other hand, am totally in love with my baby boy. He has a full head of dark hair and is aware of everything around him. Maggie says she's never seen a baby grasp so strongly or lift their head up so straight this early. He has a blue mark on his back which Ernesto says comes from the Aztec blood in him, but the mark is already fading. I sit for hours with him in my arms nursing him and listening to his coos. The girls tease me that my breasts have become as big as Trip's. Not quite, but I now get to wear a real bra without padding. I'm not sure I'll ever fit into my precious camisoles again.

Maggie says my son is a child of the mountain gods and thinks his name should be David, which means 'beloved' and will bespeak the love they all have for him. I love the name.

He'll feel loved all of his life. Ernesto is ambivalent to the name and the course the baby will take, so it's up to me. I need to make sure that David is safe and secure with the best education I can provide. I can't do this alone, at least not yet, so I'm moving to Florida with my tail between my legs. My mother is thrilled.

"I've already made arrangements to have his baptism as soon as you get here. He'll grow up Catholic," my mother states over the phone.

"Just as you di--," she begins and then stops herself.

"He'll grow up a child of the universe," I say, firmly. "Surrounded by love."

I buy the station wagon from MG, and she and Trip help me pack everything for the long drive. We travel together to the Rio Grande Valley and then say our goodbyes. These women are my soulful angels, my sisters, my found family. I will love them and Maggie and the rest of the Crash Gang forever.

The road stretches flat and open before me. A blur of small buildings and scrubby trees rush past my window. It looks the same from one state to the next... a long white line. My baby boy gurgles happily in his car seat behind me. *My spirit connects with all things.*
I drive.

I'm three years old, standing in the backseat with my arm around my dad's neck. I'm five years old, sucking a red lollipop in the backseat while my mother drives to the cemetery to visit my father's grave. I'm thirteen, my long hair still wet, riding home from my first diving competition, clutching my second place medal. I'm sixteen, with my skirt rolled up, singing at the top of my lungs to the car radio with Jackie at the wheel. I'm eighteen, sitting in the car sobbing after learning Patrick told everyone I was on the pill. I'm twenty, driving to Texas to start a new job and a new life. I'm twenty-two, flying a plane out of Mexico, running for my life.

My spirit connects with all things. The sun sets behind me and the first stars of the night appear in the darkened sky.

I drive.

With miles to go.

But I'm already home.

AKNOWLEDGEMENTS

Many of the stories in this book are true. The names have been changed to protect the guilty. I was there. I bore witness, but like the song says, "I'm frightened by the devil and I'm drawn to those ones that ain't afraid." Genny was a combination of several strong women and only a little of me.

This book is a collaborative effort and could not have been written without the constant weekly mental beatings from my writers' group. Many thanks to Kelly King, Paula Phillips, Rusty Haggard, Rachel Sanborn, Peggy Sabin, Constance Brooks, Jon Budd and Scot Courtney. All of whom are much better writers than I. I had the story, they brought it to paper.

A special thanks to Katie McNichol who encouraged me to keep writing.

Bio: With a list of crazy characters moving in and out of her life, it was time to write about them. Vicky Wicks-Goggin has lived in Ohio, Texas and Florida and decided to combine all of her experiences and people into book form. She currently lives in Texas with her eyes on Colorado next.

Made in the USA
Middletown, DE
03 May 2021